A Certain Kind of Sadness

sands press

Brockville, Ontario

A Certain Kind of Sadness

By Jillean McClory

sands press

sands press

A Division of 3244601 Canada Inc.
300 Central Avenue West
Brockville, Ontario
K6V 5V2

Toll Free 1-800-563-0911 or 613-345-2687
http://www.sandspress.com

ISBN 978-1-988281-87-2
Copyright © Jillean McClory 2020
All Rights Reserved

For information on bulk purchases of this book or any book published by Sands Press, please call 1-800-563-0911.

To book an author for your live event, please call: 1-800-563-0911

Sands Press is a literary publisher interested in new and established authors wishing to develop and market their product. For more information please visit our website at www.sandspress.com.

PROLOGUE
A ROOM OF ITS OWN

Rachel stood at the bay window of her tacky apartment watching intently. Her eyes bounced from the idling black Escalade across the road, to the street where neighbours strolled sedately, to children running through the park squeezing the last bit of joy from the twilight, to the last vestiges of her panoramic view of the red sky nestling the falling sun, but nothing could distract her from the waiting.

She lived on the outskirts of Ottawa, in a quaint little hamlet called The Glebe. It was a picturesque diamond with unique charm and an appealing trendy vibe, but even with its scenic delights and cozy small-town atmosphere, Rachel hadn't settled here. It was a canvas of hurtful reminders of everything that had gone wrong with her life a *"Howler"* that had meticulously captured every mistake she had ever made, and dispatched it to the world with glee and abandon.

Hard to believe, ten weeks ago, she was riding a wave. Possibilities drummed in her veins; her future had design and distinction. For years she'd struggled to climb her life's summit; she thought she had mastered the navigation of its deep gaping holes, but when she reached the top—a humiliating crash down a gaping hole took the last remnants of her poise. And *this* is where she landed. Alone. Stuck in a ratty three-story walkup she despised, living well below par, drinking a bottle of wine out of a brown paper bag.

Hot tears stung Rachel's eyes; she squeezed them shut, wincing with embarrassment at her stupidity. It pissed Rachel off that her mother was right. Rachel had miscalculated Maureen's sheer force of will. It was her fault. She should have known better, given her mother's drive, ambition, and cryptic brief that "mother knows best."

For a graceful, self-assured woman, Maureen had her share of deep gaping holes filled with shadows. She hated being ignored or her intelligence questioned. Rachel had done both by loving Morgan Hillier.

Maureen's disapproval included a myriad of reasons:

- Morgan's emotional baggage and ready-made family put him out of Rachel's league.
- Rachel wasn't up for the challenge. She was too young and inexperienced for a man like him—far beyond their actual seven-year age difference.
- Misfortune followed Morgan around like a duty. The tragic death of his first love. His son's death and his wife's mental breakdown. His divorce. Single fatherhood.
- Rachel's attachment to Morgan was normal but misplaced. It was a residual of her adolescent devotion and exuberance.
- Morgan's daughter Macy might want to know her estranged mother one day. Did Rachel want to be part of that mess?
- Rachel's immaturity barred her from knowing what Maureen knew, Morgan's calm exterior was mythical. Under his cool exterior was molten lava ready to explode, and she didn't want Rachel near him when the volcano erupted.
- At his sister's wedding, Morgan behaved badly. He humiliated Rachel. Drank too much. Slobbered over Helen Fielding. Embarrassed himself. Upset his daughter. Hurt Rachel. And gave Maureen tons of ammo for years to come.

Maureen's disgust mixed well with her glee. Did it matter how Morgan acted? Maureen's recriminations were limitless. For years, she had kept her criticisms on reserve. Careful by nature, she politely insisted that Morgan was a talented man, a successful man, a good father, a good son, but he wasn't the right man for Rachel. Morgan's bad behaviour at his sister's wedding had proved Maureen's point. In the process, it had shattered the fragile balance between them, and played right into Maureen's wheelhouse. She had abandoned her lady-like manners, and destroyed what little dignity Rachel had left.

Rachel's childhood memories of her mother were a painful collection. Maureen never had time for Rachel. Too many other pressing matters needed her attention. Private vacations. Errands to run. Parties to attend. Lists to check. Goals to attain. Glass ceilings to break. When Rachel assembled the puzzle pieces of her childhood, Maureen was always absent. Out of adolescent loyalty, she made concessions for her mother, rationalized her ambition. Maureen was paving the way for others while forging new trails. But no matter how she spun it, there was no denying, Maureen's absence forced Rachel to live on the outside, forced her to find refuge at the Hilliers, and forced her to take on the awkward role of *almost* family. As a result, Rachel never quite fit—anywhere. Speculation fed her childhood fears; they built a fortress leading from her heart to her head. She believed Maureen's love was conditional, and that the choices she made were never going to be good enough.

Rachel had yet to know the dimension and range of the damage, but it felt significant.

The sad complement to this shitty saga was there was no comfort in her knowing or understanding the truth of what had happened. Rachel felt no relief at being liberated from her long-held fears, no relief that she didn't have to struggle with conjecture about her mother's love. Her worries had been gouged out and replaced with the certainty that her fears were *not* a leftover invention from her childish insecurities. The truth was Maureen's love had a price and it was contingent on whether she approved of Rachel's choices.

Morgan pissed Maureen off from the beginning. Rachel saw it and adjusted accordingly— even when Maureen tried to hide it under her manipulative finesse and lady-like subtlety. But Rachel wanted Morgan in her life regardless; he had always been a stabilizing force, a beacon in the dark. He had brought her from sea to shore countless times, but now the beacon's light was no longer a port of call. The world Rachel relied on was slashed open and the pain of exposure was humbling. There was no going back; her life had been altered. She needed to grieve until the Earth adjusted to the vibration of her pain.

Rachel looked down at her hands. Tears lashed them. She was *so fucking* disappointed in herself. She let the story of her life fall through her fingers. Horrified how she had hid behind the chair like a feeb. No fight in her. Weak. She'd let Morgan leave without saying what needed to be said, too hurt, to tell the truth, too afraid to love him.

The wedding was weeks ago. Since then, everything had been moving in slow motion. People walked in slow motion; they spoke, their mouths moved, but Rachel couldn't make out their words.

How do you recover from years of relentless ache?

Blinking back her tears, she sucked in a trembling breath. After everything that had happened, Rachel was certain of four things:

- Circumstance is geography, but it often feels like fate.
- When you love someone from the deepest part of yourself, and they leave without objection, a certain kind of sadness breaks a piece off your heart. Rachel was certain everything she believed about love was hidden in that broken piece.
- Everything you love? Everything you hate? Same thing.
- Love is a war of extremes.

Rachel had first-hand experience on the war love wages between the extremes—happiness and depression, love and hatred, isolation, and intimacy—and there could be no real consoling in the throes of such beautiful chaos. A distinct loneliness collides with passion. With it comes a siege of emotions not easily understood. Emotions burn and consume even the most rational of minds. When you dust yourself off, you forge through the pain to keep ridicule at bay; you erect barricades like fortresses of natural landscape so you can bare survival.

No one knows how *you* love. No one understands the depth of *your* love. Or where that love will take *you*, until it takes *you* there. No one knows the level of insanity, sacrifice, or indulgence *you* are prepared to commit, until *you* are there, naked, your dignity tossed into the fire.

Rachel had committed countless transgressions.

She had *no choice*. She was a poor slob in love.

1

TENSION LIES BENEATH

"Hillier sends you money?"

Rachel stopped mid-motion. She heard the accusation in his voice and her body stiffened. She gripped the black metal picture frame in her hand, and with more casualness than she felt, she glanced over her shoulder. Rick had the bank confirmations in his hand. *Shit, I left them on the kitchen table.* She hadn't expected to have a good time today. Hadn't expected to ask Rick back to the apartment or enlist his help to build the bookcase. Unexpected surprises and carelessness led to that glint of judgment she saw in his eyes. It was easy to identify; Rachel had a dependable acquaintance with judgment.

She turned away, not bothering to answer him.

Rick's impassioned pleas for Rachel to stay in Ottawa, rather than run home this weekend, was boyishly insistent. Guilt kept her in town, saying yes for all the wrong reasons. The move to Ottawa had turned out to be a bigger challenge than she anticipated. She was either running to something or away from something: running back to Toronto, running to Morgan, running to work, running from memories of who she was and what she'd done. She wanted it to stop, but there was never a way out from herself. No way out of the box that people in her life kept pushing her into—even with the best of intentions. They were trying to be helpful. She knew that. But prettying up opportunity with platitudes—what a break, what an adventure, imagine a great job in a shaky economy, how lucky are you—made the pretty box they'd designed for her—a trap. No matter how pretty the box is, pretty is just decoration, and a platter of opportunity is debilitating when it's not what you want.

Rachel hated their encouragement. It appeared genuine but it *felt* like forced sincerity. And any advice came with the dreaded addendums. Starting with—Rachel, you aren't a fully baked adult and there are responsibilities you're probably unaware of—We just want to be helpful, but:

- don't deplete your holdings;
- get a good job using your connections;
- buy a house in a safe neighbourhood;
- have your assigned 1.8 kids;
- get a nanny to raise your kids;
- buy a cottage in the Muskokas;
- become a CEO of a tech company;
- steal as much as you can before you go;
- retire early, and
- leave a legacy.

Everyone who had good intentions and a blog recommendation posted their advice on the map of her life. She didn't want to follow the status-quo. She wanted value and depth in her life, but she couldn't help wondering—is there an expiry on good fortune? Her privileged life didn't allow for bellyaching. She was wealthy, connected, pretty. What more did she want? She'd graduated with people who worried about paying off their loans; getting a job *to* pay of their loans; finding a place to live—while Rachel worried over connection, talent, passion, belonging.

Was she exactly like the industrials from back in the day with a different agenda? They grabbed for power like she grabs for love. A snob of a different name? Blaming others for her deficiencies, without any insight? Was she living her own delusion? And everyone could see it except her? Or were her secrets just secrets in her mind? Rachel saw the illusions others carry unwittingly. Why would she be different? She didn't know. She never got it right, anyway. Either through her own recklessness or through the recklessness of others, she managed to be out of step. She wasn't fast enough to spot the synchronicities in time to learn from them. It was always in hindsight.

Not the case with Rick. *Him* she could read. His accusations were not buried deep beneath his eyeballs, like he thought. His stare was not calm with friendly interest. The bank statements he held were not about Rachel or the money transfer. It was about Morgan. It was about Rick. And how Morgan had slighted him. Blame needed to be accounted for and Rachel was the game afoot; Rick needed to shove her into a designer package he'd created. He didn't want her to be anyone other than the vision he had in his head. Granted, he was making an effort here, but that didn't mean it wasn't irritating. Their history was a messy one, layered with anger and pain, and to Rachel's welcomed relief, their turbulent past had remained in the past, but she felt a flood coming her way. He wouldn't be able to help himself. He had the bank statements—proof. He wouldn't hear or listen to what she said; he would be too busy owning his hatred for Morgan. She knew the drill. It had happened many times before. People don't like their opinions to be meaningless. They want you where they put you—inside their own insecurities and judgments. Where it's comfortable.

Rachel looked at the books on the shelf. Last week, she turned twenty-four. Her father sent a beautiful barrow bookcase, with mink finish, from Toronto's stylish designer district. Its clean elegant lines gave the apartment a *je ne sais quoi* vibration. Made it stylish. Her father had excellent taste. Often a prism of light shot across the room from the bay window, hitting her book collection on the floor. When she moved in, she had yanked down the heavy draperies from the windows and light had transformed the gloomy room. Stacks of her books had lined the narrow hallway leading to her bedroom for weeks; now they had a home. She ran her finger along the rim of the shelf. Sad, this was going to end badly, and after Rick was such good company today. They'd strolled through the trendy shops along Bank Street without incident—which hadn't always been the case.

Today was a retreat from themselves, a little fantasy. Rick told funny stories; his laughter infectious. Rachel got caught up in the moment. Offered him coffee and cake while they assembled the bookcase. They worked well together. Proud of their accomplishment. Settling the day on a positive note was well within Rachel's grasp, until Rick's four simple words wrecked their comfortable silence, and their happy illusion cracked.

"Hillier sends you money"—doused her with a much-needed chill and catapulted her back to the uneven pukey green walls of her walk-up, the 1975 coffee table, the lumpy sofa, dime store pictures of fox hunts, and wall-to-wall shag carpet. There was absolutely no *je ne sais quoi* vibe in this apartment. She lived in a shit shack that only a wrecking ball could make stylish.

Rick's face, his words, the controlled, angry jealousy that had been steadily moving up his body, she knew well. He was living inside their shopping day illusion—old times recreated in the present. Rationalizations were popping into his head indiscriminately. The teleplay was in motion. His emotions were tricking his mind into believing what wasn't real, and he was falling headfirst into the good relationship mirage, but when he was left with sand running through his fingers, he'd be pissed. Rachel had been there—excuses were her forte and teleplay her imaginary friend.

Rachel braced herself for what was to come. Rick had an agenda. His authoritative tone said it all.

God—I hate my life.

As much as she would have liked to absolve herself, that she had no play in this sad-sackery she found herself in, the fact was, she'd created this mess by:

- accepting a job, she didn't want;
- saying yes to an apartment she hadn't seen;
- living in a city—while lovely—she has no desire to live in, and
- leaving everything and everyone she loved behind in Toronto.

Quicksand is an unforgiving adversary. Rachel abandoned her instincts and compounded the problem by being an idiot. She may have been in the top two percent of her class but she *also* had a dependable acquaintance with being an impulsive halfwit. Rick may have found her the job, but she accepted it. Rick may have found her apartment, but she agreed to live in it. Granted, her decisions were based on a long list of obligations and insecurities, but it didn't matter now. The die had been cast. Rick already owned a piece of her shitty guilt pie for past indiscretions against him, so she'd just have to take it and stand her ground. There were always reasons, excuses, beliefs—regardless—Rachel accepted the job. She moved into the apartment. She knew the mechanics, the tactical plan of how she got there, but how did she *actually* get there?

Rachel rubbed her eye. Tiredness overwhelmed her. The air in the tiny apartment became weighty. "Hillier sends you money" hung in the air like an awkward uncertainty. She stared down at the photograph in her hand. Her parents' happy faces smiled up at her. She glanced at the clock. Seven. Everyone's at the cottage. Rachel *wanted* to be there. Ached for it. Hemmed in by the narrow walls, she looked over at the bay window and felt a sympathetic kinship with the peeling paint. The unseasonably cold autumn day was just beyond the glass, waving its wintry head. Leaves had settled on the grass. She wanted to breathe in the crisp air—she wanted, she wanted, she wanted.

With exaggerated care, she put the framed photograph on the shelf.

When the job offer came late in July, it was unexpected. By then apartments had been well picked over by the university crowd, leaving her with a dingy, furnished one bedroom with a 70s motif. Rachel was told umpteen times how lucky she was to get a place on such short notice in a premier location. She begged to differ.

Everything in her life had changed since moving to The Glebe— even *time* had changed its configuration. A snail's pace would have been preferable to how labouriously slowly time dragged. Twenty-eight days had morphed into forty thousand three hundred twenty seconds. All she could hear was the thunderous tick tock from the ugly orange-rimmed clock above the alcove. It agitated her. Forced her to pace. No matter where she stood in the apartment, she heard it ticking. The movement of the second hand was the only testament that time was *actually* passing. One murky day passed into another; it was difficult to distinguish the difference between them.

Stupid clock. Stupid Rick. Rick knew moving to Ottawa four weeks ago hadn't been an easy one. But his imposing company made it worse. He was a male version of Maureen. He knew exactly what she should do about everything. She was sick of his opinions. His guidance. His interference. His ugly voice. He suffocated her with the heat of his presence, forcing her to gasp, taking in more, hot recycled air than she cared to consume. Forget that he's an educator, charming, kind to small children, handsome; forget he's dedicated to his community and generous of spirit and philanthropic—once you forgot that, he was easy to hate.

Tick tock. Tick tock.

"Are you going to answer me?" said Rick.

Aw yes—Hillier sends you money, needs addressing—buckle up. "I don't want to talk about the wedding Rick. It's all anyone talks about these days."

She felt him behind her. He tossed the statements on the shelf in front of her. "I'm prepared to be bored."

Morgan Hillier had transferred six thousand dollars from his personal chequing account to Rachel Wharton's savings account to cover costs for his sister Elaine's wedding. The story was incredibly sad and pathetic, but Rick wasn't interested in the details or the truth, he was interested in racking up *more* reasons to hate Morgan.

Rachel examined the spine of *The Blind Assassin* with too much care, too much grip; her knuckles turned white. This was her favourite Atwood. *The Handmaid's Tale* was a close second. Elaine liked *Alias Grace*, but Grace Marks irritated Rachel. "You're suddenly interested in wedding planning?"

"Is that what this is—wedding details?" said Rick.

"What do you think it is?"

"I don't know, that's why I'm asking."

"No, you're asking because you see Morgan's name and you hate him."

"I don't trust Morgan if that's what you mean."

Rachel put the Atwood book on the shelf and grabbed the bank confirmations. She breezed past him to the small white student desk her mother had shipped a couple of weeks ago from her girlish bedroom. She opened the top drawer, stuffed the papers inside, and shoved it closed. Rachel turned, leaned against the desk; her fingers gripped the edges. She needed to change to electronic bank statements.

"You know I'm Elaine's maid of honour Rick. You know the wedding is in three weeks. This is a big wedding—lots of details to be handled and now we are getting down to the wire. What difference does it make to you if the Hilliers reimburse my expenditures?" *It was close enough to the truth.*

"I know you hate to acknowledge this, but you are a Wharton."

"I told them it wasn't necessary, but they insisted."

"It's not from the Hilliers—it's from Morgan." His eyes darted erratically.

"Same thing."

"Yes," he nodded, "he has the sweet spot, I'll give him that." She saw the tension around his mouth.

"You have a blind spot when it comes to Hillier," said Rick.

"*You* have the blind spot when it comes to Hillier."

"His interference in your life tore us apart six years ago, and nothing has changed. There's Morgan right in the middle!"

"Morgan had nothing to do with what happened six years ago, or now." Rachel turned away and walked to the bay window. On the street, a little girl held her mother's hand and happily looked up at her with adoration as she chatted a mile a minute. The mother smiled and grabbed the child in her arms tightly, twirling her. Rachel's heart rattled in her chest.

"Morgan," he insisted, "has everything to do with it. You're lying to yourself."

Rachel's white cable knit sweater strangled her. She scratched her wrists. Hot air billowed into the room, stifling her. She held her arms at her chest. "Where Morgan is concerned, I don't lie to myself." *I've tried, it doesn't work.* "But I am his sister's maid of honour," she said slowly, deliberately, and turned to face him. "This is the event of the year and what matters to him right now is keeping his sister happy. I am a minor detail."

Rick's brows pinched as he hooked his thumbs into the pockets of his jeans. "You're not a minor detail to him."

Rachel tugged at her turtleneck. "If you're talking about the week I moved here, be fair—it's been an adjustment ..."

"It *is* an adjustment and he saw an opportunity to take advantage of you at a weak moment." Rick paced the confined space in her hall entrance. "At least he's true to form."

"What are you talking about?"

Rick walked to the middle of the room, narrowing the space between them. "He knew you were upset and he knew he could exploit it for his own cause. I guarantee reimbursing you was probably another ploy to keep you close. Hillier would pick up any tab you run because he's making a long-term investment here."

"What long-term investment?"

"*You.*" He moved closer, bringing more heat. "You're his long-term investment. He's in the market for a wife and a mother for his kid, and he's picked you. You already play mother to his kid."

If only that were true. "You don't know what you're talking about. And I'm not playing at mothering Macy—I love her!" She jerked away from him but he grabbed her wrist.

"You're so blind Rach. Can't you see how he controls your life? Makes you think you need him? You never get a chance to figure out how you feel about anyone or anything because he's always standing there in the shadows, intimidating anyone in your path."

Rachel yanked out of his hold. She flicked her long strawberry blond red hair over her shoulder, her chin shot out, and her blue eyes were distant as she stared at Rick. "Morgan never tries to control my life. He could care less what I do." *I wish he did care. I wouldn't be standing here talking to you if he had shown one shred of concern that I was leaving again.*

"He's manipulating you Rachel."

"He's family."

"No Rachel, your parents and his parents are best friends—that's all."

Semantics. "Sarah Hillier raised me. I spent more time in her house than I did in my own. I played there. I ate there. I had my own room. My stuff is still there for God sake!"

"I'm not ..."

"Morgan is my best friend Rick. If he were a woman, we wouldn't be having this conversation. I refuse to defend Morgan, Aunt Sarah's, or any of the Hilliers. They are family. Any friend of mine has to accept them as part of the package."

Rick turned away from her and stuffed his hands back into his jeans. He looked tall and broad in the narrow space.

The sound of the refrigerator hummed in the background. Soft romantic music came from the neighbour's stereo. Neither of them soothing.

"I want to know where we stand. What are we doing here? What *is* this?" he said.

Rachel clenched her teeth, raking her hair back from her hot face, and laced her fingers behind her neck. *Oh God.* What went through the minds of men? Did he honestly think she'd ripped her life apart, moved to Ottawa so she could play house with him? Didn't he know by now that she hates all of those fucking questions? That there was no we? It was the furthest thing from her mind, but clearly, it wasn't far from his, and she walked right into it with blinders on.

Rick stared at her. "I'm your friend but I want to know if we can move toward something more. I want us to be together and I'm willing to wait if there's a chance, but I have no intention of competing with Morgan."

Rachel scratched her neck. "Who said you're competing?"

"You force me to compete with him."

"*I* force you?" *Don't say too much. Don't justify.*

Rick suddenly looked weathered. "You don't give me a chance Rachel. You always turn to him."

Guilt and defeat assaulted Rachel, oozing out all over her cable knit sweater. Her heart beat hard and fast. "That's not entirely true. Jason and Elaine—your sister Louise—are also my best friends. I turn to all of them, but you only see when I turn to Morgan." She leaned against the sick-in-the-pan green wall. "Contrary to what you believe, Morgan is not trying to control my life. He encourages our friendship. He encouraged me to move here. When I wanted to pack up and go home, he encouraged me to stay and give it a fair chance."

Rachel shrugged. "As for this hold you think Morgan wants over me—it's in your head."

"You're in love with him," said Rick.

With measured grace, Rachel sucked in her breath slowly to keep her screams from bursting out of her mouth with such a blast that the apartment complex would turn to rubble. She exhaled slowly— *Yes, yes, I am! I'm in love with a man I can't seem to have. Every time I think, we've reached the right place at the right time, a hurdle appears. I'm terrified that it's just chemistry for him—a temporary diversion. Regardless of Morgan's place in my life, I don't want to talk about it. I have enough interference in my life. Things are good with him right now and I want to ride the wave. If it turns out to be another disappointment, I have no idea how I will deal with it—badly comes to mind. He lives inside me. I don't know how to stop loving him. God knows I've tried. I've dusted myself off and tried to put him behind me. I've moved cities—countries for God's sake! I've dated. I've not dated. I've done charity work. I've painted until my fingers bleed. I've run myself stupid. And then I'm right back where I was before—a poor slob in love, only deeper, more attached ... I can't talk about him because I think I'm losing my mind!*

Rachel gulped back her screams to swill around in the pit of her stomach. "I don't want to fight with you Rick."

"I don't want to fight either." He lifted his eyes to hers. "I want to be the man in your life Rachel."

She closed her eyes.

"You're not interested."

"I can't."

"You mean you won't."

"Rick, be fair, there's a lot going on in my life right now. I can't go down that road when I'm so unavailable."

"I guess that's my cue then."

Heaviness sat on her shoulders; she wanted it to push her through the floor to a hole in the basement, but there was no getaway. "It's been a long day."

"You look exhausted." Rick grabbed his coat from the couch. "I'll call you."

She nodded without enthusiasm. The door latch fell into place and he was gone.

2

THE PLAYERS

Rachel stared at the door; relieved he'd left. Being Rick's friend was one thing, but she didn't intend to date him again. They were terrible together. Why couldn't he see that? Or maybe it had nothing to do with her and everything to do with Morgan. It wouldn't be the first time. Exhausted, she lay down on the orange shag rug and stared up at the rising moon. The moon was framed like a picture in her bay window. Its white brilliance stretched her puny living room. Rachel loved the moon. It was peaceful. Bright. Unassuming. It slipped into everyone's life without cause for complaint, not like the sun and clouds. The sun was too hot at times and clouds were a broody bunch. Rachel was a moonchild.

The air was stifling hot. Rachel sat up. She ripped off her sweater and hung it on the window crank. Restless, she counted the ten steps to the front door and smacked the light switch off. God, she hated this place. The furniture was in a multitude of pukie shades. The walls were a gross green colour. Plastic framed pictures covered the tired walls. When her father saw the place, he lost his mind a bit, demanded she stay at a hotel, or an executive suite. Her mother was affronted by the suggestion. Rachel insisted she would be fine. Rick lived close, she joked, in a beautiful penthouse at the corner of Second Ave and Bronson if she needed hot running water. Her father was put out that a Summerhill was living in a penthouse, while his daughter lived like a pauper. Maureen was happy with Rachel's meager surroundings—said it was good for her. The next day her father sent a care package of plush towels, Egyptian sheets, a new mattress, and a cleaning staff to scrub the place. A note was pinned to the towels—a room had been arranged for her at the Frontenac until her *new* place was thoroughly sanitized. "Just between us Sweet Pie, Love Dad."

Rachel dragged the afghan off the couch, a gift from Aunt Sarah, and snuggled into it. It smelled like the Hilliers'. She inhaled deeply, staring out the picture window. Fall had come early. The signs were unmistakable. The sun slipped away earlier. Leaves were already brilliant with autumn colours; reminders of a scorching summer were found in the curly burnt ends. When she woke this morning to frost on the grass, she'd groaned.

Nothing is a testament to the passing of time like the change of seasons.

"Everything changes," she whispered.

A telephone shrilled from the apartment next door. Paper-thin walls made privacy impossible. She went to the kitchen and cranked open the window. She plugged in the kettle and pulled out a mug. Although her loneliness never left, for the first time since moving, her solitude was preferable to Rick's wants. Crisp air stole into the galley kitchen and with it, pleasant dinner smells drifted in: beef stew, lentil soup, tourtière pie, beans, things to stick to your ribs now that the weather had turned. Laughter and heated conversations about the week's events were sandwiched between dinner choices. It reminded her of family. She swallowed hard.

Ottawa was a wonderful city but Rachel was lost without a clan to move through the jungle with. She felt exposed to the elements.

When the job offer came from St. Martin's High School, everyone assumed she would take it—even Rachel wasn't stupid enough to give up such a great opportunity. So - here she was, in Ottawa. She always believed she was fiercely independent, but the older she got the shakier that truth became. In this clapboard apartment, of all places, the realization had hit her like the big bang: *independence was easy and safe when familiar people and things are close.* With each year that passed, her safety net for soft landings was dwindling. More and more, she was a family of one. A lonely prospect.

When she arrived in Ottawa, her days were filled with too much time. She organized her classroom for fall, which gave her some relief. She met a few other teachers, but that still left plenty of time to herself, too much time. Rachel didn't want her time consumed by what ifs and missing pieces, but they dominated her thoughts. Memories sat stoically in her mind and imprinted themselves in the lonely spaces of her ordinary day. Snippets of childish hurts, indiscretions, abandonments—too many memories, too many shitty things Rachel has done. Every good or bad memory, every reason to forge ahead, hinged on her lifeline to Toronto, and her dependency on Morgan. She couldn't shake wanting him near.

Rachel didn't understand why she felt out of her depth in Ottawa. She wasn't a woman without life experiences. She'd gone to Western University in London, collected a kaleidoscope of memories, but her education wasn't restricted to the lecture hall. Her personal boundaries were crossed. Intimacies were invaded. Opportunity had given her a two-year artistic escape to Paris, and a life changing relationship with Gary Kurfont. He kept her sane. He had given her love and security when she desperately needed it. Those six years away provided her with wonderful memories and debilitating veracities, many of which had remained unresolved in the past. Now those memories were everywhere. Clamoring at her.

This move was different from her other adventures. This time, she was completely alone. Rick saw this as an opportunity to get back together, but it wouldn't work. Their rekindled friendship was layered with the unsaid, and underneath the weight of the unsaid was everything she hated about herself. When Rachel dated Rick years ago, she didn't know he hated Morgan. It didn't take long for her to see, hate emanating from him. Rachel helped cement that hatred. After their conversation today, it was clear his antagonism hadn't wavered. She made a mistake six years ago, thinking Rick was the man who would make her forget Morgan. He wasn't. Gary's Kurfont's smooth familiar beauty kept her demons at bay. She had forced Rick out of her life without conscience. He loved her and she'd betrayed him.

After years of silence, Rick Summerhill extended an olive branch. A teaching position was available at the private high school he worked at, and the job was in her disciplines—English and art. Six hundred kilometers away. She should have been grateful to him for getting her such a wonderful opportunity, but Rachel wasn't grateful. She had just moved back to Toronto after Western. She resented his intrusion, but she still let the pressure of everyone else's expectations chart her course. Now she was here and everything was different. The feel was different. It was unsettling. But why? Why did it feel so different?

The whistling kettle drew her attention. She yanked at the plug and mechanically made tea.

It can't just be geography. Her knee jerk reaction was—yes, it is, I'm living in a city I don't want to live in—but that wasn't it. Rachel was seasoned at absence. The only distinction between then and now was that her previous adventures had a stabilizing force—a safety net. Growing up, Morgan was her sounding board, the keeper of her secrets. When she went to Western, even though she shared an apartment with Lainey and Louise, Morgan was her safe haven. In Paris, she had Gary.

There was no safety net in Ottawa.

Rachel leaned against the kitchen's narrow archway. Her eyes fell to the stunning briarwood box sitting on her new bookshelf. It was handcrafted in Florence. Rachel loved it—a sweet sixteen gift from Morgan.

Wind whistled; her eyes darted to the window that dominated the east wall—the only redeeming feature in the drab apartment. The glass was hit with a rattling force; a lonely ache blew into the room and the tiny room shrank and shivered in reaction. Streetlights snapped on and bounced off her sill; happy clusters of twos and threes were on the street—friends, families, out to dinner. So Canadian to be out regardless of the blustery weather. People walking their dogs. Children playing in the frost-bitten leaves. Runners. Neighbours chatting.

The Glebe was a perfect location. Quiet character, beautiful architecture, quaint shops with eclectic charm, just south of Centertown, bordering the Queensway. Bank Street ran through The Glebe and was lined with shops, eateries, parks; the Rideau Canal was minutes away; Little Italy on the other side of the Queensway. Her apartment was off Bank Street closer to Old South. It was a short distance to the school where she taught. She liked the area. It reminded her of The Beaches in Toronto. That old world flavour. But the thought of staying here for six months? Six long, arduous, frigid months? She shuddered.

I want to go home.

How did she let this happen? Everything was so far from center. Her life was shit! She squeezed her eyes shut—don't think about it—and still, questions plagued her with no answers in sight.

Who was to blame? Who could she assign the blame too? Blame Rick for sticking his nose into her life? Blame him for finding her a dream job in the wrong city? Blame her family for their genuine happiness that the perfect job fell into her lap? Blame Morgan for congratulating her? Blame him for his encouragement? Blame him for not loving her the way she wants to be loved? Blame him for teasing her with love, for making her believe she had a chance? Blame him for wanting her to go? Blame the school for having the perfect position? Blame the teacher who had the audacity to get pregnant the year Rachel graduated? Blame herself for not believing she had a choice? Blame herself because she let the wheels of circumstance decide for her? Blame herself for her complete lack of bravery? Blame herself for not telling Morgan how she felt? Blame herself for not fighting for her own life? Blame herself for making excuses?

Don't think, don't think, don't think.

Rachel put her teacup down on the small round table in the breakfast nook, walked to her new bookcase and picked up the elegant golden-brown briarwood box with an espresso trim. She ran her fingertips over its glossy smoothness. Gently, she placed it on the kitchen table and slid into the hard chair. Every time she opened this box, she felt perched on the edge of her life, hoping to understand her past and find the answers she needed.

Her history was in this box. Sins from her past galloped alongside her present life, making her faults more pronounced. Weren't they bound to catch up with her? Did self-awareness change everything? That by acknowledging what a shitty person she was, it would miraculously make everything better? Or was it an illusion? That recognition is brief. The *Aha moment!* becomes skewed and then is quickly reframed into a historical moment that's more palpable? More forgiving? Hateful things done—are bent without breaking, to make them more manageable. Rachel's past was a tribute to manageable illusion. She had participated in so many covert operations. Avoidance was attached to every memory. She ignored what she didn't want to see at first glance so time and effort hadn't assuaged her countless falls from grace. The older she got, the harder it was to determine what was real and what was illusion.

Rachel should be a better person. She is *required* to be a better person. Every advantage life can offer, she has been afforded. She needs to live her best life and pay homage to all those who have limited choices. *I have small problems in the scale of things and they don't deserve validation because my problems are self-inflicted.* She recognizes her wonderful life, but she can't convince her heart that it's enough. Her heart is broken. Shattered into oblivion because Rachel doesn't get the love of her life, and the commitment of hearth and home. She will forever be—*almost* family, *almost* a sister, *almost* a love, *almost* a wonderful daughter. She will forever carry the weight of her ever-increasing list of almosts—like bullion. Rachel sighed. Many of her dreams had lost their way, buckled under judgment or the voices in her head. She still struggled with insecurities and choices that don't serve her or anyone else. She wants to snatch back her every regret and choose a different route.

Doesn't everyone in hindsight?

3

FROZEN MEMORIES

Rachel reached into the briarwood box. Stacks of photographs were tied with blue ribbon, her beautiful parents on top—Maureen and John Wharton, a moving force. Rachel never felt part of their love circle.

Photograph 1
Her parents were pressed together, laughing, her father's gaze seized by her mother. They epitomized love.

Rachel flipped through the pictures, her eyes smarting with tears. She counted, not for the first time, forty-three vacation spots that didn't include her.

She ran her fingertip over her mother's face. There was never a closeness between them. No lunches together. No whispered chats. No giggles. No shopping dates. She marveled at the ease it took her father to break down Maureen's rigidity. Rachel felt like a hindrance to Maureen. Something to sandwich in between more weighty pursuits.

Photograph 2
Rachel at six. It was taken at the Summerhills' cottage on Georgian Bay. Louise and Rachel had their arms tightly wrapped around each other, big smiles on their faces.

Rachel was three when she met Louise at Mrs. McMurray Tiny Tots Nursery School and they became fast friends. Now Louise was being groomed for her presidency at Delaware Confectionary, which had been in the Summerhill family for fifty years.

Rick and his friend Boyd were in the background, their tongues hanging out, giving the camera the finger trying to be all badass. It wasn't a look they could pull off; they were too blond, too tanned, too well fed. The white rambling beach estate in the background didn't help their cause. In those days, Rick was carefree. Fun. Before the heartbreaks.

Wrapped in red ribbon was a montage of Rachel's childhood. Morgan was in most of them. He was the eldest Hillier and had his own hemisphere in Rachel's puzzle pieces. Jason was the middle child. Elaine, the youngest. Morgan was Rachel's earliest recollection. Her refuge. Morgan soothed her when she was confused or insecure. He gave her piggyback rides, bought her ice cream, took her to the park; she loved him from the start. He was a peaceful force in her life; he always had been, but things got complicated when her little girl love grew up and expanded.

Photograph 3

Rachel at two, Morgan at nine. Rachel on Morgan's shoulders, her chin resting on his head and her arms tucked around his neck. Jeff and Morgan were in their green soccer uniforms, the field in the background. They all smiled into the camera.

Photograph 4

Rachel at six. Morgan at thirteen. Uncle Robert's annual picnic for his medical practice at Edwards Gardens. There was a mass exodus to the parking lot. In Morgan's arms, an exhausted Rachel was fast asleep. Her stick legs dangled, as did her arms; it was a less than graceful pose. Morgan stuck his tongue out.

Photograph 5

Rachel at ten. Morgan graduating from St. Michael's at seventeen. His friends: Jeff, Wally, Harry, and Rebecca were there. The same crew that sat around the Hillier executive table today. Everyone was smiling and happy, but Rachel stood demurely beside Morgan. By then, Maureen had explained that there were rules for double-digit girls. It was Rachel's first argument with Maureen. It taught her she had to keep secrets and hide essential parts of herself.

Maureen arrived at the Hilliers early to pick up Rachel and take her to an important business function. Her father was meeting them there. Rachel knew about the dinner but she'd forgotten and so had Aunt Sarah. It annoyed Maureen that Rachel wasn't ready. Her annoyance was compounded when Rachel insisted on taking time to say goodbye to Morgan.

"Rachel, we can't be late. We're already behind the eight ball so I don't want any of your shenanigans tonight. Forget about Morgan. Now get your things and let's go!"

It escalated from there and ended with Rachel hitting her mother and shouting, "I hate you!" The second the words were out, Rachel wanted to take them back, but she hadn't. She stood her ground.

Maureen was the picture of repose. "I'm sorry to hear that, but we have an important engagement to attend, so I suggest you get your things and come along. I'll wait outside for you."

Rachel said goodbye to Morgan, got her things, and left the Hilliers. The walk home was silent.

When she closed the door, Maureen said, "I understand you are fond of Morgan. We all are. He's a fine young man, but the fact is, he's seventeen."

"Morgan's my best friend."

"No Rachel, he's not."

"Yes, he is!"

A soft sigh escaped Maureen. "His best friend is Jeff Gilles. Jeff is seventeen. Morgan's girlfriend is Lacy Patton and she's sixteen. Do you see what I mean? They are the same age as Morgan."

"He's my best friend!"

Maureen crouched down to Rachel's level, reaching for her, but she jerked away. "You're getting to be a big girl Rachel. Too big a girl to be climbing on Morgan's lap and telling him you love him."

"But I do!"

"Yes, I know you do. We all do."

"Why are you saying mean things?"

"I'm telling you the truth. You are friends. You will always be friends. But friendships change. That's not a bad thing. It is important, necessary for Morgan to change, and grow and become a man. He'll be off to university soon. He is seven years older than you, my pet. He'll be making another life for himself soon. He'll probably meet someone special and get married. I know you're young, but you're not so young that you don't understand that Morgan will soon be a man. The same way you will soon be a young woman. You're growing up and that's wonderful. And a big part of me wants to protect you from the hurt you're going to feel when Morgan makes changes to his life."

"He's not going to leave! He's just going to university."

"I know it's hard to believe he will leave—I understand ..."

"No, you don't! Morgan will never forget about me!"

"I didn't say forget, I said change."

"He won't change."

"We can disagree about that, but what I want you to remember is that you are a young lady now. A double-digit girl. There are responsibilities and rules you must live by and climbing up on Morgan's lap is not acceptable anymore. You are not a baby. And if you don't want him to treat you like a baby, you need to take on the responsibilities of a double-digit girl." Maureen had stood and in one fluid motion, gracefully taken off her trench coat.

Her mother epitomized beauty. Lovely manners. Soft spoken. Great style. Things Rachel wanted to be. But she hated her sometimes. She hated that she couldn't just let Rachel believe Morgan was hers forever. Deep inside, she knew her mother was right, but she didn't want to hear it; she didn't want anything to change. Separation from Morgan was painful, even back then; she felt exposed without him. He was the emotional link between her life as a Hillier and her life as a Wharton. He passed between both worlds in a different way from everyone else.

After the double digits talk, Rachel reluctantly did as her mother said, and curbed her exuberance to share every detail of her life with Morgan, but it was hard. Especially the day Morgan took Elaine and Rachel to Churchill Park. Elaine jumped off the swings, got hurt and started to howl. Immediately Morgan was at Elaine's side. Soothing her. Wiping her tears with his T-shirt. Trying to make her laugh. Rachel hated it. She wanted him to make all the tears she carried inside her go away. She wanted to tell him about the talk with Maureen, about being a double-digit girl, but she worried that maybe her mother was right.

Morgan knew something was up; he kept trying to get her to talk, to find out what was wrong. She was a bundle of nerves. Morgan kept pressing her to confessed what was wrong. Sooner than later, it gushed out, "I'm a double-digit girl now and there are rules for double digit girls—and I can't be myself ever again!"

"Of course, you can be yourself," he said.

Tears filled her eyes, "I have to be different now. Keep things to myself. Maureen says I'm not your best friend. Jeff is. She said I have to stop being a baby."

"You're not a baby."

"She said I do baby stuff that double-digit girls don't do. She said you will move away and become a man. You'll change and forget about me because you're seven years older. That I was stupid to keep thinking you are my best friend and keep hugging you and telling you I love you. Like its weird or something." She looked up at him with uncertainty. "Do you think it's weird?"

Morgan rubbed his face hard. "It's not weird. We're family." He slammed the book in his hand onto the ground. "Is this why you've been upset all week?"

"Yes," she looked down at her twisting fingers, her tears splashing them.

"Look at me Punk." Morgan pointed to her—"We ..."—then to himself, "We're family. You being ten and me being seventeen doesn't have anything to do with it, we're buddies." He ran his hand harshly through his hair; a rumble came deep in his chest. "Maureen was upset, that's all. Mum forgot about her party. You weren't ready and she was afraid you guys were going to be late; that's all. It's going to be okay."

Her cool tears stung her hot face. Wearily, she stared at him. She knew he was lying. Heard it in his excellent excuses. Saw it in the way he couldn't look at her. "Everything she said is true, isn't it?"

"No Punk, it's not true." Morgan wiped her tears with his sleeve.

"Morgan ..." her heart broke and her body trembled, "please don't forget about me. You'll be done at St. Mike's soon and everything will change, so you'll have to remember that you're my best friend in the whole world and that I love you. Don't be mad at Maureen—when she told me all this stuff, she wasn't mad. She was nice—I was mad. Promise, no matter what, you won't forget."

"You're killing me here Rach."

Rachel wiped her nose with her shirt. She had never felt so defeated. "I wish I lived here for real. I wish you were my brother and we could live here as a family forever. I don't pretend when I'm here." Her chest hurt.

Morgan hugged her.

"We will always be family." He patted her back as she sobbed.

When her sobs began soft hiccups, he said. "Whew—thank God that's over."

"What's over?"

"Two more tears and I was done!"

"Done what?"

He sighed deeply. "I have a secret I need to tell you."

She pulled back to looked up at him. "A secret?"

"Just between us … you have to promise not to tell anyone."

"I promise. I really promise Morgan."

"Ok …" he whispered, "I'm …" Hesitated and looked around the room.

Rachel looked too.

"I'm … like your twin—when you're happy or sad, I feel it in my bones. When you cry like that, my legs get all weak and rubbery and I feel like I'm dying. You're like kryptonite—you know like Superman, soooo technically, when you cry—it kinda kills me."

She pushed his chest hard. He made a production of it and fell over the back of the couch.

"You lie!" she said.

"Am not!" He lay flat on his back, groaning. "It's called Racktonite. It's real!"

Heart pumping, Rachel ran around the couch to him. Was it true? Was he dying? New tears rushed down her face. "What can I do?"

He twisted on the floor, but she was sure she saw a smile. "Stay healthy. Eat good food. Get to bed on time … and try not to cry too much?" He shuddered. "The tears are killers."

He was lying! "Be serious Morgan!"

Morgan sat up. "Stop the tears! They'rrr killlin mmmme."

"Okay then promise not to forget we are best friends!"

"I'm going to pass out and die an ugly death."

She grabbed his face between her hands. "Promise!"

He groaned. "Stop crying then!"

"Promise!"

"I promise!"

"Forever?"

"Forever!"

Morgan had promised never to change and never to forget about her. An unreasonable request only a ten-year-old could make.

Because everything Maureen said was true.

***

Photograph 6

The photo that has sustained her, that captured her love for Morgan so poignantly, even before she realized its depth—at Mandy's impromptu pool party, a month before Rachel's fourteenth birthday. Morgan was twenty-one.

Mandy's brother had snapped the shot, capturing an exquisite moment that Rachel would otherwise have missed. It was a hot August evening, like so many, but this one was special, it had markers:

1. Rachel got drunk for the first time.
2. It was the night Lacy Patton died.
3. Morgan starred in her first sexual dream.
4. Morgan left two weeks later.

***

Rachel's memories of that night became sketchy after Evan gave her a tall glass of fruit juice. It had been a fun day. Rachel, Louise, and their band of girlfriends had gone to a movie and then back to Mandy's for a swim, but when they arrived Mandy's older brother and sister were having a party. They didn't seem to care that a bunch of fourteen-year-olds crashed their party.

Morgan and Jeff were there. Thank God they didn't embarrass Rachel by talking to her.

Rachel forgot her swimsuit and had to borrow one from Mandy, which was a bit skimpy, so she ended up wearing a towel most of the night. A boy she didn't know sat down on her lounger. Mandy said he was a neighbour—Evan. He was two years older, went to UCC; his father was a diplomat.

The housekeeper brought out treats and fruit punch for the girls, and her husband set up two coolers for the older kids stocked with beer and wine. Evan offered to get Rachel a drink and the party moved into high gear. Music blasted. Everyone talked loudly. Dancing got intense. Louise got pissed off when Rick showed up and went all big brother on her, smelling her fruit punch. He was dating Lacy Patton at the time. It had been years since Morgan dated Lacy, but Rachel had wondered if Morgan minded her being there with Rick. When she looked at Morgan to gauge, he wasn't looking at Lacy, he was watching her. He mouthed a message: "Be good." Rachel laughed, like that was possible with Morgan across the pool, ready to send her home at any misconduct. She remembered feeling lighthearted. Chatty. Everything seemed funny. Evan was a bit of a clown.

Rachel wasn't certain when things started to change. She remembered getting hot, then listless, and her mouth went dry. She felt a bit off. Her lips felt strange. Something was off. Her head felt strange. She thought if she walked around it would help, but when she stood, her legs were rubber. She wobbled and fell back onto her chair. She forced herself up. Evan came to her aid and grabbed her around the waist.

Suddenly she was cold. Her towel was gone. She bent to get it and her head spun. "I feel bad."

Evan whistled. "Babe, you okay?"

Rachel didn't like Evan's tight hold on her waist or his sweaty hand on her stomach; she used her elbow to push him away.

"Rachel?"

She was relieved to hear Morgan's shout.

She tried to focus. He was across the pool, a distant blur, but she couldn't yell to him, her teeth felt like they were melting. She said, "Something's wrong."

Suddenly Morgan was beside her. "Rachel?"

She felt his steady hand, his familiar smell, and she breathed in deeply. Heavy headed, she put her hand on her forehead. "I don't feel well." Then she was falling, but someone caught her before she fell.

"She's with me buddy. I think I can handle this," said Evan. Rachel heard a scuffle, harsh words. "Back off man, she's his cousin."

Morgan's skin was cool against her hot face. The erratic pound of his heart was comforting, even though somewhere in her head she recognized he was worried, but it didn't concern her. She was okay now. Morgan was there.

They were on a bench. A weeping willow cascaded over them. The party sounded far away.

His cool hands cupped her cheeks. "What's wrong sweetie?" His voice was deep, calm, and her body shivered. She wanted … she wanted something. She slid her head sideways, putting her hot lips to his cool palm that had held the side of her face. It felt good. Right. She looked up at him. He was so handsome. Morgan's blue eyes were full of concern. Her heart pounded hard, vibrating her body. She wanted desperately to swim freely in his eyeballs, and the emotion of that want overwhelmed her. Hurt her. Tears clouded her vision the pain was so intense. Sitting beside him wasn't close enough.

Rachel wrapped her arms around his neck and straddled him in one motion; her head spun; she grabbed his biceps to steady herself and was completely distracted by the feel of his skin under her fingers. Fascinated when his muscles moved under her touch.

She heard him whisper, "Holy fuck."

She felt him tremble when she glided her fingertips slowly up his arms, across his shoulders, and down his chest where his heart pounded heavily. She laughed, enjoying herself. She felt free. Uninhibited.

"Jesus Christ Rachel ... What the hell!"

To this day, she remembered feeling empowered. At the time, she moved on instinct. Her body knew what she wanted. She was an open vessel, a seeker, an emotion conduit.

Rachel pressed her palm into the beat of his heart; it pulsed under her hand like a lifeline; it connected her to him in a strange oneness.

Morgan rested his forehead at the side of her head. His face was buried against her hair. His lips whispered softly in her ear, "I think I'm losing my mind." His hot breath made her body tingle from head to toe.

"Me too—so don't leavvvve ...," she breathed with difficulty. She looked up at Morgan; he was very close and she wanted to paste herself to him.

"It's painfully obvious I can't." He cupped her cheek. Morgan was always so calm; a big brother, but that night, everything changed.

"Mummum said ..." Tears came in a rush—he will leave and find someone special. She swallowed, not feeling well.

"Christ Almighty—you're drunk!"

Her head started to spin. "I had ... had ... that fruit juice ... I really don't feeeel good though, like I'm two people," she whispered, "... like mmmy body doesn't belong to mmme ... tooo my head." She tried to focus on Morgan's face. Her words seemed wrong.

Rachel heard laughing from a distance. She heard Rick's voice snap, "Louise put the fucking drink down." She didn't remember much after that—didn't remember leaving Mandy's house or how she got home. What she did remember—fitful dreams. Sweaty. Vivid. They made her feel boneless, womanly, passionate. Morgan was everywhere in her dreams. Whispering to her. Stroking her. Kissing her. Licking her. That night, Morgan began his reign as the leading man in Rachel's every fantasy.

***

Rachel looked down at the picture. A lost moment she'd shared with Morgan, recaptured by luck. She saw innocence. Tenderness. Chemistry. It lifted off the picture. She only remembered the moment through a drunken haze. Through the lens of a camera, she saw the moment from another perspective. The naked, raw hunger on her face shocked her. Every thought, every desire Rachel ever had for Morgan was captured on this young girl's face—turned out so innocently to the camera's greedy sight; a face without inhibition.

Rachel's face burned at she looked down at herself. Mandy's revealing string bikini, no wonder she'd worn a towel, but even if Rachel had been fully clothed, it wouldn't have diminished the power of the moment—the way her body instinctively leaned within a hair's breadth of Morgan's, the way her hands sat on his bare chest. She looked pale and vulnerable: puny, scrawny—insignificant in comparison to his obvious masculinity. Even her skin, so white in comparison to his deep tan; she looked transparent, her bones—frail. Yet the way he held her, sitting on a garden bench, the sexual intimacy of the pose, her legs wrapped around his waist; his sun-kissed hand in her hair, his other hand cupping her neck. His hair—unruly. His face, his lips, inches from hers as he bent over her. Even in profile, Morgan looked intense—alarmed. Rachel's blissful weakness was equally apparent. No wonder her dreams had been so vivid that night.

Rachel was just shy of her fourteenth birthday and she knew nothing of sex and boys. At the time she thought she knew everything, but she knew nothing, and yet, unconsciously, in her drunken state, her natural femaleness reached out to Morgan in ways she didn't know she possessed, and he instinctively responded.

Raw chemistry. Even then.

The beauty of nature—without disguise.

When Rachel and Gary were in Paris, Gary saw the tenderness of the photograph. He saw the raw sensuality. He felt the intensity of the couple in the picture, their shaky, mingled breath, the tremble of their bodies; there was no denying the intimacy between them. Gary tried to steal the split-second Rachel crossed over from girl to woman. He embellished and shared a cherished moment in her life with the man she loved. She felt exposed and angry seeing the untouched passion between her and Morgan in his intimate portrait. It changed Rachel's life. It changed Gary's life. The infamous virgin—frozen in time at the click of a Nikon.

Photograph 7

Rachel at fourteen. Morgan at twenty-one. Two months after he left for Stanford, Morgan came home for Thanksgiving dinner. It was at the Hilliers. Uncle Robert's two brothers, Rutherford and Samson were there, which was a rare occasion, so Aunt Sarah insisted on a family photo. Everyone assembled against the fireplace in the living room.

Morgan looked happy. He stood on the hearth, laughing, under one arm was Jason and under the other was Jeff. To the left of the fireplace, Elaine cuddled in her mother's arms on the loveseat, and Uncle Robert sat on the arm. Aunt Sarah leaned back against him, their hands were intimately clasp, resting casually on his thigh. Rutherford and Samson were in the middle with their wives and children, and Rachel's parents were on the right. Maureen looked radiant. She stood in front of her father, his chin was tucked into her neck and his arms were around her.

Out front and well away from the family, Rachel sat alone on the ottoman, her head tilted slightly to the side. She was so pale she was almost translucent. Her arms were wrapped around her body and her elbows rested on her knees. Sadness radiated from her. Traces of tears were on her eyelashes. Her loneliness was striking.

The photo sparked so many memories, so many emotions for Rachel that tears burned her eyes. It was the first family photo taken where Rachel wasn't beside Morgan. Their volatile fight had her careening into the abyss for years.

Rachel wanted to reach into the photo and pluck her younger self out, hold her tight in her arms, because by the time this picture was taken, Morgan wasn't her friend anymore.

***

When she woke up the next morning, her head pounded. What had happened? Every part of her body hurt. Even her hair. Screams and things that smashed came from downstairs and Rachel grabbed her head, sinking back down under the covers.

Later that day, Aunt Sarah told her in soft whispers that Lacy Patton had died the night before in a house fire. Lacy fell asleep with several candles burning. One caught the drapes. The house went up in flames. Lacy was almost twenty. Although Morgan hadn't dated her in a couple of years, she was an earmarked memory for him— his first love.

Lacy's death changed Rachel's life.

It was a week of shocks. A week of pain. A week of goodbyes. Lacy's death aged Morgan. The boyish smoothness of his skin lost its tenderness; his face chiseled out into hard angles; his eyes became guarded, his body tense. He no longer looked Rachel in the eye. If his gaze did happen to collided with hers, he looked through her.

People often remarked that Lacy and Rachel could pass for sisters; Rachel reminded him of his loss every day. She consoled herself with platitudes that swirled around the Hilliers' home in a constant drone. He's grieving. It takes time to heal. It's hard to get over your first love. He's in shock. We're all in shock. She was so young, so talented, so awful. None of the well-intended words gave Rachel any comfort. She was young, but she knew Morgan better than she knew herself, and she knew something wasn't quite right. She had seen Morgan grieve before, when his grandfather died. This was more than grief, it was as if he had bricks strapped to his shoulders and glued to his feet.

Two weeks after Lacy Patton was buried at Mount Pleasant Cemetery, Morgan announced that he had accepted Stanford University's offer to join an innovative business program—an invitation he had turned down in March. His announcement was casual, over dinner, like he was asking for the bread basket. I'm leaving for Stanford this Saturday. It blindsided Rachel, especially when his announcement was met with silence. Rachel felt betrayed. Angry. It was a force unto itself. And it erupted all over the dinner table.

Not a peep came from the Hilliers. They nodded their heads in agreement.

"I thought you turned it down?" said Rachel

Morgan ignored her.

"They still have your spot?" she said.

"Yup."

Yup? Had Morgan ever used the word yup? No. Had he ever concentrated on his plate with such focus? No.

"Why now?" Rachel couldn't let it go.

"Professor Raffin wants me to."

"So?"

46

"So, it means I'm going." Still didn't bother to lift his head.

Rachel felt unreasonably hot, losing focus of the room. "Just because some guy says so?"

"He's not some guy; he's—the guy."

"Does this have something to do with Lacy's—?"

He cut her off. "No." His hands clenched into fists.

"You haven't mentioned Stanford all summer!" She whipped down her napkin. "You're a liar. I want to see your eyeballs. Or are you afraid I'll see the real reason?"

Morgan took a couple of deep breaths before his fists crashed down on the dining room table making everyone jump and the utensils and glasses dance across the tablecloth. He stood up and leaned over, his knuckles pressed into the table, his voice a forced calm. "I don't have to check with you. Who do you think you are?"

Did she hear him right? Their whole friendship was checking in with each other. Something wasn't right. He made her feel small and insignificant for the first time. It hurt. Her heart raced with panic. Something was terribly wrong, anger like she had never experience before exploded between them in a sweaty rage.

"You know exactly who I am." Her voice was calmer than she felt.

"I know you alright," he shouted, his fist slammed down on the table again. "Well here's the truth—I'm sick of you. I'm sick of seeing you. You're choking me to death. I can't even breathe in my own house! You're always around. You're just some scrawny neighbour kid who was abandoned by her egotistical parents and we took pity on. Well, I'm sick of it. I have my own life!"

Rachel's insides collapsed, whirling together into a tornado and the suction created a small hardball in the pit of her stomach. Every insecurity she had, he hit with missile-like precision. In a split second—Morgan became everyone else. She hated his words, his mean face; she hated him. "Fuck you Morgan!"

"Fuck me?" Disbelief on his face. "Fuck me?"

"That's enough from both of you," said Uncle Robert. "Morgan out!"

When he didn't move, Robert corralled Morgan while Rachel was under a firm grip being tugged away in the opposite direction, but Rachel didn't care. She screamed, "That's right Morgan! Fuck you! Don't worry, you arrogant bastard, you aren't stuck with me anymore!"

"Enough Rachel." Aunt Sarah's voice cracked loudly.

"Not even close!" Rachel yanked out of Sarah's hold to follow Morgan.

Morgan broke free from his father and launched across the room until his menacing figure was inches from her. "You little fucking shit, I can't wait to get as far away from you as I can!"

His tense body exuded energy that sunk into her, making her strong and weak simultaneously.

Tears burned her eyes. "Coward!"

Uncle Robert grabbed his arm, "Morgan. Enough."

But Morgan hit his father's hand. "Stay out of this!"

Words whirled around Rachel, but Morgan was all she saw or heard. "Go then," she shouted; shoving his chest, "I don't give a shit. Go ahead. You want to pick on me, go ahead. You want to walk around here like there's a pickle up your ass—go ahead. You're nothing but a spoiled brat from Forest Hill. Poor little Morgan, what a fucking harsh life!"

"You have no fucking idea what's going on here."

"I know the things that matter."

"You know fuck all."

"I know something is wrong! I can feel it." Her hands flew to her chest. "I can feel it Morgan. You can pretend with everyone else but you can't pretend with me, so stop treating me like I'm stupid. If you can't tell me what's wrong, fine. Go! No one's fucking stopping you! But don't pretend this is about Stanford and some professor you don't give a shit about—not with me."

With both hands, she shoved his chest. "Go!" she sobbed.

Morgan grabbed her arms, narrowing the space between them; his low voice vibrated, "You have no fucking idea how much I hate you!"

His vehemence jolted her and his features became blurred. The heat from his body pressed in hers, consuming her, burning her up, and the fight went out of her.

Morgan shook her. "Do you hear me, I hate you!"

Tears rolled silently down her hot face. "You probably wish I had died instead of her, don't you?" she said quietly into his distorted features. "Well so do I Morgan. Then you would be free."

Morgan's caught her roughly against him. The air buzzed with an eerie silence until she heard Morgan gasp, felt his hot breath against her hair, felt a rumble deep within him move up his body and explode into a scream as he shook her. "Nooooo!"

Rachel's body jerked with his anguished cry. She was numb.

Uncle Robert's voice was deep and firm. "Morgan! Let's go of her. I mean it. Let go."

Suddenly Morgan was gone. Aunt Sarah was holding her up, talking to her, but Rachel couldn't decipher her words. Her grief was too intense. Maureen's prophesy was child's play in comparison to the truth. Morgan's desperation to get away from her, his hate, vibrated through her. She hadn't just lost a friend, someone she loved above all others, she'd lost a part of herself, her mythology, and she didn't know what that would mean. She just knew something terrible had happened. It frightened her. Her isolation frightened her. She started to shake; she broke out into a sweat; her teeth chattered; nausea overwhelmed her and vomit burned her throat.

***

Rachel couldn't remember anything more about that day. She was in a fog for days and when the fog cleared, Morgan was gone. He came home at Thanksgiving and Christmas, but he had no time for her. She wanted to apologize for her behaviour that day, but he had another life by then. Rachel and Morgan were no longer friends. She was a burden. He was shaking her off. His promise of—friends no matter what—had expired. The pain of that realization had Rachel burying herself.

Photograph 8

Rachel is just shy of her sixteenth birthday. Morgan is twenty-three. They were at the yacht club. Someone from the marina crew took the shot. Morgan had lifted her out of the boat and swung her onto his back, pretending he was going to throw her in the lake. They were both laughing. They looked so young, so tanned, so carefree. It was probably the last carefree moment they had for many years to come.

Morgan wanted to play hooky from his summer job and asked Rachel to go to the yacht club. When she was a kid, they spent their summers sailing on Lake Ontario. This particular day they didn't sail, they got a speed boat. Morgan had been away at Stanford, then Oxford for what seemed like an eternity, so Rachel was game for any opportunity to spend time with him.

She knew for sure—meeting the love of your life at the point of your first recollection, and him being seven years older—forces you to bury yourself so far beneath the surface, that you are unrecognizable when you finally surface.

4

MORGAN RETURNS

From the time she was fourteen, Rachel had changed boyfriends regularly. It became a joke around the Hillier dinner table and no one loved teasing Rachel more than her childhood partner in crime, Jason Hillier, about her band of boys.

Rachel and Jason were the scalawags of the Hillier clan. Getting into mischief was their forte, and more often than not, Morgan bailed them out of their predicaments. As much as they were partners, equally, they enjoyed getting each other into trouble—they weren't coy about such things. Morgan and Elaine never participated in menacing behaviour of any kind. However, shy, reserved Elaine was easily talked into one of Rachel's business ventures. There was the bracelet-making business, the design your own bedroom business, the cookie business. Unfortunately, Rachel kept burning the cookies, and between Jason and herself, they ate the ones Elaine baked. Being a scalawag, in a scalawag team, it's important to take the good with the bad, and nothing was more hilarious to Jason than Rachel's rotating boyfriend system. But Rachel felt Morgan's absence every day. His empty seat at the dinner table was a festering sore; so, Rachel dated.

Dating was Rachel's deliberate attempt at looking normal. A rite of passage. People considered her pretty, and what did pretty girls of a certain age do? They dated. She was careful who she dated. Boys from the neighbourhood, friends of friends, brothers of friends, friends of Jason's and Elaine's, friends of her mother's were all acceptable, but she wasn't much for one on one—her favourite was dating as a group. If someone asked her out, she would immediately add friends.

No one expected boyfriends to last long, which worked in Rachel's favour. Her *relationships* lasted a month, possibly two—again she was within the norm. Regardless of how easy she made it look, it was a difficult time for Rachel. The seamless stream of boys produced a hardy laugh around the Hillier dinner table, but Rachel was distracting herself, keeping people at a distance, filling her time with goals, school, family, friends, and hobbies—everything and everyone had a place in her schedule or else the days dragged. It made it easy to get lost in time.

With Morgan at Stanford, she had to make an extra effort not to be herself, to knock her mother off her scent. If Maureen thought something was wrong, Rachel would be shipped off to school. It wasn't hard hoodwinking Maureen, she was rarely there during the years Morgan was away, but there were other considerations—nosey people, especially when it came to the Hilliers—so she had to keep her aches to herself.

Halfway through his stint at Stanford, Morgan received an opportunity to attend Oxford in England. He went. His new American girlfriend, Emily, joined him. Two years later, Morgan returned home in the spring to complete his graduate studies at the University of Toronto. Emily was in tow. Morgan was different, sophisticated, distant. He seemed taller, broader, not at all the Morgan she knew. Her heart broke a little when he spoke to her with polite reserve, as if she were a stranger. She didn't want to credit her mother for her accurate predictions that Morgan had moved on, become a man, and found someone special, leaving Rachel in the dust. Instead Rachel came up with a plan to prove Maureen wrong. Rachel didn't like Emily. She had a chip on her shoulder and a gigantic uncompromising ego. Her dislike for the young American was in the minority, which was fine by her. Emily disliked Rachel in equal amounts.

Happy to have her eldest son home, Aunt Sarah had the guesthouse prepared for Morgan's return. She wanted to give him a bit of privacy, but not so much privacy that Emily was included as a resident. Emily hadn't been pleased with this revelation; she thought Sarah was a relic. Rachel took no notice of Emily. Now that Morgan was home to stay, she concentrated on rebuilding their friendship, but he was resistant. He kept to the guesthouse. No matter—she consoled herself by focusing on their shared interests. They both loved the beach, water, boats, board games, old movies, reading, and music. She was diligent. Buried under this new polished Morgan was *her* Morgan. She was sure her mother wasn't right; she couldn't lose faith, and she couldn't accept being discarded. When he started to show up more at the breakfast table and the dinner table, she was hopeful, but she soon realized it was Alma's cooking he was after.

Their argument after Lacy's death had left an impact, but she believed he would forgive her for losing her temper. When weeks became months, he consistently brushed aside her questions, and her shiny enthusiasm faltered.

One morning at breakfast, Rachel was flipping through Uncle Robert's newspaper after he left for work. Jason wolfed down his food and Laine used charm on her mother to get Jimmy Choo pumps. Morgan was at the counter filling up his travel mug with coffee.

"The jazz festival is coming up," Rachel said and read out the headline, "The street party of the summer." She smiled, "I think I was three or four the first time we went."

She lifted her eyes to his back.

"I'm out of here," said Jason, and kissed his mother. "If you need a ride Laine hurry up."

Lainey stuffed her waffle into her mouth, chewing as she kissed her mother goodbye, and waved absently.

"Ma—where's your keys?" shouted Jason.

Aunt Sarah shouted back, "Where is your car?"

"No gas. Come on ma, where?"

Sarah looked at Rachel. "I guess I have to fill his? And unless I want him rummaging through my purse, I must get up to get my keys?"

Rachel smiled.

"Children suck the marrow from your bones." Aunt Sarah walked out of the room.

Rachel returned to the newspaper. "It was always a great day being down at the beaches. Remember? We ate too much. The boardwalk was packed. Smooth jazz everywhere." Happy days. "I had this friend, a really long time ago, who told me that rhythm and blues is music that burdens and lightens you."

Morgan made his way to the kitchen door. Her eyes followed him. "I was the only six-year- old who knew who Miles Davis, Stevie Ray Vaughan, and Nina Simone were."

His pace slowed.

"I knew the difference between big band blues, electric blues, and blues rock. I still love spirituals, chants ..."

Morgan stopped. Rachel's heart pounded.

"Narrative ballads. Remember taking me to the Rock the Park Festivals? And Sass Jordan was there—I fell in love with her raspy voice. Even when I was going to school in London she was playing at a local bar, and you came down and we went. Such a fun night. God, she was good! I'm still a big fan. I just learned how to play; *I Want to Believe.*"

He turned. For the first time in years, he looked her in the eye, and her whole body trembled.

"Hi," she smiled, "you're Morgan Hillier, right? I thought I recognized you." She stood up and held out her hand to him. "I'm

Rachel Wharton."

Rachel remembered the clipped, measured sound his shoes made on the marble floor as he walked across the kitchen to her, the smile on his face when he reached the table, the warmth of his hand against her cold one. "Hello, Rachel Wharton."

Maureen wouldn't approve of her impulse, but she couldn't help herself—he'd come back! He walked across the kitchen floor and came back. He looked at her. Spoke to her. Rachel ran around the breakfast table, plowed right into him, and wrapped her arms around his middle. His absence, her regret, missing him with such an ache that it ate her insides in fleshy chunks. Emotions she had denied herself let loose and she burst into tears. When his arms loosely came around her, her cries intensified, coming from a deep wound.

"I'm sorry," she whispered with difficulty. "I didn't mean any of it. That day—when you told us you were leaving for Stanford." She pulled back to look up at him, hiccupping. "I'm sorry. I just didn't want you to go. Mean things kept popping out of my mouth and I couldn't stop them. I just didn't want you to go. You have to forgive me. Please Morgan, please forgive me."

"Jesus Rachel, there's nothing to forgive. You didn't do anything wrong. It was me. *Me!* There's nothing to forgive."

"Yes, there is Morgan ... *there is,* you never talk to me; you treat me like a stranger. I don't know what to do with all the stuff," her hands went to her chest, "stuck inside. I ... I ... I miss going to that old movie warehouse and watching those cheesy flicks. I miss eating the bad popcorn. I miss sharing books with you. I have no one to talk to about books. No one knows who Victor Hugo is. No one knows about jazz or manual transmissions or driving fast on old Gormley Road on a Sunday. Stuff Morgan, all the stuff you did with me, stuff you taught me, stuff I love, stuff I miss. You have to forgive me, you have to! So, we can be friends again, please, you have to!" She knew it sounded bad, garbled, and maybe a little hysterical, but she had been so afraid, *so afraid.*

"Rachel," he bent down and held her arms tightly.

"I can't fight with you anymore Morgan. It's like dying. I'm sorry for the stuff I said," she hiccupped and shuddered.

"You didn't do anything wrong," he whispered pulling her into his arms. "It was my fault, mine—I'm the one who's sorry. Come on, calm down, you're going to make yourself sick ...*shh, shh,* everything's okay." He stroked her hair, whispering soothing words.

It felt good to be held by him. His heartbeat strong and fierce against her. Sounds of her crying echoed in the kitchen and he squeezed her tight. His fingers dug into her for a moment and she knew he missed her too. Her tears slowed and she shuddered out a few hiccups.

"Now—please forgive me, because I hate to make this about me, but you do know—any more tears and you will probably kill me. Which is pretty selfish since I just literally got home but given the circumstances ... unless ... did you forget about the Racktonite?"

Rachel wiped her face on the inside of her T-shirt and pulled back to look him in the eye, blinking rapidly as tears continued to run down her face.

"Forgot, didn't you?" He put on a sad face. "I know you're in the pit of despair, and I know I'm responsible, but technically, you *are* killing me with your tears." Suddenly, his body swirled then staggered back and leaned against the island. "It would help me out if you stopped crying 'cause my legs are starting to tingle a bit."

Rachel said, "You're going to you use the Racktonite thing?"

His leg buckled. "I'll understand if you want me to suffer."

Rachel laughed and cried at the same time. *Oh my God! I can't believe he's trying to make me laugh at comic book humour.*

"What?" Morgan looked up at her, startled from his buckled state, "No, no more tears— you were doing so well!"

Rachel couldn't control her tears and her fingers couldn't keep up with their continuous flow. She looked down at him as his other leg buckled, and she laughed, shaking her head, looking up at the ceiling, gulping back her tears.

"What?" he said, immediately close, pushing her hair from her wet face. "Tell me."

She dropped her head and pressed it into his chest. "I've missed you so, so much Morgan!"

Morgan let her cry.

After that day in the kitchen, Morgan no longer kept her at bay. He was still reserved, but with each day that passed, he relaxed. The day at the marina, though, was a surprise. He came home in the middle of the day with a plan to play hooky. To go to the yacht club, get a speedboat, and bum around the lake.

Rachel had no idea when she said yes how painful a journey she was beginning.

Alma packed them lunch; they threw on beachwear and headed to the marina. Under the bluest sky on the hottest day of the summer, Rachel and Morgan flew around the lake at breakneck speeds with tunes blaring. It was the best and worst day. Rachel's girlish fantasies had always included Morgan, but after that day, she no longer saw him as a dream. Her childhood confidant, her big brother, had fallen by the wayside as the years past. He was no longer capable, reliable Morgan in her eyes; he was her Morgan, the Morgan few get to see. Humourous Morgan. Tender, compassionate Morgan. The part of himself that he gave to her.

Rachel was an ordinary girl, but Morgan made her special in ways that she couldn't achieve on her own. He woke her up from her girlish crush and taught her about love, longing, and ache. He woke up the need for achievement and commitment. He woke her up to want and hate.

Morgan was standing at the front of the boat that sunny day, holding the wheel while Rachel sat in the front seat watching him.

He turned to her; he was laughing, the sun was at his back, a soft breeze moved his hair lightly; he was beautiful, confident, present. His sunglasses kept the expression in his eyes from her, but in that moment, in seeing him, really seeing him, she ached with an overwhelming love for him. Her heart pounded, her body vibrated with the first intoxicating thrill of sexual chemistry, and she knew. There were no shadows. *I am in love with Morgan Hillier.*

"Can I drive the boat?" she said.

"Absolutely." He slowed down and moved from behind the steering wheel. "Come on."

Rachel sat comfortably in the leather chair in front of the steering wheel listening intently to his instructions over the blare of Guns and Roses, *Sweet Child of Mine,* when Morgan reached across her to turn off the stereo. His forearm brushed her nipple and an electric volt zipped from the tip of her nipple to every cell in her body in the time it took to blink. When she felt the wetness between her legs, she froze. *Oh God!* Embarrassment shook her. Her eyes darted down, catapulting her into further mortification—her body had betrayed her eagerly. Rachel's nipple was the size of Mount Everest and the other one had joined the party. She turned to fire; her passion acute. Desperately she wanted a towel—a face cloth, anything to cover her body; her sudden feeling of nakedness.

Shoot me, please! Now! Rachel gripped the steering wheel. She couldn't organize her thoughts —didn't know what to do. Nothing tied together with any coherency. *What just happened?* It was too much to figure out. She was fiber-optic. Even as her sharp nipples ached, the reckless nature of her thoughts caught her unprepared. Relentless want took over her body and mind. She wanted him to fondled her nipples, suck on them. She wanted *Morgan's* lips to coax them, *his* tongue to lick them. Her emotions stirred up a pain that was both jagged and beautiful.

Morgan *must notice.* She turned her body ever so slightly, trying not to alert him that she was moving. Pressing into the shadow of the boat, she wished for invisibility

The closest she'd ever come to passion was that football guy— *Louise's pool party, last month, what was his name? Dirk, Turk—something; after kissing him for a while she really started to enjoy it. Got a bit flushed. Felt her heart in her chest. Nothing like now—my heart is beating me to death from the inside!* She'd had a cavalcade of boyfriends. Read books. Nothing like this—ever. This was intense.

"Rachel?"

Oh my God, he's going to talk about it. Heat seared her face and she sucked in her breath. Her heart pounded erratically.

"You can step on the gas a bit sweetie," he said casually. "I'm nearly positive we have extra." He stood and walked back to check. "We have tons of gas."

Rachel pressed down on the gas and they shot off. She heard Morgan lose his footing but she ignored him. The wind was forceful and hot, but intoxicating.

Morgan laughed. "Holy shit—you are dangerous behind the wheel." He made his way to the other chair and pressed his knee into the seat while he looked over the lake; his back to her. His scent reached her nose; his cologne mingled with the fresh air, a toxic combination. Her eyes glided over his broad shoulders, down his beautiful back, over the curve of his rounded bum—her cheeks burned, she was sure they were going to fall off her face from heat exposure. She wanted desperately to touch him. To run her fingers through his hair and down his chest—so, so badly. But this wasn't a dream. She wasn't safe in her bed having one of her fantasies. *Which is completely normal. I looked it up. It's normal. Healthy even. But this is real. Morgan's right here! This is wrong. So, so wrong.*

When he moved, she jumped.

He waved to a passing boater, and the guy shouted, "Hey Morgan!"

"Slow down a sec sweetie."

Rachel moved in close to the other boat. Morgan introduced her and she waved, but she was glad he was distracted, giving her enough time to throw on a coverup, pull herself together, and breathe a shaky breath of relief that he hadn't noticed her apple-sized nipple. Her dignity was safe.

After a brief chat with his friends, he said to her, "Let's take her out baby girl."

Rachel raced the boat around the lake under his tutelage. He might not notice her the way she noticed him, but being with him was always her best time, regardless of the circumstances. That day there was a new dimension carved into their friendship and she couldn't stop smiling. Happy beyond her wildest dreams, she spun and lifted the boat off the water in reckless ways, without reprimand from Morgan. Instead, they howled with laughter and he christened her Maria Andretti.

Shortly after they returned to the clubhouse, Emily showed up. Morgan kissed her lips.

"I called you." Emily's sunglasses hid her eyes but her body language spoke loudly. Her movements were stiff, her voice clipped. "Your mother said you were here." In between the lines sat Emily's unsaid accusations, but Rachel didn't care. Morgan had called her, not Emily. It felt good. Powerful.

Morgan smiled down at Emily. "Just playing hooky. It's a beautiful day."

"Hello, Rachel ... you look tanned. Did you enjoy your day on the lake?" It was clear Emily could care less about her day.

"It was the best day ... ever ... Morgan let me drive the boat." Rachel wrapped her arms around her chest. She couldn't help the blush that fused her face so she didn't dare look at Morgan, but she could feel his stare and her arms tightened around her breasts.

Emily moved closer to Morgan and slipped her arm around his

waist. "Excuse us, *would you* ... we have grown up things to discuss."

"Whatever ..." she was working on adrenalin and said, "Why don't I take off? The subway is close; it will take me twenty minutes to get home."

"No," Morgan said.

"She's almost sixteen Morgan, she isn't a child." She looked up at him, her sunglasses pulled down slightly. "Or hadn't you noticed?"

"She's my responsibility. I brought her."

Rachel started to back away. "Emily's right, I'm not a child. You guys have to talk ... so?"

Morgan's tone was deeper. "Rachel stop. You are dressed in a bikini and a dress that's see-through—I said no. You are not walking through downtown Toronto or taking the subway dressed like that, do you hear me? No."

Emily pulled out the big guns. "If you were worried about playing a superhero, maybe you should have called me to join you today."

"*Really?* You hate boats and water and sun and ..."

"Shut up Morgan. That's not the point. It's clear where your loyalties lie." She turned on her heel and walked away.

Morgan turned and pointed at Rachel. "Don't move!" Then he followed Emily.

She watched as Emily pouted and wiped at her tears. Him stroking her hair. Watching the intimate interplay had Rachel taking off before her heart broke into a billion smithereens in front of everyone sitting on deck. She had no money on her. Walking was her only alternative, short of calling Aunt Sarah or Jason to pick her up, but she didn't want that, and she didn't want to watch Morgan with Emily, or watch Emily's hurt little girl routine. It always led to her slobbering all over him. Walking was a much better plan.

She left Harbourfront and walked to Union Station. Packed with people who rushed around, looking stressed, talking on their cell phones, or frantically rushing for their trains; they seemed unaware it was a beautiful day. She walked up Bay Street and took a rest at Nathan Phillips Square. In her beach bag, she had an apple, a bottle of water, a mushy brownie, a hairbrush, a sketchpad, and sunscreen. She ate the mushy brownie while she brushed her knotted hair and studied the City Hall buildings; quickly, she sketched them. The fountain in the centre of the square made cylinder arcs. In the winter, the fountain converted into an ice rink. Many wintry, cold, Sunday afternoons of her childhood were spent at Nathan Phillips Square.

Rachel tossed her sketchbook in her bag, took a sip of water, and walked up Bay Street to Bloor, then took Bloor across to Yonge Street. She sat on the steps of the Bay Department Store and ate her apple. The shade was delightful. She was hot and tired. It was four-thirty when she left the Harbourfront.

A group of kids sat a few feet away. Rachel had no watch. "Do you know what time it is?"

The guy with blue hair said, "Seven-thirty."

"Thanks." When she got up to leave, blue hair guy said, "Hey we're going to a party tonight, wanna come?"

Rachel rolled her eyes and laughed. "I wish. My mother is making me go to my grandmother's; it's her birthday—she's ninety-six—keeps using, 'It could be her last birthday.'" The lie ran easily off her tongue, but she didn't consider it a lie, more a yarn.

Blue haired boy said, "Maybe some other time?"

"Sure." She shrugged and walked down the steps.

"Hey!" When she turned, the blue haired guy ran up to her. "Here's my number. I'm Raine."

She nodded. "Rachel. Thanks." She shoved his number in her beach bag and left. She walked up Yonge Street to St. Clair, taking St. Clair until she hit Avenue Road. She found an empty bench at the small park at the corner and drank her water.

That's where Jason found her. She didn't see him at first. She didn't see his car screeching to a halt until the woman who sat beside her said, "Is that really necessary?"

"What's that?"

"That boy, driving so recklessly."

Rachel looked where she pointed. Jason was moving quickly across the grass, looking menacing, and the woman sitting beside her scurried away. Rachel's feet were sore. She remained where she was. He stopped in front of her, his hands shoved into his jean pockets.

"Everyone is freaking out," he said calmly.

"Freaking?"

"Freaking out looking for you."

"Morgan knows where I am."

"You left."

"I told him."

"He doesn't remember it that way."

Rachel shrugged. She didn't care if everyone was freaking out.

Jason turned away. "Let's go. Your mother is going to call the police if we don't get home fast."

Rachel was incapable of getting up gracefully. Jelly shoes were not a good choice for a three-hour walk. She slipped them off and carefully got up. Her feet sunk into the cool earth.

"What's wrong?" Jason snapped.

She wanted to weep but didn't. She wanted to lie, but Jason was a liar too; he would know. "I didn't have any money so I had to walk, and my feet are sore."

"You walked from the Harbourfront?"

"Stupid, huh?"

"Why?"

Rachel shrugged.

Jason's car was cool and she sank back into the soft leather and dozed. She woke to Morgan's angry voice. Her mother was in the background. "Thank God ... we've been so worried darlin'."

Morgan stood in the open car door, peering down at her. It's very scary to wake up to a six-foot four-man, even bending, with a face on him that could haunt houses. "You ... little ... I could strangle you." He was furious. His usual calm gone. Rachel did manage to bring out the worst in him. "Do you have any idea the trouble you've caused? Get out of the car!"

Everyone was around the car, talking at the same time. Rachel was exhausted. She wanted Morgan to know she was hurting, but she played the martyr instead.

"Morgan, I don't know why you're blaming her, she was your responsibility," her mother insisted, reaching out to embrace Rachel.

"Only small children dash off into the street once your head is turned." Her mother released her; Morgan grabbed Rachel's arm and brought her close to him, lifting her face with his finger —none were gentle touches. Certainly, not the gentle touch of guidance she had received earlier that day.

"I told you, you weren't taking the subway. I gave you reasons why. Was I not clear?"

"You were clear."

"So why did you leave?"

"What difference does it make now? I'm here. I'm sorry. It won't happen again."

"Damn right it won't because I'm not taking you anywhere with me again."

She was glad she wore sunglasses; it made it easier to smile up at him. "Then it's all good, right?"

He let go of her; his face, remote.

The concrete was hot against her feet. Putting on the jelly shoes was not an option, so she walked the short distance to the Hilliers' cool grass.

"Where are you going Rachel?" asked her mother.

"Home."

"Good, I'll be right there; my things are at Auntie Sarah's."

Rachel's feet were on fire. She walked along neighbouring lawns, clenching her teeth together when she tiptoed over the concrete driveways, before sinking onto the cool grassy lawn again. When she was in front of her house, she crossed the road, relieved when she reached the edge of the grass. She had been concentrating on her burning feet so she didn't realize Morgan had followed her. He stood in front of her. She jumped the side path onto her front lawn.

"Where did you go?" said Morgan.

Too tired, she said, "Nowhere. I came home."

"It took three hours?"

"I walked."

"You what?"

"I walked."

"Why?"

Rachel sighed. "I didn't have any money."

He stuffed his hands meanly into his pockets. "Jesus, Rachel! Anything could have happened to you."

"But it didn't."

"But it could have."

"But it didn't. You don't need to worry about me, Morgan. You have Emily to worry about, and your family and your future, so don't give another thought to little old me."

Morgan laughed. "You are so full of crap, Rachel."

His laughter irritated her. "Why are you laughing?"

"You."

"What about me?"

He bent down. "You, baby girl, are so full of crap. 'You don't need to worry about little old me Morgan,'" he mimicked. "'Worry about Emily, your future, your family.' Crap Rachel—you are full of crap, and not just any crap, *melodramatic* crap."

Rachel shoved him. "Go home." She walked into the house,

sighing when her feet touched the cool marble floor.

Morgan was behind her.

"Go home Morgan!"

"No."

Frustrated, she screamed, shoving him harder, "Just go home—or to your girlfriend's or whatever it is you do—and leave me alone!" She hit him, he groaned, and she said, "I hope that hurt."

He continued to groan. "Oh yes, I'm wounded. A ninety-pound girl hit me so, so, so hard."

"Shut up, Morgan." She walked on her heels to the kitchen.

Morgan leaned against the kitchen door. "So, did you accomplish your goal?"

"What goal?" She downed a glass of water greedily then hoisted herself up on the counter, put her feet in the sink, and filled it with cold water. Her feet were grossly swollen, her soles tender, yellowish, and from the indentation of her sandals, looked like cut squares.

Morgan stood beside her. They were eye level. "Hurting me. That's what you tried to do today, isn't it?"

She looked at his blue striped shirt. "No."

"Yes, you did. Emily showed up, told you to run along and you got mad."

"Why would I care what Emily says?"

"Because she ruined your day?" Morgan flipped up her sunglasses and grabbed her chin. Their eyes met. Rachel pulled away from him and he dropped his hand.

"You scared me Rachel," he said quietly, "when I looked back and you were gone ..."

She lifted her head and saw him shake his head; he whispered, "Heart pounding panic. Downtown Toronto. Alone. Dressed as you were—you wanted me to be worried, and I was. You wanted to hurt me, and you did."

Their perfect day was perfectly ruined. "I don't want to hurt you

Morgan, well I did, but not really … It's just we had such a great day … and she showed up … and I did get mad … she can be such a … I …I'm sorry. Don't be mad."

She looked up at him. "She sees you all the time. It was just one afternoon. Don't I deserve one lousy afternoon?" Tears blurred her vision and she blinked them away. His silence hurt. "Please Morgan," she whispered, "the last time we got mad at each other … we didn't speak for two years." She felt his hand slide down her back in comfort and she reached for his forearm. "I won't do it again."

"Yes, you will." His voice was solemn. "Yes, you will."

"Well, well, well … I see the little … *girl* has been found." Emily's voice pulled Rachel away from Morgan.

"Leave it alone Emily."

Emily pointed at Rachel. "*She* created this little drama, not me." Rachel watched her face twist in disgust.

Morgan didn't respond.

"Morgan?" Emily insisted. "Did you hear me?"

Rachel looked at Morgan, but she saw he was looking in the sink. She felt him touch her feet and she jumped. "Jesus Rachel, what the hell happened?"

Maureen shouted from the hall. "Rachel? Darlin' where are you?"

Morgan yelled back. "We're in the kitchen. Rachel needs you."

Morgan swiped Rachel off the counter into his arms as Maureen rushed down the hall. "What's wrong?" Rachel didn't look at her mother or Emily.

"Her feet," Morgan snapped, sliding his hand under her calf, and held up her foot, "she walked from the Harbourfront in sandals."

"Oh darling, look at your poor feet."

Morgan carried Rachel up to her room. Over his shoulder, she watched Emily slam out of her house, making her feel much better.

Morgan laid her down on her bed while Maureen started a bath.

"I'll stop by later to see how you're doing."

She nodded. Not wanting him to go. "Morgan?"

He turned, hands in his pockets. "Yes?"

"It was a perfect day."

He nodded. "It was a perfect day."

"Thank you ... you know, since it's the last time you'll ever take me anywhere *again*. I guess the *sweet memory* will have to last me."

Morgan shook his head, his arms lifted, his fingers spread into claws, and he growled at her. "You drive me crazy." Then he was gone.

Photograph 9

Rachel was laughing into the camera looking radiantly happy. She flipped the photo over. In Morgan's familiar handwriting: "Rachel's Sweet 16 at Bass Lake. Mum, Dad, Jason, Elaine, Rachel, and Me." She turned the photo over. They were sitting in the sand. Morgan sat sideways looking at Rachel so she couldn't see his face. What had he been looking at? Thinking?

Rachel had been to so many Sweet 16 parties that year, she was Sweet 16'd out. Maureen was disappointed when Rachel said she didn't want a loud impersonal birthday. Her birthday fell on a Wednesday and her parents took her and the Hilliers to her favourite Italian restaurant. Maureen left after dinner to catch a plane to England; her sister Colleen was ill. John went to Ottawa the following day, but after his meetings, he joined Maureen. Rachel stayed with the Hilliers. On Friday, when she got home from school, Aunt Sarah said they had rented a cottage for the weekend to celebrate her birthday.

It was the best birthday. They played silly games. It was hot so they went swimming. Of course, the water was freezing, but they warmed up quickly. They watched *Paint Your Wagon* with Lee Marvin and Clint Eastwood. Ate angel food cake. Chocolate caramels. It was just the six of them. No Emily. Having Morgan home, having solidarity with him again, Rachel saw it as a victory and with the naivety of adolescence, she bricked out a future for them.

Then everything changed.

Morgan announced his engagement to Emily that Christmas and the path Rachel had designed for herself exploded without warning.

Morgan married Emily the following year.

5

MORGAN GETS MARRIED

Photograph 10

Morgan's wedding day. Emily was radiant, tucked under the protection of Morgan's arm. Rachel stared at the wedding party and slowly inhaled. Her chest heaved at the exertion. Looking at herself in the photograph, Rachel recognized her pain easily. She looked ill. Her eyes were big and dull. The bridesmaid dress looked hideous on her. Elaine stood tall and elegant beside her, smiling, her eyes soft.

It was etched in her mind; that day was a living tragedy Rachel barely lived through. She was in the bridal party—a mistake, in retrospect. Everything was big and fat about that wedding.

Emily had been particular about who sat at the head table with her and Morgan: the best man, Jeff Gilles; the maid of honour, Emily's fellow journalist, Tams Harding—Rachel never saw Tams after the wedding—Emily's mother and her third husband; and Aunt Sarah and Uncle Robert. The five groomsmen and five bridesmaids sat together a short distance away. Three hundred people sat comfortably around them.

Time stood still; she spoke only upon request. She followed without question or suggestion. Stood. Sat. Moved. Smiled on demand. Without comment, she went through the process of hair, makeup, dress, Escalade, church, and pictures. Watching Morgan gaze into Emily's eyes, kissing her, touching her, was draining. They had a receiving line that would test a saint, endless speeches, clinking glasses and demands that he kiss her yet again. One thing blurred into another. The wall she had built around herself lost its might when the bride and groom took to the floor for their first dance. Pieces of Rachel broke off quietly in that moment, and her carefully constructed wall of protection collapsed.

The lights dimmed. Morgan and Emily walked hand in hand to the center of the dance floor. Tears burned Rachel's vision; their dancing forms became watery pools of black and white.

"Hey, hey, what's this?" Jason moved his chair closer to her.

She shook her head and shrugged, trying to control her tears and the tremble of her body.

Jason looked grim as he wiped her tears with his napkin.

"I want ... to go," she whispered.

He yanked her closer, turning her chair so her back was to the bridal party. He whispered in her ear, "What's wrong?"

People were on their feet, gathering around the dance floor, clapping; flashes of light played across the walls and ceiling as they took pictures of the happy couple. Suddenly, Jason and Rachel were alone at the table. She bent her head. Her body ached from being rigid all day. She slipped her Valentino Rockstud Patent Leather Pumps off her throbbing feet. "I'm tired."

"You'll have to do better than that—I kinda know ya."

Her fingers covered her eyes as she cried softly, her heavy head falling onto his shoulder.

"Half-pint, maybe I can help."

She lost the battle. Rapid tears rolled down her hot cheeks as she looked up at him. "I ... I always thought ... he would pick *me* ...," saying the words exhausted her more than she could have imagined.

Confused, he stared at her, then she saw recognition in his blue eyes. Jason looked at the dance floor then back at her. "Oh Rach ... honey." He frowned; his eyes sad. His arm went around her and pulled her close. "How could I miss that? Yes ... of course you did!"

Her secret was out. Defeated, a quiet dullness filled Rachel's heart as they sat in silence a long time, which was a relief; she could find no others words to say.

"What's wrong?" At the snap of Morgan's voice, they both jumped apart and turned as he approached, silently watching him weave his way through the round tables.

Morgan grabbed a chair and sat in tight to them. "What's wrong?" His brow furrowed. "Why are you crying?" He stared at her. "Are you sick?"

"She's completely exhausted," Jason told him.

Morgan pushed her bangs from her face to get a better look at her. His touch burned her with all the things that would never be, and she pulled back from him. Morgan's hand sat mid-air. He froze. His jaw clenched. For the first time, an awkward strain hung in the air between the three of them.

Rachel felt tension in Jason's body, heard his shallow breathing.

Morgan's intent gaze was directed at Rachel. She stood up and she wobbled slightly. Jason stood to steady her. Rachel quickly glanced at Morgan. He sat back in his chair, his face remote, his eyes narrowed, his lips swollen slightly. She bit her lip and looked away. "I'll get my dad," she said like there were marbles in her mouth.

There was command in Morgan's voice. "Get him Jason. Sit down Rachel; you're dead on your feet."

Weakly, she sat down again. She knew she was incapable of going anywhere. She kept her back to the crowd a hundred yards away.

Jason stared down at her, indecision on his face.

Irritated, Morgan snapped again. "Go. She's in no condition to hunt down John."

Jason left to search for her father.

Morgan sat forward, his forearms on his knee. "Why do I get the impression there's more to this story?" When she looked at him, his blue eyes were cold, dead. She looked away.

"It's been a *very* long day," she mumbled, staring down at her tightly entwined fingers.

"I see."

Her tone equally clipped. "I doubt that."

Morgan leaned in close, his hot breath fanning her arm making her tremble. "Is there something going on between you and my brother?"

Her head shot up, "No!"

"You both looked very cozy a minute ago—very touching." His tone had an edge.

Adrenaline shot through her. "He was *being* nice."

"Jason?"

"We've been friends since babyhood Morgan."

"It looked serious."

"And if it was? Is that a bad thing?" She looked deep into his eyes. They were so blue and bright in the dim room; love for him assaulted her like a sting.

"Which is it then?" His edginess turned to frost.

Tears filled her eyes. "I didn't lie."

"You lie to me all the time."

"No, I don't."

His face went blank. "Enough Rachel—I'm not entering into a pubescent argument with you. I asked you a simple question. It matters little to me who you date. You appeared upset, not just exhausted—you *were* crying. I was merely concerned for your welfare, but apparently, my concern is not warranted. You have Jason to assist you."

Morgan's reprimand, the business-like detachment astounded Rachel. Pain blazed through her; dumbly, she watched his face; his eyes scanned the ballroom. His disinterest, as he sat casually back in his chair, his black tuxedo jacket open, his hands folded across his abdomen, his legs wide apart. Hate and pain bubbled up in Rachel, but only a whimper escaped her lips.

His eyes shot back to hers.

"Go back to your wedding Morgan," she said thickly, turning away from him, fresh tears spilled over. "I can't wait to get as far away from you as possible," she said. "I've spent the whole day," *with your ignorant girlfriend,* "taking orders and being good—for you Morgan. To please you. To make you happy. Not to be a headache for you today ... because you are ... so important to me, but I might as well not have bothered. Jason was just being my friend. He knows I've had enough ... he knows, so he was nice to me. But you, you're—so mean. I never thought it was possible to hate you Morgan ... but I hate you right now." Her body shook with her muffled words. She put her elbows on the table to support her heavy head. "I do!" She covered her eyes with her hands.

She felt him slide in beside her; his arm press into hers. "Rachel ...," his remoteness was gone; his hand ran along her forearm, "It has been a long day. I ... I ... Jesus ... Rachel, don't cry. Jesus ..." he whispered so low, but she heard him. "I'm fucked," he laughed, "so *fucked.*" He reached for her fingers and held them tight. "I want to comfort you, but ..."

Things had changed. So many things had changed. She had to stop turning to him, it was not appropriate to take cover with him, or to let him dry her tears; he was a married man, this was his wedding day. With resolve, she wiped her tears with Jason's napkin, taking in a deep breath, which made her shudder. Their hands were entwined intimately. Against the stark white tablecloth, it looked so right.

"I know," she said softly.

"Rachel, Rachel honey." Her mother's call reached her and their hands broke apart. They sat silently, waiting.

Maureen ran her hand along Rachel's shoulders before sitting down beside her. "Jason said … oh darling," her mother embraced her. "You do look exhausted." Her father was standing behind Maureen's chair.

Within seconds, her mother took charge of the situation. "I'll take her up to the room." She released Rachel and stood up.

"Thanks for sitting with her, Morgan, while I went to get the folks," said Jason. Rachel knew he was trying to protect her. She stared up at him, giving him her thanks, and he nodded.

Maureen helped Rachel to her feet. "Where are your shoes darling?"

"Here," said Elaine, handing them to Maureen.

Rachel glanced around the table. The Hilliers were in tow, concern on their faces. Emily stood to Morgan's right, her face twisted, her eyes spewing hatred. Jason's new girlfriend, Carrie, stood shyly on the sidelines, her face flushed, a self-conscious, embarrassed bend to her neck.

Flanked by her parents, goodnights were heard, and Rachel left for her room. Once in the room, her mother fussed over her, helped her out of her dress, and tucked her in bed.

"Go back to the party," Rachel told her parents.

"No, no, John you go back, I'll stay."

"No mum, go, I'll be fine. I just want to sleep. I'm so tired." She turned over and snuggled down into the cool sheets.

"She's safe, Mo. Let her sleep."

"But …"

"I'll feel guilty if you don't go," insisted Rachel.

"She's had a full day. Let her sleep, Maureen."

They both kissed her forehead and left. The second she heard their voices move down the corridor, gut wrenching tears exploded from Rachel, carrying her into a dead sleep.

Photograph 11

Rachel and Jessup Former. He was handsome—jet black hair, blue eyes—a shuddered ran through her at the memory he inspired.

At sixteen, Rachel had lost her virginity to Jessup Former. Jessie was a great guy. Having sex with him was one of the many mistakes in her life—at least, he was a mistake she readily recognized sooner than later. Jessup had big plans. "Girls want to own you," he had told her. She liked his plans, especially since they didn't include her. Boys like Jessie tended not to bug you for opinions or advice. Jessie was cute and athletic; she loved running her hands through his shoulder-length black hair. He was a good kisser and he was tall. Rachel liked tall. He seemed the perfect one to initiate her sexuality. But it was an unfortunate event. Even without a comparison, Rachel was certain sexual pleasure was media propaganda. Being with Jessie resembled a speeding truck bashing into you. Concerned that Jessie, although charming, might feel compelled to share their disastrous interlude as a victory, she decided to deal with it directly, and told him, "That was terrible." She thought honest was best, thinking he would agree and they would call it a day, but Jessie got huffy and became less charming. He accused her of being bad.

"Keep this to yourself Jess or I'll tell the whole embarrassing truth and you'll be dateless throughout high school, and for university you'll have to move to British Columbia."

Jessup kept it to himself, but his words lingered in her mind. Was it her fault? Was she the one who was bad? Or was sex just awful? Other than Jessie, the only true sexual encounter she'd had was with Morgan that day on the boat, which was far more intimate and sexier than what she had with Jessie. She decided to get Morgan's advice.

Morgan was in his father's study. Dinner was over. Emily was out doing whatever Emily did. "The folks"—Morgan's parents and her parents—were playing cards with the Tates down the road. Jason was at a movie with Carrie, and Elaine had gone to the ballet. Timing seemed good.

Papers were stacked in neat piles on the floor; Morgan was sitting behind his dad's huge desk in the middle of the room, tapping away at his laptop.

"Morgan?"

"Hmm?" He didn't lift his head.

She closed the door quietly. "I've been thinking …,"

She hesitated.

When he didn't kick her out, she walked over to the desk and around to his side. She perched herself on the corner—ready to run if need be—and spoke quietly in case the folks came back and walked into the room. "Romance novels make sex sound great."

Morgan froze over his keyboard.

She had his attention; she saw the rigidity in his body.

Rachel swallowed hard. "Regardless of propaganda … I think … I think … sex, well … it isn't so great. Terrible actually. Painful."

She took a deep breath, her heart pumping so loud it thumped in her ears. She barreled on, "You've had sex … I mean … you're having sex regularly, right?"

Silence.

The grandfather clock ticked heavily in the background. She turned to the left. Jean Francois Millet's oil painting of French peasants hung on the wall. Somber emotions emanated from the painting: the peasants were set against the fields; evening was coming from the horizon. She stole a glance at Morgan. His face was eerily blank. She bit her lip. Her hands shook so she sat on them. "What do you think?"

Morgan closed his laptop and sat back in the leather chair, waiting for her to continue. His attention was unnerving. This was delicate stuff. Old people couldn't handle it, but Morgan wasn't old, certainly not too old to remember what it was like being sixteen; plus, he was married—at least those were the reasons she told herself at the time.

"I need to know if it's just me or does everyone feel the same way about sex?"

Rachel's words sat in the air—waiting.

There was no turning back now. Nervously, she licked her lips and rushed on, ignoring his penetrating stare and the charged silence. "Maybe people lie about it because, if they don't lie, they're—like freaks or something. I don't mind being a freak if it's the truth. Or maybe its media bullshit? Like those silly romance novels making it seem great. Or movies making it look sexy and flowing when it's just plain hard work. I don't know why people are weird about sex. I understand the baby thing and the disease thing. It's about being careful. Responsible. It's the lying and the *stigma* that freaks me out."

Sex had so many attachments, so many judgments; it was hard to differentiate them all. Messages were mixed and wide. Don't have sex too young. Sex when you're too young is bad. Abstinence is best. If you have sex with more than one guy, you're a slut. STDs. HIV. Pregnancy. Sex is something you have with someone you love. Anything beyond that is seedy and wrong. Why is something so natural demonized? It's not necessary. Sex plays its head games. It leaves you with a space, she thought sadly. The intimacy of sex is so personal—too personal to share with Morgan? Sex with Jessie was not pleasurable. Awkward. Painful. Unrelenting. The worse part— him being inside her—was indescribably demeaning. Was that normal? Who else could she ask but Morgan? She didn't know, she just knew he knew everything about her.

"It's the ..."She looked at Morgan, his blank stare, his stillness. It intimidated her. "Morgan ...?"

The words wouldn't come.

Rachel shook her head. *Have I lost my mind? What am I doing here! Stop! This was a very bad idea. Bad. Bad. Bad idea.* "I'm sorry … you're busy."

The air crackled with tension. Rachel's pounding heart made its special drone to the tick of the grandfather clock. She slid off his desk.

Morgan's hand shot out to stop her.

"Don't …" his voice was deep, and it cracked. "Don't go." He sat forward. "This is important. I know it's important, but I'm … a little out of my depth here, and I'd rather do almost anything than have this conversation … but I know it's important, and I want you to tell me what's on your mind. What you're upset about."

She lost her nerve. She wanted to cry; embarrassed suddenly for having sex with Jessie, and embarrassed that she was talking to Morgan about it. "This was a mistake."

Morgan was on his feet; he cupped her forearms. "You can tell me."

"I made a mistake coming here. I think I've lost my mind or something."

He crouched down to look into her eyes. "You took me by surprise. Give me a chance to catch up."

"I thought I could … I just don't have anyone else to ask."

"I panicked." His smile was self-deprecating as he wiped her tears with his thumbs.

His familiar face, the crook of his smile, she couldn't help but ask, "This is you panicking?"

His smile deepened; he shook her playfully. "Don't tell anyone I panicked; it will wreck the reputation I'm working on."

Her heart squeezed in her chest. She looked away.

"You had sex." It was more of a statement than a question. "Was this your choice?" His voice was deep, measured, reasonable.

Rachel nodded. She heard his sharp intake of breath. Heat fused her body from head to toe with humiliation.

"Okay, why don't we have a comfortable seat." He guided her to the leather couch and he sat in the armchair beside it. Tension was gone from his body as if his limbs had suddenly lost bone density. "Give me a minute," he whispered. Morgan cleared his throat. "How old was the boy?"

"Seventeen."

"Did he have any experience?"

"Yes ... well, he had done it with another girl and I knew the ..."

"Logistics?"

"Yes ... but ..." she looked at the wall. "Everything you read or see, it makes it out that my whole generation is doing *it* all the time, but I think," she looked down at her clasped fingers, "that's an urban legend—a handful decide for the rest of us, I guess. Because it ...*it was bad.*"

"The sex was bad or you are bad for having sex?"

"No ... the sex was bad ..." Visuals of Jessie burst into her memory—him coming at her like an epileptic hummer. It was like she wasn't there. Just a body he pounded away at.

Rachel slumped forward, her hands covered her face; hot tears burned a path down her boiling face. "It was awful."

"It's okay," He yanked his chair closer to her and rubbed her arm. "I'm sorry. Inexperienced sex can be bad, but often having sex with someone for the first time can be difficult for many reasons. You may have both known what to do or what to expect based on what you've learned at school or from your friends—about the mechanics of sex—but experience does play a role."

"It gets better then?"

"Once you know your own body, learn what you like, what feels good."

"I thought he was a good kisser."

"How did you feel when he kissed you?" he asked quietly.

"It felt nice."

"How did your body react?"

"I was nervous."

"No ... I meant ... has your mother talked to you?"

"*Your* mum explained everything about my period and sex, and then I took it in school."

"No, I meant sexual desire."

"Love?"

"You can feel desire without love. Chemistry and love are very different."

"Is it one or the other?"

"No, when you are romantically involved, it means both, but it *can* just be chemistry and still be good—it can be great in fact."

"What?"

"Chemistry is tricky. If you're young and innocent and the person you're with is older and experienced, they'll know how to arouse you because it's new to you. But here's the tricky part; even if you're in love with someone, it doesn't mean they'll know how to arouse you. Bad sex can happen even if you are with someone you love. The problem is you might want to have sex with someone because they are a good kisser—like what happened to you—but then the sex turns out to be bad; you second-guess yourself. But it's difficult to figure out no matter what you feel. When it feels good, it's easy to get confused and believe, because it feels good, that your partner is good for you. Maybe you're in love; maybe it will change your life in important ways, but that isn't always the case."

That day on the boat, Morgan had barely touched her—and her body had reacted. "So, whether you are in love or not, there's a fifty-fifty chance that nothing will happen?"

"That's why I said, if your partner is experienced and knows how to make your heart race, because it's a new experience for you, and you have nothing to compare with—that's one thing, but it doesn't mean you're in love. It just means you two have chemistry."

"What about having sex with someone you love? How do you know if it's different?"

"The difference is, you want to please your partner and that gives you pleasure. If the sex is bad, you will want to work on it to make it better. You're not born knowing how to arouse your partner or to know what they like, but when you love them, your response is different because the feeling is deeper. Your heart doesn't just race, it pounds. Your body trembles, but you feel like you're burning up; it feels so good it hurts—like you're on a roller coaster and your stomach is about to cave in."

Rachel's head shot up to look at him. "Really?" She didn't like his answer.

He moved a piece of hair from her mouth. "Really."

She looked at him closely. "So that's how you feel with—*her*?"

Rachel saw his immediate discomfort; he looked away, his face going blank.

She wanted him to feel uncomfortable. She hated that he felt that way about Emily. "Don't do that Morgan. This is important, isn't it? I don't want to make the same mistake I did with Jessie. My body did react. I was nervous and it felt good when he kissed me, but it went bad quickly. There was no heart pounding or trembling, at least, not in a good way. I need to know if something is wrong with me. Who am I going to ask? You're my best friend."

Morgan's discomfort turned to irritation. His eyes suddenly bore into hers. "Jason is your best friend." A statement, not a question.

"You were mean to me—cold. I hate when you do that. You hurt my feelings so I got mad." Rachel met his stare.

He leaned back in the armchair. "I ..."

"What?"

"It's childish ..."

"You're going to panic *and* be childish all on the same day?" She clapped her hands together. "Lucky day!"

He laughed at her and her heart raced. "That pleases you, does it?"

"So, so much! You have to tell me now. It's the rule."

"What rule?"

"Share and share alike. So how are you being childish?"

Morgan hesitated, clenching and unclenching his left fist. "I didn't like you confiding in Jason." His fist moved quicker.

Rachel was young, but she could see how difficult it was for Morgan to admit this. She recalled his coolness the night of the wedding, his arrogance when he spoke to her.

"You *were* kind of busy Morgan."

"I know you Rachel. For you to be that upset, something more was going on, something you told Jason. I could see it from across the room, so don't tell me you were exhausted. It was more than that—you were distraught."

"You're right," her voice was clipped. "There was more going on, but you are the last person I would tell."

"What did you say?"

She trembled at the snap of his voice. "You heard me."

"A minute ago, I was the most important person in your life."

Her chin stuck out. "You are."

"You're not making any sense."

Anger bubbled up in her—frustration. "Because *you* don't understand it—it doesn't make sense?"

"That's not what I said Rachel."

Her heart pounded. "It was your wedding day Morgan, hardly an appropriate time to discuss my *pubescent* troubles."

"Well, that's a new one—throwing my words back in my face."

Rachel didn't appreciate his sarcasm. "You want to know?"

He hesitated before he said, "Yes."

"Nothing is *ever* going to be the same again. From now on— everything changes."

"*Rachel* ..."

She felt his hand on her arm, but she knocked it away.

Morgan sighed. "Change is difficult, especially when you're a teenager."

"Stop it!" she shouted.

"Stop what?" His voice was smooth like silk, soft, inviting; it made her angry.

"Being all understanding. I don't want you to understand. I came here to get some advice, so if you're not going to help me, I'm leaving." She got up, but he stopped her.

"You need to calm down." His voice had a steel edge.

"Let go!" she pushed at his hand on her knee.

"What do you want to know?" he snapped, his grip on her remained tight.

She took in a shuddering breath—victory. The haze in her eyes lifted; she stared up into his angry pools of blue. "You said your body has a reaction when you kiss ..."

"Not always."

She breathed heavily. Getting in deeper. "What about you?"

He paused, meeting her stare. "I'm a guy. It's different."

"I'm not talking about chemistry sex Morgan." *Don't ask. Don't say it.* "I'm talking about—so good it's painful sex. Have you had that kind of sex?"

Something flitted across his eyes, then it was gone. Reluctance replaced it. "Yes," he hissed.

Morgan had enjoyed "so good it's painful sex" with two women—Lacy and Emily. Until the day Morgan had accidentally touched her nipple, Rachel's sexual experiences were safely tucked in her imagination. A nipple graze could hardly qualify as sex. "Mine didn't."

"It can be difficult for a woman … girl the first time."

"No, I mean it has never happened. Tons of boyfriends—it was pleasant at best. And my first sexual experience was horrible." *Maybe there is something wrong with me?*

"Like I said, experience can play a role."

Boldly, she led him exactly where she wanted him from the moment she walked through the door. "So, I'll get experienced. You're experienced—why don't you show me how?"

"No." his voice was stern. "And you shouldn't be having sex anyway, you're too young.

"How old were you?"

"That's not the point."

"You're right; the point is I'm going to find out with or without your help. I was right the first time—it was a mistake telling you. It doesn't matter anyway. Jessie was willing, I'm sure I'll find someone else who's willing to show me how. Someone *with* experience. Maybe I'll become a sexual aficionado."

"I don't think so, Rachel. This ends here." His blue eyes were dark, tense. "If you don't agree, I'll be forced to tell your mother."

She sucked in her breath, shocked at his admission. "You wouldn't!" Rachel tried to yank free of him.

"Promise me, Rachel. This ends here."

She could only stare at him.

"Promise me!" he insisted.

She tossed her head. "Fine."

"What does that mean?"

"It ends here."

"Good."

She wanted to get away from him. "Let go!"

"Calm down first."

Rachel sat rigidly. Her cheeks were on fire with frustration and betrayal. She wasn't going to cry. She was done crying over this bastard.

"Jesus Christ … look, Rachel, men and sex are a dangerous combination for a beautiful girl like you. I have to be sure—even if you said what you did to get me to do what you wanted—at least with me you're safe. Boys are incapable of thinking of anything but themselves, and men are not boys."

She sat like stone. She turned cold eyes on him. "Morgan let go."

Morgan sighed heavily but released her.

Rachel stood up and turned to leave the room. Over her shoulder, she looked at him. "Don't worry Morgan, I can navigate my way through this without your input."

He grabbed her by the arm, swung her around, and before she realized his intent, his lips came down on hers, trapping her hands against his chest.

The kiss was intimate and frightening. Her body reacted immediately. Her heart accelerated; each pound bashed into the next pound so that the beats were indistinguishable. She couldn't catch her breath. His tongue made her tingle. Her vagina burned. She was completely out of her depth as she melted into his body. It was like nothing she had ever experienced; she was completely at his mercy. He had made his point, and Rachel wanted nothing more than to experience everything he could teach her. His hand caressed her back, her bum; his fingers were in her hair. She felt like she was drifting on the open sea. Desperate to touch him, she pushed her trapped hands free from between them and reached up to his shoulders, the curve of his neck, to run her hands through his black hair; kissing him back. Morgan deepened the kiss. Overcome, she expressed it the only way she could; with her tongue, her fingers, her hips, her moans of pleasure. Pressing herself into his hard grooves, she felt his passion and it took the kiss to a wild recklessness.

Morgan yanked his head back and pressed his face into her shoulder, away from her. His chest heaved; his breathing laboured.

Rachel's body was a mass of nerves. She wanted to beg him not to stop —the slight space between them, was an indescribable pain. And yet, fear had her shaking at her abandoned response, her want for him, and the confusion that it brought her.

Even as she yanked out of his hold and ran from the room, she couldn't help worrying—did he enjoy it?

Rachel relived that kiss many, many times. Unable to be in the room with him without recalling the raw emotions she felt in his arms—the hardness of his body pressed into hers, his tongue licking at her, his hands in her hair, her breasts crushed against his chest—so she avoided him.

More importantly, she understood what he had meant. He wanted to teach her a lesson and he succeeded. His experience made her inexperience shockingly apparent. Nothing else would have convinced her. It also made her aware of how vulnerable she was with Morgan. Emotions had gripped her. Abandonment of good sense had taken her on a wild ride of emotions. She was no longer in love with the boy next door; she was in love with a married man. Jason knew how she felt, but no one else could, especially her mother. She needed to protect her heart and her secret or Maureen would make sure Rachel never saw Morgan.

After the reckless kiss, Rachel dedicated herself to her dating life. Looking normal was key. She liked dating in a group. There was safety in numbers and it kept possessive relationships at bay or brought them to the surface. Family was her foundation. School was her priority, then her art. On more than a few occasions, boys she had refused a date would tell her, "You're saying no? What's wrong with you? Girls kill to be with me." If she did say no to a date or a party everyone was going to, ridiculous things popped out of boys' mouths: "If you don't come with me, I'll have to take someone else. I mean it." Rachel understood that's how it worked. "No, I don't think you understand. I mean it. I'll take Jenny." It amazed Rachel, how a guy—the same age as her—a guy she knew casually, thought *he* had the power to dissolve her into bits. Where did that come from, she wondered. More times than she could count, she stopped dating a guy because of his bad manners and then he would telephone incessantly, pleading to get back into her good books, but she ignored them. She wasn't being cruel. They had made their decision. They decided to play archaic male games that she wasn't buying into and it bit them on the ass. When they realized she wasn't bluffing, *they* decided to forgive *her*.

Boys were a curious bunch. *Where does that type of arrogance come from? Or was it insecurity?*

Avoiding Morgan lasted a couple of weeks, then she fell back into the fold without incident. He never mentioned the kiss and neither did she, but their time spent together changed. They were never alone, always part of a crowd.

In those days, Morgan and Jeff Gilles had a band, playing at local bars, weddings; Morgan seemed to need the outlet. As the years passed, their playing turned into jam sessions at Morgan's house. Emily hated the band, hated the time it took. Emily traveled a lot with her job as a journalist so when she was in town, she wanted Morgan to spend time with her, but Emily missed an important part of her husband by not watching him play. Morgan playing to an audience was exhilarating to watch for Rachel. Morgan didn't chat; he didn't wear his emotions on his sleeve; he was private, but when he sang, when he played, emotion emanated from him. And the songs he chose were often sad, romantic, yearning tunes.

One night in particular, center stage, Jeff and Morgan sat on stools beneath a red spotlight; their acoustic guitars blended, Wally on drums, Jason on bass. Morgan sang *Nights in White Satin* by the Moody Blues. During the chorus, Morgan looked at her and she felt it in her toes, but so did the girl directly behind her.

Rachel heard her, "Did you see? He looked right at me. He's

gorgeous."

When the song ended, the crowd went wild.

Elaine shouted over the applause. "That was great!"

Louise laughed. "I see Morgan in a whole new light."

Sonny Reeves, Elaine's boyfriend, whistled under his breath, "Someone's getting laid tonight."

Elaine hit him affectionately.

Emily was in Alaska working on a seal story.

"Lucky Emily," said Louise.

Rachel agreed. "Yes, lucky girl." She knew firsthand what a passionate man Morgan was under that cool exterior. When she closed her eyes, she could still feel the way he had made her body come alive. His touch, his taste, his smell was etched on her skin and her tongue. She'd felt things with him she didn't know were possible, and in the process, she fell more deeply in love with him. For the first time in her life, she had felt passion, and there was no settling for second best. The next person she slept with, she had to make sure all her parts came alive, the way they did with Morgan.

6

YOUTHFUL FOOLISHNESS

Photograph 12
Rachel and Elaine were sitting on the hood of Morgan's
Escalade. They were decked out in Western wear with a London
or Bust sign hanging from Jason's neck.

Rachel started Western University in London and turned
eighteen that September. She had declined the Ontario College of
Art's offer of acceptance. Her parents and her friends thought she
hadn't got in to OCAD. She didn't correct them. Western was *just*
far enough away from Toronto that she didn't have to watch Morgan
be happily married. At Western, she focussed on a double degree in
visual arts and psychology. Rachel had never been away from home
before and although she had pangs of homesickness. She consoled
herself with the fact that both Elaine and Louise were with her—
more than enough support from home. She knew moving to London
was the right thing to do under the circumstances. There was no
other way. It was also her chance at freedom. To be independent.

She had lived her whole life between two households: the
Whartons and the Hilliers. That dictated a certain amount of
discussion to coordinate her activities between her parents and the
Hilliers. Her upbringing resembled a tribunal. She was well loved,
granted, but there were two sets of rules, two sets of discussions, two
sets of clothes, two beds, two closets—two of everything—like she
was a child of divorce. It was annoying and left Rachel with a bitter

taste in her mouth, like a saliva duct that oozed sourness. When she took up residency at Western, her ties to parental advice became non-existent. Rachel's personal assembly of conferrers had suddenly disbanded with the distance it took to drive from Toronto to London. After years of juggling and dodging two sets of parents, Rachel thought she would love her independence, but it left her with a vague state of being.

In the wake of her new life, Rachel fought her weakness to run home every weekend, and forced herself to belief—this was her time. She ignored the pangs of loneliness. She filled her days with school, studying, and parties. Her infamous dating rotation system was at its finest. But with each day that passed, it became harder and harder to admit the truth. Flying without a net wasn't all it was cracked up to be. The dating, the parties, the late nights, lost their lustre with a speed that surprised her. Homesickness reared its ugly head repeatedly. A thousand times, she wanted to call Morgan, but she resisted. This was her new independent life away from him. Away from the family.

When Rick Summerhill stopped by their dorm with books for his sister Louise, Rachel didn't recognize him at first. He looked good. Sophisticated. Confident. It was his last year at Western, getting his honours in mathematics before continuing his master's and Ph.D. at McGill. He asked her to coffee; coffee turned into lunch, which turned into dinner. They started spending all their free time together. Rick's attention provided her with a sense of security. He was funny, outgoing, looked out for her, concerned, considerate; his sister approved and the days flew by. Then she mentioned Morgan in casual conversation, and things turned sour. Rick abandoned decorum, becoming belligerent.

"What did Morgan do to you? He's a letch."

Morgan was many things, but a letch wasn't the noun she would use to describe him. "Why?"

"Your precious Morgan is the worst kind of letch because he rides under the radar where no one can see what a fucking prick he is—Mr. Golden Boy isn't so golden." The venom on Rick's face chilled her as he paced around the room. "That fucking prick stole from me. He stole everything and then blamed me! I can't ever get it back. Do you understand? *I can never get back what he stole!* It's his fault. So, spare me the accolades. I know you two are close—Morgan and Rachel, you're notorious—so just spare me."

"If you know that, why are you dating me?"

"You didn't do anything to me but I hate your pal. So, let's just cut him out of the picture."

Cutting Morgan out of the picture was not an option, and Rick's hatred interfered with their relationship, putting Rachel in the position of defending Morgan, which made her miss Morgan and hate Rick a little more each time. Living in London became a grind. Going home to the Hilliers' became necessary for her state of mind, but Rick was convinced it was to see Morgan. Even though Morgan didn't live at the Hilliers', Rick insisted he was the reason for her visits. In his mind, she continually picked spending time with Morgan over him, and it pissed him off. He wasn't wrong; she would have gladly spent time with Morgan, but the sad truth was Morgan had made a new life for himself, and it didn't include her. When he did visit his parents, it was during the week. On his way home from work. On his way home from the airport. On his way to the airport. When she took her spot at the Hillier table on the weekend, she heard Morgan was building a new company, that he was working hard, and that he had taken Emily to a resort up north for a little relaxation; she liked hearing about his life.

The Hilliers took the sting away. Her parents were rarely home these days. A teacher's strike had her dad working double duty around the province, and Maureen's bank had bought out Canadian Reliant Management. She was in charge of merging the bank's services with Reliant's financial planning and investment portfolio services. To be fair, at first, her dad had assumed she was still at school—they were paying for residence, and it's true most kids just went home for the holidays—but in her weekly call to him, Rachel said residence was loud and unruly and she needed some quiet. He was spending most of his time in Ottawa, so he was glad she was staying with the Hilliers, but he would be home for Thanksgiving. He missed both his girls.

Aunt Sarah showered her with attention on her weekend visits, cheered her up, gave her hugs and kisses, went to the movies with her, listened to what she said, treated her like the daughter she desperately wanted to be. Sarah seemed to know things weren't right.

"You know when Elaine first went to Western, she would call me crying her eyes out. She hated it." Aunt Sarah shook her head and reached for Rachel's hand. "It overwhelming. Even the strongest get a little depressed."

"I bet Morgan didn't."

Aunt Smiled. "Then you would be wrong, but don't ask me for any details because I would have to kill you."

Uncle Robert followed Sarah's lead and distracted Rachel with a new skill. He taught her how to fence. They practiced at the fencing club on Saturday mornings. If Rachel lost their love and support, she had no idea what would happen to her. Robert and Sarah were her foundation. They always had been.

On the rare occasions when Morgan showed up on the weekend, it was when Emily was on assignment, and Rachel didn't pass up those opportunities. At the time, she concocted storylines for herself that relieved her of any burden; she was a master. The truth was too nasty. Consequences and facts were never her strong suit, but the fact was, Rachel was in love with a married man and when her resolve to keep him at a distance crashed, which was every time she was in his company, she worked around him being married and her being away at school like she was taking a detour. She didn't think. She didn't discuss Morgan with anyone, including herself, but when Rick tried to move their relationship into high gear, she freaked. He wanted to defer McGill for a year and stay in London, find a job, rent a new apartment downtown. No more roommates. Somewhere near campus, to be close to her. Rachel panicked. She struggled with which cereal to eat in the morning, and Rick was talking jobs and apartments?

Rachel thought dating one person, someone older, someone she knew, would keep her from missing what she'd left behind and provide her with a new path, but Rick didn't do what she needed. He had needs of his own. He was looking for a serious relationship; he was looking for opinions and decisions. When she showed no interest in his plans, they fought. Their fights turned mean and dirty. It became too much for Rachel. Her life decisions were in her future, not in her present, but Rick couldn't bring himself to hear her. Hate clouded his judgment. No, longer was it insular, it had expanded and incorporated each facet of their lives.

The map Rachel had created in her head became quicksand. She felt trapped. Obligated. She worried about what Louise would think if she broke up with her brother. Would it affect their friendship? Probably. Especially if her brother started in on Morgan. Blood is thicker than any friendship. Reluctantly, she held on for all the wrong reasons and she hated herself. On top of the fighting and the worrying, she still had an obligation to herself to do well in school, but her diligence turned carelessness. She started skipping class. Food didn't interest her. Sleep eluded her. Morgan filled her dreams. Her distance from him made everything worse. She ached for him.

She tried to stay away. Tried not to call. But she caved.

The second she heard his voice, she burst into tears and a weight lifted from her shoulders. Her sadness spilled out like a garbled mess: homesick, Rick, fighting, her fall from scholastic grace, and Morgan did what she needed. He talked her off the ledge.

Maureen invited Rick to Thanksgiving dinner. She had no idea they were having problems. The bright side was, her mother was a great cook. Aunt Sarah had Alma. Sarah hated the kitchen—a fair trade since the kitchen hated Sarah. Rachel loved the holidays. The Whartons' lonely house lost its quiet, untouchable quality, transformed by chatty laughter and abundance. More importantly, Morgan was in every room she was in and he didn't have to speak or interact with her, his presence was enough. Rick fit in with an ease that day and they spun a snappy repartee between them that was flirty and affectionate, reminiscent of their childhood, reminiscent of how it was when they first started dating, which was a welcome relief and a happy surprise. It was a good day. Even Emily's irritating presence didn't bug Rachel.

After dinner, Trivial Pursuit was yanked out and everyone separated into teams. Rachel's happy contentment and sleep deprivation over the last month had her dozing off at the final stretch.

As usual, Morgan carried her up to bed and Elaine opened doors and pulled down the duvet. This had happened a billion times over her life since she rarely could stay up past ten. Rachel was a deep sleeper so she had no recollection of them putting her to bed, no recollection of speaking to Morgan, of fighting with Jason that she hadn't abandoned the team, of putting her arms around Morgan's neck, of smiling at what he said, of kissing his cheek, but Rick didn't miss one intonation, one touch, one sleepy smile. When they got back to London, his hatred spewed out of him in a venomous rage. It scared the crap out of Rachel. She ran. She followed her instinct and called Morgan; her fingers couldn't tap out the numbers fast enough. He was able to calm her down, but the raw emotions stayed with her.

The next day was gruelling. Everything she touched turned to shit. In her studio class, when she sketched the female model draped in a long, beautiful, blue see-through scarf, it wasn't a replica, but an original piece with the model squeezed to death by a cloak of a hundred little penises.

Her professor stopped while making the rounds and said, "Thanksgiving has that effect on me too."

Walking home, she didn't notice Morgan's jag sitting outside her residence until he swung open his car door and stood on the path. There was no Maureen, no Rick, no Emily, no family looming and watching, and Rachel was so happy to see him she was incapable of control. She didn't even remember forming a thought, she just ran. She dropped her books, her bag, her coat, and flung herself into his arms.

Over stir-fry, Rachel poured out her sad tale.

Morgan listened.

"You're telling me what he is doing, what he wants—how do *you* feel?"

"It's like he's building his whole life around me," she said.

"And that makes you nervous?"

"Yes."

"Why?"

She looked around the room, pressing her fingers into her mouth before saying, "I like him, he's fun, smart … direct. He likes to try new things. He's a doer. I like doers." She looked down at her bowl.

"You're a doer," said Morgan.

She nodded without looking at him. "So are you," she said softly, then moved on quickly. "But he's older and he wants things I can't give him."

"Like?"

"Commitment."

"By commitment you mean dating him exclusively?"

"I am dating just him ..."

"Tell him that."

"I have ... but he thinks my lack of interest in his future means I'm indifferent to him."

"Is that what it means?"

Rachel whined. "I don't care what it means!"

Morgan laughed. "That sounds about right."

Rachel lifted her expectant gaze to him.

"Sweetie," he smiled, "your eighteen, I don't think you're supposed to care what it means."

"He hates you."

Morgan shrugged. "I know."

"You know?"

"He has his reasons."

"It doesn't bother you?"

"Do you hate me?"

"No!"

"That would bother me."

"Morgan ..." Looking into his eyes, seeing his tender concern, it was hard to remember he was a married man. She looked away. She wanted to touch him so badly it hurt.

"There's more to this, isn't there?" asked Morgan.

"I can't give him what he wants—ever."

"Maybe not now and maybe not him, but someday you'll give it to someone."

Her eyes snapped back to his. "No, you don't understand—*not ever.*" She swallowed the lump in her throat.

"Rach ..." Morgan slid into her side of the booth. "I know it doesn't feel like it right now—"

"Please don't say these are the best years of my life."

He laughed. "No, I wasn't—but good point because they really are—no, it's just everything is so overwhelming at this time in your life." He grabbed her hand and squeezed it. "It's important to try and figure out ways to deal with your stress. I hear you've taken up fencing?"

"I have."

"Dad says you're good."

Rachel smiled. "He's being generous."

Morgan dropped her at the University gates. She waved goodbye as he sped back to Toronto, back to his wife, back to his life, and Rachel moved on. She went to see Rick. Regardless of the wants she couldn't give him; he didn't deserve the callous words she'd yelled at him during their last fight. His behaviour was bad, but so was hers.

When he opened the door, his first words were, "Met up with the superhero I heard?" "I'm not here to fight. I want to apologize."

They made up, spending a couple of hours skiing at Boler Mountain in Byron, then watched an old movie—*The Greatest Show on Earth*—and shared a bowl of popcorn.

Gary Kurfont came home half way through the movie. Gary's eldest brother, Chris, was also a roommate. Gary was in second year and a fellow art student.

She didn't realize she was monopolizing Gary's company until Rick said, "If you aren't going to watch this movie, I'd rather watch the game."

"Sorry man," said Gary, giving him a lopsided smile. "My fault. Not very often I meet a beautiful girl who knows who Chagall is. Lost my head."

Gary smiled at her, his blue eyes tender, familiar, his black hair longer than fashionable, messy—again, familiar; her body tingled.

Gary stood. "Did you ever see Heston in *Mega Man*?"

"Seven times. Loved it," she said excitedly. Morgan was the only other person she knew who liked old movies. "There's this theatre in Toronto that plays old flicks. Morgan and I use to go all the time."

Gary nodded. "There's one in Montreal."

"I'm turning on the game," snapped Rick.

Gary threw up his hands. "I'm leaving, I'm leaving."

Fighting with Rick became an unhealthy sport. It was relentless. Destructive. After one too many fights, it came to ahead. Morgan was at the bottom of the dispute as usual. The Whartons and Hilliers came to London mid-week for a surprise visit. Elaine and Rachel cut class to join them at the Delta Armouries. Rachel, of course, was thrilled to see Morgan under any circumstances. The family stayed two nights.

Rick freaked when she showed up at his door Friday evening. He demanded to know where she had been. She told him. Parental presence made no difference to him. Morgan was there. Emily was not. Rachel knew what Rick's reaction would be, which was why she hadn't invited him. He would have turned their fun mini-break into a tension-filled nightmare, or worse, spun a tale of guilt to stop her from going. Instead, she said nothing. Rick's resentment was profound. He said her relationship with Morgan was weird. That Morgan had ulterior motives.

"You're my girlfriend, but you can't find time for my family?"

"That's not—"

"Then come to Toronto. We'll go to dinner with my sister and parents."

"I have to catch up on what I missed. My parents are off to Chicago with the Hilliers and Elaine is staying here. Morgan is off on business and Jason took Carrie to Quebec City."

Rick lost complete control, threw an overnight bag together, and slammed out of the apartment. She was still sitting on the couch, dazed at what had just happened when Gary strolled in ten minutes later.

Gary's uncomplicated presence was nirvana against the turbulence. Opportunity made them available to each other. Rick's other roommates, Gary's brother Chris, Boyd Cameron, and a girl she had never met were all away for the weekend. Rachel and Gary spent the night hanging out. They ordered pizza. Watched old movies.

One flirtatious kiss, that Rachel felt everywhere, led to another. They spent the weekend together.

Sex with Gary was great and she never regretted it for a second. Gary made her feel carefree, sexy, beautiful. He was easy. Easy smile. Made no demands. No commitments. He didn't have expectations. He didn't care what her plans for the future were. He didn't care who Morgan was; he lived in the moment, where Rachel like to live. What she did regret was the hurt expression she saw on Rick's face when he came back early from Toronto on Sunday afternoon with Gary's brother Chris, to find Rachel and Gary cuddled on the couch, naked, snoring contentedly under a Toronto Maple Leaf blanket. Rick's hurt turned to fury in thirty seconds.

Gary was punched repeatedly—hardly a fair fight with a groggy naked boy as an opponent, so Chris intervened. "He's had enough. You made your point,"

Rick whipped Gary's pants at him as he lay doubled up on the floor.

Terrified, Rachel clutched the blanket around her. Her brain was silent as she watched Rick struggle to catch his breath. He picked up his duffel bag and left the apartment. The floor shook when he slammed out of the apartment.

Somehow, Rachel made it into Gary's room and got dressed. When she came out, she heard Chris say, "You don't think I can see that? And you've gone and fucked it up. Now we'll have to move because you couldn't keep your pecker in your pants."

"My pecker has been in my pants. It just ... sort of happened. A surprise. Still, I'm glad it was you guys and not—"

"Christ—don't even say it! You don't make it easy little brother. Neither does Rick. I told the bastard to leave it alone, but he thinks he's in love with her. He can't see the fucking truth staring him in the face. Beautiful women—Jesus Christ!"

"She is beautiful—in every fucking way."

"Shut up," said Chris and Rachel heard a slap. "You're lucky you're not dead."

"He'll get over it."

"When he hasn't had what you've had?"

"He hasn't slept with her?"

"Nope."

"Christ ..."

"Get your things and get out of here—fast. We'll crash at Jimmy's until we can figure this out."

Rachel gripped her Manolo shoes tightly and walked into the living room. The two men were silent, looking off into space; Chris was smoking. She grabbed her coat and purse. Gary came up behind her as she was slipping on her shoes. "I'm sorry about this baby."

She turned to look up at him. His beautiful face was cut and an ugly bruise had started around his eye. His face looked pensive. "I'm so sorry Gary."

He reached down and pulled her up into his arms. She wrapped her arms around his neck as he lifted her off the ground. He kissed her neck. "I had a fantastic weekend. I'm sorry it ended badly." He kissed her—she loved kissing him.

"Okay guys, let's move it along," said Chris.

Gary walked her to the door. "Want a ride home?"

"No."

"You have my number?"

She nodded and kissed him quickly.

Outside, she hurried along the path. When she looked up to run across the road, she saw Rick's car. Parked in front of the building. He was in the driver's seat, staring at her. She shivered. The violence she'd seen in him earlier frightened her. He started the car. Frozen, she stood on the pavement, waiting for him to decide what he wanted to do—kill her or drive away. He threw his Porsche into first and flew passed her.

Working on autopilot, Rachel went to the airport. By Sunday night, she was standing in the lobby of the Ritz Carlton Hotel in the same Manolos and jeans, waiting for Morgan. The front desk said he was out. After three hours in the elegant lobby, Morgan came through the revolving doors with Jeff Gilles, two men she didn't know, and a woman. She stood up. Even though it had only been a couple of days since she had seen him, her body trembled with relief. She watched him move across the marbled floor, watched him smile, having him close shifted the weight of her dread and fear.

Morgan turned his head and saw her. She saw his surprise, his pleasure, and she laughed.at the recognition she saw on his face. He laughed too.

He kept his eyes on her. She watched his lips say to his companions, "Excuse me please," and walked in her direction. She met him halfway.

"This is a surprise," he said, reaching out to kiss her cheek. She had the grace to accept the ludicrous behaviour of her showing at the most unlikely place—imagine! "Yes, an expected detour on the way to my dorm." She swallowed the ache lodged in her throat and force herself not to fling herself into his arms.

He put his hand at the small of her back and moved her toward the elevators. "Everyone okay at home?"

"Yes, everyone's well." Her hands were in constant movement. Her eyes bouncing around the room. "This is a surprise, I know—you're working, I'm sorry. I ..."

"We'll talk?" he said, holding the door open. She nodded and the elevator whisked them up to his suite.

Once behind closed doors, he said, "What happened?"

"I've done a horrible thing."

"Only one? Lucky girl." He removed his tie, flinging it over the chair.

"You're not going to like me when I tell you. I don't like me."

Morgan stuffed his hands put his pockets. "What did you do to warrant such recrimination?"

Rachel looked away. "I slept with Rick's roommate and I haven't slept with him." She slithered to the couch. "Rick and I had a huge fight and he slammed out of his place and, well, I just sat there, staring off to space when Gary Kurfont walked in and we—just hit it off, and one thing lead to another—and we spent the weekend together."

The silence was unnerving and she turned to look at his reaction. His expression was blank. He just stared at her.

"It was just so nice. We talked about art and books and it felt right. I didn't plan it; he didn't plan it—was just a lovely surprise. Do you know what I mean?"

Morgan nodded. "I do."

"And those moments are such a rare find." It was the first time, in so long, she was in the rhythm of belonging. "You can't let them slip through your fingers." She looked down at her jeans and ran her hand along her thigh. "I guess it depends on the value of the moment and the complexity of the consequences, but I didn't consider either of those things."

"What was the value of the moment?"

"The moments," she lifted her eyes to his briefly, "that linger in your memory. They keep you warm when you're lonely. Isn't your ability to imagine priceless?" she said quietly.

"Yes." He moved to the chair across from her. "What do you want to do?"

"I don't know. I don't want to go back to London," she trembled, "but going home seems pointless, everyone is either away or at school." She put her hand on her left shoulder, her arm resting across her chest. "Louise is going to hate me." Her eyes darted back to Morgan's. "If you had seen his face ..."

There was a fleck of something in Morgan's eyes, but before Rachel could decipher its meaning, he looked way. "I can imagine." He stood, paced around the room. "Keep your distance from Summerhill. He may have taken his frustration out on Kurfont, but I doubt that will satisfy him for long." He turned away, staring out the window that ran the length of the room. "He holds grudges."

"Really?"

He took up pacing again. "He needs to cool off. There's no point going home. You would be alone." He stopped to look at her. "Stay here—it's safer and I won't have to worry."

"About Rick?"

Morgan seemed agitated. Distracted. "He beat up the roommate but he wanted ... am I thinking of the right guy? I met Kurfont, right? —briefly—at the souvlakia place?"

"Yes. He was with his older brother Chris. He's also a roommate."

Morgan nodded over and over again. "Yes, yes I remember." He jerked back like something hit him before switching gears again. "I'll get you a room."

On shaky legs, she stood up awkwardly. "Can't I stay here?" Her brow knit, "Do you think ... Rick would ...?"

"Good idea, stay here. You'll need some clothes and things." He pulled out his wallet and passed her his credit card.

"I have money, Morgan."

"Just take it. I need to do something so don't give me a hard time."

Rachel took his card. "When do you leave?"

"Thursday."

"Can I stay till Thursday?"

"Stay until Thursday."

Rachel slept on the couch, not bothering with the pull-out, her dreams filled with staying the week with Morgan. Monday morning Jeff stopped at their hotel room for breakfast. The two men discussed business: the Montreal office, differentials, clients, strategies. Rachel spent the day at the library doing research on a couple of essays that were due the following week, and picked up a book from her reading list: *Crime and Punishment* by Dostoyevsky.

They both arrived back at the hotel at the same time.

Thrilled to see him stepping out of a cab, Rachel laughed, "Do we have perfect timing or what?"

He glanced in her direction, not recognizing her or understanding why she was talking to him, he arrogantly looked away, but his head snapped back. He slammed the cab door, stood in the middle of the hotel driveway, and stared at her. "Perfect," he smiled.

Working all day did not alter his neat appearance. He wore black sunglasses, his dark blue suit remained pressed, his crisp white shirt pristine, his yellow tie—perfect. The hotel's glass doors gave Rachel a glimpse at herself and she gasped. No wonder he didn't recognize her. Her hair was a flyaway mess; she looked pale, ridiculously pubescent, and her clothes were wrinkled beyond recognition.

"I look a mess." Rachel tried to smooth out her clothes.

Morgan grabbed her hand, yanking her along with him. "You look beautiful."

"More like you lie your ass off."

"More like a sight for sore eyes," he said.

Rachel tugged his arm, halting him. "Really?"

His face was blank but his eyes were spears of lights. "Really."

"Bad day?"

Morgan drew her into the side of his body, his arm around her waist as he manoeuvred her to the elevators. "Tell me about your day."

Once inside the suite, Rachel showed Morgan her purchases.

He wasn't impressed. "I give you my credit card and you buy a couple of T-shirts and soap?"

She held them up against her chest. "But look how cute they are?"

"Yes, very cute, but tomorrow night I have to go to dinner with Monsieur Marchand and his beautiful wife. I thought you could join us … unless you would prefer not to, which is fine, too."

"I would love to go!"

"As sexy as you are in jeans and a T, this is Montreal and the Marchand's dress for dinner, so I think a cocktail dress is in order."

"You're asking me to spend ridiculous amounts of your money? Because a cocktail dress—in Montreal …"

"I think I can handle it."

"What about tonight?"

"There's a little bistro Jeff wanted to try." He stood up and slipped off his suit jacket. "Kathy flew in tonight; maybe we could all go together?"

"Are my jeans and very cute T suitable, my lord?"

Morgan laughed. "I'm going to have a shower."

***

Montreal broke Rachel's heart.

That first night, Morgan insisted she take the bedroom and he would take the pull-out in the sitting room. She refused. She had come unannounced; it hardly seemed fair that he crunch his large frame into a pull-out. The second night, her intentions quickly spun in a new direction when she lay in her lonely bed. The wind howled around the hotel and the windows trembled. The front door rattled at every movement in the hall. She heard the tap tap of Morgan's fingers hitting his laptop keys in the next room. Staring at the warmth of the light under his door, she fought with herself. She didn't want to sleep here—alone. But he was married. Not cool. But when was she going to have another opportunity like this? To spend so much uninterrupted time with him without recrimination? She threw back the covers. The second she pushed his door open, her story tumbled out of her mouth. She pleaded her case while slipping into bed beside him. "You go ahead, read your notes; bang away at your laptop; I'll be as quiet as a mouse, you'll see. So, so, quiet. Just don't make me go out there. It's lonely out there. It's noisy. The wind is howling and the rain is beating the hell out of the glass—really, I'll be as quiet as a mouse.

Morgan laughed, "You haven't stopped talking."

"Quiet as a mouse," she whispered, sinking down under the bedclothes.

In the night, she woke up to find Morgan pressed into her back, his face buried in her hair, his hand splayed across her belly; she'd never felt so wonderfully safe, and easily fell into a deep sleep. He was gone when she woke. For the remaining nights, Morgan insisted she take the bedroom, no negotiations, and he endured the pull-out.

That week with Morgan, she put her fall from grace out of her mind. She revelled in being with him. She thought nothing of his wife in some far-off land in the Middle East getting the story to end all stories. She thought nothing of Gary or Rick. It was the first time Morgan and Rachel had been completely alone in years, and she loved every minute. They had breakfast together in their room near a balcony window, chatting about the coming day before Jeff joined them for coffee. When they finished, she got a kiss on the forehead and he was gone. They met up after their day of work, chatted, got ready for dinner, and they were off.

They never spoke of Rick or Gary—what a selfish bitch she was—or her lack of redeeming character. They had a blast instead. The moment was all that mattered. Little things brought her joy. She marvelled each time she walked through his suite door, that she was here, in Montreal, with him. Looking at him, smiling at him, eating with him, laughing with him, bitching at him not to leave his shoes in the middle of the floor, an intimate portrait of joy personified. They had a rhythm predicated on give and take, and a need to please the other.

But time is a runaway train. The moments raced by without consent, and the time had come for them to leave.

Silence permeated the room as they packed. They were silent as they rode down in the elevator. In the taxi. The airport. There was no discussion on the plane. Rachel concentrated on the book she read, her movements, other people's movements, drinking, eating, until the time came for the silence to end.

Standing in the airport, Jeff Gilles stood awkwardly beside Morgan.

Unperturbed, Morgan looked down at her. "Are you coming home or are you going on to London?"

"I *am* here, but," she said hesitantly, suddenly unsure of herself, darting a glance at Jeff.

"Elaine and Jason are coming home. I'm sure Carrie will be over." Morgan looked disinterested as he scanned the baggage carousel. "Jeff there's your bag."

Jeff weaved through the crowd.

Morgan turned to her, cupping her cheek, his forehead furrowed as he whispered, "Listen sweetie, given the circumstances, I would prefer it if you stayed here. I'm sure Summerhill has been blowing off steam all week, but it's the weekend. Time and opportunity are on his side if he wants to drag out his anger, but you know him best. It's up to you."

"I'll stay." It was so easy to say those words.

It was so easy to follow Morgan to the car, slip into the front seat beside him, walk through the Hilliers' front door, and smile at Jason. When Morgan said he would barbecue, it was so easy to agree.

When he said Emily was away, he might as well stay the night, it was easy to make popcorn, and watch an old movie with him. It was so easy with Morgan.

Yet when she went to bed, nothing about it was easy. At three, she dozed off, but it wasn't restful. A nightmare so real, she woke with a start, thinking she was still in the throes of her dream. Morgan was missing—no, he'd left her.

It took her a minute to realize she was home and quickly got out of bed. Morgan hadn't stayed in the guesthouse; he was easy to find in his childhood bedroom.

"What's wrong?" he said.

"I had a nightmare. I couldn't find you."

"I'm right here."

She crawled in beside him. "In the dream …," she snuggled down beside him; his arm came round her waist, "we were on vacation … somewhere warm. We were standing in the airport and you told me you were going to get the car." In the dream, he had smiled at her; kissed her, told her he loved her. Tears sprung into her eyes at the memory, at the elation she felt when he said he loved her. "You said you'd be right back; not to move. I waited and waited and you never came back, so I went outside, but the parking lot was empty. The lot was fenced in. Big chains were on the gate. I tried to get them loose but I couldn't. I ran back to the airport but the doors had the same big chains on them. I kept screaming for you …"

"Abandoning you in an airport? Now does that sound like me?" he said, his tone, bantering.

"I was so scared."

"But you're safe now."

"What if it's true? That I'm a lost cause and destined to be abandoned?"

"But you're not. You're safe. Right here with me."

"But …"

"But you're not. You're here and I'm not going to let you get lost. We were at the airport earlier and you're probably feeling the effect of what happened last week."

"You think so?"

"Yes."

She grabbed his hand and held it to her chest. "Do you think I'm a bad person because ... of what happened?"

"No," his tone was hushed, "I know you're young, but making mistakes is not exclusive to youth. We all make poor choices."

"You should have seen his face. There was so much violence and anger inside him when he hit Gary—it was terrifying. I don't blame him. But Morgan ..." She rolled around to look at him. "I didn't even think about him once. I didn't even consider what it meant. Even caught, I didn't think about it. Not really. I just ran. Doesn't that say something about me? That maybe something is missing inside me? Like a conscience?"

"Sweetie, you have a conscience. Nothing is missing inside you. You're young—not dead. The tug of war between you and Rick ... it's been going on for a while, I'm surprised it's lasted this long."

"I thought ... he'd make me feel ...?"

"What?"

"Safer," she said sadly, pushing her face into his chest.

"You don't feel safe?

She hesitated.

"Rachel?"

Sighing, she whispered. "It's been lonely. Even with Elaine and Louise there, I've ... missed home, and Rick is nice .... He didn't deserve what I did." She put her hand under her cheek. "I've made a mess of things."

"This is your first shot at independence. Every day you gain a little more experience, than the day before, but even then," he looked down at her, "you'll still do and say stupid things. We all do. Making mistakes doesn't mean you're a bad person. It means you're taking risks—good or bad—that's for you to decide. Right now, you're questioning your judgment. If you didn't have a conscience, we wouldn't be having this conversation." His eyes were solemn in the dim light, his face twisted. "You got caught up in the moment; I've been there." Morgan stared up at the ceiling then closed his eyes. "I'm the last person to judge you or anyone if stupidity is the measurement stick."

"I never hear you say stupid things or do stupid things."

"I do—trust me."

Something in his demeanour, the sorrow in his face; she knew he carried his demons. "Do you regret your stupid things?"

He looked at her. "No." There was a heavy rumble in his tone.

Rachel wanted to ask him what caused him so much pain, but she knew him well enough to know excavating it would take time.

"Really?"

"Really."

"I'm sure what I did makes me a horrible person, but I don't regret being with Gary. He's so uncomplicated and beautiful." She laid her head on Morgan's shoulder, not wanting to see his disapproval. "I wanted to be with him. I hadn't been ... with anyone since Jessup. Gary made it so easy. With Rick, he made everything so difficult. Gary made me feel good about myself. I wasn't self-conscious or worried. I didn't feel like I was ... lacking something. It felt good. Do you know what I mean?"

"I know exactly what you mean. To regret something that felt so right is like saying it should never have happened, but because it happened, it made an important impact on you. Even if it was wrong."

She smiled up at him. "Exactly."

"Sometimes things happen when you least expect them. That's certainly happened to me."

She shifted her head slightly. That was the second time he'd mentioned his regrets. "What happened?"

She watched him collect his thoughts. Hesitating, he said, "Just that ... sometimes," his arms held her securely, "you meet the right person but the timing is off. You're too young or she's too young, and the only thing wrong is one of you needs to grow up. Maybe you can wait for them. Maybe not. Maybe life crowds you. You let circumstance guide you. And *sometimes*," his voice was soft and far away, "knowing what you want comes too late, and the chance to make a change comes too late."

"I thought it was never too late?"

He was very solemn. "Sometimes it is."

Terrified, she snapped, "Don't say that!"

He looked at her, his gaze intense; he took a long time to answer. "It's never too late."

She snuggled closer to him, wanting to believe him, needing to, but she was afraid he was right, that sometimes you *do* run out of time, and it's too late.

***

Jason found Morgan and Rachel, in his bed the next morning. Morgan was quick to explain she'd had a bad dream. Jason ignored them and prattled on that Carrie was coming over to spend the weekend. Alma had made breakfast and they were to get out of bed because he was hungry. Reluctantly, they did. They went down for breakfast, everything was light and easy. Morgan showered, kissed her on the forehead, said he would see her after work—maybe he would get home early if he got through the backlog on his desk.

The second Morgan's car zoomed away; Jason grabbed Rachel by the arm, "We need to talk," he said, practically pulling her arm out of its socket as he pushed her out the door leading to the back garden.

Jason was pissed. "What are you playing at, Rachel?"

Confused, Rachel stared blankly at him. "What do you mean?"

"He's fucking married! Or have you forgotten that?"

Rachel steeled herself. "No, I haven't forgotten."

Jason hit his head with his palm. "I must be confused 'cause you looked quite content this morning curled up to him, in his old room, in his old bed, while his wife is on the other side of the world." He paced. "You went to Montreal, didn't you? That bullshit story about meeting at the airport —and don't fucking bother lying, because I knew you would, so I called Jeff."

"You called Jeff!"

"I called him to play racquetball—asked him how the Quebec deal went and he mentioned you showed up."

Rachel yanked at her shirt. "Something happened at school. I needed to talk to Morgan."

"*So, you flew to Montreal?* It must have been a big fucking something."

"I couldn't do it over the phone."

"You did it on purpose Rachel, so spare me the fucking lies."

"I did not."

He shook his head. "This has to stop."

"Rick and I fought. It was bad. Real bad. Violent ... I needed to get out of town ... I wasn't sure what he would ..."

"And you couldn't wait to tell Morgan?"

"Shut-up Jason! You know nothing about it."

"I do know Rachel. I know too damn much. This little scenario you've built in your head is fucked up." He grabbed her. "People are going to get hurt!"

"The only one who's getting hurt is *me*." She yanked her arm away from him.

"Do you believe that? What was your fight with Rick about?"

"None of your business."

"Tell me Rachel or I'll call the fucking guy myself."

She had never seen Jason so angry. She believed he would call. "I slept with his roommate."

"And you think Rick isn't hurt? Having sex with him and then having sex with this other guy?"

"I didn't have sex with Rick."

"Oh well, that makes it so much better!"

"Mind your own fucking business!"

"He's my brother! And you're fucking around with his life. He married her—you have to accept it. I know you love him, but he's not going to leave her, not now."

"You don't know that."

"Yes, Rachel, I do. He's been married for two years. The business he and Jeff are putting together is taking off. Morgan's planning a coup with Henri Marchand. He's driven. He's sunk everything he owns into this venture. He's too pragmatic to fuck it up now. Even if he wanted to divorce her, he wouldn't. She's an asset to him. It would be a mistake. He can't afford an expensive, messy divorce right now. He won't risk it."

"He loves me. I know he does."

Jason sighed. "He does—but he loves you like a little sister. Has he done anything to give you the indication that he's sexually attracted to you? Grabbed a tit? Made a sexual innuendo? Anything? In any way? Or has he been the same old big brother Morgan—listening, guiding, helping."

"I hate you! Why don't you mind your own fucking business? This is between Morgan and me." She punched him, kicked at him. "Don't you have your own life to worry about? Why are you getting involved in mine?"

"This isn't meant to be and you need to stop pretending it's something it's not! God knows what you've tried to pull behind closed doors because the fact is Rachel, you're a manipulator. You use your tits and tears to get what you want."

Rachel slapped him hard across the face. When she raised her hand again, Jason easily grabbed her wrist. A welt was forming on his cheek.

Jason slowly lifted his gaze to hers. "You need to make a life for yourself away from him. This is unhealthy Rachel. You know I love you, and I want to protect you, even if it's to protect you from yourself, but this isn't meant to be, honey."

"You're wrong!" she cried, and she tried to yank her hand free. "It is!"

"No, sweetie, it's not." His hold tightened.

"It's not possible to love someone this much and for it not to be real. You're wrong!"

That's when he told what he had come into the garden to tell her. "They're starting a family Rach."

"You're such a liar! He would have told me." *Morgan can't have a baby with her; that would make them a family. He can't be a family with her.* "Not a baby Jason! He was supposed to have a baby with me!" The fight went out of her.

"I know Sweetie. I know." Jason hugged her while she cried.

Rachel had to leave. She couldn't watch Morgan become a doting father; touching Emily's growing belly; watching the surprised look on their faces when their baby kicked inside her; displaying their ultrasound picture on the fridge. She had to go. It was over. Her one-sided love affair with Morgan Hillier was over. Once she was capable of functioning, she gathered her things to leave.

Rachel left without a word and return to school. Leaving had to start right away.

When she returned to Western, she looked for a school she could transfer to—preferably a school that put a large body of water or land between her and Morgan. She had to make it impossible to fly home for a weekend. She didn't trust herself.

7

CITY OF LIGHT

Photograph 13

Rachel and Gary snuggled together outside the Ritz Carlton in Paris on a cold afternoon in November. They were celebrating their arrival. She was eighteen. He was twenty. Far away from home, they were ready to start a new adventure.

After the heart-wrenching yelling match with Jason, Rachel returned to London, but she never went back to her dorm. Chris continued to stay at Rick's, but Gary moved out, staying with his brother's friend Jimmy who lived in an old house with a vacant attic just off Richmond Street—a ten-minute walk to Western.

Rachel went to class during the day, saw her friends, talked to her mother often, and stayed with Gary at night. There was no pressure. Their passionate relationship saved Rachel from going crazy. Gary became a stabling force in her life.

Gary was an amazing artist. He filled his new space with incredible murals. He encouraged Rachel to do the same. Her murals were angry testaments with bold colours and erotic themes. Gary thought they were brilliant.

"They make me hard." Gary's forthright manner had shocked Rachel at first, but she soon fed off him and explored her sexuality.

"How hard?"

"Rock hard." He unzipped his jeans and put her hand on his crouch.

"So, it's my paintings you like?"

Gary laughed, undressing her quickly, picking her up and throwing her on their makeshift bed, which consisted of a mattress on the floor with mismatched sheets and blankets. He yanked off his -shirt. Gary had a wonderful body, muscled, large shoulders, narrow waist. His blue eyes sparkled mischievously, he pushed back his black hair from his face with his fingers; his arms cut. "I'd still fuck you senseless even if you painted by numbers."

The attic on Victoria Street was their alcove from the world. It had a small kitchen that looked out over the living room and a large bedroom. Gary used the bedroom for his studio and the living room was their bedroom; it contained a bed, a couch, a TV they never watched, and two desks pushed together where they studied. There was no time, no room to think in her new life.

Go to school, have sex, eat, study, have sex, go out with friends, have sex. No thinking. No hard and fast rules. There was, however, one exception.

"Rach?"

Soft music played in the background. She looked across their desks at him., he was turning a page of *What is History?* His casual appearance wasn't casual. He didn't look at her. A rarity. Immediately, her body tensed.

"Yes?"

Gary looked at her. There was none of the usual merriment in his eyes—their colour was deep —midnight blue. "No fucking anyone else, okay baby?"

Rachel looked down at her book. "I had never done anything like that before. I ... I had never cheated. I'm not a cheater." Her face was hot.

"I'm not a player. I'm a one-woman kind of guy who likes to be in a relationship—I know, I'm a dinosaur." He concentrated on his book again. "I want to make sure we are on the same page, I know how easy ..." there was a quiet sadness about his tone, "it is, for things to get fucked up fast."

His words hung in the air.

"Gary?"

His head remained down. "Hmm?"

"Gary."

He lifted his gaze.

"Who hurt you so badly?"

His smile had a certain kind of sadness that she knew well. "First love is a bitch."

"You're preaching to the choir brother!"

Gary laughed and shook his head. "Anyway, like I said, just want to make sure. I mean, I know you're not a cheater—I could tell it wasn't a usual thing."

Her eyes widened. "What does that mean?"

"Let's say you were innocently eager?"

Her brows hit her forehead; her face burned. Can you tell stuff like that? "Really?"

Gary laughed. "Why are you embarrassed?"

She huffed. "I'm not."

"Yes, you are."

"Don't laugh at me."

"I'm not laughing. I think you're adorable. Come here baby girl." He sounded so familiar. In the soft light of the room, he looked so familiar.

"No."

"Why?"

"You just want to have sex."

"I can't hug you without having sex with you?"

Unreasonably, she said, "You don't want to have sex with me?"

Gary slapped the desk and howled. "Come here and you can tell me what you want? A hug? A kiss? A fuck?"

"Why do you always call it that?"

"What? Fuck?"

"Yes—can't you just say sex?"

"I like the way *fuck* sounds." His voice was low. "Sex just doesn't do it for me—it's not passionate enough. Fuck—it's passionate. Fuck me baby."

Rachel was wet. Hot. His husky voice vibrated through her. "We've already had sex today—twice."

"We fucked five times yesterday. I could barely stand."

Softly in the background, Carlos Santana played a slow sultry tune that made the room hum.

"Really? Barely stand? That sounds serious." Rachel stood and climbed up on her desk, moving to the music, peeling off her clothes and whipping them in his direction. She heard him swear. She smiled, fondling herself as she pushed her undies down to her ankles and then kicked them at him with her toe. They made love on his steno chair under the duress of out of control laughter.

Later they lay in bed, her head on his chest, moonlight streaming in through the large bay window beside them. He stroked her hair. He was quiet. She could feel tension in his body. His request earlier, she realized, had more to it.

"Why are you looking at other schools, baby?" He shifted to lie facing her, giving her his full attention.

Rachel was surprised he noticed, but glad he had. Their earlier conversation made more sense. "Being adventurous ..."

"Were you going to tell me?"

She lay on her back. "I don't really have a plan so there's nothing to tell."

"Were you going to ask me to go with you?"

Surprised, she turned to see if he was serious. "Would you go?"

"Were you going to ask?"

Tears stung her eyes. They were sudden. Unexpected. "You're

the only thing keeping me here."

"What is it?" he whispered and that made her cry more. His warm body was close; his arms pulled her into him. "Why do you feel you need to go?"

"Run."

"Run? Rachel, what are you afraid of?"

"I'm not afraid. I just need to go. I need to get away from here."

Gary held her for a long time before he said. "I have an opportunity—with École des Beaux-Arts in Paris. I've been debating whether to go. I'm lost here. Art is my life—but my parents—my dad is a stockbroker and has a lucrative business; we have nothing in common. My mother is a corporate lawyer. I'm getting a business degree and taking art electives. The only reason I'm here is because my brother is here."

Rachel didn't know what to say.

"I want to get out of here—just go and leave all the bullshit behind," he whispered.

Rachel sat up in bed and stared down at him. He pushed his pillow against the wall and sat up against it. "I mentioned you—gave them your background—transferring wouldn't be a problem."

She smiled. "Riding on your coat tails?"

Gary's face was an animated one, but it had become decidedly blank. "Do you want to come with me?"

She didn't hesitate. "Yes."

"You don't need to talk to your parents?"

"I want to go with you ... and my mother knows I'm looking for a change."

"It's another language."

"I speak French."

"No friends. No family."

"Doesn't sound like you want me to go."

Gary snapped back the blankets and got out of bed. "No games

Rachel. I'm asking you to come with me. We'll share a house with other students, but I have no idea what we'd be walking into. The artist in me wants to go. Especially since, well, Sergi Gauguin has extended the invitation." He pulled a Molson out of the fridge.

Rachel was impressed. Sergi Gauguin made a splash in the art world thirty years ago with his painting *Nerf*—an explosion of nerves woven into the canvass like a traffic accident against the backdrop of a serene garden.

"Sergi Gauguin. Wow," she whispered.

"He saw a couple of my paintings at a Montreal gallery. A friend of mine, his mother, owns the gallery; that's the only way I would have got a chance at a showing. It was just after I started here. Gauguin asked to see me, wanted to see my portfolio. I met with him and he asked me to go to Paris."

"That's quite an honour. You'd be crazy not to go."

Gary shoulders sagged; his head bent. "When you were looking at other schools ... I thought ..."

She got out of bed, "You thought what?" Covering the space between them to stand in front of him, "What?"

"That our *thing* was over and I should go to Paris and paint away my demons."

"How very dramatic," she laughed.

"Isn't it?" he smiled ruefully, putting down his beer. He grabbed her waist, tugging her closer. He kissed her neck. "Are you coming?"

"Not yet, but I know I will soon."

He laughed. "And I'm the sex maniac?" He forced her mouth open, his tongue lapping her up like she was fresh fruit. His fingers played with her nipples.

"If you're going to do that ... they're large so you'll have let them know you want to play."

"Really? Big tits aren't sensitive?"

"They play hard to get."

He slipped his hand between her legs. "Now here … *very* sensitive."

"Oh …" She jumped at his insistent fingers.

Gary lifted her onto the counter and buried his head between her legs. He teased her relentlessly, his tongue insistent until she came.

She sat up, grabbing at him, kissing him.

"You want me, don't you Rachel?"

"Yes."

"Tell me what you want."

"Gary!"

"Come on baby girl … beg me." His head dipped down to her breasts; his tongue, his teeth, were aggressive. She closed her eyes. His sweet endearment rang in her ears. How many times had she heard that from Morgan's lips, millions?

"Come on baby girl … tell me what you want."

"You—"

"Say it." His tongue was inside her again.

Her head thrashed around on the counter. "I want you to—"

"Say it!"

"Darling … please."

He lifted her off the counter and put her in front of the sink, entering her from behind.

His hands went to her hips to hold her there. His hot breath was in her ear. "Does that feel good baby?"

"*Yes.*"

"You'll come to Paris with me?"

"*Yes.*"

His hands ran up and down the front of her body, playing with her breasts before slipping his fingers inside her; she came immediately.

***

Rachel went home the next weekend armed with her news of Paris. It had been a month since their Montreal mini-break, a month since they had spoken since they cuddled together in his boyhood bed. Morgan and Rachel were different people by the time she walked through the Hilliers' front door. At Sunday dinner, they didn't speak. Futility was the barren, pregnant silence between them. It didn't ease the sorrow, but the detachment they shared, made it possible for her to be in the same room as him. When Emily announced she was three months pregnant, Rachel died a little. Words of congratulations were incubated at the north side of the dinner table, then fed through fibre optic wires to the south side, and connected to a serrated knife where it was systemically buried inside Rachel's gut.

Jason announced that he and Carrie were also expecting and they would be getting married the following month.

Maureen said, "Rachel has good news too. She's off to Paris for a year."

Congratulations were all around. Morgan's head remained a shadow over his plate.

Later that evening, Jason took Rachel aside. "You did good."

She did what was necessary. The ache she harboured had not diminished, melodrama aside, she had not died—possibility had died. "Congratulations. You're happy about the baby?"

"Very happy."

"I'm glad," she said. "I'm not going to be here for your wedding."

"I know."

"It's best."

His eyes looked beyond her. "Yes," he whispered.

***

Paris provided a passage from Rachel's vacancy. She discarded her memories of Morgan on the tarmac of Pearson International Airport and embraced the City of Light.

Rachel loved the landscape of Paris, the geography. The Seine River flowed through the city—east to west—entering Paris from the southeast, then looping north, and curving west before leaving the city. A perfect symmetry. The river divided Paris into the infamous left and right banks. The right bank, to the north side, had small industries, office buildings, and shops. The left bank, to the south side, was an ancient haunt for artists and students to chat arrogantly of their latest and greatest work or debate on beauty, sex, drink, and food.

Rachel and Gary had arrived late in the school year. Housing for students was non-existent. Sergi provided a solution. He owned several properties and assured them he would locate the perfect spot. The first house, he immediately dismissed upon arrival, recognizing it as unsuitable. Gary and Rachel thought it was perfect. Sergi begged for their pardon, citing that the attic was in deplorable shape and no one had used it since the 1800s. It was a five-bedroom three-story house in Saint-Germain-des-Pres; a beautiful, old neighbourhood that was minutes from the Seine, close to school on Rue Bonaparte, close to amenities, and had seven historical monuments within walking distance. Four couples lived in the house. Two British, one Italian, and one French. Dilapidated attic or not, they insisted on seeing it.

Reluctantly, Sergi slammed his left shoulder into the door several times to dislodge it. Standing amongst the grime and debris, spiders' webs woven with a silky artistry, and plank floors, Gary looked at Rachel, an excited grin on his face. "It's just about perfect."

She nodded. "Just about."

"*Non!*" Sergi was appalled, but they soothed him with visuals of how they would spin the attic with spun gold.

Their housemates were very agreeable—took them to the

student canteens nearby, arranged for them to visit exhibitions, parties, and introduced them to other foreign students to mingle with; Gary and Rachel fell into Parisian life easily. They made friends. They did all the tourist things. Walking along the Pont des Arts, Gary and Rachel held hands and took goofy pictures for Rachel to send to her mother. No packets of photos went to the Kurfonts.

On their visit to the Louvre, Rachel was captivated. It was a monumental task to drink in; not a task to be slovenly thrown back in the throat like cheap *du vin*. It was a wonder that required commitment and concentration. It was to be enjoyed at a leisurely pace for savouring purposes, a pleasure Rachel did savour. She read everything about the Louvre, discovering that, originally, it was a King's residence. The renaissance palace became the world's largest and most famous art museum. It covered more than forty-eight acres by the mid-nineteenth century. Rachel loved the architectural masterpiece that it was, she loved that each monarch who had lived there added their own additions: sometimes sculptural and structural adornments.

Even the contemporary additions, such as, *La Pyramide,* she loved. Not everyone felt the same way. Traditionalists hated the enormous transparent dome. Rachel had no idea how much until a month after their arrival; a debate broke out in a quaint café close to home. The question for debate: the glassy dome's modishness is crude against the regal Louvre. An offensive piece! It should be removed! Rachel and Gary's new housemates were a mixed bag of opinions. The English couples loved mixing the old with the new, however, the French and Italian couples were passionate people; debating with a fierceness that the glass structure was insulting, completely dragging the architectural elegance of the Louvre into a sinkhole. Rachel reserved her judgments with her new European friends, as they heatedly argued ancient versus contemporary. Vulgar versus dazzling. Tradition versus modern.

Gary held his glass of red wine up in the air. "I'm on art's side; the artist's vision is in their discretion. Pei had a vision. It may not be your vision or mine but it's not supposed to be." The café had been decidedly quiet.

"The debate is academic," Rachel said quietly, "La Pyramide and the Musée du Louvre are synonymous with each other now."

"Always the diplomats—you two are so *Canadien.*"

Gary clinked his wine glass with her teacup. *"Enchante!"* he whispered in her ear.

The proximity of Paris to other great cities had a complimentary advantage for Rachel and Gary. Sergi's genuine fondness for the two budding artists spawned an enhancement to their education. Sergi's reach was everywhere. He had many friends who welcomed the young couple in their homes and shared their traditions in Rome, Florence, London, Berlin, Vienna, Amsterdam

Notre Dame was, by far, the fondest memory Rachel had of Paris. In the Wharton household, it was the best-known Gothic cathedral. Not one of her housemates agreed with her. They cited— at great length—other Gothic cathedrals that, in their estimation, far exceeded Notre Dame. But her love for the cathedral icon had nothing to do with its bricks and mortar, and everything to do with her father.

When he was a high school teacher, John Wharton spent as much time with Rachel as possible. Her childhood memories of her dad were filled with ice cream runs, laughter, movies, and books he read to her. Summers were spent at their cottage on Lake Simcoe. The Hilliers spent the summer with them. Uncle Robert always came up on Friday night. Sometimes Maureen made it north.

John Wharton was the second son born to Randall and Amanda. After graduating from university, John joined the family business— Wharton Newspapers. John's older brother Geoff was CFO and Randall was CEO. Back then, the Wharton building was on Bay

Street near the old Woolworth's. When they built Wharton Plaza on Front Street, John had an office between his father and Geoff. A year after John joined the company, his parents died in their private plane off the coast of Newfoundland. After that everything changed. Suddenly men in suits, angry whispering, phone calls and papers—lots and lots of papers needed to be signed. In the end, her dad left Wharton Newspapers and became a teacher. Rachel never knew what created the rift between the brothers.

Rachel's days with her father lasted until she was six. John Wharton's natural charm and instinctive ambition spread. Her dad believed the school system was a machine that brooked no progressive change; it had become fat. Within twenty years, it would date itself. Instead of losing heart, he started an educational foundation that explored new pathways. He spoke around the country, but his message soon spread around the world, at symposium's, Fortune 500 companies, and political parties started to take note and wanted him on their side.

But back then, he was the centre of her world and Notre Dame was his backdrop. Her father's passion for this place echoed in her ear when she walked through the old cathedral's threshold fifteen years later. Standing under rows of carved flying buttresses, with crowned peaks that gave the basilica a delicate profile, Rachel fell in love.

She whispered to Gary, "When I was six years old, my father read *The Hunchback of Notre Dame* to me."

Her father had animated the tale, jumping on furniture, whipping cushions about the family room. He had engaged her completely, yanked at her heartstrings with laughter and tears. She would sit quietly, listening to his every word, watching his every move.

"My Dad loved the story. He gave Victor Hugo's lusty descriptions of Quasimodo's love for his sacred place depth and meaning. I can still hear my dad's voice ringing in my ears …

"His cathedral was enough for Quasimodo. Saints and demons; Quasimodo lived safely amongst them. The beautiful marbled statues did not judge or deplete. Saints blessed him. Monsters protected him. Passing many hours, Quasimodo would squat before his friends, having long chats about the state of the day. At the centre of the cathedral that enshrined the mediaeval tale of a city's dreams—a city's soul."

"Then you're going to love this," said Gary, moving her to the centre of the cathedral. "Stand right here."

"Why?"

"*Shh* … listen."

Rachel stood, inhaling the scent of history as she waited—and then she heard it. She jumped, startled by the first boom; the music of Quasimodo's grand bells vibrated through her. Tears stung her eyes as she listened. Quasimodo's true love—the big bell.

The first time John Wharton read Hugo's beautifully vivid picture of Quasimodo's excessive champion of love for his cathedral, and the treatment he received from those who didn't understand him, Rachel had exhausted herself from her rapt attention. In that moment, standing at the centre of Notre Dame, listening to the bells, Rachel realized Quasimodo had not inspired her love for Gothic and medieval sculpture; it was her father. His passion had led her to research the period in both art and literature, and her passion followed close behind. France was the best place to indulge in her fascination.

Rachel loved painting. Loved painters. Painters had traditions of style. There was a foundation paved by painters before them and from old traditions, new traditions formed.

But France introduced her to a new love. Medieval carvers. In the twelfth century, carvers had yet to discover all that stone had to offer. In its artistic infancy, challenges plagued these carving sculptors. Capturing their visions of ornamentation and pattern into complicated angles with limited space was a necessary trial and error evolution. When Rachel and Gary went to see the medieval sculptor Gislebertus' *The Last Judgement* at the Autun Cathedral, the challenges of the medium were apparent. What further challenged these artists was that their compositions were not renditions of their own beliefs or plight, but rather commissioned carvings to educate the masses on sacred Christian scripture. Clergy and artist laboured together to bring theological belief into the mainstream. They adorned churches all over Europe with scriptural commentaries in stone. When these artists became more comfortable with their medium, pushing themselves to the arduous step of free movement, Gothic marvels in stone were born. Carver's changed how they carved their figures. Harsh angles smoothed out. Managing confined space became second nature.

Rachel stood on the north porch of Chartres Cathedral, in awe of the carving *Prophets and Saints*. She knew that the bored vacationers that whipped by this masterpiece had no idea of the skill and power that went into these carvings. They had no idea of the dedication and love required to execute the sculptor's vision with such mastery. For it to be attained in the thirteenth century when life was a shadow of today? It mesmerized Rachel—blew her away. This carving had been a major production. Christian patrons, regardless of social disposition, assisted labourers in dragging the stone to its destination, for no other reason than the magnificence of the endeavour; Rachel couldn't imagine how many men it took.

Living inside art, living inside their work, living inside the spectacular architecture that surrounded them, profoundly affected Gary and Rachel. It pounded through them, bonding them. Freedom of expression transformed Gary in ways that endeared him to her. For the first time in his life, Gary lived and breathed his art. He too had left discarded pieces of himself on Pearson's tarmac. His parents' disapproval of his choice to be an artist hurt him deeply. *Why can't they just love me and wish me the best? They aren't even paying for it.*

The Kurfonts believed making pretty pictures was not a profession. Certainly not a profitable one. They told him running off to Paris at the invitation of Sergi Gauguin was foolish. Gary didn't even *know* Gauguin. That Gary's inexperience and impracticality would have him back in Canada within three months. Penniless. And he would have lost precious time at the Ivey School of Business. His parents' disapproval left him raw, but Sergi's belief in Gary was categorical, and it assuaged that rawness. Sergi nurtured the talent he saw in Gary's work in Montreal. He pushed Gary to draw out the artist that lay hidden behind parochial landscapes and urban chaos, which confused and frustrated Gary.

"I don't know what the old man wants!" he ranted one evening, pacing the room. "Nothing I do pleases him." Gary looked at Rachel. "He slashed my canvass today—*slashed it!* Can you fucking believe it?" He shook his head. "Any day now he's going to rescind my full ride."

"He's not going to rescind anything. You are, by far, the most talented in the class."

"Bullshit! You're the talented one. He loves your stuff."

"I'm good—but you're *great.*"

"Bullshit! Your stuff is earthy and sexy. You should have got the scholarship." He stopped pacing and stood in the middle of the room. "My parents were right."

Rachel stood. "No, they're not."

He looked her in the eye and shouted. "They are! He hates me! What is it you're not getting here?"

Rachel hesitated. This was important to him. She knew. He had never raised his voice to her, never been sarcastic.

"*What?* What's the look for?" he demanded.

"You want my opinion?"

"Why the fuck do you think I'm talking to you?"

"To let off steam. To rant. To have me stand here and agree that Sergi is a fuckhead like a simpleton."

His face twisted. "You fucking agree with him!"

"I understand you're upset Gary." She walked to him, speaking softly. "I understand how important this is to you. But the truth is, if the artist in you was as honest as the man you are, you wouldn't just be the most talented guy in the class, you would be trying to find your stride and your greatness. But right now, as an artist, you're an arrogant prick. You can't see for looking."

Gary was stunned; his eyes riveted to her face. "What?" he whispered.

She remained calm. Her voice measured. "Your ego clouds your judgment."

"What?"

"You do the assignments and technically—they are perfect. Everyone thinks you are amazing, that your work is amazing, but they're just replicas of your talent. You know you're good. You paint like you're good."

"Isn't that a good thing?"

"No."

"What?"

"Not with talent like yours." She took a deep breath. She was going in, complete honesty. "Your ego's hurt because Sergi slashed a beautiful piece today. I know what's going on inside your head — 'Jesus, can't the fuckhead see how fucking talented I am? How fucking great that painting was?' —But he knows you're brilliant. He wants you to dig deeper. Art isn't just a beautiful talent; it's a beautiful expression, even if the emotion is ugly. So, take your ego out of the equation and take an emotional risk. You're holding back. There's a barrier. He likes my paintings because all my insecurities and emotions are on my canvasses. I'm an open book." She pushed his hair back from his forehead. "I think if you put your tenderness into your art—put more of the loving, passionate man you are into your art—he wouldn't slash any more paintings." She kissed his cheek tenderly. "Think about it." She left the room to give him some privacy.

A couple of hours later, she returned to find him sitting on the floor in the dark, under the window. The silence was eerie. His sketchbooks and canvasses scattered about the room. Work she had never seen before—of beautiful babies and white-haired angels—there was something different about the paintings. A rawness. She knelt in front of him, saw his face was streaked with tears; his eyes were full. Cries burst out, a heart-breaking pain shook him, and he fell into Rachel's arms. She held him tight.

Gary painted his pain and his joy with tenderness after that day. He revelled in his art. His passions took hold. His work expanded. He looked for the intimate moments in life and then magnified them on canvass. He immersed himself into the psychology of colour, its vividness and its dullness. Skin tone became his fascination. Nudes were his focus and they were a testament to his devotion to the female form. Rachel noticed, he always did a working piece first, and he always painted the same woman. He painted her anger, hate, love, joy, and sorrow. He developed new texts for her skin; he used an assortment of embellishments, enjoying the experimentation process, mixing and dusting; he tried everything, but on her first. She never made it to the final piece. A different model took her place. His first love, Rachel suspected. The results of his experiments changed his work. Gary's nudes took on a dreamlike imagery. When he dusted crystal particles onto the alabaster skin of a peasant virgin girl with luminous eyes, Gary had no idea where it would lead.

The *Virgin Peasant* was first in a series that Gary called *The Virgin Bibles*. The Virgin unsettled Rachel. Her innocence was in the dimensions of her bright ethereal eyes. In the whiteness of her skin, in the softness of her face; she had no guile. Her arms cradled her large breasts on her small body like she was cradling a baby; her fingers were long and delicate, her legs were open wide, her sex succulently pink, her stance suggestive but not vulgar. The second piece had the virgin peasant languid on a colourful cushion; her back arched, her arms flung over her head. Beads of sweat glistened on her skin; her breasts like song peaks. Her lover, nothing more than a dark flow of hair between her widespread legs partaking in her already established succulent flesh. The virgin looked out from the canvass, nestled against her delicate arm, her eyes shimmered with pleasure and longing.

The first time she saw the piece, Rachel lived the passion of the peasant girl. It was impossible not to feel the eddy of emotion Gary inspired.

"You can almost hear him sipping her in, *non?*" Sergi Gauguin stood beside Rachel.

Yanked completely into the painting, she had not heard his arrival. She blushed, embarrassed by her adoration of the young virgin's abandoned pleasure under the watchful eye of Sergi Gauguin.

She swallowed. "The movement of his hair suggests a more … energetic approach, don't you think?"

"My delicacy." He bowed, a lopsided smile on his craggy yet attractive face. "I should have known better. Your embarrassment has not clouded your accurate assessment."

"I'm only embarrassed at being caught in the moment of her passion in such a public place and Gary is awkwardly absent," she smiled.

Sergi's laugh was deep. "How delightful you are *Raquel.* Most women would have denied an amorous response—women who are not French, that is." He sighed deeply, caught in a memory. "I had the pleasure of seeing both pieces in my home. And yes, I had to make love to Chantal for many hours. First viewing is intoxicating."

Rachel nodded, looking back at the painting. "Gary has been very secretive."

"She is extraordinarily beautiful," he said.

"In an unsettling way."

"You are unsettled by her?"

"She has the mark of innocence and yet she's not innocent. She's known heartache. Her eyes ... the inflection of so many colours; her eyes are alive with frankness. Her nude body doesn't make her naked; her eyes do. Her passion for her lover is haunting. I think I'm a little envious of her," Rachel whispered. "It's ... you can see her embarrassment that her passion is naked for everyone to see, like she has sinned by a standard she didn't create, but she accepts the judgment. Even what Gary named the paintings, *The Virgin Bibles,* inferring that the virgin has her own Bible she lives by and it has trapped and freed her?"

"You do not know the model."

It wasn't a question but a statement, and it tugged her from her admiration. She stared up at him. Sergi Gauguin was impeccably dressed in a black suit, white shirt and tie, a white handkerchief in his front pocket. He was tall for a Frenchmen.

"No."

His curious and confused expression did not match his question. "Does this disturb you?"

"No."

His brows shot up. "Western women, usually, are threatened when their lover shares with another."

Rachel stepped back, startled for a moment. "You think Gary is sleeping with his model?"

Sergi put his hands behind his back. "My apologies, Raquel, this discussion has become derailed. I do not think Gary is sleeping with another woman. His devotion to you is exceptionally plain. I am interested in the idea of a western woman's acceptance that her lover has painted an intimate portrait of another woman, without recrimination or threat. Not surprisingly, you are the exception, *mon cheri.*"

"French women are more forgiving than western women?"

"They are not innocent to the ways of life."

"So, if Chantal takes a lover you will understand her need for sexual freedom?"

"Chantal is more than my lover and the mother of my children, but if she did take a lover, it's because she is missing something I cannot provide. It does not mean she no longer loves me."

An outer door slammed and Gary came rushing in. His hair was windblown, his jean jacket was under his leather jacket, his black pants had paint on them. He dropped his portfolio and duffel bag on the floor just inside the French doors and quickly made his way across the room.

"Hey baby," he smiled and picked her up in a bear hug. "You like it? Jesus tell me you like it."

Tears sprung unexpectedly into her eyes. "It's brilliant."

He kissed her. "I'm relieved ... I didn't know if you would—"

Sergi cut in, "She is enamoured with your work. We were just discussing it when you came in. She finds your beautiful virgin unsettling."

Gary put Rachel down; his arm clutching her to him and she pressed her ear into his chest. His heart was beating fast, furiously.

"Unsettling?"

"Her eyes," Sergi said, "they are haunting. What did you say, Raquel? 'The virgin has her bible she lives by and it has trapped and freed her?' We should use that in the program." Sergi walked slowly toward them, his pace slow, his words measured. "Raquel did not know the model ... I had indelicately given her the wrong impression that you had slept with the model. I am a buffoon for giving her such an impression for your devotion to her is clear. My apologizes. I caught her in a moment of living the beautiful virgin's passion. Her amorous response to your work must be indulged." He handed the gallery's keys to Gary. "Vincent is around here somewhere. Ensure you lock up when you leave?"

Rachel watched the two men stare at each other. Something passed between them. She had seen these types of exchanges many times in her life. Men saying things to each other without words. Rachel had cast men in a secondary role to women when it came to emotional intelligence. Gary and Sergi's unspoken exchange, as with many she has witnessed over the years between Morgan and Jason, her father and Uncle Robert, defied her belief.

When the gallery door closed, she said, "What was that look?"

He looked down at her. "What look?"

"Sergi's look?"

"The—you better make sure my gallery is locked up or I'll kick your ass look?"

"*Gary.*"

"I don't want to talk about the old man. I want to talk about how you look in this light."

She laughed. "Who are you trying to impress?"

"I was trying to be romantic."

"You have to prepare me for romance. I'm used to—let's get down to business."

"You know, you're blowing it for yourself. Kiss romance good-bye you *silly bitch*."

She relented. "I loved your painting—very erotic."

"Made you *amorous*, eh?"

"I was looking at the second one. Her lover is enjoying himself." Rachel glanced back at the virgin. "Are you sleeping with her? Sergi may not have wanted to leave that impression," she wrapped her arms around her breasts, "but the more I look at the painting ...

You've slept with that girl, your strokes on her body are delicate, loving."

"Jealous?"

"You enjoyed being with her."

"No one modelled for me. It was private."

Rachel laughed. "Privacy has been abandoned at this point buddy. Everyone will want to know who she is, and there I will be standing beside you, while people file in and out of here. Someone will make it their business to find out who she is; it's better if you tell me now so I'm prepared."

"No one modelled for me," he whispered. "The beautiful virgin lives inside my head." His hand cupped her face and kissed her lightly. "Every move, every sigh, every whisper, every gaze, she lives inside my head. Her smell, her response, lives inside my memories." He opened his mouth over her lips, biting at her, licking her, but she refused to open her mouth; not prepared to give in to him when he was talking about another woman.

His hot breath made her shiver. "*You* are the virgin."

She opened her mouth to share her shock and recrimination when he bent his head; there was a savage passion in his kiss. His wet tongue invaded and demanded. His hands cupped her bum, pulling her close.

"Look at yourself," his breath was heavy, as he spun her around so she was facing the painting.

Rachel glanced at the young girl—the only two canvasses on the wall. In the soft light, the virgin's pronounced innocence was in the starving and passionate ache in her eyes. She didn't know how she looked in the throes of passion. Gary played with her ear; the scorch of his breath made her tingle.

"*That* is not me," she whispered, "my hair is blonder with red highlights and hers is a darker red, her eyes are blue and mine are green, and her skin is paler, and she … she's not just smarter, she knows more than I do. For someone so young, she's seen great pain. And truth radiates from her. Look at her eyes. They're haunting. I plunder around like a blind elephant."

His hands splayed across her abdomen.

"It's like she's two people."

His hands followed the curve of her hips and then reached under her skirt.

"*Gary* ... I won't be able to concentrate if you do that." her head fell back on his chest and she closed her eyes, enjoying his roughly tender insistence.

He pressed his head against hers. "Don't think. Don't wake up. Just feel baby."

She saw the furrow on his brow. "What's wrong?"

He shook his head; his face twisted.

"Why are you unhappy?" She turned to face him. "You should be so proud of yourself. Your piece is spectacular. Not to mention, we're in Paris and your first major piece is, not at the gallery at school but in *Sergi Gauguin's* Art Gallery, and Sergi is pulling out all the stops from here to New York." She smoothed out his frown. It was unlike Gary to be nervous or stressed. "What is it, beautiful boy?"

He shrugged. He let her go, walked over to his work, and stared at the painting.

She said, "What did you mean—don't wake up?"

"It's nothing Rachel."

"Yes, it is. Do you think I'm in asleep?"

"Yes."

"And when I wake up, what will happen?"

"You're just caught in a dream. When you wake up from it, you will leave."

"I have nowhere to go."

"Yes, you do. You just don't think you do."

"Is this an elaborate way of trying to get rid of me? We've only been here for five months, but I'd thought we were getting along great."

Gary turned to look at her. "We are—and no, I'm not trying to get rid of you. I need you to stay. To be with me … or …"

"Or what?"

"I think I will lose my mind."

"Well, I'm not going anywhere."

"Good."

"I am annoyed though."

"About?"

Rachel put her hands on her waist and dropped her hip. "Well, a few minutes ago you had your hand down my panties and now you're on the other side of the room."

Intensity emanated from Gary's eyes. "Take off your clothes," he whispered.

Rachel gave him a saucy smile. "You first."

8

THE VIRGIN BIBLES

Critics loved *The Virgin Bibles*. Sergi pulled out all the stops: social media, chat shows, radio, every art school form England to Asia had a visit. Gary was a hit. Accolades of a brilliant future were on the tip of everyone's tongue; Sergi's protégé was on his way. Rachel sent the many clippings of his success to Gary's parents and his brother Chris. She even sent a copy to her mother—not a picture of the paintings though. No sense in bringing it out into the forefront. Maureen sent her congratulations. Gary's parents remained silent, but Chris surprised them by flying to Paris to spend four days with them.

Chris burst into the kitchen with, "Where's the little perv?" Thumping and bear hugs were exchanged between the brothers. Over Chris's shoulder, Gary looked at Rachel, bathing her in such a look of love and gratitude. She had been nervous about contacting his family about his success, but in that moment, although her motives were not altogether pure and guilt was a stone's throw away, she knew some good had come from it—she had done the right thing for Gary.

The Virgin Bibles was on the lips of everyone and anyone in Paris town. Gary was the sexy rock star of the art world. A fan club was started in his honour. Even "the virgin" began to receive mail at Sergi's Gallery—marriage proposals, presents, demands that the identity of the beautiful model be revealed. When the paintings were brought to auction, an aggressive bidding war started, unheard of for an unknown painter, but it ended with a sale to a private collector for five hundred and fifty thousand American dollars. Gary was catatonic. Sergi was elated. Rachel was relieved. Watching the crate being closed and strapped together lifted a weight off her. The paintings were off to their new home in New York. Far from her sight.

Gary's work took on a primal focus after that, as did their sex life. While scouring a pot, he came up behind Rachel and pushed her dress up over her bum and kissed her cheeks, his fingers soon made their way around, slipping into her. His fingers were magic, knew exactly where her spot was. She was a quivering mess within minutes. Henri caught them one day when they thought they were alone.

Henri was not flustered. He poured himself a coffee and said, "I am envious."

Rachel was embarrassed. She was far from streets lined with oak trees in stuffy Forest Hill. Gary appeased her, promising to jam a chair against the kitchen door in future, but he wasn't giving up the pleasure of fucking her in the kitchen.

Later that night, they were lying in bed when someone knocked on the door. It was Henri. In rapid French, Henri made his request: "Collette and I want to switch partners with you."

Rachel sat behind Gary.

"No," said Gary.

"No?" Henri was shocked.

"No," said Gary.

"What is Raquel's wish?"

"No," Gary insisted.

Henri was confused: "We are French. We are young. What is the problem?"

"We appreciate the offer—but no."

"Regrettable." Henri left.

"What if I wanted to switch?" Rachel teased.

He rolled his eyes. "Yes, you're so worldly, Rach."

"I'm not?" She thought she was. She was in Paris having tons of sex and drinking almost a full glass of wine without passing out. She could even stay up past one—at least once a week.

He laughed. "Having sex in Paris doesn't constitute worldly. Say, fuck me Gary." He had that expectant look she hated so much, like he knew best. "Go on, say it, fuck me till dawn, Gary."

She looked him square in the eye. "And that constitutes worldly? Knowing how to say the words? Okay, you sex maniac—Gary, I want you to … to … to …"

"My poor baby. My beautiful little virgin girl."

"Stop saying that. I'm not a virgin."

He pushed her onto the bed and nuzzled her neck, working up to her ear. She could feel his smile against her skin. "Yes, you are my love. Let's put it this way—the first time we did it, it felt virginal."

"You think you're so smart. I lost my virginity at sixteen."

He stared at her—devious charm. "Was he sixteen too?"

She couldn't help but laugh. "It was terrible. I was sore for a week."

They both laughed. He pulled her under him. "Do you want to have sex with Henri?"

She wrinkled her nose. "He smells funny."

They laughed again.

Photograph 14

James Hillier's birth announcement card. He was a few weeks old when the picture was taken. He was so peaceful—jet black hair. Rachel hated that beautiful baby.

Spring in Paris brought news from Rachel's parents. Morgan and Emily had a little boy, James Robert. The manifested appearance of a new Hillier brought bitterness that Rachel had difficulty reconciling. She set aside her love for children, allowed her bitterness to ferment. It was categorical; she hated baby James.

Rachel sent an appropriate congratulatory telegram in reply to the Hilliers' happy news. She sat in front of the picture window overlooking the narrow back garden for six hours composing: "Congratulations on the arrival of your son. Our thoughts are with you and your family during this happy time."

Then she debated. *How should I end this puny sentiment—with Love? Sincerely?* She moved back and forth on whether to include Gary. Would that disturb Morgan? Would he care either way? She laughed at her lunacy. He just had a baby with his wife. She ended with, "Our Best wishes to you and yours, Love Rachel." Once it was sent, she rejoined her life with more animation than she conceded to feeling. She painted large canvasses of bare trees, murky rivers, deserted streets, lone women facing acts of God, and a collection of dissimilar chairs: vacant, colourless, their only adornment—vases empty of flowers.

Shocking news came from Toronto six months later. James Robert Hillier had died.

Rachel collapsed on the sofa.

Thoughts were impossible. She became motion instead. She arranged for the flight home. She thwarted Gary's pleas to attend the funeral with her.

When she arrived in Toronto that November, being home was a mesh of surreal events strung together without compliment. The day of the funeral was miserably cold. Standing at the gravesite, the wind howled into a weeping whirl that weaved through the small congregation of mourners—a matching sentiment to Emily's hysterical tirade. Stoic and safe behind armour Rachel didn't recognize she possessed; she kept her eyes down, her thoughts blank. Each member of the Hillier family, bar Emily, threw dirt on top of the small casket. Rachel lifted her eyes in Morgan's direction when

Emily begged him to bring her boy back. His silence bred Emily's contempt.

"It's your fault!" screamed Emily, beating at him. "You bastard! It's your fault! Why weren't you there! I didn't know what to do! Why weren't you there!"

Morgan was a haunting figure, a shadow of the man she had known her whole life. Emily's estranged mother, recently back in the fold since the demise of her third marriage, cooed Emily into her arms, walking her to the Escalade at the curb. All eyes cast down at her retreat.

Morgan watched as they lowered his son deeper into the open wound in the ground, and he looked up. Rachel met his gaze. Since her arrival, there had only been blankness in his eyes, and now, it suddenly disappeared. Morgan's sorrow was powerful. It reached across James' tiny casket and into Rachel's body. Pain exploded in her chest and shot into every corner of her body; she broke out into a cold sweat. Her hand went to her heart; tears flooded her eyes. He mirrored her action. They shared their suffering, their communion transporting them into each other.

The moment ended when the baby's casket hit bottom.

The mourners moved to their cars.

"Why don't you drive with me darling? Daddy can drive your rental." Her mother's pale complexion and strawberry blonde hair were stark against her dark suit and the gloomy fall day.

"You go ahead ... I want to drive myself."

Maureen wiped Rachel's tears with her leather glove. "We'll meet you at the Hilliers?"

She nodded.

The procession of cars left Mount Pleasant Cemetery. Alone with little James, she whispered, tears taking complete hold of her. "I'm sorry ... James. I've hated you without knowing you and now I find myself at a loss."

"This wasn't your fault."

She twisted round to face Jason. "I hated him," the honesty of her disgrace forced her to see what she had ignored for so long. "Me? Hating a defenceless child!"

"He had a genetic heart condition. They operated. He died. Emily's brother died of the same thing, only he lived a bit longer. Everyone did their best."

"You don't understand."

"I understand completely. Do you? You think because you resented the *idea* of James, you're responsible in some way for pushing his young life along into death? You didn't." Jason meant his words to sooth, like an offering, a path back into respectable behaviour, but guilt crushed her regardless of his sentiments.

When she returned to Paris, Rachel was defeated. She couldn't sleep or eat. Running became her escape. She hoped that one of the narrow streets led to a secret passage where redemption lived. But there was none.

Each night she ran through the city's dark empty streets. Ran through streets where candy vendors had long since gone, side paths had long been swept, cafés had lost their lovers and friends to cozy lounges and feather beds. The Eiffel Tower, the epitome of the City of Light, was in the distance. Its illuminated beauty held no power for her on her nightly runs. When she ran alongside the Seine, its melancholy smell filled her senses, clouding her mind with a temporary distraction. She took no notice of the Louvre; she drove herself hard and blocked out all her loves. Notre Dame had a foreboding quality in the dimness of night. Under the Arc de Triomphe, she passed quickly and avoided the sacred pleasure of the deserted Tuileries Garden. For three weeks, she ran and walked the streets of Paris, returning at dawn. As November became December, rain pelted her. She wanted to feel the cold rain on her overheated body. She wanted every muscle and joint to ache. The night the running stopped, she had arrived back at their house, soaked. The grandfather clock in the front hall struck five.

Gary was waiting, sitting on the staircase, hot tea in hand. "This has to stop Rachel. You're going to kill yourself." He pushed the mug into her hand. "Drink."

"No." She handed it back.

"At least it's a decision." He scooped her up and carried her upstairs to their room.

Street lights brightened their dark room. Gary put her down on the sofa and she peeled off her wet clothes and put his sweater on her chilled body.

"What is it baby?"

There were no more tears inside her, no more restraint from the truth. "It's Morgan."

"The guy whose baby died?"

"Yes. Morgan Hillier. He's married to Emily."

"Morgan Hillier?"

"Yes."

"Is this the same Morgan you and Rick fought about all the time?"

"Yes."

"So, what's the story Rachel?"

Her voice was emotionless. She stared at the far wall. "I'm in love with him. I've been in love with him since I was fifteen, but he married someone else."

There was a long pause. "Does he know how you feel?"

"No. He thinks of me like a little sister."

"When did he marry?"

"I was sixteen."

Gary's voice was measured. "Is he the reason you wanted to run?"

"Yes. He was starting a family with her. I couldn't stay. I hated that baby."

"And you feel responsible?"

"Yes."

Gary sat down on the bed and leaned his forearms on his knees. The room had a distant buzz. Laughter echoed from the street below. "So where are you running to now?"

"I'm running in circles."

He got up from the bed and walked to the bureau, a towel in his hand. He dried her neck and face, her legs and feet, then threw it over her head and dried her hair. When he was done, he picked her up, carried her to the bed, and put the blankets around her. He slipped in behind her and put his arm around her. Rachel fell asleep instantly.

Rachel lived in a blur, not getting out of bed. Exhaustion consumed her. Vaguely she recalled Gary speaking to her, bringing her food she didn't eat. It required too much effort to focus.

When her focus finally did return—she woke with a start.

Gary knelt beside the bed looking at her. For a second, she thought it was Morgan and her heart hammered against her chest.

"It's me," he said.

"Who else would it be?"

He gave her a crooked smile. "I Googled the Morgan guy. His name was familiar. He has an impressive resume," His eyes held hers, "Could pass for my brother. But then I'm sure you noticed that."

Rachel held her breath when he moved to get up and walk to the narrow window across from the bed; he watched the street as he leaned against the cool pane. "Sergi is pleased with the success of *The Virgin Bibles*. I know we were only staying for a year, but Sergi wants me to stay another year ... finish my degree here. There's no point in returning to Western to please my parents, not after being here. I could go back to Canada, go to art school in Toronto, BC or Montreal. It would be cheaper than Paris, but the sale of *The Virgin Bibles* makes everything possible. Either way, I want to stay. I'll leave it up to you whether you stay or go."

She slid to the bottom of the bed and sat on her legs. "Do you want me to go?"

"I'm not a complicated guy Rachel—the artist in me? Yeah, that's complicated, but me, the man, not so much. I like to keep it simple." He turned to stare at her in the dimness. "The way I see it, we have a great time together; we have the same interests; we enjoy each other's body. I'm not looking around. So, you love a guy you can't have? You don't get everything you want—welcome to adulthood. But we're young and in Paris. Why not enjoy it?" He glanced down at the street before gazing up at the sky. "I'm going to have a shower and head to the studio."

He grabbed his jeans and a towel. Rachel desperately needed a connection with him. She was scared. Lonely. Her depression gripped her and incapacitated her. She needed to feel his warmth against her. She spoke softly, "Do you want company?"

Gary leaned against the door; his thumb hooked into his track pants. "That depends."

"Depends?"

"You were away for a week in the T dot. You were compulsive for three weeks, and you've been catatonic for another week, so that's five weeks. If you shower with me … I'll have expectations."

Tears clouded her vision. Gary was so wonderful. She loved him in ways that were deep in her soul, a loving combination of friendship, gratitude, respect, and chemistry. She smiled at him, and her tears spilled over. She wanted to tell him, what he meant to her, but that wouldn't have been fair.

Within seconds, Rachel was flat on her back and her clothes gone.

"I thought you had shower expectations not bed expectations?"

"You can't look at me like that after a five-week drought and not know …"

"Know what?"

"God, you're such a baby."

She watched as he frantically stripped off his track pants. "I take it there won't be any foreplay?"

Gary tucked his head into the curve of her neck and laughed. His fingers moved inside her. "I'll make it up to you." He moved on top of her; his thrusts were powerful and urgent. "I've missed you."

It felt good to have him inside her. Good to feel the release.

"Baby ... pull me into you."

She tightened her pelvis muscles and heard his cry of pleasure— sex tips from *Cosmo*. When it worked, no one was more surprised than Rachel. Gary had gone wild. He insisted on knowing where she learned that and she threw him the magazine. Of course, once he read it, they had to do everything on the list. It made him happy. Men were so easily pleased. They lived in a physical world that comprised of sex and sports. In Gary's case, it was sex and art—but he executed his art like it was an exciting fast-paced sport. He put his whole body into the strokes, the mixing, the contemplative pacing. His moods were hard to gauge at times. When he was frustrated, they had sex. If he was euphoric, they had sex. When his energy was explosive, they had sex. Sex with Gary was great, but the longer she was with him the more she realized his secrets were trapped under the frenzy of their sex life. Gary wasn't a slow easy strokes kind of guy; he was passionate and hungry, always hungry, always needing the connection. *Why I wonder?*

Rachel stayed another year.

***

Elaine called with the happy news that Emily was pregnant again. It cemented the reality. Jason was right; Morgan was never going to leave Emily. Deep down she had held onto the hope that he would leave her, that it was impossible to feel this connection with him without it being real. Her craving for Morgan's love came in the form of a playful, satisfying, sex life with a man who filled the void. Fantasies needed to be angled into the light of plausibility.

The news of Emily's pregnancy had Rachel re-constructing herself. She discarded her shitty bits and rebuilt herself into a more profound, connected self. She painted her aches on canvass. She was a martyr, forever a poor slob who had ever sacrificed happiness for another, and cupid's broken arrows were the nails that pounded her into the canvass. She immersed herself into her art to the point of saturation.

Gary was the hero for her newly formed concoction of discarded and rebuilt pieces of herself. He was her illumination, a street lamp to stand under, to keep the darkness at bay. Gary's status as hero was unwittingly accomplished for over a year, but Rachel's martyrdom was too difficult to maintain, and before too long, the fairy dust he sprinkled on her—blew away. Her discarded pieces were calibrated again and when Rachel surfaced, she knew she had to go. Not something she conceptualized—*I'm leaving*—but then she never acknowledged—*I'm using him*—either. Possibly, there was a subconscious recognition that this was a path well worn, but the notion was fleeting.

At the time, Rachel had been approaching her twentieth birthday; her history was a packed minefield of discarded men. Was she callous? Self-involved? She had never thought so; she was waiting for Morgan, waiting to grow up, waiting to finish school, waiting and waiting. During her time in Paris, she believed that one day Morgan would be hers—even though he was married and their communication narrowed to Christmas presents and birthdays, even after she picked herself up after James' death, the thread of hope started to spin its web again. She clung to those silver-lined hopes with optimism. She needed to be patient—*apparitions incubated with a healthy dose of denial*. But it was clear her prospects had reached their full conclusion with the announcement of Morgan's second child. Life had most assuredly moved on, as it should.

No brick houses needed to fall on her, she got it.

Her parents spent Christmas with her. Rachel and Gary flew to England to stay with her mum's younger sister Gemma in a cozy flat in Notting Hill. Her parents stayed with Maureen's eldest sister Colleen.

Morgan had sent a present along with her mother, which Rachel tucked into her suitcase. She would open it when she was alone. On Christmas night, Aunt Colleen's house was full of family and friends. Rachel escaped to a quiet room upstairs and sat on a pile of coats. With trembling hands, she untied the royal blue bow and unwrapped the silver paper. She gasped when she opened the box to find emerald earrings surrounded by diamonds.

Rachel took off her pearls very slowly and replaced them with the emeralds, tenderly touching them where he had touched them. The tiny card, trimmed with a holly border, was no more than six centimetres square. It said, "The colour of leaves in spring and your eyes, Love Morgan." She ran her fingers over his words. And like magic, the silver-lined web of hope got stronger.

The four of them left for Paris on Boxing Day, and they rang in the New Year at Sergi's. Her parents were returning home on the third. Rachel went to their hotel the night before to help her mother pack. The men went to play billiards. Maureen prattled on about family gossip. Rachel half-listened to how Elaine broke up with her boyfriend. Jason's baby boy, Daniel, was precious—then came the update which peaked her ears.

"My heart went out to Emily. James' death—losing a child? I can't imagine the pain. I sympathized. Having to watch Carrie with Daniel was difficult for Emily, but the abuse Carrie took from her was scathing. Morgan was constantly checking Emily—you know, in that polite asking a question type of way he does, 'Do you think that's a fair assessment? Don't you think that's the prerogative of his mother?' You know how he is. No one realized how serious her animosity was until the two women got into an argument and Emily punched Carrie."

"Emily punched Carrie?"

"Punched. Kicked. Screamed. Said she didn't deserve Daniel. Sarah and I were there, but we couldn't get her off Carrie. Morgan had to."

Rachel flopped down on the bed. "What happened?"

"Morgan got her out of there, and they were missing links for a month. Sarah had told me Emily wanted another baby. That having another child might help her—not replace the one she lost, but help her heal and move on. Frankly, given her mental state, it didn't seem wise, but she was under the care of a therapist at the time." Maureen shrugged, "The next thing, they show up for Sunday dinner and announced their happy news. Emily glowed. She seemed back to her normal self. But Morgan ..."

"What?"

"Morgan is ... a very detached man."

Rachel's back stiffened. "No, he's not."

Her mother sighed as she folded her cashmere cardigan with care. "I know you two once shared a special bond when you were younger, but things change, people change. He just buried his son—it changes you—and his marriage is on tenuous ground. Not to mention, he's making quite the name for himself in the business world. He has quite the reputation. But Morgan has always been—older than his years." Maureen stopped packing. "For such a young man, tragedy seems to follow him around."

"That's not true."

"You probably don't remember. He dated her when you were small, Lacy Patton? She died tragically?"

Rachel's body stiffened. "I remember her."

"Such a shock. When someone so young dies it's hard to fathom. I know Sarah was so worried about Morgan. He wouldn't talk about it. She wasn't surprised when he up and decided to go to Stanford after all, but he didn't stay long as I recall."

"He went to Oxford."

"Yes, that's right," she sighed. "Tragic. Now there's James. On top of an unstable wife, who's pregnant." She shook her head. "Then add being a Hillier. Goodness knows it has inescapable challenges."

Maureen stared thoughtfully at Rachel. "Those are pretty earrings? From Gary?"

Rachel fingered them. "Morgan."

Her mother looked down at her sweater. "They're very beautiful. Emeralds and diamonds."

Realizing immediately, her mother didn't approve, Rachel said carefully, "You know Morgan."

Carefully Maureen folded another sweater. "Yes, I do. He reminds me of his grandfather, Altman. He was an ambitious risk-taker."

"I never met his grandfather."

"Robert was never close to his father. Altman Hillier was a hard man. His wife was a sweet woman. I have no idea how she put up with him. He had all the right criteria for a prospective husband: handsome, powerful, wealthy, good family. Given the generation, any young woman of the time would have jumped at the opportunity to be his wife, but he was a cold man. Not like Robert at all." Her mother wrapped the sweater in tissue paper. "Altman was extremely disappointed Robert became a doctor. *Can you imagine?*" Maureen shook her head and frowned. "He wanted him in the family business; they were shipbuilders."

"Yes, I know."

Maureen smiled absently without looking up. "Yes, I'm sure you do," she said, putting her wrapped sweater in her case. "The unfortunate thing for Altman is that his other two sons were useless and ran Hillier Shipyards into hard times, so he had his eye on Morgan to do great things. Altman adored him. When Morgan opened his own company and then teamed up with Marchand Industries, Altman would have been impressed and proud. Morgan has made quite a name for himself apart from his family's lineage of success and reputation. I'm sure wherever Altman is, he has been tracking his grandson's every step."

"Morgan never talks about him." Rachel lay down on the bed, watching her mother. "Everything was always so secret. He never came to visit; they always went to him."

"That was Altman. Anti-social. Eccentric. Years and years ago, the old man would have these fabulous parties, but he never came out of his study to greet his guests or join in the festivities. It was probably for the best; he had a wicked temper." Her mother's blank stare met Rachel's. "Not like Morgan. Even with Emily, who has completely lost herself, Morgan is …" her mother turned to stare out the window, "controlled. Everything he does is controlled." She looked back to Rachel, and the hairs on Rachel neck stood on end. "No anger. No passion. Controlled. It's not good. What is under all that control? And when and what will break it?"

Maureen Wharton moved swiftly to her case again, her head down. "Morgan is a brilliant young man and there is no doubt he has large shoes to fill, but he'll never get away from the comparison."

Rachel sat up, licking her lips. "What comparison?"

"To Altman, of course." Her mother laughed slightly. "Morgan certainly isn't his father's son—Jason is. No, Morgan is a carbon copy of Altman. Just like the old man in so many ways, right down to how he took over the family business. When Morgan had his success; he cavalierly took over the failing Hillier Shipyards. He couldn't have timed it more perfectly. Immediately, he fired Rutherford and Samson Hillier …" Maureen packed her shoes in a narrow case and zipped them carefully. "I'm sure Morgan owns their asses and their children's asses. When the two brothers showed up at Morgan's press conference with big smiles and the directive that the family was melding together during their time of strife, well it was entertaining. I would have loved to have been at that negotiation."

"They were greedy," Rachel said softly. "Rutherford and Samson stole from the company with their greed. They didn't care about the people who worked for them or their families. They didn't even care enough about their own family. They weren't even decent. Some of those people had worked there for thirty years and Rutherford and Samson tried to screw them. If it weren't for Morgan stepping in when he did those poor people would have got nothing. I hope he nailed his uncles to the wall. I hope he *does* own their asses."

Her mother's eyes narrowed. "You've talked to Morgan?"

Rachel stood, squaring her shoulder. "I haven't spoken to Morgan since I left for Paris—not even at James' funeral—but I read about it and I watched the press conference. It was Rutherford and Samson that gushed like slime. Morgan was very matter-of-fact in a big picture sort of way—this is where we are, this is what we're going to do."

Her mother was slow to answer, then she smiled brightly, too brightly. "I'm relieved you're here, well away from all that mess. It's Morgan's mess, not yours." She pushed back Rachel's hair. "You have so many things to look forward to. You don't need to take on Morgan's business problems or bad decisions."

Rachel buried her resentment.

***

Three months after her mother returned home, Rachel got a surprising and disturbing call from her.

"I wanted to tell you, prepare you, before Elaine calls or anyone calls … things have taken a rocky turn here. Emily found out on Friday she's having a girl and she's … more than unhappy. At dinner tonight, she blurted out that she was going to kill herself and the baby and then knocked everything off the buffet table onto the floor; smashed Sarah's china and crystal when she walked by the sideboard. I can't tell you how relieved I am that you're there, darling. I know how fond you are of the Hilliers and this must be very upsetting, but you must concentrate on your studies. I know the impulse to come home will pop into your head, but the Hilliers have rallied together and are getting Emily the help she needs."

When she hung up, Rachel stood in the hallway for some time, her hand still on the phone, trying to catch her breath. Her heart pounded hard.

"Rach?"

Gary came up behind her. "Rachel? Was it bad news?"

She trembled. "Yes, but please, I don't want to talk about it."

He took her hand. "Come back to bed."

***

Winter turned to spring. Rachel loved spring. Paris became a buzz. People took to the streets in droves. Blossoms were budding and trees were filling out. Cafés filled up. Romantic melodies and sleepy French circulated through tables and spilled out onto the Champs Elysees. Their second school year was ending and Henri and Collette were relocating to Rome to continue their studies, which gave them a perfect reason to have a party.

The front room was packed with friends. Sitting on the bench by the open windows, Rachel strummed the guitar Morgan had given her for Christmas years ago. Watching the children on the street skip to their little ditties, she couldn't take her eyes off James, a cousin of one of the local children visiting from England. He was four. He was crouched down, intent on playing a game of marbles. The song she had not planned on singing whirled around in her head. Her eyes trained on James, the James who lived.

She strummed the guitar, the melody of Hoobastank's song "The Reason" came: "I'm not a perfect person ... be the one to catch all your tears ..."

When she strummed the last chord, she didn't realize she had gained an audience. She didn't hear the silence of the room or the applause that followed. She didn't see neighbours listening from their stoops. Rachel watched the curly, black-haired boy, playing marbles with fascination. His posh English accent had the boys rolling their eyes and the girls giggling behind their hands. James was a beautiful little boy. Only when Gary sat on the bench beside her and touched her face, did she return to the room.

Rachel leaned her guitar against the bench and smiled at him. Her skirt had inched up her thigh. He gently pulled it down, massaging her knee. He leaned down and tenderly kissed her. "Just when I think I know you; I realize I have no idea who you are, do I?"

She tugged at his open collar, smiling, whispering to him, "How can you? I don't even know."

He smiled, but his eyes were sad. "I love you Rachel."

A poignant ache lodged in her throat. Rachel looped her arms around his neck, pulled him down to her lips and kissed him. "I love you, too."

"I think you saved my life," he said.

"You saved mine, too." She gathered him close. Rachel had never seen him so emotional. She didn't regret her admission; she did love him and he did save her. He came into her life at a time when she was battered. She had clung to him like a needy child. He let her. He knew about Morgan and he accepted it; he accepted her. If there had been no Morgan ...

Gary was right. She had been sleeping. How can you eat, drink, sleep, love, and not be aware that you're sleeping?

Easy.

The sleepy edges around her eyes started to clear when the photograph of her and Morgan at Mandy's party went missing. During the search for that photograph she found a missing piece of her puzzle, and she woke up. Out of the blue. And everything changed colour.

Rachel had looked everywhere for the missing photography—searched every nook and cranny.

When she went hunting through Gary's studio for charcoal one day, she found his sketches of *The Virgin Bibles*—piles of them. She laid them out on the floor and saw the progression of his work; saw his search to find "the virgin"—to find her lover. Intently, she studied the sketches. She took her time. Read his notes. At the bottom of the pile, there were five pastel sketches of the virgin and her lover.

These sketches were different from the rest. The virgin sat on her lover's lap in this one, her legs wrapped around his waist, her nude body lovingly close to him, her forehead resting against his jaw; her face turned out slightly to the world; her expressive eyes echoed her love and pain; her red lips, moist, pouting, a hint of delight on her face at being in his arms. And him—he—was splendid in his beauty; his broad back, muscular, exquisitely carved, his face—desire etched on his furrowed brow, in his eyes, tortured, intense—his mouth slightly open. The lover revelled in her soft curves, she could see it on his face. His nude body wrapped hers in a protective cove, his left hand buried in her red hair, his right hand fondled her exposed breast. The way they sat, turned into each other and out to the world, the sensuality, their eagerness for each other, the naked emotion was discerningly familiar.

Rachel had believed the virgin's lover was Gary, but the lover's stature was wrong. It was—*oh God*—and that's when it happened. Rachel jolted out of her sleep. She knew exactly who Gary had sketched. She knew exactly where he got his inspiration.

"No!" She whispered.

Her heart pounded.

She started to search.

Gary's desk.

His drawers.

Books.

Supplies.

"How could he!"

She hunted.

Rachel thought she had misplaced the photograph. Had hunted endlessly. Searching every cubbyhole. Every pile, every drawer, trying to find it. Tears of recrimination and frustration had hounded her for weeks as she scoured to find it. The loss of the picture had even taken hold of her sleep. Filling her dreams with defeat and abandonment. *I need it to get through the days. To prove Morgan's existence.* But she hadn't lost it. Gary took it. Used it. *He stole a piece of my life. An important piece. Somewhere—here, somewhere in this studio!*

Tapping her fingers, her body trembled, she paced—where?

Then she blanched. *Did he put the sketch to canvass? Are the Bibles not a pair? Were the first two just an exercise that turned into gold?* Rachel crossed the room, flipping through Gary's canvasses neatly piled against the wall, six deep.

The third painting of *The Virgin Bibles* was in pile six. When Rachel saw it, she fell back. Her heart drummed in her ears. The sketch of the lovers was in living colour. Stroked lovingly. Tenderly. He painted unbearable, forbidden passion. It exuded from the lovers. There was no mistake. It was Morgan. She knew the contours of his body better than her own. And this virgin—she was different from the other two. Two virgins hadn't been blended into one. There was no mistaking, it was Rachel. It was her skin tone. Her hair. Her eyes. Her body. Her want. Her passion. Her face burned at the rawness she saw on her face. Far more revealing than the photograph. The painter had a delicate touch. The texture of her skin, the way it glistened in the twilight. The eloquence of Morgan's concern for her. Everything Rachel felt, everything she wanted from Morgan, Gary had captured in his beautiful painting. It was a masterpiece. The other two paled in comparison.

Rachel's eyes stung. She turned the painting away, unable to deal with the explosion of emotions that gripped her. She choked for breath, doubling over, her hand on her stomach—and saw the photograph tucked into the wooden frame.

Gently, with loving fingers, Rachel removed it. The sensual chemistry between the two people in the photograph was apparent, but Gary's masterpiece gave it depth, feeling—made it palpable. She pressed the photo into her chest.

The next morning, after Gary left for Sergi's studio, Rachel swiftly packed her things, leaving behind what he had given her over the last two years. She took the pastels and the painting from Gary's studio, crated it and shipped it to her lawyer Rupert Landon with instructions. She emailed Rupert to expect the package. She contacted her father to inform him that she was investing in an art piece. She wrote a cheque for $250,000 and tacked it to Gary's art board. She called her mother, explaining she was attending an art class in London and would stay with Aunt Gemma. She left no note for Gary, just the lyrics of the song she sang at Henri and Collette's going away party.

Without a word, she closed the door on the old house, took a plane to England and sat in her Aunt Gemma's front room until the end of summer. Gemma didn't ask questions. She didn't linger by Rachel's side. She didn't hold her hand. But she did field calls from Maureen until she was ready to talk. She did build a safe harbour from Gary's pleas. She did let Rachel be catatonic.

When the fog of indecision lifted, Gem drove her to the airport, and Rachel got on a plane back to Canada.

Macy was two days old when she arrived at the Hilliers' front door.

9

TIME TO GO HOME

Photograph 15

At the beach in Georgian Bay. Morgan sat in the sand. His forearms were on his knees, his hands casually clasped between his legs. A soft breeze pushed his hair around his face. She knew his face so well: his square jaw, his high cheekbones, his blue eyes brilliant in his darkly tanned face—dazzling. His white smile was wide. The orange sun was low in the distance, a ray of pink shot across the sky.

Rachel and Gary were meant to say goodbye. Gary had loved her perfectly. He had been a safe harbour while she regained her perspective and strength. He let her sleep while her eyes were wide open. And she loved him, but not enough to stay, not enough to rob him of the chance to meet someone who would commit to him and love him and not enough for her to close the door on Morgan. Once she woke up from her dream, once she found Gary's hidden canvass, she knew that the prophecy he had made in Sergi's gallery was right, and she could no longer lie to herself or him.

Gary had used the picture of her and Morgan as his inspiration for the first two paintings. He painted a version of her and saved the truth for the last one. He couldn't bring himself to paint the third one. He waited. Saved the truth until he was ready to paint it so he never made it part of his collection. It took almost two years before he conceded and put his brush to canvas. In the painting, he paid tribute to love, a love that Rachel shared with another man. And yet, he painted it lovingly. Rachel knew the painter in him needed to paint the final scene. He stood outside himself and watched over each brushstroke. The painting was poignant. A passion of pain and love. It was everywhere on the canvass.

Creating additional heartache for Gary was not what Rachel wanted to do or feel, but the idea of standing in front of him, looking into his eyes, saying the words she had to say, seeing his beautiful face smooth out into acceptance and understanding, was too gut-wrenching. She intended to spare him, to let him go, to let him find the love of his life. He deserved better than what she could give him. And she didn't want him to take, or accept, what she could offer. So, she left like a thief. She ran to England to figure out her next step. The thought of painting terrified her. The pain she felt would be exposed for everyone to see, like a neon sign, telling her whole life story. She couldn't do that so she retired her brushes. She needed to retreat, to step out of the world, reflect, be alone with herself, figure out who she was, what she wanted because all she could paint at that time was anger and pain.

Rachel hoped Gary was angry at her abrupt departure, angry that she took his sketches, his painting. She wanted him to hate her, but he didn't. He must have called her mother because he found her at Aunt Gemma's. Guilt had set in by that time and then and she couldn't bring herself to talk to him. Gemma relayed his messages. They were all the same: "I love you; the last piece was for you, when you were ready—happy birthday baby; I'm here if you need me—any time, I'm here."

He returned the cheque, but she sent it back with a brief note that said, "The painting is brilliant." His last message was "Be happy." Rachel comforted herself with the belief that one day, he would hate her.

***

Rachel arrived in Toronto a week before Labour Day. No one was expecting her. Her parents had showed up in the UK for a visit just as she was leaving. They wanted her to stay in England, but with school starting in September at Western, she insisted she needed to get organized. Rachel was glad her house was empty. When she looked over at the Hilliers, as usual, the driveway was packed with cars. On shaky legs, she crossed the street.

Jason opened the front door.

"Half-pint." Surprised, he pulled her into a bear hug. "You have impeccable timing—Morgan's new baby girl just came home."

Preparing to hear those words and hearing them, and knowing they were not about her anymore, Rachel steeled herself. Nervously, she entered the living room. Her eyes quickly scanned the faces for Morgan's. He was already making his way to her and scooped her up into his arms. She still fit—perfectly.

When Morgan put his baby daughter into Rachel's arms, she was completely captivated by her teeny fingers so perfectly sculptured. Soft, feather-like curls, framed her adorable face. The weight of her body in Rachel's arms made her heart swell. "Oh my God, Morgan, she's so precious,"

Morgan's warm hand held her shoulder, holding her while she held his child, and she looked up at him, giddy at the overwhelming bliss she felt. "She's so beautiful!"

Joy emanated from Morgan's eyes as he stared back at Rachel and the feeling of love whirled around them. Baby Hillier sighed and they both laughed. Morgan stroked his daughter head, the wide grin on his face was boyish. "She is beautiful," he breathed.

Emily appeared briefly in the foyer that day. Her appearance shocked Rachel. Emily was unrecognizable. She looked drawn; her eyes dead. Clothes hung on her. Her usual flawless style—gone. Rachel never saw Emily her again. A few days after her return home, Morgan called and told her he was divorced. The decree had come in the mail that day. He said they had started proceedings long before Macy's birth, but he hadn't told anyone other than his parents until it was final. The break-up of Morgan's marriage was very clean, simple. Rachel was surprised how easy it was to dissolve a marriage. Within a day of Macy's birth, Emily immediately put distance between herself, Morgan and the child, taking a job in a newsroom in Budapest. Morgan received custody of their daughter. Macy was a week old when her parents divorced. Rachel didn't ask about the details; she knew he would tell her when he was ready. Although Macy was too young to understand how her life had changed forever, Rachel wanted her life to be happy, and she wanted to be a part of it. When Morgan put the baby's little body into her arms—such a feeling of love overwhelmed her. This tiny person was part of Morgan; a part she could love without reservation.

When he told her he was divorced, he sounded exhausted, so she wasn't surprised when he said he needed a break, to get out of town, and take the opportunity to bond with his daughter. He rented a cottage in Georgian Bay and asked her, "Do you have Labour Day plans?"

"Louise mentioned getting the gang together for a girl's weekend at her cottage in Tiny Beaches."

"Of course, she did. I'm sure your friends are anxious to see you. You just got back …"

Morgan sounded distant like the phone was held far from his mouth.

"Where is the cottage you've rented?"

"Allen Beach."

"Well, that's just down the street. Do you mind if I stop by because honestly, I'll need a place of refuge."

"Why?"

"Just between you and me?"

"Is there any other way?"

"You'll think I've lost my mind."

He laughed. "I doubt that; tell me. I would love the diversion of someone else's madness."

"It'll just be exhausting. They'll ask sorts of questions about Paris. There will be a lot of gossiping and drinking. It's an eclectic group and I don't think I'm up for it. I mean, I love hanging with Louise, but the others? Hey, did I tell you, Louise and I rented a house near campus? It looks like a gingerbread house! Very cute. We have to go down the first week of September to get gas and cable hooked up."

"Well aren't you so organized."

"I know—being all mature and practical probably sounds like crazy talk coming out of my mouth."

Rachel spent more time at the beach house Morgan rented than she did at the Summerhill's. Their days were spent doing day trips, taking walks with Macy tucked in a carriage. Rachel entertained Morgan with her girlish babble on anecdotes for world peace, art, and Paris. It made him laugh. They reacquainted themselves with each other and their friendship took on a new dimension. It deepened. Never had she felt in perfect balance with anyone. What she had been missing in Paris, what she couldn't have with Gary, she found on the white sands of Georgian Bay.

Morgan grounded her, filled her with silver linings.

The signs of Morgan's failed marriage were not noticeable to the naked eye. Knowing Morgan, he went out of his way to keep his pain at bay, but she saw the battlefield his life had become the first night she stopped by to see him. He didn't answer her knocks and the screen door was unlocked so she let herself in. He stood on the wide wrapped around veranda with a drink in his hand looking over the bay. He was a stoic figure. To the outside world, he had remained the same, she was sure. Neither a hair nor a word was out of place. Not a skewed collar, not an errant thread, nothing gave him away.

From her spot in the kitchen, she watched as his body slowly weaken with his pain. The slump of his shoulders, the weary weight of his head; he snapped the tumbler in his hand into a million shards of glass as he struggled to control the whirlwind of emotions that fought to be free. Rachel went back to the screen door and snapped it back so he could hear her.

"Hello, hello," she called.

"On the porch," he called.

Rachel grabbed a basket off the kitchen counter and filled it with glasses. She went out to the porch and he was in control again. His face smoothed out.

"I think we should start this vacation right!" She held out a glass to him. She saw the question in his eyes. When he didn't take it, she smashed it, then handed him another.

"You want me to break the glass?"

She ignored his sarcastic question. "Break it."

"No."

She ignored his arrogant tone and smashed the glass with force herself. She handed him another one.

"You're not going to stop until I smash the glass?"

"Glass*es*."

"Rachel ..." his weariness was evident.

"Come on Morgan—smash it."

"No!"

"Yes!"

"No!"

"Yes!"

Frustrated, he swiped the glass from her hand and smashed it. She handed him another. At first, the crashing of glass was angry but soon all you heard was their laughter and the crunch of twenty-six broken glasses under their feet. Within a few days, the tension in Morgan's shoulders relaxed, his smile came back. He got a tan; he swam in the bay. There was still a dark hole inside him and she knew she had made the right decision to come home. To be his friend. To help him heal. To start over. Their friendship made it easier to deal with the commitments of daily life. After the last two years, they were both ready for calm and easy.

Smashing away his rental cups solidified their attachment to each other. They had challenges to face. Morgan was a single parent with a company to run. Rachel needed to leave Paris behind and restart her life in Canada. When she transferred back to Western, she altered her degree path to include an Honours in English Literature and shifted her honours specialization in Visual Art to Museum and Curatorial Studies. Her decision got her out of the studio. There would be a heavy load with changing direction—possibly an additional year, but luckily, her two years in Paris were under review. Whatever the outcome, she was happy to be back. She was looking forward to being Morgan's friend and loving Macy. Their friendship was needed, wanted; their newly formed alliance made them stronger.

***

Shortly after he announced his divorce, Morgan went on the hunt for a new house. He took Rachel along. Every house they saw was missing that certain something that screamed home. Just when they were ready to give up, they found one they were looking for. She recalled standing beside him in the botanical back garden, the pool a few feet away, and he said, "What do you think sweetie?"

"I *love* it." She pressed her fingers tips to her lips.

He looked down at her. "I can see myself living here, can you?"

"Absolutely."

"I never liked the first house I bought."

Rachel agreed, but she didn't say anything, knowing that Emily had picked it out. Emily's divorce settlement included the house, all its contents, and fifteen million, as stipulated in the pre-nup.

Morgan bought the house that day.

Once the house was settled, Morgan went on the hunt for something else. To Rachel's genuine surprise, Morgan started dating. Each weekend, Rachel came home from university to find a different woman on his arm. They were always tall, beautiful, articulate. Accomplished talents with successful careers: doctors, captains of industry, lawyers. His dating irritated Rachel. They were wrong for him, wrong for Macy. When Rachel told him, he laughed. Rachel was crushed. She didn't know how to handle this new development or the emotions it inspired. Morgan had no such problem; he was on a dating rampage, which meant after he spent time with his daughter and his family, there was no time for Rachel. This wasn't what she had planned. The only good news was she babysat Macy while he was out, but before long she noticed he was taking advantage of her good nature. When she arrived at his house, he barely noticed her and gave her an off-handed goodbye as he rushed out the door, and far too many times, he got home in the wee hours of the morning.

Rachel hated meeting the women he dated. At the end of the date, they always made themselves comfortable. He poured the wine, the—woman—always sat on the couch, shoes kicked off, and called Morgan baby: "Where can I freshen up baby?" "Red wine for me baby." Rachel had had enough. Her days of falling asleep beside her laptop doing homework, or face first in a book, were over. Not to mention his dating life foiled her plans. She was lonely, depressed, and tired all the time. She cried so often she was sure she had a rare disease.

After "red wine for me baby" left, Rachel hit him with both barrels. "You know what Morgan—I think you can take this job and shove it! I'm all for helping out but I'm underpaid and underappreciated. I come home each weekend to spend time with you and Macy and you, you ignore me. Barely a thank you. I love

Macy, but dealing with the cavalcade of women you parade through here, well frankly you can just stuff it. Consider yourself notified. I'm done. Find yourself another babysitter."

The next day he showed up at her house looking contrite, waving a white flag, and two tickets to go see the Broadway musical, *Wicked*. He was forgiven.

Morgan had a Christmas party downtown. Rachel looked after Macy. Jeff and Kathy were going. It was business. After Rachel put Macy to bed, rather than go to the spare room, she went into Morgan's and laid on top of his bed. His room was adjacent to the nursery. When she woke in the morning, she was under the covers. He was home? But there was no evidence of him in the room. She raced to Macy's room. She was sleeping in her crib. She went looking for Morgan. She checked the spare room across the hall—no Morgan. The one beside Morgan's room—empty. Her hand was on the handle of the next one; it was the pretty room. She whispered softly, "Please don't let me find him in bed with some girl."

Empty.

Heart pounding, she walked to the two remaining spare rooms. They were empty. She crept downstairs, stopping every couple of steps to listen—any noises to make her unhappy? Silence. A few more steps. Silence. Each pause, she was greeted with silence. Maybe Morgan wasn't home at all? Maybe her mother came to check on her? Took off her pants? That would mean Morgan stayed out all night with the—who did he say it was tonight? Did he say? *He's never stayed out all night. Why didn't he call? What if something happened? What if he drank too much, smacked up the Jag, is lying in a puddle of blood somewhere, and can't call?*

Foyer—empty. His study—empty—so were the living room and the dining room. Where was he? She pressed her fingers to her lips and broke into a run, heading for the kitchen. She needed a phone. Panicked, she struggled to think who to call—Ishmael? Did Morgan even take the Escalade? No, no, she would call Jason. She burst through the kitchen door. At first, she didn't notice the other people, just Morgan sitting at the kitchen table reading the paper. She was relieved to see him and pissed off all at the same time.

His head jerked up in surprise, then he saw her; his brow suddenly knit, "Hey." He stood up. Her mind registered that he was concerned. "What's wrong?"

She walked across the room to the table. "You're alright?"

"Of course." He chuckled. "Why?"

The chuckle sent her over the edge. "*Why?*" Her relief vanished. "Where the hell have you been? What time did you get home? I tried to stay up but I couldn't keep my eyes open—God knows what time you came home. *Not even a call!*"

With her hands on her hips, "When I woke up this morning there was no sign of you. No phone calls. No note. I started to think …" Annoyed, she could feel tears burn her eyes; she wanted to say, shacking up with someone, but instead, "You were lying dead somewhere. Didn't you think I would be worried?"

He yanked out a chair. "Sit."

When she didn't move, he insisted. "*Sit.*"

He bent his head slightly so they were looking squarely at each other. "Do you remember Monsieur and Madame Marchand?"

"Yes," she mumbled.

"I took them to the Christmas reception at the Royal York with Jeff and Kathy—"

"But I thought you went with that—"

"I know what you thought … am I telling the story?"

"Yes." She folded her arms around her chest.

"There was heavy snowfall; the roads were in bad shape, the Escalade slid into a telephone pole trying to avoid a Buick. There was an ambulance, there were police, we were freezing. Because Kathy is pregnant, she went to the hospital and the police took us there. Kathy is fine. The police dropped us off at Jeff and Kathy's place about four. I called you four times. Two here and you will find messages on your cell, which I'm sure you have misplaced." Which she had. "I called Jason at six to pick us up at Jeff's, and then we came here. I brought the Marchand's here because I had told them they could stay with me after the reception. There was no point going to sleep when we were so rattled. When I came home, I found you on top of the bed so I put a blanket around you and came down here and made some breakfast. And just before you came into the room, I was going to show the Marchand's to their room. Does that answer all of your questions?"

"Yes."

"So, we're good?"

She pulled her chair closer to him. "We're good." He was so close, his lips so close; she wanted to kiss him so badly.

"We should leave these two young people to get reacquainted, no?" said a thick male voice.

Rachel startled.

"Oui, Cherie," agreed Madame Marchand.

When Rachel turned, she recognized the Marchand's immediately. They had met in Montreal several years ago. Jason stood in the background, a playful smile on his face. He was enjoying this—bastard. Rachel was mortified that they had witnessed her outburst.

Rachel whispered, "Excusez-moi Monsieur et Madame Marchand."

Madame Marchand smiled taking charge of the room. "Do not concern yourself sweet girl. I have … how you say? Been there." She turned to her husband. "Henri, Morgan said the first room at the top of the stairs on the left. The bags are in the hall."

"I'll get them, Henri," said Morgan.

"Non, non," Henri waved his hand. "Merci beaucoup Morgan,

but the boss has spoken." He took his wife's arm and escorted her out of the kitchen.

The minute the kitchen door closed Rachel whispered, "I'm sorry."

Morgan smiled. "Now you sweet talk me."

10

PASSION

Photograph 16

Rachel at twenty-one. Morgan was twenty-eight. She was in an exquisite sleeveless black lace gown. Morgan was devastating in his tuxedo. They were at a business function of Morgan's. His dating spree had come to an end and he had asked Rachel if she would attend these work functions with him. This picture was the first of many to come.

Taking a date to company events had become complicated. He wanted to work the room, not be attentive to a companion, but he didn't want to show up alone. It put notions into the minds of women who either wanted to set up the poor single father with their sister—their daughter, best friend, or themselves. Rachel was his stand-in girl Friday. It did cross her mind that she was his in-between girl—the girl in between wife one and wife two—the convenient one, the one he didn't have to try with to get what he wanted.

This was a difficult year for a myriad of reasons. It was the year they crossed the line. It was the year Larry Bernhardt arrived out of nowhere. He came in quietly, but she noticed. Even when others tried to dissuade her suspicions. When she picked up the phone that afternoon, she had no idea that Larry Bernhardt would change the trajectory of her movements. She was reading the sordid tale of Helen Queen of Sparta when Larry slowly insinuated himself into her life. Lesson: how large—your small world is.

***

Rachel worked diligently on finishing her last undergrad year, and tutored elementary and high school students part-time. She was flirting with the idea of teaching like her dad. She was organized. Focused. Larry Bernhardt, however, was a persistent irritant. He always had a reason for calling: When did the library close? When was Professor Sims in his office? Did I get T.S. Elliot?

Instinctively, she was cautious even though he seemed shy on the phone, apologetic, but he was an unidentified caller. When she asked around about him, no one seemed to know Larry Bernhardt. That wasn't unusual, Western is a big campus. Rachel didn't want to encourage him so she kept the chats short. The calls increased and so did the tone; they were no longer apologetic or girly, but more intimate.

Larry called. "I liked that short skirt you were wearing today—nice pleats. *Very nice.*"

Rachel asked Professor Sims if he knew Larry Bernhardt—it didn't sound familiar to him, but that wasn't so unusual with so many students in his class. She knew if she pressed him to check his records, she would have to tell him more, and Larry Bernhardt hadn't done anything. Still, there was something weird about Larry. It made Rachel uneasy. She asked her roommates to listen on the extension to see if they picked up anything familiar or strange, but Larry was back to his girlie, polite self.

It was as if Larry knew her roommates could hear their conversation. Her instincts said he did know. Her instincts said to be alert. Friends she had made at Western were her new roommates since Elaine had graduated the year before, and Louise had moved in with Stephen a couple of blocks away. When she told Louise about her mysterious caller, she laughed, "You aren't in the Big Smoke anymore, nothing ever happens in London."

Was she being paranoid? Irrational? Rachel shrugged it off, but she still felt like someone was watching her. Closely. The hairs on her neck stood when she was at Weldon Library and she quickly scanned the large room. Concern had her looking over her shoulder often. Had her paying attention to her peripheral vision. Nothing in particular had happened to suggest she was in danger, but something was off. Prudence, made her change her jogging paths, double bolt the apartment door and insist others do the same. She even bought an alarm attached to the door.

It made her uneasy that those around her thought she was wrong, that it was her imagination. Even though it threw her off balance, it was also the year Rachel's life was in bloom. Her relationship with Morgan was changing constantly, adding new dimensions. It was exciting but it frightened her too. She had more to lose now with Morgan than she ever did, but she forced herself to enjoy him and not to lose her focus on school.

Her safety concerns made her cautious and her caution became more obsessive as the months passed. Checking and rechecking locks. She contacted The Running Room and joined one of their groups so she wasn't running alone. She rarely went out, worked diligently on her dissertation, and didn't answer the door when she was alone.

She counted the days to the weekends. She loved the sound of the train pulling out of London's VIA Rail station, heading for Toronto. She had applied to the teachers' college at Western and hoped she didn't get in. She wanted to go home. She wanted to leave school behind and start her new life.

***

By late October Rachel was exhausted from being on safety alert twenty-four-seven. She went home to Toronto for the weekend. The two families, as always, had Sunday dinner together. After dinner, Rachel had reluctantly slipped upstairs to get her suitcase to return to London. When she returned, she heard them talking.

"This is my first corporate party," Elaine gushed, unable to keep the excitement out of her voice, which was a rarity for the calm, cool Elaine.

Elaine had followed Jason's lead and was now working at Morgan's ad agency. The agency was one of many businesses in Morgan's conglomerate.

There had been a considerable amount of gushing from Elaine since Shawn Gable appeared. Not that she blamed her. Everything was coming together for Elaine. Great job. Shawn proposing to her a few weeks ago. The wedding planned for 2010—two years away—but Elaine was willing to wait for St. Paul's and the exclusive Atrium Hotel. The Gables, Elaine's in-laws-to-be, owned a family resort called The Oaks on Lake Rosseau in the Muskoka Lakes, and they'd offered to host a wedding party weekend a couple of weeks before the nuptials. It was quickly becoming the social occasion of the decade.

"I hope you like my dress," said Elaine.

"If you're wearing it," said her fiancée, "I'll love it."

"I think you'll be more than pleased, Shawn," said Aunt Sarah. "Elaine is stunning in it."

"The price was pretty stunning too," grumbled Uncle Robert.

"Oh stop," insisted Morgan's mother. "I'm looking forward to this and I don't want you bursting my bubble."

Uncle Robert said, "I'm only trying to illustrate to Shawn the expenses he will incur when he marries my daughter if it works anything like it does in my house."

What party? Rachel didn't know about a party. She would remember a party that required a stunning dress.

Rachel's father laughed. "Right you are my friend—not to mention the new shoes, new purse, new coat, a day at the spa ..."

Carrie said, "Jason loved my dress."

"I'm with Sarah," said Maureen Wharton. "You're tearing the backside out of this."

Her parents were going. The only one not invited was Rachel. On wobbly legs, she walked into the living room. "What party?"

Everyone was comfortably scattered around. Morgan was sitting in the high back chair near where she stood, his head buried in a book. He lifted his gaze when she spoke and he smiled.

"What party?" she asked again, searching his eyes.

"The advertising awards dinner at the Metro Centre is next Thursday."

She felt out of place standing there in the archway of her living room. "The whole family is going?"

Morgan's gaze didn't wavier as he looked at her. "Yes."

His cool stare bothered her. *He always seemed so bloody calm—like whatever could be wrong? Or was she humouring herself? Or was he thinking— what is it now?* She blushed. She hated that she blushed.

But embarrassment happens when you're not included or not thought of as relevant—you're just a nuisance, stupid. Intellectually, she understood. She heard him say Thursday night. Just because she was in London, she wasn't welcome?

She wanted to cry. She wanted to demand why he hadn't invited her—not even to ask! Rachel had been going to the award dinners for years with him and any other function he requested her attendance. Suddenly, she'd lost her girl-in-between job? When did that happen? Not even a text? So, it wasn't on Saturday night this year—not even an invitation? Angry words were on the tip of her tongue, but Jason's words from years ago whirled in her head, "You use your tits and tears to get what you want, Rachel."

She became aware of the eerie silence in the room; she became aware of everyone's eyes bouncing from him to her. Rachel's blush deepened. There was a roaring sound in her ears and she felt like she was going to be sick she was so embarrassed. She ignored it. "I better get my skates on or I'll miss my train."

"Do you want to come?" Morgan asked softly when she returned to the living room.

Yes, she wanted to say, but he was asking out of guilt, and her pride won over her instinct to join the party. She looked over her shoulder at him. "Everything is organized; it would be a shame to upset the applecart. Maybe next time?"

The eerie stillness in the room became an oppressive silence. Rachel kissed her mother and Aunt Sarah. Macy was lying on her stomach on the floor playing checkers with Daniel. Rachel leaned down and kissed the top of her head.

Macy immediately rolled over, stretching out her tiny arms. "Huggies pweease."

Rachel hugged her tightly whispering, "Be a good girl," in her ear.

"Loves yous," Macy whispered back.

"Love you too."

Rachel quickly looked over at Carrie. She was tucking Robby into his bassinet. Carrie didn't like Rachel getting too close to her sons—or Jason for that matter. She wasn't sure why Carrie hated her since she'd been instrumental in Jason winning her over, but there was no mistaking her dislike. It hadn't been gradual, it was immediate. Rachel took the opportunity to kiss Daniel goodbye while she was busy. She whispered in his ear, "I'll see you, beautiful boy." Rachel stood.

Jason said, "No kiss for me?"

"Com'mere and I'll give ya a wet one."

"Spaz," said Jason.

Rachel laughed. "Goof."

"Nerd."

"Dumbass," was Rachel's parting response before she left the room. She immediately launched into her get-ready-to-go tasks.

Morgan came into the hall. "I'm taking you."

A protest was on her lips, but the determination on Morgan's square jaw made her hold her tongue. He grabbed his leather jacket; her suitcase was already in his hand and he held open the door to let her pass.

They drove to the train station in a tense silence.

When they arrived at Union Station, Morgan cut the engine of his Jaguar and turned in his seat to look at her. "I want you to come."

Rachel folded her hands primly on her lap. She averted her head taking great interest in the construction on Front Street.

Morgan sighed deeply and covered her hand with his. Rachel shoved his hand away and jerked back from him. Morgan always soft-soaped her out of her moods—not tonight. She wanted to feel hurt and lonely and for him to feel guilty about it.

Morgan grabbed Rachel's coat lapel and tugged. Startled, she stared blankly at him.

His face was tight, his blue eyes accusing. "Don't ever do that again!"

"Do what?"

"Don't be *cute*." His breath was hot on her cheeks. "I know you're hurt and wanting to put me in my place, no matter how unreasonable that may be. So cut the bullshit and tell me what's going on because I know this isn't about a boring awards dinner."

Whenever she thought about it later, she cringed at how she had burst into ugly sobs. Her hands had been tight fists. Her head—heavy. She fell forward, tucking her hot face into her hands.

Morgan swore and reached for her, pulling her into his side until her sobs turned to shallow shudders. Embarrassed, she drew back from him, wiping her face with her sleeve.

Morgan yanked out a tissue from the box in the center console. "Here," he said and started the car. "I'll drive you to London." Morgan snapped up his cell phone and made arrangements for Macy, then wheeled the car around and headed west.

They weren't on the road long before he stopped and her head snapped up to see Lake Ontario up ahead and a deserted promenade. "Are you ready to talk about this?"

"There's nothing to talk about." She shrugged unable to look at him. Telling him about Larry seemed ridiculous—nothing had happened. He hadn't been rude or forceful. What could she say? I have a funny feeling? I'm driving myself crazy? And it wasn't just Larry. It was the future. The unknown. It was Morgan and the status of their relationship. Being away from him—the distance. Change. Goals. After honours, there was another year of teachers' college. Another year away from him. "It's nothing. I'm just overly emotional right now."

"Rachel." Morgan's firm tone said he wasn't satisfied with her answer.

"I don't know—it's just, I get tired of being away from home." Tears filled her eyes again. "My life is here but sometimes I feel— very far away."

Tears traveled rapidly down her hot cheeks. He twisted in his seat and leaned into her. "I didn't mean to make you feel further away."

"I know." She *did* know it wasn't his intention to exclude her but knowing that didn't make the sting less. It was a trigger. She turned to look at him. He cocooned her; his arm was over the steering wheel and dashboard and his other along the back of her bucket seat. Her eyes dropped to his chest. She noticed the way the material stretched across his chest; curling hair peeked out. "I heard them talking about their pretty dresses and how they were looking forward to the party …" She shrugged, unable to finish.

"The only reason I didn't invite you is because the dinner is on Thursday night instead of Saturday. I know you have some flexibility in your schedule but it seemed like a great deal of rearranging for you to come down for one night. You've been working so hard." Morgan rubbed his eyes. "I should have mentioned it, at least, give you the option. I *was* trying to be considerate."

"We'll just leave it the way it is." Rachel wondered who he was taking. When he took Rachel with him, he worked the room and she danced and flirted to her heart's content.

"Tell me why you won't come?"

She shook her head. "You're right; I do have a lot going on right now. Who are you taking?"

"No one." Morgan pushed a button on the console beside him and the bucket seat motored backward giving him more space, stretching his long legs out, commanding the space. Rachel swallowed hard. "You used to be a dating fool, but you haven't been dating much the last couple of years."

Rachel snapped up a tissue from the box beside her and wiped her nose. "No." She'd had a few dates in the last year—a sad effort when she was mad at Morgan. The second they left her sight, she forgot about them. When they called to go out again, she wasn't interested. Some accepted her answer and moved on; some didn't and tried to woo her, which was exhausting. She didn't care if she went out with them or not and for some reason, that made her more attractive. It suffocated her.

"Why?"

"Too much work." She tortured the tissue she held. "It's not just that—after I date a guy, I start feeling closed in."

"How?"

Rachel averted her face. "They demand more time, expect things."

His tone was soft. "What kind of things?"

"The things that attract them in the first place are the things they want to change. Or else it's just about sex, like you're obligated in some way to have sex with them because they buy you dinner. Now

I just pick up the tab or go Dutch."

"I see." Morgan leaned back further in his seat, a playful smile on his face. "I'm no expert, but he didn't do it right if obligation is part of your vocabulary. Mind you, boys can be—abrupt and more than a little selfish. Did you get a selfish one?"

Rachel folded her arms tightly across her generous chest. "That's hardly your business."

Morgan's brows cocked; a surprised smile crossed his face.

"You find this amusing?" she snapped. Morgan's effort to suppress his smirk irritated Rachel. "When a guy holds sex up like a weapon—like its proof of some description, I hardly find that amusing. My body isn't a rental unit."

"Of course not."

Rachel's expectant gaze fell on him. "How long do you date a woman before you sleep with her?"

"That's hardly your business," he smiled mockingly.

Rachel gazed out at the bleak night, depressed. "Don't make fun." She thought of the lonely apartment waiting for her in London. Even with three roommates, she was lonely. She felt disconnected and abandoned, and yet, she chose this. She could have gone to school in Toronto and lived at home. The reasons at the time were good ones, but things were different now. This was her fourth year away from home, soon to be five. She was tired of independence.

"What are you looking for in a man?"

She twisted in her seat to face him. His eyes were bright, they sparkled in the darkness, his humour gone. There was quietness in his stare that unnerved Rachel.

She lied. "I don't know." Her head dropped slightly. "I don't have a shopping list of attributes if that's what you mean. Every girl I know has a list: handsome, cool car, nice to his mother, good career. I'm so tired of hearing the list, I'm so tired of hearing how the guy tallies up—I don't *want* that."

"I thought those were the things a woman wanted?"

"How can you find the right person from a list?"

"It's amazing how easily you convince yourself that it can be done," Morgan said quietly. "You believe the person is what you want based on your expectations, your family's expectations, your friends' expectations, correct timing—it's easy."

She told him, "If you're weighed down by expectation, that doesn't give you any room to find love. I don't have a list. I don't care how much *money* he makes or how many *things* he has; I'm looking for—I don't know—a connection. Passion. Love. A relationship! Not some lukewarm runner up, but a real deep-down emotional relationship. I want to brush my teeth with him, make coffee with him, cuddle, fight, love him, hate him. I don't want to know why I love, just that I do."

Rachel shook her head. "Maybe it doesn't happen for everyone. Maybe people settle because its time and other needs become more important. Maybe I'm one of those people it doesn't happen for. With the amount of dates, I've had over the years, you would think I was an expert or feel something for longer than a few months. Not that it hasn't been pleasant, it has. Other than what happened with Rick, I've had a good dating life. The guys I've dated have been very nice to me, but they always felt more than I did."

She looked at Morgan. "How can that be? How could they feel more? It can't be one-sided all the time. It can't just be about chemistry. Chemistry is good, but shouldn't there be more? My parents have chemistry, but they have something else. I don't know what it is, an intimacy or something. Your parents have it, Jason and Carrie have it. I don't know about Elaine and Shawn yet because I haven't been around them, but knowing Elaine, I can't see her settling."

Rachel put her palms on her eyes. *It must be me. There must be something wrong with me! Why doesn't Morgan want me?* "Maybe I'm defective in some way."

Morgan put his arms around her and gently held her. His raspy reply indicated his impatience. "You're not defective."

Rachel lifted her eyes to his, searching for a mocking glint, but there was none. His eyes were clear and tender, intense with light, and Rachel's breath caught in her throat. She felt his heart pounding under her fingers, felt the heat from his body.

"You're a sexy, desirable woman, with absolutely no airs about you, and that can drive a man crazy because he never knows where he stands, but there's nothing wrong with you."

The vibration of his voice made her heartbeat frantically in her chest. Rachel whispered, "Elaine is engaged. Louise is engaged. Mandy is hoping to be engaged at Christmas. Not to mention the four weddings I was at last summer!" She looked at the collar of his shirt; it was mauve, which looked perfect with his black leather jacket. She could smell his cologne. He had a clean man scent. "I'm—" she lost her train of thought.

"You're what?"

Rachel pushed away from him but her hands lingered on his chest. She stared at her hands against his mauve shirt and moved them away slowly. "I'm envious," she said finally.

Morgan laughed. "You've never been envious a day in your life."

Sadness and longing caught her off guard. "But I am," she said softly, leaning her side into the leather seat. "Maybe I am one of those people who are destined to be alone and married to their career or else settle for less because time runs out."

Her parents were a testament to the endurance of love. Married thirty years. Morgan's parents—married for thirty-six years. Was meeting your soul mate luck or fate? Was Rachel destined to love a man she couldn't have?

"What about you and Emily? What broke you up? Losing James?" asked Rachel.

Morgan was solemn. "That was different."

"How?"

"It was over long before James was born." He shook his head. "Having James was our attempt at trying to make the marriage work—not the best circumstance for bringing a child into the world. James did bring us closer for a while, but then he died. It was devastating for us both. We couldn't recover from a deep loss. We couldn't recover from being married." He dropped his head back against the bucket seat and closed his eyes. "So many regrets."

Compassion overwhelmed her. "I'm sorry." She could feel his pain and guilt like a tangible thing. He was distant suddenly. She reached for his hand and squeezed it and he immediately laced his long piano fingers through hers. He turned his head in the bucket seat, his eyes met hers then he dropped his head onto her shoulder. Twisted in his chair, his arms reached for her, gathering her close to his chest. He breathed in deeply. She stroked his black hair, loving the feel of it, the thickness, while she whispered words of comfort. Words he had used many times to soothe her. A feeling of well-being washed over her. Morgan had been a beacon in the darkness during many of her adolescent hurts and hurdles; she felt she had come full circle, having him need her. Their bodies pressed together, his closeness intoxicating her.

Morgan's hands ran up her back and tunneled under her long strawberry curls, and cradled the back of her head. He pulled back to rest his forehead on hers. She thought the sharp, heavy breathing she heard was his, but she soon realized it was her own. Her heart pounded like crazy. Their breath mingled. The moment was so— arresting. Even now as she reflected on that night, Rachel wasn't sure how it happened. She remembered their lips touched, felt his mouth on hers, just barely touching them, probing gently, cautiously, letting her feel the touch of his mouth, the shape of his lips. Rachel trembled violently; the soft brushing movements of his warm mouth drove her crazy. This wasn't just a kiss. It was a life. The clenched emotions she held deep erupted and exploded all over Morgan.

It wasn't their first kiss but it should have been. It was also their first step past the line drawn between them since that day in Uncle Robert's study.

Morgan moved away and she whimpered. His eyes held hers as he silently pushed her coat from her shoulders and threw it in the backseat. Following his lead, she tugged at his coat, and he helped her remove it, and toss it. They stared at each other and laughed. Falling into each other's arms, Morgan kissed her quickly, again and again, before his mouth roughly caught hers, parting her lips in a deep hungry kiss that had her head spinning. She could scarcely breathe. Morgan's hoarse moans excited her as he ran his lips along the curve of her neck. The press of his hand smoothed down her silky blouse to her breast. He played with the hard tip through the fabric and then released her. His eyes locked with hers. Her bright green eyes stared willingly into his. Morgan reached up, took her hand, and brought it down to her breast, placing her hand where his had been. He eased his fingers between hers. His free hand moved to her other breast rubbing the tip a little harder. She jerked against him.

"Does that excite you, Rachel?" he said roughly.

Rachel looked up at him and saw his pleasure. She sat up in her seat and pushed herself up, with her free her hand she held his shoulder to steady herself, and she moved to straddle him, sinking into his body. She met his gaze and smiled. "Does it excite you, watching me, Morgan?"

"Yes." When his mouth came down on hers this time it was hot, forceful, and wet. Her answering passion threatened to drown her. Under the touch of his hands, she became aggressive. Her hands moved confidently over his body. Her thoughts were gone. She unbuttoned her blouse, and then unbuttoned his shirt. She ran her hands appreciatively over the matted hair on his chest, feeling the thunderous pound of his heart under her fingertips. She closed her eyes and bit her lip; her emotions were so fierce they frightened her.

When she opened her eyes, Morgan was watching her, his stillness brought a blush to her face. Was he having second thoughts? Were the wonderful sensations that filled her body going to come to an embarrassing end? She held her breath. Did her reckless behaviour turn him off? How many times had the reckless passion of a boyfriend turned her off, and make her feel like she was alone and any female body would have done? More than she could count. The difference here—Morgan was returning each touch, each kiss passionately. Hadn't she done that before too, with the misguided notion that if you act it, you'll feel it? Again—more than she could count.

"You are so beautiful," Morgan whispered, reaching for her. She exhaled a shudder of relief. His lips kissed a path down her throat and along her shoulder nudging her blouse aside. Her blouse was gone. Her bra was gone with a speed that had her panting. Morgan leaned her back against the steering wheel and his wet tongue. He traced the top of her breast and she gasped, "Morgan!"

He drew his lips around the tip of her breast and licked it repeatedly, and a small scream that turned into a cry escaped her. Morgan's hand pushed at the curve of her breast, opening his mouth wide, he took her nipple inside his mouth, flicking it hotly with his tongue. Rachel watched him at her breast and a surge of pleasure gripped her. She whimpered at the pleasure his hands gave her, as they moved down her rib cage, caressing her with a lingering slowness.

Rachel ran her fingers through his hair and yanked up his head. Her hand ran along his neck and down his shoulders to his arms. She swayed against him. Steadying herself by sinking her nails into the tense muscles in his forearms, she pressed her abdomen into his stomach then moved back. The tips of her soft breasts scratched against his chest. Morgan's shudder moved them both. "Jesus Christ," he gasped, roughly hauling her into his crushing embrace. His mouth opened hotly over hers in a driving force that was wild. He kissed her cheek, her ear; his hands where everywhere, probing, demanding, making her breathless and aching. Pressed so closely against him, she felt his arousal and her stomach flipped; her body tingled. She wanted him, to feel him in every cell of her body. She slipped her hand between them to feel his hardness. She wanted his hardness to be a part of her. When she cautiously ran her hand along the zip on his pants Morgan jerked back.

Rachel froze, afraid to breathe. Her face was on fire with embarrassment, but she made no sound.

Morgan framed her face with his hands. "Don't look at me like that, sweetie," he said, his face so close to hers. She didn't know where she ended and he started, but the steady, familiar warmth of his eyes brought her some calm. He breathed into her mouth in soft whispers, "You're too unbelievably sweet for this to happen in my car." His smile was tense.

Morgan smoothed his hands down her back and pulled her back into his secure embrace, holding her tightly until the unbearable ache inside her subsided, and the chaotic world of a few moments ago righted itself. In silence, he dressed her and put on her coat. He didn't move her off his knee but just dressed quietly, a frown across his forehead. She could only watch him numbly.

The stare he gave her was intense. He kissed her hard on the lips then lifted her back into her seat.

During the two-hour drive to London, they didn't speak, and yet, it wasn't an uncomfortable silence. When they arrived at her apartment, Morgan carried her suitcase. The smell of popcorn met them when they walked in on her two roommates watching a movie. Rachel noticed the appreciative glances they gave Morgan but she chose to ignore them. Dragging out his stay was her only goal.

Rachel said, "Who wants a cuppa tea?"

Everyone said yes, but Carla whispered, "Oh Rach, use the water in the fridge. The sinks clogged. The super's fixing it."

"Okay." The superintendent and his son were coming out when she reached the kitchen. "Hello Mr. Horvat, everything all fixed up?" He was a kind little old man from the former Yugoslavia, who had been managing buildings for Deckglow Properties Inc. since he emigrated from his country twenty-five years ago.

"*Bok*," he said in a strong Croatian accent as he bowed slightly, "*kako si, mala?*"

Over the year, he had taught her a few phrases, hello, how are you, and thank you. Although she didn't have the accent down, she understood the words. "I'm well Mr. Horvat, *hvala.*"

He stepped into the front hall. "My son you know, *da?*"

"Of course," she smiled at the shy, solemn man, who also bowed. "It was so kind of you both to come out on a Sunday night."

Mr. Horvat waved his hand away. "No trouble to fix."

Morgan came down the hall and extended his hand to the two men as Rachel introduced them. Once they were gone, Rachel made tea, but too quickly the tea was over and Morgan said he needed to head back. Sadness and panic gripped her. She couldn't help it; fat tears sat on the brim of her eyes, spilling over. She remembers whispering to him as they stood in the hallway. Her arms hugged her body and she curved into his. Jason was right, she did use tits and tears to get what she wanted. "Stay." She dropped her throbbing head onto his chest. "Please stay." Her words sounded painful even to her ears.

Morgan stroked her hair. His arm slipped around her and drew her into his side. "Lead the way," he said quietly.

She led him to her bedroom. The second she opened the door and let him pass, she became an awkward fool. She had shared close quarters with Morgan before. Not on the heels of an intense passionate exchange; it suddenly made her edgy. *He'd said grown men are not boys. What did my plea mean to him? What did it mean to me?* Just a few short hours ago, she wanted to have sex with him. But right now, she was anxious. Her emotions sat just under her skin, confusing her, scaring her, and she needed her childhood friend now, not the man who could push her sexual buttons.

Rachel decided not to think—that was her best and only plan on occasions when she didn't have a hope in hell of figuring out her next move. She got ready for bed. It had been a long time since she shared a bed with Morgan. Nervous, she didn't look at him when she crawled in. He reached for her and she trembled. He pulled her into his arms, laying her head on his chest. He whispered, "Go to sleep."

Morgan kissed her forehead and switched out the light. Rachel closed her eyes, her hand on his chest, comforted by the steady beat of his heart. She slipped into her first blissful sleep in months.

Saying goodbye to Morgan was not a new experience for Rachel. The next morning as she watched him drive away from her, she couldn't control her tears. In a daze, she walked down Richmond Street, surprised when she stood outside the university gates. Oblivious to the rain and cool temperature, Rachel sank on a bench and sobbed.

***

Larry's friendly calls had become a burden. A series of inane discussions that led nowhere. At times, she felt like he was breaking her down for his amusement, then out of nowhere, his social misfittery would reveal itself and her empathy for him compelled her to be polite. It distracted her. Made her puny. Clouded her judgment. She needed to be aware of the real threat and not allow him to suck her into his neurosis. To occupy her mind and keep her focus, she compartmentalized Larry by profiling him. Analyzed his speech patterns. Words. Phrases. Listened for background noises. Inflections in his tone. Searched social media. Investigated the Bernhardt name, its geography, and statistics. Most importantly, she didn't want Larry to divert her attention from her life. A shift had taken place between Morgan and her, and she wanted to savour it. This was an important year for her. Next year she wanted to get into Western's distinguished Althouse College. Competition was intense and standards were high. She needed to remain diligent.

After that night in Morgan's car, Rachel had anticipated awkwardness when they met again, that he would want to take it back and remain friends, that crossing the imaginary line into this new realm was a mistake, but she was wrong. The affection between them grew and deepened. They were careful to keep the new dimensions of their relationship private. Exposing her budding relationship with Morgan to Maureen's scrutiny was not an option Rachel wanted to exercise.

Rachel had found more than her sexual stride in Morgan's arms. Everything changed for her. Never had she experienced total commitment to another person, but she did with him. It was hard to ignore the romantic fantasy she had built in her head after their kiss. Her heart was crisp with the disturbing emotions she felt, a raw, unforgiving prideless passion.

The explosion of sexual chemistry didn't even take her by surprise. She wanted him constantly, thought about him constantly. Her greediness for him brought new and complicated dimensions to her life; dimensions she had only entertained in her imagination— fairytale love. The second Morgan's lips touched hers, she moved into a new realm. Without much success, she had tried to put him and the cravings he left her with out of her mind, but the feel of his hands caressing her body was vivid: the rough tenderness of his lips, the hardness of his body under hers, the feel of his muscles contracting where she touched. Their passion had been hot and wet.

She had no thoughts of right or wrong, yes or no. Control eluded her. Her emotions had been too sensational for thoughts or words.

Rachel had been shameless with wanting him, but there was more than a sexual awareness between them. It had been a long time since she shared her deepest fears, her deepest longings with another person. She had not shared her secrets with Morgan in a long time.

School kept her sane while this shift in their relationship took place. They didn't acknowledge the shift. They didn't talk about the shift. They lived in a state of being. The intimacy between them brought Rachel comfort, more than she thought possible. She knew she wanted him but she found she needed him, too, to trust him with her thoughts again.

Rachel's anxieties about Larry escalated. He dragged out their conversations. He commented on her clothes. Where she jogged. Then his calls increased substantially. It prompted her to confide her worries to Morgan.

Sunday dinner was at the Hilliers'. Everyone disbursed. Morgan was in the sitting room off the kitchen. He sat in the armchair beside the fireplace, a government white paper in his hands. Elaine and Shawn were whispering to each other on the couch on the far side of the room. Jason was outside with his boys. The women were in the kitchen. Macy was baking with Auntie Maureen.

"Morgan?"

"Hmm?"

She played with her nails, snapping them nervously. "Morgan …" How did she explain?

He raised his head. "Hey." He tossed the report on the ottoman and stood. "Hey." He reached out for her hand. "What is it, sweetie?" he whispered.

She shook her head, her eyes darting over to Elaine and Shawn.

"Come on." Morgan grabbed her hand and took the lead, steering them to the study.

He leaned against the desk. She stood in front of him. "What is it?" he said.

"Do you ever feel in your gut that something isn't right, but everyone tells you, you're wrong, that you're being paranoid?"

Morgan laughed. "Every day."

"Does it make you deviate?"

"Rarely."

"Have you been wrong?"

"Rarely."

"What makes you believe you're right?"

He shrugged. "Instinct."

"What if your instincts are wrong?"

"There is no wrong answer when you listen to your instincts, because you will learn from the experience."

"Definitely—especially if the instinct is strong?"

"If your instinct is strong listen to it, pay attention, test out your ideas to collect information. It helps to expand your ideas."

"Yes ... I've been doing that." She tapped her finger against her lips, taking in his words, "but I do need more information because what I'm collecting isn't leading me anywhere."

"Want to tell me what this about?"

Her distracted gaze fell on his familiar face. She moved to stand between his legs. For the first time in weeks, the tension in her body left. "A couple of months ago this guy started calling, says he's in one of my classes, but I've never met him and he's never approached me. He's friendly on the phone. Polite. Informed about my classes— I assume they're his classes too, but something ..." she inhaled deeply, "... nags at me that they're not. My roommates think I'm too *urban* for London. I can't go to the police because he hasn't harassed me or done anything other than become a bit of a pest. But I've become careful. Locking doors and windows. I bought an alarm. Change my route to class every day. I even joined a running group, and—this might sound a little crazy—but I've started recording the conversations with Larry. One of my roommates is working on her master's—a thesis on the audio-lingual patterns of autistic children—and she has all this auditory equipment. I borrowed what she isn't using. She thinks I'm crazy too, and maybe I am, but … there's something."

"Follow your instincts Rachel."

She looked at him, relieved. "Really? You don't think I'm crazy?"

"Someone who acts like your friend, when they're not, is suspicious."

"That's it. That's what bothers me. He acts like we're friends. He has an advantage over me and it makes me feel vulnerable." She moved closer to him. Her arms went around his neck and she pulled his head down. She noticed his clenched jaw. "Thank you, Morgan." She kissed his lips softly. They'd kissed often since the night at the train station.

"You're upset?" she observed. "About what I told you? Or for kissing you?"

The hands he had on her back came to life, reaching down and cupping her backside and yanking her closer to him. He leaned down, the hungry pressure of his lips and the wet, soft attack of his tongue caused a disturbingly familiar chaos inside Rachel.

"Not the kiss, obviously," she whispered into his mouth.

His voice was heavy, deep. "No. "

"Shouldn't I have told you?"

"Jesus, yes! Always." He rested his forehead on hers. "I know you've taken precautions, but he hasn't said or done anything that gives you a hint?

"No, nothing. Its friendly but he knows about my life."

"Have you mentioned it to your parents?"

"I don't want to worry them since there isn't anything to tell. It just makes me uneasy."

"Do you want me to send someone there to check it out?"

"No, but if his pattern changes again, I will."

"How has his pattern been changing?"

"He called once every couple of weeks at the beginning, then once a week, and now he calls a couple of times a week. They aren't long calls, but he'll say he saw me running when he was driving to work and asks me running questions. Yesterday he said he liked my coat or a sweater I'm wearing." Rachel felt Morgan tense under her fingers. "Innocent enough, but creepy."

"Promise me you'll be careful. Never go anywhere alone. Keep monitoring his calls. Have you lost your cell phone again? I haven't seen it this weekend."

She gave him a crooked smile. "I forgot it in London."

His finger traced the line of her cheekbone. "Keep it with you at all times, okay Rach?"

"I will." She hesitated, "this might sound crazy, but before I hooked the recording equipment; I asked the girls to listen on the other line to see if he sounded familiar."

"And?"

She shook her head. "It was like he knew they were there."

A hard rap on the door made Rachel jump back from Morgan.

"Morgan?" said his mother.

Morgan pushed his hair back with angry fingers and slid off the edge of the desk, and walked around to the leather chair. The door opened.

"Jeff is—," Aunt Sarah started to say, but stopped, looking at them both in a bouncing back and forth motion. Her gaze curious.

"Yes mother?"

Mother and son stared at each other for a few seconds, but it seemed longer; Rachel was nervous.

"Jeff is on the phone from Montreal. Line two. He said it's important." Sarah held her arm up to Rachel in the promise of a hug.

"Why don't we let them talk?"

Rachel went with her but wasn't happy about it. She glanced over her shoulder at Morgan and he winked at her before pushing the button and picking up the phone. "Jeff?"

***

It wasn't long before Rachel received a disturbing call from Larry. It solidified her paranoia.

"I loved the red halter top with the blue cashmere sweater you were wearing the other day. You seemed to be enjoying the park too. Who was the guy? Too young to be your father. Too intimate to be a brother. Boyfriend?"

Rachel wanted to hang up; instead, she stayed calm and said, "Yes, it's my boyfriend. He's the protective type, drives me crazy," she laughed.

"Yes, I think I've seen him with you before."

"Really?" Her heart pounded a little harder.

"How about meeting me for coffee?"

"Sorry, but I'm almost finished my dissertation. I've been working on it like a fool, so I just want to get it over with, do you know what I mean?"

"*Do* I."

"Listen I've got to go, duty calls. With a trembling hand, she gently replaced the receiver and gulped in the air. Morgan had come to London during the week and taken Rachel to an early dinner and then they went for a walk in Springbank Park. Larry Bernhardt hadn't just noticed her while going about his day—he had been watching her.

Fear tingled down Rachel's body in a constant flux. Larry's pattern had changed again. Should she involve the police? She knew they would probably laugh her out of the building— how many of her friends had reported serious harassment from employers and ex-boyfriends to no avail? Too many. When she looked up the statistics, they staggered her. Although 90% of sexual assault victims are women, only 5% of assaults are reported and, of those crimes reported, only 11% lead to convictions. Those numbers gave her no incentive to go to the police.

Women don't trust the people who are supposed to protect them. Prejudices and treatment by police, lawyers, judges, and the personal repercussions victims of these crimes must shoulder if they went to the police was too high. Every report she read made that abundantly clear. Risk and cost outweighed the meager advantages. And this was in 2008. Rachel couldn't imagine what it was like for women before. She wondered what it was like for her mother. Maureen finished university in 1982. She was smart. Ambitious. Beautiful. She was certain her mother had fended off wondering hands and lewd suggestions. Thirty years later, Louise was playing a different ball game completely, she was being groomed to be president of the Summerhill empire. Thousands and thousands of women that came before them made their privileges possible. Rachel admired so many, Read their books. Listened to their music. Watched their films. Margaret Atwood. Nellie Bly. Billy Holiday. Emily Murphy. Toni Morrison. Sarah McLachlan. Judy Holliday. Jennie Robertson. Oprah Winfrey. Maggie Smith. Katherine Graham. Golda Meir. Madame Curie. Alice Walker. Nellie McClung, Ida Lupino. Margaret Sanger. Mary Pickford, Babe Didrikson. Emily Stowe, Josephine Baker. The list was endless of women who prevailed regardless of the challenges.

Rachel was a doer by nature. Whether police took her seriously or not, it wasn't the point. If Larry did this to someone else, her report would be right there, and the information she had profiled. She needed to see it from a new angle. An experiment with no expectations and one more precaution.

***

The police station receptionist sat behind plexiglass, her vacancy was punctuated by banging her knuckle against the cubical, asking in a listless tone, the purpose of Rachel visit, asking her to repeat herself, to stand at the red line, to speak louder into the microphone adhered to the plexiglass. Every word Rachel uttered bounced off the plastic cone in surround sound, shot up to the ceiling, and exploded in stereo around the empty thirty by sixty room. She was in little danger of not hearing her, but what she didn't know, obnoxious and condescending people didn't faze Rachel. Standing on the outside looking in, that was her forte. In her best breathy Marilyn Monroe voice, Rachel answered her and ignored her pissed off face, until she heard someone call her name.

"Rachel?"

At the door marked police personnel, a man stood, looking at her expectantly. It took a minute to place him in the unfamiliar surroundings, then she smiled. "Mr. Harper, it's good to see you." She walked over to him. Rachel tutored his daughter, Mabel, in English. Mabel was a great mathematics student but struggled with Shakespeare. "How is Mabel?"

"She just texted me, an A on her essay thanks to you – shit, I'm sure she wanted to tell you herself. Act surprised when she calls?"

"Of course," she laughed.

With sympathetic fatherly eyes, he said, "Terry giving you a hard time I hear."

Her eyes pricked with a sting, in that moment, she missed her father so acutely, she couldn't find her words. She shrugged off her loneliness with a smile., careful not to meet his gaze.

Mr. Harper yelled over to the receptionist. "Terry, I'm going to take Rachel back."

"I bet you will," she muttered to herself, but they both heard her.

Mr. Harper walked over to Terry, his tone deep and sharp.

"Excuse me?"

Startled, Terry changed her tune, an apology on her lips, but he didn't leave it there and walked behind the plexiglass. Rachel turned away to read the public service announcements on the bulletin board. Within minutes, he returned.

"Mabel never mentioned you worked for the police."

"That doesn't surprise me. She hates that I'm a detective, so does my wife, even after twenty years on the force." He escorted her down a large hall. "Do you mind if we take the stairs? My wife said Cary Grant took the stairs everywhere he went to stay in shape," he leaned down in a conspiratorial way. "Think she was trying to tell me something?"

Rachel laughed. "I'm a bit jealous, people tend to insult me directly to my face without beating around the bush." Mr. Harper was in his mid to late forties, over six foot, with a few gray flecks in his hair, dressed in a blue suit and a pink and white striped Ralph Lauren shirt, looking very Cary Grant debonair. Rachel doubted his wife was dropping him exercise tips. "Mrs. Harper is a Cary Grant fan?"

"Huge."

"I don't blame her. I loved *Notorious*, *An Affair to Remember*, and *Houseboat* with Sophia Loren – she's beautiful and plucky and he's suave and can't help himself from falling in love with her. Mrs. Harper has great taste in men."

He busted out in a belly laugh, flashing a beautiful set of teeth, turning a bit red in the face as they reached the top of the stairs. He pulled open the door leading to a large room packed with officers. Everyone stopped what they were doing for a split second and had a good start before the flurry of activity reconvened. A woman with a pointy face and angular body suddenly appeared, handing Mr. Harper messages, and speaking rapidly.

"Harper," a man shouted from behind them, "the pathologist

wants to meet at 4. Heads up, he's in a pissy mood."

"That can't be good," he sighed, thumbing through his messages.

"Who are you?" said the pointy faced woman.

"Rachel Wharton."

She dropped her head slightly assessing Rachel over the rim of her glasses. "Why are you here Rachel Wharton?"

"She's giving a statement Jess."

"Can't someone else do it?"

"No, they can't."

"When you're done, we need to talk about Bolson." Over her shoulder, she shouted at a group of officers standing in a circle around a coffee pot station. "Stop gawking. Get back to work or I'll be in a pissy mood."

They snickered but broke ranks immediately.

"This way Rachel." He guided her to a corner office overlooking the north end of the city. Two desks were pushed into the center of the room facing each other. An assortment of little kid art plastered the back wall with macaroni sculptures, paintings, and farm animals made from nylons. "I love your art installation," she said.

Mr. Harper smiled. "My ode to fatherhood." Papers littered the chair beside his desk but he threw them on the floor. "Have a seat ... I heard what you said to Terry, but why don't we start at the beginning?" He yanked his keyboard from under his monitor.

His fingers flew over the keys, as Rachel described Larry Bernhardt's insidious intrusion and the reason why she came. "He knew where I went for dinner and with who. Our brief conversations had always been about school, homework, events on campus. I mean sometimes he would comment on what I was wearing, but it was always around school. This was different. We went to three different places that night. He didn't just see me passing, he was following, watching me. I know all he's done is be a bit creepy ..."

He quickly interrupted her. "Trust me, a bit creepy can quickly escalate. I'm just glad ...," he pushed his hand through his hair agitation, "you came in and I was here."

The silence between them crackled with all the things he wanted to say but didn't. "Thanks for saying that Mr. Harper. I hesitated coming here. He might be harmless. I want to believe he's harmless, but every instinct tells me I need to alert." She reached into her backpack, pulled out her notes, and put them on his desk. "Which is the reason, I did some checking." She leaned into his desk. "There are no phone listings for Larry Bernhardt in the London Middlesex or Elgin County area. Not even in the GTA. I did find a Bernhardt family who lived in Stratford. A woman named Lilly Bernhardt. But she didn't have a husband or a son."

"How do you know?"

"I called her looking for my long lost Uncle Larry. Her husband died years ago and she's a single mum with three daughters between the ages of ten to fifteen and none of them have boyfriends, including her."

His gaze had a trace of something she couldn't put her finger on, what was that look? She always had such a difficult time deciphering tells on men.

"She just gave you this information?"

She held his stare. It wasn't a skeptical look – cautious? Curious? "Yes, she did." She flipped the page of her notebook. "I also checked social media statistics."

When his eyebrows shot up, she said, "In first year, I had to take statistics, see how I'm using my education? You should be relieved. Anyway, I broke down the demographics: see, 13-17; 18-24; 25-34 – the largest demographic is 18-34, which is roughly fifty-one million people – and there is no Larry Bernhardt. Not even when I followed a lead in the obits, but guess who that lead me to?"

"Lilly Bernhardt?"

She laughed. "Yes, imagine that, an easy connector. The interesting thing? The largest increase of users from 2009 is from alumni. By 29%. Do you know there are only forty-odd thousand Bernhardt's in the world? Its origin is German and where is the largest population of Bernhardt's? Germany."

He sat back in his chair. "This a lot of information, but what does it mean?"

"It gives you a profile of Larry."

He sat back in his chair, "Tell me what you see."

Rachel hesitated, immediately second guessing herself. "You don't think so?"

"I'm interested to hear what you have to say. Fire away. No judgment."

"Well, the fake name gives us lots of information. Even if we didn't know there were no phone matches, picking the name Larry Bernhardt tells us he's in the 40-50 age."

"That's an interesting conclusion."

"It's not a name a twenty-something would pick. How many kids do you know named Larry? None. It was popular in 1947. I checked. Michael and Matthew were the popular names in the nineties, which would have been a better choice if you want to hide in a crowd rather than stand out in one. I think he picked Bernhardt for two reasons, one because it's a common name in his culture or it's a comfort connection – use what you know."

Rachel ran her finger over the word Germany. She thought back on their conversations. How Larry sounded. "I don't think English is his first language. There was a slight heaviness in his tone. A hard D sound."

"My mother-in-law is from Slovenia so I know what you mean."

"Yes, and my superintendent is from Croatia and he has the same tone, so there's something there."

"Any other impressions?"

"Ninety percent of university students are on social media, and if Larry was part of it, he would know the uni crowd. Their interests. Idioms. Chatter. It always sounds like he was forcing it when he calls, plus, he didn't know Western's online student system or have a solid grasp of the course work. So, I think Larry is European or first generation. He's not a university student or grad and not on social media. He's single. Lives with his immigrant parents. Sexually repressed. I doubt if he has an email address."

"Impressive. You're a natural detective." He picked up her notes. "Do you mind if I keep these?"

"Really?"

"Absolutely. You've done a remarkable job here. Your instincts are great. Fixing the holes in your security, your research, taping him – I'm going to want those tapes – but all excellent work."

"Wow, I didn't expect this … and of course, I can bring the tapes tomorrow."

He nodded. "Excellent. Do you have a cellphone?"

"Yes, but I must admit, I haven't got used to needing it."

"I had the same problem. Kept forgetting it, but it's a tool that empowers you to get help if you need it." He handed his card to her. "You call me, day or night if something else comes to you, or his behaviour changes again. Just like you did today when he added stalking your movements to his calling schedule. People come to the police for all kinds of different reasons, but I want to ensure we are on the same page, that we can build a game plan, so this might sound like a silly question, but what would you like us to do for you?".

"I make him stop. To stop following me. I feel like I'm being watched twenty-four hours a day. I check my locks constantly. Look for cameras in vents, light sockets, walls, but I can't find anything. I'm driving myself crazy."

"I want him to stop too but I can't do anything without you reporting it, so I'm glad you came today. Early stalking behaviour is early intervention, so first things first, have you asked him to stop calling?"

"Well ...I never encouraged the calls ..." It seemed so obvious, tell him to stop calling. Why didn't she? "I get off the phone as quickly as possible, but no, I haven't come right out and said stop calling."

"Don't beat yourself up for being polite and giving him the benefit of the doubt. You did nothing to make this happen. What you did do? You trusted yourself. You took precautions even when others questioned your judgment. But now, the game plan changes. I want you to tell him to stop calling. If he continues to call you? That's criminal harassment."

He pulled out his Blackberry. "What's your cell number?" He typed in her number and took her picture. "I love the camera on this thing. Great for work. Imagine what Blackberry will invent by 2020."

Eleven years from now, it seemed like a lifetime away. Where will she be? Teaching? Married? With babies?

"I hope phones are bigger in my fifties," he said, dropping the phone into his breast pocket.

"Mr. Harper," she hesitated, "I want to thank you if you hadn't come along when you did, I'm not sure ... if today would have been as successful. Everything I've read is in direct contradiction to our conversation. So, I'm curious, you've been on the force for twenty years if a woman came in with a complaint like mine, would she have been taken seriously?"

He hesitated. "I ..."

"Okay, maybe that's not a fair question. In your twenty years of experience, has a woman reported a sexual assault or a rape and wasn't taken seriously?"

Mr. Harper sat back in his chair inhaling deeply, his hands pushed back his hair, and expelled a deep breath. "There have been incidents, in my twenty years, where women have come in to report crimes, and officers didn't do their jobs, and the women were injured or killed. It's extremely frustrating."

"Fighting archaic stereotypes is always hard to overcome."

"It is. When men see harassment as a woman getting harmless male attention, or sexual assault as boys being boys, it undermines a very serious problem. Saying it's better than it was, is a cope out. That's not good enough for me. Not near good enough. We should be better in 2009 but we're not." He looked at her. "I have a beautiful wife and three beautiful daughters, so my perspective and experience tell me, it's worth filling out a report and working the case."

Mr. Harper embodied everything good about men. Smart, polite, kind, respectful, and can rock a pink pinstripe. "Your frustration is comforting sir. It gives me hope." Rachel stood and held out her hand. "I have taken enough of your time. Thank you so much for listening and for making me feel a bit safer." As she turned to go, she stopped and looked back at him. "Does your wife watch Cary Grant's movies late at night, when you're not around?"

He looked surprised. "Yes, how did you know that?"

"I do the same thing when I miss the man I love," she smiled. "This is just an observation, so please forgive me if I'm out of line, but I think *you* remind your wife of Cary Grant, not the other way around." She backed out of the room slowly and pointed at him. "Cary always dances with his leading lady, so you might want to add that to your moves. You won't regret it."

Telling the police, making it official, was more emotional than she had anticipated. By the time she walked to the bus, she was crying. With shaky fingers, she called Morgan.

11

LEAH WHARTON'S WEDDING

Photograph 17

Her cousin Leah was on the left and Rachel was on the right. Rachel was so happy in the picture until Leah and Geoffrey Wharton turned it to shit.

After she dropped off Larry's tapes, Detective Harper confirmed her phone records had been requested, and they were following a few leads. He would be in touch.

The next day Larry called and she was ready for him. "Larry, I want you to stop calling me."

"I thought we were friends."

"No, Larry, we aren't friends. I don't even know you. And I have to be honest, I have quite a bit on my plate with school. And I work. I have friends and …"

"Your man."

"Yes, Larry, my man. I'm going to finish up my work here and go home. So, let's just say goodbye now."

Larry slammed down the phone. A landline.

A week went by. Nothing from him. Week two. Nothing. Things were looking up. Her case was moving forward. Larry hadn't called. And she was in love. Then the unexpected happened. Her long-lost cousin Leah showed up at one of Morgan's business dinners. This chance reunion gave Leah and her father information they couldn't ignore and changed the molecular structure of the silver lining Rachel had designed for herself. A game was afoot that Rachel didn't even know they were playing, and just like that, her romantic bubble was interrupted.

Rachel had met Leah three other times in her life: a wedding when she was ten, a funeral for her father's cousin, and a museum reception. It never occurred to Rachel that she would meet Leah in a neighbourhood bistro, on an especially frigid Saturday night, outside Montreal. Rachel didn't think Leah could pick her out in a line-up. Rachel, however, noticed her well-photographed cousin before she approached their table. When Leah crossed the room, she waited until the men noticed her. More importantly, she waited until Morgan noticed her.

Once Morgan looked up, Leah's attention immediately turned to Rachel. She smiled. "It's good to see you again, Rachel."

"And you, Leah."

Morgan stood.

Leah walked around the table, holding out her hand to Morgan. "Leah Wharton, Rachel's cousin. You look familiar, but I don't believe we've met."

Morgan shook her hand. "Morgan Hillier."

Pleasantries exchanged; Morgan politely moved Leah along.

When Rachel received an invitation to Leah's wedding five weeks later, she was curious. Leah was a beautiful, outgoing woman with an easy laugh, impeccable fashion sense, and a media darling. Newspaper articles, the covers of *Forbes, Chatelaine, Flare, Business Week, MacLean's*—there was Leah, her sparkling smile, and old Canadian lineage for everyone to see and sigh at. When Geoffrey Wharton named Leah his successor, it made front-page news. Leah's younger brother Christian was shy and stayed out of the limelight. Since John Wharton's estrangement with his brother, Rachel's associations with her dad's family were limited. They were rarely in the same room together and when they were, it was all very polite and civilized. Even though her parents didn't receive an invitation to Leah's wedding, her father encouraged Rachel to go, saying the riff with his brother had nothing to do with her. Rachel asked Morgan to go with her and John Wharton was delighted. Her mother disagreed.

Her father's position: "It will be a media circus. Who better to handle the onslaught than Morgan?"

"He'll create it you mean," snapped her mother.

"Great!" laughed her father. "He's perfect then. He'll deflect it from the target." "What target, Daddy?" asked Rachel

Maureen was annoyed. Uncle Geoffrey wasn't her favourite person. "Why did you agree with this John?"

Her parents exchanged a stare. Her father said, "He has always been able to deflect attention from her. He will protect her."

"From what?" insisted Rachel. "What are you talking about?" She looked at her mother. Rachel heard the doorbell.

John Wharton turned to Rachel. "Sweet Pie, you are a Wharton. In this town, that means something, but your mother and I have done everything we can to protect you from media exposure. It's an unforgiving master. My father was a private man, not unlike Morgan, but he loved the newspaper business, as did your grandfather, and your great-grandfather. In those days, people were curious, but respectful. Times have changed. Family dictates have changed, too. My brother has a different style than my father, a different style than me. He thinks any media is good media. People will approach you at the wedding, wanting to know who you are, your connections—your family, your friends—to determine how it can be used to their best advantage. Morgan is experienced with the media and people. I'm pleased you asked him because if you find yourself in a difficult position, he will be able to walk you through it."

"Questions about you and Uncle Geoffrey?"

"Possibly," he said slowly, "but it could be about anything. It depends on what they want."

Betty, the Wharton housekeeper, knocked on the open study door. "Excuse me Mr. Wharton, but Mr. Hillier is here to see Rachel."

Rachel jumped out of her chair and dashed to the foyer. When her eyes lit on him, his tie was pulled down slightly, his hands were in his pockets, his suit jacket pushed back over his thighs; he looked tired. Compassion for him overwhelmed her.

Her heart pounded as she moved closer to him. "Hey, tall man," she whispered, reaching out for his arm to guide him into the living room. "We were just talking about you." Once they were safely in the living room, she quickly kissed him, standing close.

He cupped her face with his palm; his thumb traced her lips, his face solemn.

Her hand smoothed down his tie. "Rough day?"

"It's good to see your face." Morgan tipped his head slightly to the side, listening intently, then dropped his hand; his jaw clenched and his brow furrowed. She heard it, too—her mother's high heels. Rachel stepped away from him, moving to stand behind the straight-backed chair.

Her father was the first to stand in the archway. "Morgan." He held out his hand to the younger man. Her mother was right behind him.

Morgan smiled. "Good to see you sir." They shook hands.

"We were just talking about you," said John.

Morgan nodded, throwing a glance at Rachel. "So, I understand. I hope it was good."

Her father slapped Morgan's back. "I was just telling Rachel how pleased I am you are taking her to Leah's wedding. I was a little concerned for her. The media will be there in full force and it might be a little overwhelming for Rachel if people know who she is."

Morgan nodded.

Her mother had no pleasantries to spare. "What brings you over Morgan?"

"The wedding is the reason I stopped by; I'm having a scheduling problem ..." He turned back to Rachel. "I will be in New York that week."

Rachel tried to keep her disappointment out of her face. She walked around the chair.

"That's too bad," said Maureen.

Morgan went to stand in front of Rachel. "I'm not cancelling transparent girl, but I'm having a few logistic problems. I will be at a meeting until early Saturday morning. At the moment, I'm on the eleven o'clock flight. That's cutting it close to get to the church—"

Her mother interrupted him. "We can work something else out Morgan," she smiled. "There's no need for you to rearrange your schedule for a family wedding," she laughed.

Rachel wanted to go with Morgan. It would just be the two of them and that rarely happened. Quickly she suggested, "I can go to the church alone and we can meet at the reception?"

Morgan shoved his hands in his pockets. His face, blank. "There's another option. Elaine—"

"Really Morgan," insisted Maureen, "don't worry, Rachel can find someone."

Morgan slowly turned sideways to look at her mother. "Maureen," he said quietly, "I would appreciate discussing this with Rachel."

Rachel stiffened at Morgan's polite but firm tone. The charged silence deafened her. She was too afraid to look in her mother's direction. Her eyes were glued to the side of Morgan's head.

John said, "Of course you do, we'll leave you two to work out the details."

Morgan nodded. "Thank you, John, Maureen." Once her parents left the room, he turned his attention back to Rachel.

Immediately, he picked up where he'd left off. "Elaine wants to go to New York with me to look at wedding dresses. I leave Thursday morning. Are you interested in joining us?"

Rachel jumped, grabbing the sleeve of his suit jacket. "Yes!" Then she frowned, "But we'd miss the wedding."

He shook his head. "If the three of us are going, I'll arrange for a private plane. That way we have more flexibility and can leave New York earlier, get ready on the plane, and be at the church on time. Sound good?"

That was an understatement.

John thought it was a great solution. Unfortunately, Maureen disapproved of the trip. Two glaring facts held her in check: Rachel was over twenty-one and Elaine was with them.

While they were in New York, Elaine's presence set the tone for the trip. Morgan worked and they shopped. They met for dinner each night at a different hot spot.

The flight home went as Morgan had anticipated. Ishmael had the Escalade waiting on the tarmac at Pearson airport when they arrived in Toronto. They dropped Elaine home, before heading to the church. Like clockwork.

Rachel took care in picking out her church outfit, wearing a light and cheerful red and white Chanel jacket with matching straight skirt and bronze peep-toe pumps. Riding to the church, her father's words in the study whirled around in Rachel's head and it made her nervous. She fiddled with her hat, putting it on the seat beside her, putting it on her lap, torturing the brim until finally Morgan took the hat away and grasped her hands in his. "It will be okay."

Crowds were everywhere when they arrived. Photographers and television crews lined the street. The activity excited Rachel. She had never been to such an elaborate wedding. Morgan told Ishmael to pass the church and go around the block.

"There is a west door," Morgan whispered to her.

When they rounded the last corner of the block the congestion wasn't as bad, but there was still quite a horde of people. "Right here is great, Ishmael." He handed Rachel her hat and said, "Please take our bags to my house and then we'll meet you here in an hour and a half?"

Ishmael nodded, "Yes sir."

Morgan tapped the top of Ishmael's seat in confirmation. "Thank you."

"Yes sir."

Holding her hand tightly, Morgan guided Rachel through the mass of people. His long strides had her running beside him. He then stepped out of the crowd to cross the grass in order to get to the west door.

Rachel laughed, enjoying the bustling atmosphere. She smiled up at Morgan. "This is exciting. I feel like I'm in a movie."

Morgan stopped abruptly and she knocked into him. He caught her easily with one arm and her flyaway hat with the other, which sent her into peals of laughter at his dexterity. When she looked at him, he had that familiar annoying blankness was on his face; Rachel didn't care. She was glad to be with him. Still heady from their new intimacy, still heady from him believing her about her mysterious caller, still heady from their trip to New York, heady from having this time alone with him without their families; she couldn't stop smiling at him.

"What did you say?" he asked, his arm still around her.

"I said," she smoothed down his tie, "our trip to New York, the private jet back, hustling to the wedding, cameras everywhere, on this cool beautiful March afternoon, it's like being in a movie. The best part of all, it's not a movie. I'm with you; the sun is shining, and I'm wearing the prettiest shoes ever—all my favourite things!"

His arm tightened around her. His eyes softened. His demeanour changed, and her Morgan materialized, not the capable one, not the business magnet, the man who shared a secret world with her.

"You," his deep voice was barely above a whisper, but it vibrated under her hand, "are the most beautiful woman I have ever met."

Rachel remembered heat rushing to her face, not because of the words he said, or the look on his face, or how close his body was to hers—it was the whole package, and she fell in love with him again for the hundred and sixty-seventh time in her life.

"Morgan?" A man shouted from across the grass and the moment ended.

An older man approached them. "Hello Stuart," said Morgan, immediately becoming capable Morgan. They shook hands. "This is Rachel. Stuart Hanson."

He extended his hand to Rachel.

"You aren't one of those young ladies that don't have a last name, are you?" smiled Mr. Hanson.

"Wharton. Rachel Wharton."

Rachel stiffened when his brows shot up and his eyes shone. "Another beautiful Wharton. Do tell me more," laughed Stuart.

"No relation, *I wish*. Just a friend," said Rachel, following Morgan's example of polite distance.

"Of the bride or the groom?" asked Stuart.

She smiled. "The bride. Our mail use to get mixed up all the time."

***

Leah's wedding was one of a long series of weddings that Rachel had attended during the last year, which were wonderful events, but Leah's wedding was the benchmark of perfection for all others. When the church door opened, Rachel could smell the flowers. Bouquets decorated the alter. At the end of each pew, white roses and baby's breath strung together with lemon satin ribbon. A choir sang to the guests while they waited. Once Morgan and Rachel sat in the bride's side of the church, she slipped her hand into his. She whispered in his ear. "I'm so happy Morgan." He kissed her hand.

Leah had a big wedding party. Rachel counted seven bridesmaids and seven groomsmen. The bride was breathtaking in an updated version of Maria's dress from *The Sound of Music.* Uncle Geoffrey held Leah's arm in a detached way. He didn't act like the proud father, more like he was walking into the House of Commons with his constant nodding, flashing smile, and occasional wave. He hadn't aged gracefully, Rachel didn't mind noting; he was nowhere near as charming and handsome as her father. After the ceremony, Morgan and Rachel went to lunch at Seville's before heading back to Morgan's house to change for the evening. She had bought two dresses in New York. One for Louise's wedding in June, which was a sexy emerald green dress with a plunging neckline, that fit her like a glove. The one for Leah's was demur in comparison, a black strapless cocktail length dress with a gold flap on the chest and a narrow gold pleat in the skirt.

She felt beautiful that night, blossoming under Morgan's intense stare, eating fabulous food, sipping French wine, dancing. Rachel was in a glow so her guard was down when her Uncle Geoffrey approached her.

"Hello Rachel," said Geoffrey.

She smiled brightly at him, addressing him casually. "Hello, Geoffrey."

He smiled back. "Seems you're working hard at not giving the wrong impression."

"The wrong impression?"

His brows lifted, a crooked smile on his face. "I understand you're a friend of the bride's and not my niece." Geoffrey looked out over the crowd, throwing her a side-glance. "Stuart Hanson is a long-time friend—he was interested in knowing who the young woman was that had captured Morgan Hillier's attention."

Rachel laughed, putting down her wine glass, feeling no pain. "No one captures Morgan Hillier's attention for more than a New York minute."

It was Geoffrey's turn to laugh. "You're very modest for such a beautiful young woman." He sipped his champagne. "How's school? Almost finished?"

Politely they stood together watching everyone dance. "In a couple of months."

"Interested in joining the newspaper business?"

"Actually, I start graduate school in the fall at Western. I want to teach like my father."

"What do you want to teach?"

"Art and literature."

Geoffrey Wharton nodded slowly. "Yes, yes, I recall your mother mentioning you went to school in Paris—beautiful city. Did you like it?"

She laughed. "It is a beautiful city."

"Sergi Gauguin was your mentor, right?"

Caught off guard again, she smiled to cover it. "Yes. The great Sergi Gauguin."

Not understanding why Geoffrey Wharton would be interested enough to find out about her, and not knowing what direction he was taking the conversation, she changed its course quickly and scanned the sea of guests to find Morgan. "Your daughter looks beautiful."

Morgan was talking to a couple near the bar, a whisky and a glass of white wine in his hands.

"She takes after her mother, as do you."

Rachel nodded. "My mother is very beautiful."

"Leah mentioned she bumped into you and Morgan a couple of months ago at dinner?"

Rachel played dumb. "Really?"

"You and Morgan were having a dinner meeting with the Bargen Group—in Montreal, I think she said?"

Rachel stiffened, the fog from the wine lifted; her mind was suddenly alert. "A meeting? I'm not the meeting type. And Barks? Doesn't sound familiar."

Casually he said, "Bargen's. They make yachts in BC. They're in a bit of a financial pickle—expanded too quickly, but rumour has it they've had a resurgence. Is Morgan buying a yacht? Or maybe he's investing in their future?"

Three brothers owned Bargen Yachts. The night Leah saw them briefly, Morgan, Rachel, the three brothers, and their wives, were celebrating the merger of Morgan's Freightliners with Bargen's Yachts. The brothers and their wives arrived separately in Montreal—care went into the plan. That afternoon, the brothers signed the papers, and dinner followed that evening at a secluded restaurant.

"We don't discuss 'yachts' or 'Barks,' Geoffrey," she said mildly, finally seeing the strings attached to the wedding invitation.

Geoffrey enjoyed that one; his laugh was loud and hardy, drawing attention. Rachel saw Morgan turn to look at her. For a moment, he stared at her.

Rachel felt ridiculous. She had flirted with the idea that she might be the catalyst for change between her father and his brother. Her uncle had never spoken to her before. His sudden interest flattered her at bit. He knew so much about her life. Was he being polite? Was he setting up a peace treaty for her father? But she was wrong. The Whartons were not interested in making amends. They wanted to know about Morgan's business ventures.

"I guess that's true," Geoffrey chuckled. "It's been a while since I was a young man—the mind gets rusty about what young people talk about." He wasn't prepared to give in yet, however. "You should look at the Bargen's website. I seem to recall Morgan liking boats—the brothers make beautiful boats. Canadian icons."

A glass of white wine appeared in front of her. "For the lady," said Morgan, suddenly standing beside her. Rachel took the glass from him.

"Who makes beautiful boats?" Morgan sipped his whisky.

"Geoffrey was asking if you were buying a boat from the 'Barks' people in BC?" Rachel shrugged; playing dumb wasn't so hard, especially in the company of a man like Geoffrey Wharton. Giving Morgan as much information as she could in the least amount of words, she said, "Apparently we had dinner with them that night we bumped into Leah?" She shrugged and opened her eyes wide at Morgan. "You know how business bores me. Now, if we're talking about art? Or a good book?"

Rachel smiled at Morgan. "I need to powder my nose." She put the glass down. "I'll be right back."

***

The joy of the day had been sucked away in a second. After returning to the dining room, she asked Morgan to take her home.

Rachel sat in the corner of the Escalade staring at the window button pensively.

Finally, she said, "I thought the invitation was a first step to making amends with my father. Can you believe that? How stupid am I?" She looked at him. He stared ahead. The back of the Escalade was dark and she couldn't read his face, but she suspected it was blank. "He wanted information on the Bargen deal. Like an idiot, I'm too busy having fun, drinking wine, dancing, I thought he was showing some interest in my life. *His niece!* No. He uses me to get information about you. Even when I dissuaded him, he came full circle. I shouldn't be surprised; it's not the first time. My dad tried to tell me—prepare me, but I had no idea what he meant. I thought I did. I thought I was ready."

Morgan leaned over and said. "Ishmael could we have some privacy please."

"Yes sir." A black partition motored up, separating them from the driver.

"Did you know?"

"I suspected."

"You suspected because it was obvious to you that Leah didn't just happen to have the good fortune to be in a small family restaurant an hour north of Montreal at the most opportune time?"

Morgan looked at her. "Yes. They must have been tracking one of the Bargens and hit pay dirt."

"And when she heard I was with you, she saw an opportunity—a weak link?"

"Not the way you think ... God, Leah must have booked it from Montreal once the scout told her you were with me."

How could she have been so blind? Not to see the potential? "And you didn't think to let me in on your suspicious?"

"I could have been wrong."

"But your instincts told you that you were right?"

"I was thinking of you."

Her patience snapped and the hurt she felt bubbled up in her throat. "Thinking of me? I find that hard to believe, Morgan."

"Then you would be wrong." He slid across to her; his arm rested on the back of the seat. "I knew how much you were looking forward to the wedding. I didn't want to spoil your evening. I suspected that they would approach me. I can handle whatever they throw my way. But yes, I was suspicious. Suspicious when they insisted on knowing who you were taking to the wedding—for security purposes. You put my name on the reply card, right?"

"Yes," she whispered.

"I thought they were using you to get me to the wedding because

Leah saw us at the restaurant together. She's done her homework and found out that we've been seen around town together. Been photographed together. Your attendance at my side has been consistent. People are showing an interest. I've refused to give Wharton any press time, and the Bargens and the Hilliers going into business together is big news. Leah saw us with the Bargens. She knew something was up and has been like a dog with a bone ever since. That they approached you was the surprise. And you are not a weak link. I wasn't concerned how you would handle yourself, at *any* point."

Her breathing was shallow. She could feel his breath. The beat of his heart. The heat from his body. He reached out to softly caress her face. "I didn't say anything because you wouldn't have enjoyed New York or today if you had been prepared. You were nervous enough. And I wouldn't trade my memories of you today, for anything. You were so beautiful. I had the most fantastic day and it was for no other reason than because I was with you. I'm sorry it's been ruined."

"I thought ..." Her heart broke into her voice.

"I know," he whispered, pulling her into his arms. "Sweetie, I'm sorry. I knew when I looked over at you—I knew. I saw it on your face. I could feel it. But even though you were hurt, you didn't let it show; you didn't give him the satisfaction. You handled yourself like a pro. I am so proud of you. You were brilliant."

Morgan kissed her mouth softly, but the touch of his mouth had her wanting him with a fierceness she had no desire to conceal. Her hand reached into his hair, bringing him closer. Her tongue darted along his lips; she demanded what she couldn't ask for. Morgan quickly took charge. He scooped her up and pulled her onto his lap and pressed her back down onto the soft leather of the seat. She pushed off his jacket and tugged his tie down. She didn't remember unbuttoning his shirt until her hands ran along his bare chest and she felt the ripple of his muscles under her fingers. He moved away from her and she bit her lip to stifle her cry of frustration. She looked up at him in the dimness of the car; his eyes sparkled as he looked down at her. Spreading her legs apart, he lay down on her and she sighed.

When his mouth came down, it was like no other kiss they had shared. It was wild, out of control, his hardness pressed into her. She heard the zipper of her dress move down the side of her body, felt his hands on her body, her breasts; his rough tenderness turned her on fire. His hands ran up her bare legs and then slid down her panties. His expert fingers played with her with such exquisite slowness; she panted and begged him. Sweat broke out on her body. Then his hands cupped her bum and lifted her, his head moving between her legs. His mouth fastened on her, his tongue moving around the curves of her sensitive pink flesh. She could barely breathe. She remembers bucking against him, but he held her securely. She had never felt anything so consuming. His tongue tortured her, pushing her beyond thought; she could live inside the sensations he stirred in her. When her release came, she felt like she was taking a catapulting dive threw the air. He held her, his arms wrapped around her body. He buried his face in her belly, still licking and kissing her as she shook in a frenzy. The intensity of the moment shattered Rachel. When the tremors stopped, he sat up, gently pulling her with him, her legs wrapped around his waist. Her hands tenderly moved through his hair and down his shoulders as he took a handkerchief from his trouser pocket and he gently wiped between her legs. She watched him. When he lifted his head, he reached up and captured her nipple in his mouth, sucking hard on it, biting it gently. It was all so intimate, so personal, that she longed for him with renewed force. She pressed into him, feeling his hardness, unashamed of her nakedness, wanting him to see her, touch her, play with her.

Watching him at her breast, she stroked his face, whispered to him, "Morgan, I need more of you." She kissed his forehead. He lifted his head, cupping her breasts before he buried his face in between them then looked up at her.

She sunk into him, their faces inches apart. Gently she moved her hips against him in a slow steady motion. "I need more of you."

Morgan pushed his face into hers, his breath hot. "How much more?"

Rachel reached down between them, caressing his hardness. "All of you darling." Over the speaker, Ishmael said, "Excuse me, sir." Rachel practically jumped out her skin, suddenly aware of their surroundings.

Morgan leaned forward and pressed a button. "Yes!" he snapped.

Cautiously, Ishmael softly explained. "We are minutes from Miss Rachel's home."

Morgan's face shut down. There was a pause. She waited for him to say something but he remained silent. He didn't give Ishmael another destination or make a suggestion to her. She thought the evening was just starting, but apparently, it was over.

Rachel looked away from Morgan. She felt flushed with embarrassment. She grabbed her discarded dress and she moved off his lap. He didn't stop her.

"Thank you, Ishmael."

Rachel quickly put on her dress and zipped up the side. She heard the rustle of clothes. She had no idea where her underwear was and she wasn't about to look for it. Her hair was no longer piled on the top of her head—the clip gone.

Morgan was distant. Certainly not the man who had seduced her moments ago.

Rachel was a mess.

The car stopped.

Ishmael announced, "Miss Elaine is crossing the road." He got out of the car swiftly ready to greet her.

Feebly, Rachel whispered to Morgan. "Are you coming?"

"No."

He was so remote; it made her chest cave. Her nerves were shot. To her horror, she started to cry. Elaine's arrival was imminent, but Rachel couldn't control herself. The loving—the incredible intimacy they'd shared was gone in an instant. How could he be so cold? She dropped her head into her lap and used her dress to wipe her face and nose.

"For Christ sake, Rachel, I'm in no position to comfort—"

The door clicked open. She heard Elaine's voice. "Hey, it's still early. I want to know everything, come over to the house."

Morgan spoke low, firm. "Give us a minute Laine."

A brief pause, then the door closed. She cried. He sat. How long, she wasn't sure. She was too mortified to care. Even though she was clothed, she felt naked.

When his hand touched her hair, she jerked back. "Please don't touch me, please, please." She pushed closer to the door.

"Rachel," he sighed heavily but reached for her. She gave a half-heart struggle and then let him hold her close to his chest and eventually she gained control.

Ishmael got back in the car and drove over to the Hilliers' driveway. In her current state, she couldn't go home. Elaine met them in the foyer and immediately folded Rachel into her arms. She struggled not to cry, but it was no use. Elaine took her to her room and then left her alone. No questions. Her clothes were still in the drawers and closet, her toiletries still in the bathroom. She didn't bother to look in the mirror; she knew instinctively how horrifying she looked. She took the longest shower of her life. The soothing heat, the steam, the calming sound of the water brought back her equilibrium.

When she went downstairs, Aunt Sarah and Uncle Robert were

in the TV room at the back of the house. Morgan was there. Wrapping her arms around herself nervously, she stood in the breakfast nook like an idiot, not knowing what to do or say. How could she explain her behaviour to her surrogate parents? Even though they didn't greet them at the car, Rachel was sure Elaine had described to her parents the state she'd arrived home. Short of blurting out to her friend, *your brother drives me crazy and I'm so sexually frustrated and demoralized with wanting him that, that* ... She gulped back her emotions. *Look at him, I'm going mad and it doesn't even faze him.* Didn't she have enough trouble with a stalker and blood relatives who were first-rate bastards—adding on Morgan Hillier's hot and cold demeanour was insane!

Morgan stood, noticing her first, his back to his parents. She felt frail and pubescent under his intense stare. He had showered and changed into jeans and a blue cotton shirt; his hands were in the front pockets of his jeans. It hurt to see his casual beauty. He stepped in her direction and she jolted back, afraid she would fall completely apart if he came near her. She could still feel the touch of his hands on her, the touch of his tongue in her body, the scent of his skin. Morgan was a danger to her piece of mind.

Morgan's face changed at her retreat; it twisted. He looked down, nodding to himself. Aunt Sarah caught his movements, and looked up, seeing Rachel. Immediately she was at Rachel's side, cradling her with her arm, drawing her into the room, but Rachel couldn't sit. She moved restlessly about the room. Morgan was stationary.

"Morgan told us what happened," she said quietly.

Her whole body fused with embarrassment and her eyes swung to Morgan's. She inhaled.

Morgan gave her a mocking stare. "I didn't think you would mind my parents knowing that the invitation was to get information on the Bargen's deal."

Rachel breathed in his explanation. He explained away her overwrought behaviour. How clever was he? She should feel grateful, but she didn't. Instead, she felt like a stupid will-less doll. "Yes well," she said slowly, "it certainly completes an embarrassing night."

His eyes sparkled with anger. "That wasn't my intention."

"I know what your intention was," she said mildly. *The Whartons may have hurt my feelings, but you are killing me! A slow steady death!* "That was sweet of you to be concerned about my reputation."

His brow cocked. It was Morgan's turn to be surprised. Putting down his coffee on the sofa table, he walked over to his mother. "I'm leaving." He reached down and kissed her cheek. He nodded to his father. "Dad."

"I thought you were staying? Macy will be disappointed if you're not here in the morning," pouted his mother.

"I have to leave," he said, moving swiftly around the room, picking up his wallet and keys, his jacket, anger in every line of his body.

"Why?" insisted his mother.

"He wants to get away from me," Rachel said, the words popped out before she had the good sense to censure them.

Sarah and Robert Hillier were at attention. They stood. The room filled with tension.

Morgan stopped dead in his tracks, venom pouring out of his eyes. "You want to take me on Rachel? At this stage of the evening?" he snapped.

She was amazed at her brashness. "What? A silly little school girl like me?"

Morgan took slow measured steps toward her. When he was three feet away from her, he stopped. "What the *fuck* do you want Rachel?"

Rachel trembled; her bravado gone. Not since that horrible day he announced he was leaving for Stanford, had he spoken to her with such bitterness.

"Morgan," his mother scolded.

"Sadie," whispered Robert, "come on honey, let them work it out."

Rachel didn't want to provoke him; they were good together. Being together was wonderful. Isn't that what he said. He's wonderful. Understanding. Affectionate. Tonight, wasn't his fault. What she wanted was for him to take her in his arms and tell her he loved her, that after what they shared in the car was just as good for him. That he was distant because ... she knew it was the back of a Escalade, but they could have gone to his place. What was holding him back? Weren't they in this? Together?

Morgan looked down the hall. "They're gone—so what is it Rachel?" He walked her back until she was up against the wall. "For Christ's sake—tell me what you want. Is it blood? A pound of flesh? What!" He pressed his body into hers and smashed his fist into the wall. His breathing erratic; hers too. Fear gripped her at what she had unleashed.

"Get out," he said, making a narrow space between them. "I don't trust myself. Get out!" he yelled.

***

Ottawa air had a colder snap to it than Toronto. Rachel leaned over and cranked the window shut, rubbed at her arms, and plugged the kettle in again. The night of Leah's wedding reception, how could she not see, what was now so plain? Morgan gave her so much pleasure that night but took none for himself. He wasn't angry with her, she realizes now, he was frustrated. She intended to go home with him, but they were interrupted. They always were, yet, she couldn't help reminding herself, it had still been early; they could have gone to his house, but he made no suggestions. And neither did she. Physical frustration combined with emotional frustration is deadly.

The weekend in New York, he was hers. His attention was wonderful. Even with work and Elaine, he was still hers. Rachel didn't have to monitor her every movement with Elaine; she did leave them alone at times and Rachel spoiled herself with Morgan, touching him, laughing with him, eating with him. In the Escalade, to reach a pinnacle in his arms, only for it to be snatched away? Hurt led to her anger. She took it out on Morgan, when she should have talked to him, told him how she felt.

Had he been feeling the same way—angry and frustrated?

It shouldn't have surprised her that Leah's wedding had been a hunting exercise to find out if Morgan was doing business with the Bargen's. For years, she has been guarding Hillier secrets, especially Morgan's secrets. She was privy to all aspects of his life. She should have anticipated the Whartons' interest was not based on family harmony. Her intuition was impeded at the time. Her eagerness to live each precious moment with Morgan blurred her vision.

Things were very cool between Rachel and Morgan after Leah's wedding. Embarrassed and appalled by her behaviour, she didn't attend Sunday dinner and she could see it pleased Maureen. When she asked her mother how dinner had gone, she said, "Morgan and Macy weren't there." Rachel's heart sank. She returned to school and dragged herself around campus.

Cool March air became a warm April. Summer started early. April first brought record heat.

12

THE STALKER

Photograph 18

Six weeks after Leah Wharton's wedding, *The Free Press* newspaper in London, Ontario, ran a picture of seven women lined up, their backs to the camera Rachel was in the line-up.

Larry Bernhardt hadn't called in over a month. Her mind churned with what that meant. Their last conversation ended abruptly but her point was clear, she wasn't interested. Was he just respecting her decision? Maybe he knew she'd gone to the police? No matter how hard she tried to convince herself that his silence was a good thing, her instincts screamed it was a ruse. He might not be calling but she still felt his presence, and it was starting to take its toll. Strange things started to happen. Her orderly desk, with everything in its place, wasn't quite in its place. Clothes went missing. A drawer was left open just a touch. Each incident had her asking questions of her roommates, the superintendent, the cleaner they'd hired, but her queries led nowhere. Larry's tactics had changed yet again so she called Detective Harper and he agreed with her, this wasn't over.

"Go nowhere alone and call if he calls, really if anything changes, call me," said the detective. "Put me on speed dial."

Rachel hadn't been home since Leah's wedding. Elaine visited a few times; she didn't bring up Morgan, which was a relief, but she missed him. He left a few messages for her. A thousand times she wanted to call, but each day that passed made it harder to reach out, and then too much time had elapsed. The emotions from that evening bridged so many sensations on so many levels it was hard to decipher them all, but they wavered between intoxicating and embarrassing. Right now, she craved the comfort and sense of calm he gave her. She was so exhausted. Her body was on constant alert.

Late one afternoon, she was alone in the apartment—both roommates had left for Grand Bend early that day—when a decisive rap on the door took her by surprise. No one had buzzed. She went to the door and looked through the peephole. It was a man she didn't know.

"Hello?" she yelled.

"Package for Rachel Wharton."

"I'm sick. Just leave the package at the door please."

"I need a signature."

"Sure, I'll sign yours, if you sign mine that I disclosed to you that I have mono and you refused to accept my cautionary advice?"

"Where your signature goes, I'm making a note that you have mono."

"Excellent."

"Excellent."

Once he retreated, she heard the ding for the elevator and opened the door, looking both ways first before picking up the large manila box with pink ribbon. She locked the door. *Olive branch from Morgan?* Excited at the idea, she ripped open the box and peeked inside, but it wasn't from Morgan. The box was filled with corsets, edible undies, fishnets, garters, G-strings, and five packages of boobie tassels in an array of colours. Her fingers trembled as they slipped through the silky garments before closing the box. Her heart pounded in her ears. There was no card but she didn't need a card. Every instinct told her it was Larry. Goosebumps took over her body. Sweat broke out across her brow. *Be calm. Pay attention. Why would he send these? Because he wants me to wear them of course. Okay. We haven't met but he has asked to meet me. I said no. Breathe. He knows where I live. He has my phone number. The house line is not listed in the phone directory—it's under Carla's name. He's motivated. That means he targeting me for some reason, so I need to pay attention.*

Breathe.

Rachel called Morgan but his home phone was rerouted to his assistant.

"He's in a meeting Miss Wharton."

Rachel didn't recognize the woman's voice. "No problem, I'll call his cell."

"He's the keynote speaker at UFT's commencement today so I don't think that's wise."

"I appreciate your help."

She called Louise, but Stephen answered.

"Hey, Rach, still coming to dinner tonight?"

She breathed deep. "Yes, I am but I was hoping to talk to Louise to ask what I can bring." Tears stung her eyes.

"She's at the store getting the stuff for tonight. Sorry I have no idea what she needs. You can call her cell."

"Thanks," she said.

Her skin crawled. She felt like she was being watched. She went to the window and scanned the buildings around her. Nothing out of the ordinary. She noted the people walking, the cars on the street, but no one was looking up, no one noticed her. Was he watching her right now? Taking in her reactions? Just because she couldn't see him, didn't mean he wasn't there. What if he was watching her right now? She turned and looked around the room. For months she had checked every hole, grate, and light for cameras and listening devices and found nothing. But that wasn't to say the place wasn't laced with them, cameras the size of dots. *Why me? And how could he get in to plant them?* Did it matter? She sucked in a deep breath. Calm was needed.

Breathe. Think. The package arrived. It's from a local courier. Larry could have requested a certain delivery time. If he's watching me, he knows the girls are away and I'm alone. Let's see if he's watching me right now. Then he'll know if I do this ... She walked to the big box of sexy lingerie, pulled out a crotchless lace teddy, and held it up to her body.

The phone rang.

She picked it up.

"You make me hot." He was breathing heavy.

There were no preliminaries anymore. He was watching her from inside the apartment. She was prey.

She deliberately misunderstood him to keep him on the phone, hoping the police were tracing the call. "Larry is that you?"

"Yes, it's me."

"Are you sick? The weather's been hot one day and cold and rainy the next. It's so easy to get a cold. My mother says hot water, honey and garlic do the trick. You should try it."

"You're concerned for me? Why?"

"Cause ... I'm ...human."

"You certainly are." He panted, grunted, and then he let out a cry and she carefully put the phone down. *Be calm.* She returned the teddy to the box, picked up her purse; she checked to make sure her cell was in there and she breathed smoothly when she saw it. She needed to get out of there. Now. She got her coat and left. Wherever Larry was, he was busy.

She ran fast in between houses and buildings. Luck was on her side. A cab had just dropped someone off at a building three down from hers. She took it to Masonville Mall. She made it in less than ten minutes. Too fast for him to track her down. She was safe.

Rachel called Morgan's cell and left a message. "Larry sent me a box of lingerie, Morgan. Corsets and everything crotchless." She couldn't keep the panic out of her voice, but no tears. There was no time to cry. "He's watching me. I think he has access to my apartment. I'm glad I reported it and gave the tapes to Detective Harper. "

She leaned against the wall of Hudson's Bay and bent over to calm herself. "He's close Morgan ... because ... I held up the lingerie to myself. Just to see. To know how close, he is real close. He called right away. Morgan ... he ...he ... he was masturbating! I think he's watching me from inside the apartment. I've checked for devices and found nothing, but they could be anywhere." People were close so she moved further from the door. "I was sure to appear calm when I left. I'm at Masonville. Louise is here. I'll sneak back later and get my stuff. I don't want him to know how scared I am. I'm sorry I'm calling you like this. They told me you were at the university for commencement, that you were the keynote speaker and not to bother you. But I wanted ... to tell you—for someone to know— I'm in trouble." She doubled over; tears flooded her eyes despite herself. "I'm scared. I'm sorry I'm such a pain in the ass ... I ... miss you sooo much."

I miss you, had become, *I love you* language, to Rachel.

Detective Harper was her next call but she got his voice mail. She brought him up to speed. Told him she would be at Louise's, gave him her number, and that she would return home later that night to get her things. Once she was settled in a hotel, she would let him know.

Louise was next. When she called Louise's cell, her friend was so excited about the dinner party that Rachel couldn't burst her happy bubble. The good thing was Louise was at the Superstore across from the mall, so Rachel met her. Together they finished the grocery shopping, and then Rachel went back to Louise's place to help her get ready for the party. Once inside, she felt safe. Several times Louise asked her if everything was okay and she lied. Instead she kept herself busy chopping vegetables and setting the table. Stephen entertained her with his marketing presentation, due

Wednesday, on hockey rinks in South America.

Rather than go home to change, Louise suggested she borrow something of hers. She didn't care what it was; she let Louise pick as she stripped out of her shorts and T-shirt. She threw on the dress, fluffed her hair, and met Louise and Stephen's friends from Ivy, who only talked shop: business, how it's changing, how technology plays a role, and whose marketing platform they admired. Rachel kept checking her phone to see if Detective Harper had called in amongst the liberal posturing taking place amongst Louise's Ivy friends—my daddy has more money than your daddy. No one seemed to know that Louise was the heir to the Summerhill fortune and future CEO of one of the top three international confectionaries. Their posturing fortunes were chump chain to the Summerhills. It made Rachel smile. She knew there was a reason she liked Louise. They even discussed Morgan and his innovative approach to project-based business. Louise didn't say a word and neither did Rachel.

After everyone left, Rachel helped her friend clean up. When she handed Louise her plate she said, "Little Miss Confectionary is on the down low?"

"Yes," Louise shrugged with a giggle, "I'm doing a Rachel. It's very liberating. I had no idea *how* liberating."

"It certainly lowers the expectations," Rachel agreed. "Are you going to tell them?"

"Noooo, when graduate school is done, I will probably never see these people again."

"Why?"

Louise stared out the window. "I will go back to my real life. You know what it's like." Rachel nodded, she did. "But it's been fun being anonymous. I …" she bit her lip, "I had the registrar use my mother's maiden name."

"I didn't realize anonymity was so important to you."

"It wasn't. I like being Louise Summerhill, but soon I will be done and before you know it, I will take over for my father, so this is my last chance."

"Last chance?"

"To have the life I've never had. It sounds nuts, but I've never lived in an apartment building." She lifted her hands out of the water, "or washed dishes, or lived modestly. Our room is so tiny that we can only fit a single bed in there. I wake up squished against a wall, Stephen spooning me, grabbing onto my boob in his sleep, and I love every minute. I just had my first dinner party and *I* went to the grocery store to get the food, and *I* cooked it myself. It was good right?"

"It was fabulous."

"If I told anyone else this, they would call me a snob."

"You aren't."

"I'm—"

"Happy?"

Louise looked at Rachel and it was all over her face. "So happy, Rach. And I'm so in love with him."

"He doesn't know you're a Summerhill, does he? And he hasn't met Stephanie and Del?"

Louise shook her head, and whispered, "We use coupons! Can you believe it? Stephanie would have a cow!"

Rachel busted out laughing. "You grocery slut!"

"I *so* am! I get all excited over a dollar off. Very intoxicating, Rach."

Rachel nodded. "The value of the deal. Buy one, get one free?"

"Yes!" she hissed.

Rachel dried the last plate and turned to her friend.

Louise's eyes were misty, her laughter gone. "I love you; you know. Anyone else would have made me feel like an asshole for pretending to be someone else and lying to the man I love, but you ... make me feel like anything I do is ok."

Rachel put her arm around Louise's waist. "Because it is, my friend. You're on an adventure. You just need to take a little time off from being Louise Summerhill before you put on your big girl pants."

Louise stared at her. "Is everything okay, Rach?"

"Of course, why?"

"You were a trembling fool at the Superstore this aft. Jumpy. Tense. Looking over your shoulder. You keep checking your cellphone. I didn't even know you had one. I can see you're not sleeping. You're too thin even for you."

"One – maybe two reasons were enough."

"Spill it. What's going on?"

She told her everything. "... I've never really been afraid before. Not like that. For once I ran for a good reason, but I need to go back and pack a bag. I'll stay at a hotel for now."

"You're not going alone. I'm taking you. Ten minutes to get your stuff and get the hell out of there and you'll stay with us."

"You don't have the room."

"The couch is a pullout. You're not going to be alone. Hopefully, this detective guy will call soon. I'm going to tell Stephen."

"No." She jumped off the counter.

"Just that you're staying the night. It's all good, 'kay." She hugged Rachel tight.

Stephen tossed the keys to Rachel. "She's been drinking you'll have to drive. It might be a piece of shit, but it will get you there."

Larry wouldn't expect her to drive home in Stephen's car, dressed differently, would he? *No, he wouldn't.* She pointed to Louise's closet. "Can I borrow your ball cap and those overalls?"

With Louise in the passenger seat, Rachel sat behind the wheel of a true shit box. They didn't talk. Blood pumped hard and fast through her heart. She parked on the street.

"Rach, I think you should park in Visitors, it's closer."

"I want a little distance from the building."

Louise looked up at the building, "Your apartment is dark. When do the girls come back?"

"Monday."

"We'll call them tomorrow and let them know what's going on. Okay, let's do this."

Rachel shook her head. "It will be quicker if I go up alone. No distractions."

Her friend pointed at her. "If you're not down in ten minutes I'm coming up. I'll get in the driver's seat in case we have to make a quick getaway."

"Louise …"

"I know … but no thinking. Let's hurry and get out of here. And for God's sake be careful."

Stephen had a baseball bat in the front seat. Rachel grabbed it. Her eyes darted up and down the road as she made her way to the foyer—keys in one hand, bat in the other. She quickly looked over her shoulder when she opened the outside door. No one was on the street. Hot muggy summer air forced everyone inside. The air buzzed. It was eerie. No one was in the foyer. She let herself in, walking quickly to the elevator.

"Miss Wharton, *kako si?*"

Rachel jumped and her nerves cracked out a scream before she could translate, how are you in Croatian. She spun around to find Mr. Horvat smiling kindly. "You startled me." Her breath was out of control. "But I'm well—tired—but well."

He nodded knowingly. "Da," he said and walked down the hall to his apartment.

"*Dobra večer*, Goodnight to you as well," she called.

Rachel watched the elevator numbers intently as she made her way up to her floor. Her grip on the bat was solid when the doors swished opened. She stepped out and looked both ways. Nothing.

She rushed to her apartment. Her fingers shook so badly it was hard to get the key in the lock. *Breathe. Close your eyes and breathe.* The key slipped in and she turned the knob and pushed her way into the apartment. Pressed back against the door she tried to organize her thoughts. Don't turn on the light. Dark was better. If he was watching, he couldn't see her—a shadow at best. She needed to pack and get the hell out.

The phone rang and she tensed. *Maybe it's Morgan. What if it isn't? I'll wait for the three rings and the answering machine will kick in.* Carla's voice clicked on: "We're not available to answer right now. You know what to do."

"I know you're therrrre," Larry laughed.

Rachel snapped up the phone. They were tracing the call. "Larry? Isn't this a surprise. Why are you calling? I thought you were a nice guy, but I'm thinking maybe I'm wrong."

"I am a nice guy—a good boy. But I can't help it, I love watching your beautiful tits bounce when you walk."

"That's rude."

Softly, she put the phone down on the side table. Getting out of there was her primary goal. She shoved bare necessities into her bag. Louise had the car running. *I'm certain I can outrun the bastard.* She needed running shoes.

Rachel went back to the phone and picked it up, dropping her bag at the door. Larry was grunting. She checked the front closet for her running shoes. Not there.

"Come out, come out wherever you are. I can't see you, but I've got a surprise for you."

"What do you want Larry?"

"You know what I want? I want my big fat cock in your tiny—"

"Have you ever heard of foreplay, Larry?"

Rachel put the phone on the table and ran to the bedroom to get her running shoes.

A bang came from the front of the apartment. Rachel crouched low, her eyes moving wildly from her shoes to the bedroom door. *Bang, bang, bang!* She double-knotted her laces and yanked her cell from her pocket. She hit Detective Harper's number and grabbed the bat. She waited. Listened. His voicemail clicked in.

"Mr. Harper it's Rachel Wharton again. Someone's trying to get in the apartment. I think it's him. I don't know if you got my earlier message but he sent me lewd underwear and masturbated on the phone." She didn't allow herself to think. *Process later.* She strained to hear what was going on beyond her door. *A voice? Voices? What was that?* She quickly moved to the bedroom door and looked down the hall. Tiptoeing along the hall, she reached the doorway of the living room. Another bang shook the door. Muffled swears. A male voice. Keys jingled. "Mr. Harper—Oh my God! He has keys. *Shit this is it.* Please send someone!"

She grabbed the landline but Larry had hung up. She dialed 911. "My stalker is trying to get into my apartment. I already called Detective Harper." She cut off the operator's questions and quickly gave her address. "I can't talk. I must go. He's going to get in and I need both hands." She dropped the phone to the ground.

Rachel watched the lock turn. She held her breath and pulled the bat up over her shoulder. Her feet were planted in the plush carpet. Ready.

The door flung open and a suitcase was thrown into the narrow hall with force. Her eyes were on the familiar case when the lights switched on, blinding her. She put her arm up to shield her eyes, holding tight to the bat. She blinked furiously trying to gain her vision.

"Rachel?"

She tried to focus. "Morgan?" She pointed the bat in the direction of the door. "I can't see! I've been in the dark too long."

The lights switched off.

"It's me, sweetie," he spoke softly. "I came as soon as I got your message."

"Morgan? Morgan!" Her body shook. "You're here!" Rachel dropped the bat. "You came," she sobbed. Seeing the outline of his body she ran into his arms. Morgan held her tight. She couldn't believe he came. *He came.*

"Morgan, we have to get out of here!"

***

Minutes later, sirens wailed. Police surrounded the building and subdued Larry as he tried to escape out the back door.

Larry Bernhardt turned out to be Rodney Horvat, the building superintendent's forty-something son. An electronic sweep of the apartment showed there were cameras in the bathroom, living room, and Rachel's bedroom. Fourteen out of sixty apartments in the building had spy cams installed in them and were recovered by investigators. Twenty-one women were affected.

Rodney Horvat's father cried when the police patiently explained, this wasn't about Rodney playing with his computers.

"You knew him," said Detective Harper.

"Yes. He worked around the building. He was polite. Kept to himself. Shy. He seemed so harmless. His father was so proud of him. Such a sweet old man. He taught me Croatian greetings. Called me *mala*. It's a term of endearment." She put her hands over her eyes. "I lived in this building last year too but a different apartment." Her head snapped round to look at Louise. "With you and Elaine."

"Apartment 402." Louise looked at Detective Harper. "You'll let us know if we … if he …"

He nodded curtly. "Of course."

Overwhelmed, Rachel buried her face in Louise's lap. Her friend gently stroked her hair. "You had no way of knowing. This wasn't your fault."

It didn't feel that way. You see someone every day. Exchange greetings. She never would have suspected him. Morgan had booked them into a hotel, took their luggage, and went to get his car, leaving Rachel on the lobby couch, while Louise called Stephen. A policewoman threw her jacket and baseball cap over the back of the couch. "You've been interviewed?" she said.

"Yes."

Police milled about, talking to tenants, putting their minds to rest. Rodney Horvat's control center was his bedroom. She watched as a convoy of officers carried out two file boxes each. *What did they find?* Activity surged in the lobby. People shouted out questions. Media arrived and police pushed them back. "You know better. Move to the boulevard."

In the commotion, no one noticed Rachel slip on officer Davey's police jacket and tuck her hair into the cap. Her legs were heavy as she walked to Horvat's apartment. No one stopped her. She tucked her hands into the pockets. There was a notebook and a pencil. She took it out and started to blindly flip through it. For five months fear had become a permanent taste in her mouth. It was part of her now. Who was Rodney Horvat? A mild man on the outside. What did he look like on the inside? Would a visual give her a hint? Would knowing appease her fears? A few officers were stacking boxes in the living room. Detective Harper was talking to the broken shell that was now Mr. Horvat. She walked past the kitchen and into Rodney's cramped smelly bedroom, filled with cameras, TVs, and computers. No one was there. Bookcases lined the room. Half were emptied. Years of VHS tapes, CD Roms, and boxes of USBs. Hundreds of unsuspecting women videoed as they bathed, dressed, had sex—all neat and catalogued by date and name. His bedroom had a cheater door that led to a small room. Nothing prepared her for what she saw there. Naked pictures of her filled the room. Showering. Dressing. Doing homework. On the phone.

Rachel walked around the room. Stared at pictures of her private parts—her breasts, her bum, her vagina—for everyone to see. Notes he made to himself about what he wanted to do to her were written on the wall in violent terms. Detective Harper and his police officers had seen all this. Other people would see this. Humiliation fused her body but she just kept looking, unable to stop. Shocked. Mortified. It wasn't until she saw the life-size picture of herself and a hole in the wall where her vagina was, that she screamed. She couldn't stop screaming. The floor vibrated under her feet. She heard the pound of running over her screams. Detective Harper was shouting, *"Jesus Christ, how the hell did she get in here! Get her out! Now!"*

Morgan was there suddenly. Talking to her. Trying to hold her, but she pushed him, hit him, screamed at him. When the tears came, she cried like something had broken inside her.

***

A big part of her wanted to run home and never leave, but Western had accepted her into Althouse. She had worked too hard to run. Her bravado slipped when Detective Harper told her that, after cross-checking victims' names with other crimes, they had found six women had been raped by Horvat. It gave her comfort to know that apartment 402 did not have cameras. Louise and Elaine were never filmed.

Rachel and her roommates moved out of the apartment into a condominium on a quiet street off Western Road. Morgan had the condo swept for electronic devices each week.

Rodney Horvat may have been caught, but Rachael was still trapped inside her fears. She built safety walls around herself and buried herself behind them. Until that point, her insecurities had been exclusive to Morgan. After Rodney Horvat, her insecurities grew out of proportion.

13

THE JOB OFFER

Morgan bought a one level beachfront property in Tiny Beaches the year Rachel returned from Paris, but he didn't tear it down until she graduated with honours that spring. Graduate studies at Western didn't commence until the fall, so they worked on the project together. She immersed herself in every detail of building the cottage. To this day, she felt happiest there.

Although they had the cottage livable by July, the summer was busy with finishing the inside and giving it the final touches it needed. When the summer came to an end, it was a heartbreak for Rachel to leave after Labour Day to return to London, but she consoled herself with knowing she would come home often and head for Tiny Beaches.

Best laid plans quickly evaporated when circumstances took control of Rachel's life. Halfway through teacher's college, a couple of weeks before Christmas, Rick Summerhill showed up at her house. Since he'd walked into his London apartment and found Rachel snuggled under a skimpy blanket with Gary, she had seen him only once, at his sister's wedding, and now he was in their living room. She braced herself before she entered the room, but there was no evidence of hate or anger on his face. He had a job offer. A teaching position had become available at his high school in Ottawa. It was a co-ed private school, that had a maternity leave opening for the English and art teacher—Rachel's specialties. The teacher who covering the maternity leave had found a full-time position, so they needed someone for September. Rachel was stunned at Rick's suggestion. Her parents were over the moon.

Out of a sense of guilt more than interest, Rachel posted for the job and she went to the interview in Ottawa, checked out the school, the location, but she did it for her parents and to satisfy Rick's unwelcome assistance. She took solace in the fact that her application showed her lack of experienced. She was sure the principal needed an experienced teacher. Rachel was counting on it, but it didn't work out that way. She got the job. Rick stopped by the cottage to deliver the news on Family Day in February. It was as if she had just yanked an electrical cord out of the wall and received an enormous shock. Congratulations came in droves. From her parents. The Hilliers. Rick. Louise. She appreciated their enthusiasm—except Morgan's.

Morgan's congratulations grated on her nerves. She wanted him to be upset at the thought of her leaving again. It crushed her when he wasn't. She was devastated. But what was the source of her devastation? Was it just about Morgan? Of losing their new-found closeness? The prospect of another new city, without family or friends? Or is it because she felt like a fake? Letting others run her life. She was weighted down with obligation to make others happy. Rachel didn't want to go to Ottawa. The mere thought of leaving, yet again, was unacceptable to her.

Although Rachel didn't want the job, some facts couldn't be denied. This was a choice position in the two disciplines she wanted to teach, and no student straight out of school receives such an opportunity. Rick had—unwelcome or not—secured her an outstanding opportunity at St. Martin's High School—despite the way she had treated him. Shouldn't she take the olive branch? Could she disappoint her parents? Herself? She wanted to turn it down. She wrestled with what turning it down would mean. Questions hounded her. Would this be her only opportunity? Given her newbie teaching status, the best she could look forward to was substituting a day here, a day there. Had Rick influenced this decision? How could she turn her nose up at it?

Her romance with Morgan was a new frontier. He was a free man. She was a free woman. Ottawa's distance could put a strain on their relationship, ending it before it started. Since last April they have spent a lot of time together. Their affection for each other had grown since last winter, but only in private, no public displays, which Rachel preferred until she was surer of Morgan. Their friends and family were certainly used to seeing them together, but was that because they *were* together? Or was it because they'd always been together and everyone was just used to it? They didn't talk about their status with each other and Rachel was too scared to ask. It might burst the cocoon she was in wide open. Or were her worst fears being realized?

Questions whirled around in her head and she couldn't turn to Morgan. He owned part of the questions. Even if she appeased herself with coming home, frequent weekend visits wouldn't be possible if she moved to Ottawa. A six-hour, seven-hour drive? Her weekends would be in the car. Flying was her only option. How could she afford that on a new high school teacher's starting salary? She had promised her mother to curb her spending, to learn how to budget.

After Rick's announcement, everything moved at linear speed. It never occurred to anyone that she might turn the job down.

***

Rachel used Elaine's wedding as an obstacle to St. Martin's Principal. She needed the Friday off for the bridal shower being held at the Gables' resort, The Oaks, in the Muskoka Lakes, and the Friday before the wedding. But the principal agreed to her requests. Confused and hurt, Rachel accepted the position. She made no effort to move to Ottawa. Instead, she spent the summer at the cottage with Morgan and Macy until she had to leave. In the meanwhile, Rick found her a furnished apartment near the high school, but he warned her it wasn't up to much.

August seemed to come too soon. Her mother organized her things and had them shipped to her new address. Rachel paced the house and slept badly. Anxiety gripped her; she couldn't seem to get control of it. Every time the phone rang, she jumped for it—waiting for a call, but she didn't know from whom. The school? To say what? It's a mistake? She didn't need to go?

There was no one to turn to. Louise was not an option; Rick was her brother. Elaine lived in a different world these days—knee-deep in wedding plans.

Maureen opened the lines of communication a week before she left.

"I hate the thought of you leaving again when I just got you home, but this will be good for you. I know you helped Morgan with his cottage," she looked at Rachel. "I'm sure you just wanted to do something nice for him after all the help he gave you in London with ..." She shook her head, not looking at Rachel. "Of course, working on his cottage must have been a thrill. A blank canvas. Different perspectives and textures. Architectural plans. Then there was the shopping and decorating. What a wonderful experience. And being near the beach too, but now you've finished school, this is your first summer without the thought of returning; it's time for you to concentrate on Rachel."

Maureen pushed Rachel's hair back over her shoulder. "You go to Ottawa, darling. Your father and I are so proud of you. It doesn't surprise us that you've become a teacher. You know, Daddy misses teaching every day. And this is a wonderful opportunity. How often does that happen straight out of school? It's only six months but it will get your feet wet and when you come back, I'm sure Daddy will help you get into the system here. Goodness, he knows enough people." She kissed Rachel's cheek.

Rachel knew her mother was right. It was only six months and a wonderful opportunity. But she didn't know if her mother encouraged her because she thought it was the right move for her career or if it had more to do with her disapproval of Morgan. She didn't ask. She paced the floor instead, churning the questions around in her head. The hope for a reprieve never happened. Time ran out. By mid-August, it was time for Rachel to go.

The two families had a celebratory weekend before Rachel left. Morgan had a fourth birthday party for Macy. It was an awful day. Macy clung to Rachel and Rachel clung to her. Leaving her behind again was going to be difficult. The following day it was Rachel's turn. Maureen and John threw her a going-away barbecue. After the party, Rachel kissed and hugged everyone through her tears. Her plane was leaving in a few short hours; time for stalling had evaporated. When she got to Morgan, she steeled herself from touching him. Afraid she would break, "Take care of yourself," was all she could manage. She didn't want anyone taking her to the airport. The emotional upheaval of the last few weeks was plenty for Rachel. She slid into the backseat of the taxi and Morgan's jag bolted passed them. Rachel swallowed, trying not to cry.

Don't think about it.

Rachel waved to everyone through her pasted-on smile. She asked the driver to leave quickly. The second she left her street she slumped into her seat and let her tears cloud her vision. *He couldn't even wait until I left.* Engrossed in her hurt, she didn't notice the taxi had stopped.

The sound of Morgan's voice had her head snapping up.

"I'll take it from here." Morgan leaned in to the window and handed the cabby a roll of bills. "Could you get her bags?" Rachel quickly wiped her tears just as Morgan opened the passenger door and held his hand out to her. Stunned, she took it. His jag sat in front of the taxi. Trunk open. Engine running. The cabby was running with her luggage as Morgan opened the passenger door. "I thought I would take you to the airport. Do you mind?"

With difficulty, she found her voice. "No."

He smiled. "I hoped you would say that."

Rachel's heart pounded relentlessly. When he slid into the car beside her, he moved close to her face, his gaze steady, "This is between *you* and *me*."

Her breath was shaky. "Yes."

They were silent.

At the airport, he parked the car and they walked silently to the terminal. They found an empty alcove. They stood silently. Soon their alcove filled with other passengers. Characteristically, Morgan had his hands in his pockets, his black hair messy, in a sexy rugged way. His blue eyes twinkled as he smiled down at her. "You okay?"

No. I want to go home with you, but she nodded. He walked her over to the ticket booth and waited while she got her boarding pass; she was the last passenger in line. Except for a few employees and passengers racing after errant children, there was no one around. They stood together silently in front of the security gate as she fumbled with her purse then looked up. Standing in front of him, she could do nothing else but notice everything. How solid he was. His shape. How tall he was. He loomed over her, making her feel safe; he always made her feel safe. His square shoulders. The strength of his arms. The way he smelled. His smile.

"Be a good girl," he said softly, moving to stand close to her. "Remember, if you need anything you just have to call."

"I'll remember." Rachel bent her head; her hair covered her flushed face as she played with the buttons on her shirt. As she studied her button, her mind was quiet as she listened to her breath moving in and out, hearing Morgan's, feeling the breeze of it against her hair.

"Do you want to go?" said Morgan.

His *sudden* perceptiveness irritated her. Rachel's head shot up defiantly. "Think I'll fail?"

Morgan's blue eyes held her gaze with an intensity that made her chest contract. "You'll be amazing." The husk in his voice made Rachel tremble. She caught her bottom lip in her teeth.

"No goodbye hug?" he said sharply.

She averted her eyes. "No."

"Afraid to?" The playfulness was back in his voice.

"Why would I be afraid of you?" Rachel looked around as the airport signs started to blur.

Morgan put his hand on her neck. She jumped at the contact, her eyes darting up to his. He bent his head. She was disappointed when he kissed her cheek. The touch of his lips on her skin sent a tingle down her spine. It had been weeks and weeks since he touched her; she didn't want it to end.

"Morgan," she whispered, hearing the weakness in her voice. "Kiss me goodbye."

Morgan released her neck; his hand ran down her back, drawing her nearer. Everything became misty, like a slow-motion dream. This was between them. No one else. Just them. His mouth came down. The hungry coaxing motion of his mouth brought a strange melting heat coursing through Rachel. A groan escaped her, somewhere deep and uninhibited. Her hands trapped against his chest. She pushed at his coat and she splayed her fingers across his cotton shirt. She felt his muscles contract, felt him trembling when she moved her hips against his, felt his heart pound like her own. Rachel's head sank back on his shoulder and Morgan deepened the kiss. His arms wrapped around her like a protective steel coating, lifting her off her feet. Her arms stole up to his neck and looped around it, drawing him closer. She clung to him, returning the demanding pressure of his mouth with her demands, savouring the warm, hard crush of him, and she drifted and drifted and drifted.

Abruptly, he released her lips, kissed her cheek, and held her securely against his hard body. An exquisite ache in the pit of her stomach bruised her heart, as she held him fiercely. Morgan drew down her arms from around his neck and kissed her hands. He didn't speak to her—just stared—and she waited, watching him, but he said nothing. She grit her teeth in frustration. *Say something! How can you kiss me like that, like you mean it, and just let me walk away from you?*

His silence was her evidence. Rachel whipped her hands out of his and stepped back. Angry green eyes bore into blank blue ones. Still, she waited, watching him. Nothing. An invasion of coldness took control of her.

"See ya around Morgan."

Rachel walked away without a backward glance. She remembered thinking; she'd show the bastard! She would love Ottawa. She would find a man to love passionately and never return to Toronto. If Morgan didn't want her? Fine! She wasn't going to beg for his attention! He was either interested or he wasn't. He wasn't. Unless of course, it was for a quick feel—that appeared to be the height of his interest. And yet, lust didn't pass between them. Giving and receiving with such intensity, with such a need to please the other person—it wasn't lust. Lust was taking without conscience or emotion. Until Morgan, Rachel's experience amounted to lustful moments. Lust was good. It had its place, but it wasn't the only place she wanted to go. The consuming passion she felt in Morgan's arms was the only real place she wanted to go.

On the plane ride to Ottawa, her thoughts were somber. Reality compelled her to come to terms with the truth—the chemistry between them was incredible, but it was apparent Morgan's intentions had nothing to do with romance or love. Since childhood, Rachel has worshipped him. Was her desire real? Or meshed together with childish worship? *I don't know.* Genuflecting to the wisdom of her sexuality was Rachel's natural instinct. What would the equation equal at the end of a sexually satisfying affair? Heartache? Heartache so dense, that repose would surely be out of her grasp and forever remain an unconquerable enigma. Denying blatant reason wasted good energy. A party of one can't hold a relationship together. How many women did she know who clung to men who didn't want them with urgency and vulgar petition? Too many; living in the land of obscurity, wondering what they'd done wrong? *Why doesn't he love me? Am I not good enough?* The pocket-sized truth that no one acknowledged—yes, you are not enough for him to love. Not to say you aren't enough for someone else, just not enough for him.

***

Rachel's resolved to love Ottawa deflated within the first week of her arrival. The silence; the ugly walls; the lack of connection to anyone or anything sent her into full-scale wallowing. That first Sunday in Ottawa was excruciating. The minutes dragged. The clock banged in her ears.

She called home.

Jason picked up the phone. Rachel heard laughter, the TV in the background, and she struggled to keep her tears under control.

"Hey, how's Ottawa?" said Jason.

"Settling in." She didn't want to talk to Jason. "It sounds chaotic there."

"Jason who's on the phone?" asked Uncle Robert.

"Rachel. Everyone yell, 'Hello.'" As instructed, they yelled hello.

Rachel shook with the effort to swallow her tears. She opened her mouth but no words came. The pause stretched too long, she knew it did, but she couldn't yank the moment along.

"Rach? What is it half-pint?" Jason's voice was gentle, and it made her grab at her shirt.

She spoke slowly so her tears wouldn't spill over and drown her. "You know—stuff."

"This growing up crap is a pain in the ass, isn't it?"

"J … Jace." She realized her mistake immediately. Casual conversation was not going to be possible. "Jace …" she struggled. "I have to go."

Morgan was on the line. "Get off the phone Jason," he ordered. "What's wrong Rachel?"

At the sound of his voice, so familiar, so close, she lost what little control she had and burst into tears. "Morgan!"

There was urgency in his voice. "Did something happen?"

"No. I just …"

"Just?" he encouraged.

"I hate it here!" she said in a gush. "I'm … I'm … so lonely."

"Why didn't you come home this weekend?" he demanded.

Rachel hesitated. "I … I can't just yet. Lainey's party is coming up, and then the wedding. My mother has clamped down on me. Said I was spending too much money and cut me off. She's put me on a budget and I've already blown through this week's money and next week's, and I haven't even started working yet. Of course, I can't cook so I eat out a lot—by myself. Everything is *by myself*. Maybe after I get paid …"

"Money is the reason you didn't come home?" he snapped. "Why didn't you tell me before you twisted yourself in a ball!"

"Don't yell at me Morgan!" she sobbed. "I'm barely holding on here." She paced the room. "I've never lived completely on my own before. I thought I could handle it, but it's hard, that's all. I just needed to talk to someone. I haven't talked to anyone all week. Well, I talked to my dad, I mean I haven't talked to anyone standing in front of me. Well, I saw Rick, but it's not the same." Her breathing was becoming difficult to control. "I'm sorry. It's going to be alright. I'm just having a bad moment. Sunday's are always special; we always have dinner … I shouldn't have called. Don't worry. Tomorrow will be better."

She leaned against the kitchen counter. She dropped the phone from her ear to her shoulder, but she still heard him curse.

"If you hang up on me Rachel Wharton, I'll personally come up there and ring your stupid little neck. I've never wanted to beat the shit out of anyone more than I want to beat the shit out of you at times. Do you hear me?"

She brought the receiver close to her ear once again. She couldn't muster angry indignation at his arrogant tone. She paced the apartment blindly—around the living room into the kitchen, around the living room into the kitchen.

"Do you hear me?"

Rachel blinked back her tears. "Yes."

"Just stop with the melodrama for Christ sake—it's not going to fix anything." He knocked something over. "You piss me off you little shit and I don't know what to be more pissed off about."

Rachel was silent.

"Stop pacing for Christ sake!" he shouted.

Dejected, she stopped and slumped down on the antique armchair near the bay window. Annoyed that he knew her so well.

A heavy pause sat between them before he said quietly. "Have you stopped pacing?"

"Yes." Rachel sat forward, resting her elbows on her knees, her head heavy with emotion.

Morgan sighed deeply. "We're going to figure this out, okay?"

She held the phone like a lifeline. "Okay."

"Good."

"Are you alone or is everyone there?" she asked.

"I'm alone, in your dad's study."

Overwrought with emotions that clouded her better judgment, she said quietly, "I miss you."

"I miss you," he said equally quietly like it was a secret between them. "Do you want me to come there?"

"I want that—it's embarrassing how badly, but ..." she sniffled. "But what?"

"I know I'm being a baby, but living alone sucks the big one." Morgan laughed and it gave her the courage to continue. "This apartment is full of time. The days are bad enough but the nights are like an eternity."

"I know." His voice echoed her loneliness.

"Are you lonely Morgan?"

"I've been lonely for years sweetie."

"I'm sorry." Her heart broke for him. Her heart broke for them. "I'm sorry I make it worse."

"You make it better," he said.

"I'm being melodramatic."

In an incredulous tone, he said, "You're melodramatic? I hadn't heard."

She laughed. "Bugger."

"You're still my favourite prima donna."

"I'll grow out of it, right?"

"The prognosis isn't good."

"Morgan, all this time to think is killing me."

Morgan sounded far away. "It's a big adjustment, but once you get into the swing of things it will get better. Be gentle with yourself. It's going to take time."

At his words, her face ignited with the burn of her unshed tears. "I'm ... I'm much better."

"Don't lie to me, Rachel."

Tears spilled out of her eyes silently.

"It's going to be all right. Come on sweetie, don't cry."

"I'm sorry for bugging you like this."

"I thought we were friends?" he asked.

She tried to suppress the loss she felt. "You're my *best* friend Morgan."

"And you're mine, so don't apologize to me for how you feel. What I don't understand, is why you didn't call?"

"I thought maybe you wouldn't want to talk to me."

"When have I *ever* not wanted to talk to you?"

She watched her wiggling foot. "At the airport, I was sad to leave and ... well, I ..."

"Sweetie, I know you didn't want to go. It's always hard to leave, but I never want you to feel forced to stay anywhere or feel stranded."

"Things have been very confusing—between us. I wanted to talk to you, to tell you, but all this other stuff got in the way and now I'm just so tired. My head hurts. I never know what the right thing to do is. I've never felt so disconnected from everything and everyone."

Something in Morgan's long pause made her sad. "Give it time. You owe it to yourself to give this opportunity a little more time. I know you're struggling right now." He paused before saying quietly, "I certainly don't ever want you to feel that you can't come and talk to me. Regardless of what's going on, I don't want to compromise our friendship. Promise me you'll call if you need me—any time."

"Okay."

"Promise me."

"I promise."

"That doesn't mean we can't try to make this transition to a new city as painless as possible. So, don't give me a hard time here, but I'm going to send you some money so you can come home anytime you want, okay?"

"You know I can't accept that Morgan."

"I'm not arguing with you Rachel."

"Morgan—"

"If the situation were reversed and I needed your help, wouldn't you help me?"

"Of course!"

"Then be gracious."

"*Oh Morgan—*"

"*Oh Morgan*," he mimicked. "I want to do this. This is between you and me. I'm certain Maureen has her reasons for turning this into a learning curve, but I know my sister, and I know the bills she runs up and I'm equally certain a Hillier wedding, when you live in another city, is hard to afford on a budget."

"Thank you for understanding." A knock came to the door and she jumped. "There's someone at my door." Confused she stood up. "I don't know anyone in Ottawa."

"Let's see who it is."

Rachel clutched the phone to her ear and looked through the peephole. She opened the door. "Rick, hello."

"Summerhill." Morgan's tone changed. It had a snap to it, like a hospital PA system: Dr. Hillier to pediatrics *stat*. "Put him on the phone, we have business."

"Sure." Rachel handed Rick the phone without question. "Morgan wants to talk to you." She stood back. "Come in." She hung his coat over the ugly pea green armchair.

There were no pleasantries in Rick's greeting. "Hillier, you barked."

Rachel slipped to the bathroom. The mirror was less than forgiving; she looked awful. She splashed cold water on her face making a puddle of water around the vanity. She brushed blush on her cheeks to lift the sadness off her paleness. A stretch really, for her eyes matched her red hair with an unattractive brightness. Her heart jittered rapidly in her chest. She needed to relax. *Breathe. Breathe.* She wasn't trapped in this God-forsaken place. With Morgan's help, she could go home. Just between them, he said. Her mother wouldn't know she was bending their budget agreement. She gripped the edges of the vanity. She needed this help right now. *Just until I am settled. Morgan said it was hard starting a new job never mind a new city. It's going to be all right. After Elaine's wedding, I'll be able to afford my plane ticket—not every week, but I'll be able to go home.*

Rick was still on the phone when she returned to the living room. He nodded to her. "No, I just stopped by to see how she was getting along in our fair city." He gave her a boyish smile. "A cup of coffee for my concern would hit the spot."

Rachel laughed. "Wait—let me crawl from under the brick house that fell on me and I'll make it."

His laughter was deep and low.

Rick had been a perfect gentleman that night. He took her to dinner and a late movie. A couple of days later the first bank confirmation came.

Ottawa made Rachel aware that pieces of her were missing. Pieces deliberately discarded to get her through the week. In tiny steps, in unnoticeable ways, she had been losing pieces of herself for years. Things she took for granted were suddenly noticeable. She began to crave them in her own life. Couples stealing kisses as they walked hand in hand. Families playing in the park. Cravings she never allowed herself to indulge in suddenly became her priority. She craved having a family of her own. A man she loved and who loved her back. She wanted to make her life messy with commitment.

Seasons change; time grows longer, darker. Knowing what you want, doesn't lead you where you want to go. Morgan was the man she wanted but the tarot cards were turning up empty cups. Time seemed long. Would she find the love her parents found in each other? Would Rachel be a bitter old maid with twenty-three cats like Miss Donaldson on the third floor? Future aspirations and the picture they made had never been a concern of Rachel's, but the lonely apartment that waited for her each night consumed her with its emptiness.

Karma is a bitch. What goes around comes around. How many people had she hurt over the years? Her list of discarded men was long: some she misled, some she ignored, some she tried to love.

Sadness ate Rachel. She had lived on the surface of her life for years out of necessity. Forced her to remain missing by keeping herself at a distance, leaving discarded pieces of herself in London, Paris, Toronto, and establishing new personas. She evaporated time to evaporate her thoughts. She made life busy. Now time sat like a giant clock in the center of her pukie apartment, mocking her, chiding her for her flaws. Rachel was no longer innocent from feeling the depth of her life. There was no escape from her certain kind of sadness. She couldn't exchange it, so she milled around in its surplus, aimlessly.

14

THE VISIT

Bang, bang, bang!

Rachel bolted upright. Her flailing arms hit her teacup and it crashed to the floor. She felt disorientated and sore. Pushing her hair from her face, trying to get her bearings, she held her hand in front of her eyes. The brightness of the sun had chased away the loneliness of the night. Photographs littered the small breakfast table and the floor.

Another sharp rap startled her. "Rachel?"

She said, "Who is it?"

"Rick."

"I'm coming."

Using the table, she pulled herself up with difficulty. Her body was stiff from sleeping at such an awkward angle. The briarwood box was still open. Photographs littered the small breakfast table and the floor. She piled the pictures from the table and floor with deft hands, not wanting Rick to see her life, stuffing them into their briarwood box before answering the door.

Rachel squinted up at him. "Have you been knocking long?" She stepped aside to let him in.

"A few minutes," he shrugged. "I was getting worried."

"I was asleep." She walked quickly to the table. "Take off your coat and I'll make coffee." She went back to the table, picking up the box of photographs; she put them on her shelf, but even that small task hurt Rachel's head.

Rick was behind her.

"I'm sorry about yesterday," he whispered. "I didn't want to fight with you or talk about Morgan or put you in a position of defending him, but I meant what I said; I want to build a future with you Rachel."

"I want things too, Rick," she said softly.

"What things?"

It took too much effort to lie. "What everyone wants: love, family, passion, dreams coming true, but I don't know if I can have all those things right now."

"Let me help?"

"How?"

"By getting involved in your life *here*."

She faced him.

His face was blank, his body stiff. "I know the city. I can be your guide. Who knows where it might lead? There's no pressure."

Rachel sank into one of the ugly green chairs. *That made it worse.*

"We never really talked about what happened …." His words hung in the air.

Rachel wrapped her arms protectively around herself. *Oh God*

There was a long pause. "And not something we'll do today." Rick sat on the sofa, his arm stretched out along the back, his ankle resting on his knee, his gaze steady. "No one knew what happened."

Rachel surmised as much. When Louise got married, the two friends had touched on the break-up.

Louise told her, "I know it's been years since you and Rick broke up but I get the feeling there's unfinished business between you?"

It took everything in Rachel not to throw up.

"I'll take that as a yes. I'd kill to know the story." Louise patted Rachel's twisting hands. "Don't panic, I won't torture it out of you. Your life. Your business. You are my best friend and I know we made a teenage pact to be in each other's wedding, but Rick's in the wedding party. It's more important that you be there and comfortable than fulfilling a teenage pledge, so what do you want to do," she pushed Rachel playfully, "wedding party or guest?"

Relieved at the options, Rachel said, "Guest."

Louise was a good friend. "Done."

It was a beautiful wedding.

"You're a million miles away," said Rick.

Rachel shrugged. "Your sister has always been a good friend to me. Thank you for not telling her."

"I'm glad you came to the wedding."

"Louise made it easy."

"You looked beautiful."

"You ignored me."

"I noticed you," he dryly. "Morgan never took his eyes off you."

"Morgan is an observer."

Rick shook his head. "He watched who you talked to, who you danced with, it seemed …"

Morgan was her escort for a reason. "I know where you're going with this and you're wrong."

His stare was grave. "There was an indulgence in his waiting, like—a man waiting his turn."

"You're wrong."

Rick ignored her. "And it wasn't a question of if—more of when."

"Waiting for what? Getting his turn at what?"

"The prize."

You are so wrong. "And what is the prize, Rick?"

"You."

Rachel sighed, sick of these little scenarios Rick assigned to Morgan. How she would give anything if they were true. "That's not why. There had been some trouble in London." She breathed deeply. "A guy stalked me for months. Police caught him just in time, but he left his mark."

"What? Louise didn't say anything."

"She had moved in with Stephen by then, but she was there the night they caught him." Rachel's palms were wet. Goosebumps ran up her arm. She bent her head. Her hands were in tight fists.

"When did this happen?"

"A year ago," she said. "Your sister's wedding was the first social occasion I had attended since it happened. I asked Morgan to come so I could enjoy myself."

"I'm glad you did." Rick leaned forward. "You looked beautiful. I couldn't keep my eyes off you." His tone made her uneasy.

Why can't I love him?

"I do want you to enjoy your time here but I think the reason you haven't settled here," he said, "is because you have a bad attitude about it."

"I know." The minute school let out on Friday, she rushed to the airport to catch her plane back to Toronto. Ottawa ceased to exist the second she stepped into the airport.

"You've always lived in the moment Rach, but since you moved here, you live for the weekend. No wonder you're so unhappy."

"To be fair, a lot is going on right now. The Gables' resort is next weekend; my cousin is graduating from medical school, and then it's Elaine's wedding. Maybe after the wedding, we can assimilate me into life in Ottawa?"

Rick's pleasure was unmistakable. "Excellent!"

Guilt got her off the sofa. "Good. But I need to kick you out. My parents are flying in today." She smiled. "They're taking me to lunch."

Rick stood. "I'm out of here."

15

JET PLANE

Rachel tapped her foot incessantly, drummed her fingers against the arm of her seat with a graceful carelessness. She strained to see out the window of the small plane as the captain informed his passengers that they were approaching Toronto momentarily. The captain said the weather was unseasonably hot at 28 Celsius. "Enjoy the day."

Perfect for their drive north.

Rachel checked her purse for the twentieth time: wallet, cell, cards, and gifts for the bridesmaids and Elaine, directions to the Gables' resort, the photograph from her memory box of Morgan and her, and a sketchbook. Sketching was making its way back into her life again. After that first horrible flight from Toronto to Ottawa four weeks ago the thought of the lonely apartment that waited for her was overwhelming; Rachel had picked up an airplane napkin, borrowed a pencil from a fellow traveller, and Morgan's familiar features materialized from under the tips of her fingers. The sure even strokes she sketched made the distance between Ottawa and Toronto more manageable.

The move to Ottawa had been especially difficult after the summer she'd had with Morgan. Promise was in the air and Rachel couldn't help but get excited that things seemed like they were coming together. Finally. Then Rick showed up and everything changed. Rachel looked out the small window as the plane descended. Below, flat, green land stretched far to the north, in beautifully manicured, precise squares. She had learned to hate traveling. Lately, every arrival and departure seemed to gouge another piece of her.

Don't think about it.

The plane hit the tarmac, reduced speed, and taxied to the jetway. Rachel sat straight. Elaine's soon to be in-laws had invited the wedding party to their resort, The Oaks, north of Toronto. Three whole days. She closed her eyes and breathed in deeply. Three whole days with Morgan. Last night, she was so excited she couldn't settle into sleep. She called Morgan and chatted a mile a minute, then she rang off and fiddled with packing her gifts for Elaine and the bridesmaids. Still sleepless, she called Morgan again. He laughed as she explained she had moved the gifts out of her bag and into their bag.

She fell asleep finally—on the floor, between the two suitcases, phone in hand.

Trying to be polite, she waited patiently to disembark the plane, waited patiently for her bags to shoot out and down the carousel, waited her turn for the escalator to take her to the arrival doors. When the automatic doors swished open to admit her into Pearson's Terminal III, throngs of business travellers surrounded her. She didn't spy her dad immediately and frowned.

"Rachel!"

Her head snapped round; her long hair framed her pale face. She was the picture of innocent beauty. Oblivious to the appreciative stares from men, or the envious glances from women, her spontaneous delight at seeing Morgan gave her goosebumps. He stood on the outskirts of a clump of people stationed around the arrival square. He filled her gaze. She stood poised, enjoying the sight of him. Dressed in casual khaki pants, hands in his pockets, he wore a green striped shirt, brown leather jacket. He was—beautiful. Her eyes met his and an injection of pleasure shot through her when his gaze ran over her body. Glad she wore her new fitted light beige leather jacket, brown pants with a flat front that hugged her hips, and a white V-neck sweater—a birthday gift from her mother. Rachel had abandoned her sense of style a while back and rarely wore clothes that accentuated her natural assets. Watching him watching her, she smiled, delighted with her mother's good taste. *What are mothers for anyway?*

Her green eyes were brilliant with sparkle.

Morgan lifted his gaze to her stare and there was no mistaking the desire lurking in the depths of his blue eyes—fleeting as it was. He gave her a lopsided smile and laughter bubbled up from somewhere in the pit of her stomach. Pain, loneliness, insecurity: in an instant, he made the vacant space inside her disappear.

Rachel's heart pounded in her ears as she walked across the shiny floor on shaky legs. He met her halfway.

He slipped her overnight bag off her shoulder, an amused glint in his eyes, as he lowered his mouth to hers. Morgan briefly branded her with the hot demand of his tongue, and then he moved away, making it appear as though he had kissed her cheek.

"Jason and Jeff are over there." Morgan threw a glance at his brother and friend standing patiently where Morgan had stood moments ago. "I had to pick them up so I told your dad I'd pick you up, too."

Rachel marvelled at how casual he was, how calm. She was incapable of speech, her face burned, her breathing came in a rush and her body throbbed from his kiss, from his closeness.

Morgan grabbed her hand to guide her through the crowd, and numbly she followed. It didn't distress her to acknowledge that she would follow wherever he led.

By the time they reached Jeff and Jason, Rachel was semi-functional. "Hi guys."

Jason shoved her with his shoulder. "Hey, half-pint."

Jeff smiled. "Hi yourself." They fell into step with Rachel and Morgan.

Jason stuck out his tongue at Rachel. "I've missed you creep. No one to rag on. Why didn't you come home last weekend?" He threw a scowl at his brother. "You know Morgan, he sucks at sharing information."

Rick had begged her to stay. His charm and her guilt compelled her to stay. It seemed like an age since she had seen Morgan. "I do have laundry to do you know."

Jason laughed. "Ha—you don't do your laundry."

"Sadly, it's my mother's new plan to turn me into a responsible adult."

He feigned horror. 'No!"

She nodded. "Afraid so."

When Maureen realized John had been increasing Rachel's allowance since their daughter turned sixteen, she cut Rachel's generous allowance and took all her credit cards before she moved to Ottawa.

"Your spending is completely out of control." Maureen flapped Rachel's credit card bill in the air. "Fifteen hundred dollars for a purse, and seven hundred and fifty for a pair of shoes!"

"They are classics, Mother," said Rachel.

"Classics!" Maureen turned to her father. "Do you hear this? This is your fault."

"Maureen darling—"

"Don't Maureen darling me John Wharton. Both of you may have been born with a silver spoon, but there is no excuse for being frivolous."

Both father and daughter said, "I am not frivolous!"

"She needs to understand the value of a dollar." Maureen breathed in deeply. "You are financially immaturity Rachel Wharton. You need to be responsible. You need to reduce your wardrobe and shoe collection. When you are twenty-five you will become one of the richest women in Canada and you won't know how to balance your cheque book."

"Mum, I got 95.6% in calculus. I think I can balance a cheque book."

"Don't be sassy Rachel. You need money management skills. You need a budget. You start a new job in three weeks; it's a perfect opportunity to learn."

"This is unnecessary," John said. "The interest Rachel makes in a month far outweighs her meagre expenditures. She knows that we've discussed her portfolio at length. She understands the parameters—"

"We are doing this my way, John." Her mother had strong opinions about money, but Rachel didn't think that was what was bothering Maureen. Rachel saw resentment in her mother's eyes, that Rachel dared to buy shoes and a purse at two thousand dollars when Maureen could not. No matter how much money Maureen made, she would never buy a fifteen hundred-dollar purse.

Rachel built the budget to please her mother, but she did find herself in a financial crunch with Elaine's wedding. Put the name *Hillier* in front of *wedding* and watch the dollar signs soar. Rachel would rather eat dirt than plead for leniency to Maureen. The added expenses of gifts, travelling back and forth to Toronto, her dress, and Macy's dress did not fit into her new teacher's salary. It irritated Rachel that Rick was tenderly close to the truth the other day—on more than one level.

Of course, Jason would never believe she lived on a very strict budget. When he grabbed her new jacket between his two fingers, he whistled, "I need convincing that you watch your pennies."

She slapped his hand away, laughing. "It's a birthday present from my mother. I do live on a budget."

"Sure, you do," he mocked. "Jetting from Ottawa to Toronto

every weekend, you would have to live on a budget."

Morgan squeezed her hand and she looked up, but he was staring at his brother. Jason held up his hands. "Okay, okay, I'll leave her alone, but she missed a week. I have to catch up." He nudged Rachel. "You know that, right half-pint? There can be no protective bands."

Morgan didn't reply just looked straight ahead. He was one of those guys—words were not always necessary; a look was all it took. It would be nice to be one of those "one look says it all guys," but Rachel knew, it was never going to happen for her.

One more thing not to add to her New Year's Resolution list: useless words.

"I hear the Gables' place is quite spectacular," said Jeff. "Kathy and I took the kids to The Oaks last year on holiday, but I didn't know they lived on the property."

"A couple of kilometres away from the resort," said Morgan.

Rachel smiled. "I'm looking forward to it."

"You're returning to Ottawa, Sunday or Monday?" asked Morgan.

Here we go, she thought. "Sunday."

Morgan tossed his keys to Jason. "You're on baggage."

Jason dragged his leg and hobbled over to Rachel. "Your bags, Miss. Don't want to lose me bread and butter, now do I, eh?"

Rachel handed Jason her carry on. "Or you'll have to live on a budget, too?"

"Awe Miss," Jason smiled, sincerity and charm oozed out of him, "I dream of havin' enough money ta live on a budget."

Rachel's laughter echoed through the parking lot. "Jason Hillier—I did miss you!"

Jeff took pity on baggage boy and helped him assemble the luggage properly so a firing would not be necessary.

In the front seat of Morgan's Escalade, Rachel dug the picture out of her purse. "I found this the other day." She handed it to Morgan. "Do you remember?"

Morgan pushed back into his leather seat and stared at the picture. "Yes."

She thought he would smile at the memory of that weekend, but he remained solemn. She leaned closer. "The man who rented us the cottage took the picture." Shifting to sit on the storage compartment between the bucket seats, she pointed at Morgan and laughed. "Everyone was looking at the camera except you. You must have turned just as he snapped the shot. You're smiling, but it's only a side shot, what were you looking at?"

Morgan slid his arm over her left leg intimately and she blushed. Jeff and Jason were battling something when they slammed the back hatch shut. Morgan turned to face her. Their gaze on par with each other.

"You," he whispered, holding the picture up. "Look how happy you are?"

She looked at herself. She was happy. That weekend was perfect. Turning sixteen was perfect. Morgan did all her favourite things— ran along the beach, played volleyball and scrabble, watched a *Fred and Ginger* movie, and he read aloud her favourite poets: Rossetti, Poe, Browning, Woodsworth.

"I was *so* happy," she whispered back, lifting her eyes to his.

His left hand reached out and stroked her cheek tenderly. "Me too."

"I've missed you so—"

Morgan's lips grabbed hers. His mouth was insistent, wet, passionate; she felt it in every part of her body.

Jason's laughter cut through her reverie as he opened the passenger door. "… it certainly put the smug son-of-a-bitch in his place."

Morgan broke the kiss, dropped his hand, and she slid her back into her seat. He looked out the windscreen blankly. Incapable of thought, she followed suit.

Jeff laughed. "The timing was perfect. It's like you personally ordered it."

Jason clicked his tongue. "Lucky is my middle name."

Morgan turned the ignition and handed the picture to Rachel without a glance.

"Whose picture?" asked Jason.

A composed Morgan said, "Rachel found it—her sweet sixteen party at Bass Lake."

"Let's see?" asked Jason. Rachel handed it to him. "We haven't been to Bass Lake since." He whistled. "Good God, we all look so young!" After Jeff had a look, Jason held it between the bucket seats. "That was a great weekend, wasn't it, Rach?"

Rachel politely said, "Yes." She reached for the photo.

But Jason held onto the picture. "What's up half-pint?"

"Nothing. Nothing at all."

"I wouldn't say anything." Rachel heard suspicion in his voice.

"I'm tired ... I ... I haven't been sleeping well."

"You? The girl who can sleep on demand?"

"Oh, I'm a whole new woman since I moved to Ottawa. All kinds of bad habits. Drinking, smoking, staying out all night."

"Sur-vey says!" yelled Jason.

"Okay, if you must know, the walls of my apartment are like tissue paper and the neighbours are amorous newlyweds, so sleeping is hard, and being a high school teacher isn't a clean job. I've learned the art of humility—cocky students tend to do that." *It sounded so much better than I've been pining for your brother beyond what is decent.*

Jason knew she was lying. "You humble?"

"Yes, ya bastard—me. I'm a double newbie—new to the school and a new teacher; they're kids, and being kids means they can smell fear." She threw him back a glance. "Put *you* in my class at sixteen."

He nodded, giving her a crooked smile and sat back in his seat. "See what you mean."

"Not much teaching is taking place, they're too busy trying to make me look stupid." Rachel twisted round and stuck her head between the bucket seats to ask Jeff, "How's your new baby boy?"

The blank planes of Jeff's face disappeared into pleasure. "He can stand up, but no first steps yet."

Watching Jeff Gilles regale his seven-month-old son's accomplishments, the marked difference between Morgan and Jeff, struck her. Jeff was quiet, his gentle face narrow and boyish. He had a healthy toss of brown hair and his eyes were a soft golden brown. He was a tall, but slight man: a thoughtful, serious man. Rachel had known him her whole life. He was mild-mannered compared to Morgan's more compelling personality. Although Morgan had had a privileged childhood, there was an edge to him, a relentless ambition. His dark colouring added to his fierceness. The hard angles of his handsome face, hard-jawed, high cheekbones, cool blue eyes. Morgan was a hard man to miss; she had to admit, he wore his masculine sexuality with ease, but his beauty went beyond his handsome face—he was complicated. He was incredibly gentle and understanding, but he was also arrogant and cold, a man who liked to hold himself at a distance. He played pretty close to his chest. He rarely raised his voice, but when he did, his truth was cutting.

Morgan's demeanour might be quiet and calm, but was neither quiet nor calm. It was deliberate and controlled. His notorious reputation in the business world for being demanding and ruthless to get what he wanted, didn't shock or surprise Rachel. Morgan was financially successful at birth, but it was not his only currency. The Hillier legacy was strapped to him whether he liked it or not. Rachel knew better than anyone the lengths people would go to cash in on that legacy and everything that came with it, but again, those were the external forces he didn't care about. The ones he did care about were his close family. His sustaining and enduring friendships.

Morgan's ability to listen, his ability to bring out the best in people, his vision, to pick what mattered to him and do it, were his best successes. He didn't need everyone to like him or what he did. If there was a disconnect it meant it wasn't meant to be; not everything is for everyone.

Rachel nestled her cheek against the leather seat. "When does Kathy go back to work? A year is a long time to be away from the rat race. How does she feel about going back?"

Jeff handed her his accordion of pictures, then clasped his hands around his knees.

"She wants to stay home with the kids."

"You're happy about her decision?"

Jeff conceded with a sigh. "I have to admit; I've enjoyed having her at home this past year. We finally live in the house we practically killed ourselves building." Jeff shrugged. "You know how it is. We both worked late hours; Jackson was in bed by the time we got home. The weekends were a wash between family, friends, business. Now when I come home it's alive with activity. Jackson is running around with his little friends tearing after him; the baby is crying; the phone is ringing—it's great. I love it. The quality of our life is better. We're not keeping to the same schedule."

Jeff averted his face, staring out the window.

Rachel grabbed his hand through the bucket seats. "I'm happy for you Jeff. If it's what you and Kathy want, that's the most important thing, right?"

Jeff smiled. "You're the only one I've told, beside Morgan, who hasn't questioned our judgment."

"It's a hard decision," said Jason thoughtfully. "When Carrie and I had Daniel, we were young, still in school, it wasn't the most ideal situation, but we made it. Now Daniel's in school part-time and she has time with Robby, but she still works part-time. She doesn't want

271

to lose touch with speech pathology, but she wants to be home with the kids. Carrie's a perfectionist. It's hard to find a balance."

Rachel said quietly, "If I had children I would want to stay home and raise them. Their bad habits would be my bad habits."

"Not everyone is in that position," said Jeff.

"I know," she agreed. "But you are. You didn't force Kathy to make this decision. She sees an opportunity and wants to take it."

"I don't want her to think I have all these crazy medieval expectations because she's at home. I want her to be happy, not feel like she's my unpaid slave."

"Doesn't sound like it," Rachel smiled.

Jeff stared at her nervously. "I can't ... believe I told you all that."

"Me either," Morgan said, his gaze turned to Rachel; he winked at her before turning his eyes back to the road. "I've known you for thirty years and I don't think I've ever heard you say so much."

"What about you Rachel?" Jason had a cheeky smirk on his face. "Have you heard the rumours that you're dating Rick Summerhill again."

She looked at Jason between the bucket seats. "Who told you that?"

Jeff said, "Kathy is on the board of directors for Children's Hopes and Rick's mother is on the same board."

Rachel laughed. "I'm not dating Rick."

"Is there a rekindling in your future?" said Jason.

"To think, I was glad to see you, Jason Hillier."

"He never got married, did he?"

"I'm surprised you're still married."

"Girlfriend?"

"Not that I know of, but then again, Rick doesn't discuss that with me."

"Do you spend time together?"

"We work at the same school so I see him every day. We have spent some time together but not a lot."

"But he did find you the job?"

"You're labouring point?"

"Apartment too, right? Not far from his I'm sure."

Morgan cut in, "Why do care Jason? Do you want to date Summerhill?"

Jason sighed. "No, I'm just saying."

"Is this sport or interest?" asked Rachel.

Jason ploughed on. "I'm not trying to be a pest here. But I know you Rachel, and you tend to take people at face value. I didn't think you knew about the rumours; I think the poor bastard hasn't got over you, and I thought you should know," said Jason.

She blushed. Her conversation with Rick was fresh in her memory. Rick's wants. Her reluctance. His judgment. Her deflections. His accusations. Her justifications.

Jason said quietly, "Several people have asked me if the gossip is true. I said, no."

"Good answer."

"Half-pint, don't take this the wrong way, and I'm not trying to upset you, but a man doesn't go to so much trouble just to be a nice guy. He didn't just find you a job. He found you a job in another city—one he's living in, and not just any job, a job where he works. What might be obvious to me might not be obvious to you."

It's obvious—now, after Rick laid his cards down, quite decisively, on her ugly, beat-up 1972 coffee table, that he wanted to be the man in her life again— naïve? That's an understatement.

"Yes … you're right, of course," she said quietly, embarrassed, she bent her head slightly so her long hair covered her face. She ran her index finger along the crisp crease of her pant leg. "I was naïve— and it's obvious now that you've explained it." Jason had said things she hadn't thought of that worried her. "I'm terrible at assigning motivations to people. I never see it coming."

"I want you to be prepared." Jason touched her shoulder. "Everyone's going to be at the house. It might come up."

Rachel patted his hand. "I'm glad you told me." She dropped her head back against her seat, and she turned to look out her window. Cars swished by, blurring her vision. The rapid movement made her feel sick. Instead, she concentrated on the apartment buildings in the distance—sporadically but decoratively positioned along the 401— but when they started to sway, she looked away. She crossed her legs, tightened her arms around her body, and leaned into the passenger door, staring at the glove box. She'd walked into the job in Ottawa blindly. The consequences? She had no idea. What she did know is that Rick wasn't going to stop trying to win her over. Rachel's eyes burned and her right temple started to throb. If it was obvious to Jason, then it was obvious to Morgan, and he said nothing. He'd watched her board the plane to Ottawa without difficulty. No guidance. No warning. If he had, would she have listened?

No, she wouldn't have. It had to be Jason to explain the things that she hadn't even considered.

Morgan veered off the 401 taking Avenue Road, going south. Friday traffic was stiff with cars, delivery trucks, and couriers.

Rachel didn't want to think about Rick or Ottawa, but her mind kept drifting back. Rick did find her job and apartment, but he didn't impregnate his colleague so Rachel could have her job. The opportunity inspired him and he thought of her. Maybe he thought, now that she was older, well-traveled, she might be more ready for a mature relationship, and this opportunity would bring her to his city, and they could restart what didn't have a chance six years ago. He didn't force her to accept the position. No fireside chats. No pressure. And yes, Rick lived a couple of kilometers away; she ran past his place every morning, but it was also a few kilometers from the school, which was completely helpful since she didn't take her car to Ottawa. But Jason suggested there was manipulation in his gesture—he could be right. She didn't see, but it didn't change the reality. She couldn't wait for her six months to be up—and she was in love with another man.

Her brow furrowed. Rick's hatred for Morgan was no secret. What if Morgan was the motivating factor behind the opportunity? It wouldn't be the first time. Why though? Was it his way of separating her from Morgan? That separating her from Morgan would help Rick gain ground with her? That seemed extreme. Would he even go that far? For her? *No,* she thought.

Where would Stephanie get the notion they were together? Was Stephanie being overzealous? She could be a bit overbearing, not to mention interfering with built-in expectations of Rick's girlfriends. It had made Rachel nervous when she did date Rick. Or was she not being overzealous at all, but repeating what Rick had told her? How many people knew? She'd told Kathy. Kathy told Jeff. Jeff told Morgan. Morgan told Jason. Jason told Carrie … Aunt Sarah told Rachel's mother?

Rachel sucked in a deep breath and exhaled slowly, dropping her head back against the headrest. Complicated. With each day that passed, things get more complicated. Complication was becoming a permanent fixture in her life. She rubbed her forehead. Her breath laboured. Could Rick's manipulations further complicate her already complicated relationship with Morgan? She had been so close to Morgan, closer than they had ever been before, but then circumstances took over. The fiasco at Leah Wharton's wedding, Rodney Horvat, grad school, and just when she was regaining ground with Morgan building the cottage, making that their first home without ever saying it, Ottawa happened. Was she kidding herself? Was she always going to be on the outside of a relationship with Morgan? She pressed her folded arms into her chest, gripping the sleeves of her jacket, making the leather crackle.

Rachel emptied her mind. *Breathe. Don't panic.*

Panic attacks had become a part of Rachel's life after Rodney Horvat. With help from a therapist, she had been able to control them. In the beginning, the attacks were severe. Fear overwhelmed her—trapped her. She constantly looked over her shoulder. Dressed in a dark closet. Eating, sleeping—were impossible tasks. Unexpected things would trigger her panic: a crowd, a smell, a movie. She felt trapped all the time. She felt trapped now.

The movement of the car was making her feel worse. She hated being car sick. She reached into her pocket for another Gravol but the package was empty.

She needed to empty her mind, concentrate on her breathing. *Everything is good. Breathe.* The mix of her queasy stomach and her panic pressed down hard. She pressed the window button. The cool breeze was glorious against her hot skin.

Morgan's hand rested on her knee. "Rachel?"

She couldn't answer him, nausea overwhelmed her, and her heart pounded.

"What's wrong?" said Jason.

Morgan told his brother. "Car sickness."

Morgan's hand closed over hers. Rachel felt the calming strength in his long fingers. She wanted her racing heart to slow down. She wanted the pressure to lift. *Breathe. Breathe deeply.*

Morgan pulled the car down a side street and parked. He took her hand, putting it on his chest. She could feel the steady beat of his heart; heard the steady pace of his breathing. Everything was still but those two things. *Breathe.* The stopped car helped. Each breath she took, her mind started to calm. How long they sat there, she didn't know, but her body started to cool down. Her breathing was under control, and her panic and nausea slipped away.

Morgan opened the console beside them and took out some Gravol, handing it to her. "Macy misses you like crazy," he said.

She shifted in her seat to look at him, inhaling deeply. "I miss her like crazy, too."

How much longer would Macy miss her though? She was four. The realities of what that meant cut Rachel's wounds deeper and made them more susceptible to infection. With each day that passed, the further back Rachel would go in Macy's little mind. Six months was a long time in a four--year-old's life. Rachel was so replaceable in their lives. They were so irreplaceable in hers.

Do you miss me Morgan?

A silly thought, she knew, Morgan was a busy man—a little girl to raise, a house to run, a business, a son to be, a brother; he didn't have time nor was he inclined to miss her. God, she had become everything she never thought possible. She was an embarrassment to herself. Not only did she yearn for a man to the point of weakness and sanity, the judgments she had spewed on unsuspecting love-drunk girls from her past proved Rachel to be a fraud.

16

SAY SOMETHING

Morgan moved the Escalade back into the flow of traffic. He saw the desolation on her face; it worried him. He knew she didn't want to be in Ottawa. He knew she was waiting for him to make a move, to smooth it out, and as easy and as appealing as that sounded, he couldn't do it. He wasn't going to decide for her. He was here. He supported whatever she wanted to do, and she was the one who had decided to go to Ottawa. She hadn't included him in her decision or asked for his opinion. He knew exactly what Summerhill was up to, but Morgan hesitated telling her. Rachel was a mess before she left for Ottawa. Her anxiety was at a peak. Telling her what Summerhill was up to would only have added to her stress and worry. It wasn't worth it for a few brownie points, but he was glad Jason had told her. Prepared her.

Standing by, watching her suffer through the stalker, watching her suffer through moving to Ottawa, frustrated him, but she had to trust herself and trust him. She didn't. He had shown her in a multitude of ways how important she was to him, that he missed her, that he would help her in any way possible to make the transition to Ottawa as stress free as possible. He met her halfway. Creating anxiety was not his intention, but she had to decide what she wanted. The circumstances she found herself in were the consequences of her decisions. But Rachel sucked at consequences, and his protective nature where she was concerned, was ingrained in him. He wanted her to be happy. He wanted her to experience a full, satisfying life, but at the expense of her not experiencing life? He didn't want her to miss opportunities or be plagued by stress or commitments she wasn't ready for, or couldn't make, or didn't feel. Hadn't she told him that—more than once. Morgan knew better than anyone what pitfalls to avoid when it came to Rachel, but he also knew she didn't want space from him. The reasons why, eluded him, there could be one of many.

At the red light, Morgan turned to her. "Better?"

She nodded, sitting back, but he could see the conflict on her heart-shaped face. "Last night on the phone you were looking forward to this weekend. And now you're here, your parents can't wait to see you, and I know Macy is driving everyone crazy asking, 'Is she here yet? Is she here yet?'"

She lifted her beautiful green eyes to his; they were steady but guarded. When her eyes dropped down to his lips, he broke out in a cold sweat. The heat from her body made him shift uncomfortably. He still tasted her on his lips from the kisses he'd stolen. She might be a half-pint size, but beyond her beautiful face and a body that inspired sinful gluttony, she had an innocent wonder and wit. When mixed with her brand of sensuality—it was toxic. It took mammoth strength to ignore what he wanted. He turned away.

If only they were alone. But they were rarely alone.

Rachel wasn't the only one feeling the heat of gossip. Jeff was no match against his curious wife. Kathy would grill Jeff when she saw Rachel in the car. Look how she'd grilled him two nights ago!

***

Morgan sat alone in the Gilles' living room when Kathy returned from the kitchen. "More coffee, Morgan?"

"Thanks." He held out his cup. She poured from a silver teapot. A wedding gift, no doubt.

"How is Rachel doing in Ottawa?" The question was casual but

Morgan knew there were few casual things about Kathy.

"Settling in."

Kathy poured herself a cup and sat on the couch across from him. "I'm on the board for the Children's Hope Foundation. So is Rick Summerhill's mother."

Cat and mouse games weren't Morgan's style. Kathy knew that, but it didn't stop her from believing in her charm and she continued with her fishing expedition. "Can we consider 'settling in' sufficient?" he said.

Kathy rolled her eyes, expending an exaggerated sigh. "I know, I've been on maternity leave too long. I'm turning into my mother! I'm a lawyer for God sake! A criminal lawyer … and yes I *do* have to keep saying that so I don't forget." She tapped her cup impatiently. "This whole other world—the stay at home mummy's world that I have never been a part of, and it's turned me into a nosey little bitch."

They both smiled politely.

Morgan decided to send the right information out. "So, what do you want to know?"

"Stephanie Summerhill said Rachel was dating Rick." Her head tilted to one side. "I remember years ago they dated. The next thing, they broke up; he moved to Montreal and she moved to Paris. So, I was surprised and curious that they were back together."

"And you think I know the story?"

Kathy smiled. "Morgan, I know you're technically Jeffrey's friend but I've grown extremely fond of you over the years. Hopefully, you feel the same, so I hope you're prepared to indulge me, because I'm interested in all things that are none of my business, and you know everything there is to know about Rachel."

"Why is Rachel's life of interest?"

"She fascinates me."

Morgan looked at his black coffee. He knew the feeling. "As far as I know she's not dating Rick. They're friends."

"Do you know why they broke up years ago?"

He lied. "No." He liked Kathy. Intelligent, sharp, witty, outgoing, beautiful, loving mother and he too considered her a friend, but he would rather eat shit than have this conversation. Rachel was not extracurricular material for the gossipmongers at the Children's Hope Foundation.

"Why don't you ask what you want to know so this conversation can be over?"

She laughed. "That's what I love about you Morgan—no bushwhacking bullshit."

"I'm glad you approve."

"I don't mean to come off like your mother, but I'm worried about you. You're a single parent, working long hours. You never date. Before Rachel came back, work was all you did. Yes, yes, the parties, the receptions, but they were work. And then you built that bloody cottage ... and I just know it's because of her. You make it all look so easy, but it's a big fat lie. I know how hard it is," she held out her arms, "because it takes two of us to make this work."

"I appreciate your concern, but there's no need."

Kathy ignored him. "I think you're in danger Morgan. I like Rachel but ... she's a creative sort, all beautifully melodramatic and high maintenance. There's no point in denying how you feel about her. Remember? All those years ago, I spent several days with you both in Montreal. Neither of you stepped out of line, you didn't even touch each other, but you looked like a couple—acted like a couple. She ate off your plate all the time. You finished her sentences. You communicated without words. Thoughtful of each other ... and it didn't seem to matter that you were married to Emily at the time or that she was dating Rick. And then she takes off to Paris because the mood strikes her. You bury a son and she fly's in and fly's out. You get divorced and she turns up, dabbles in your life, and now your daughter's life, and she's off again, to Ottawa this time."

Morgan was relieved to hear Macy and Jeff coming downstairs. Macy's little girl voice echoed in the hall.

"How many times do you change a baby like that?" she asked, stomping on each step.

"About every two hours," said Jeff.

"In a whole day, how many times then?"

"In my professional opinion?"

"Yeah, in your pernessional opinion."

"Seven, eight times a day."

"What about feeding a baby like that?"

"Maybe six times a day?"

"So how do you get babies?"

He hesitated. "Cause I think my daddy needs a baby like that."

"Why do you say that?"

"Cause he seems really sad and you look really happy when you were with that baby ... and maybe my daddy needs your kind of babies."

Morgan heard the stomping stop.

"My kind of babies? What do you mean Macy?" Jeff's voice had lost its playfulness and fatherly concern replaced it. Morgan braced himself.

"You know—boy babies. I'm a girl, but maybe he would be happy like you if he had boy babies." Morgan heart jerked in his chest.

"Macy, there is no way your daddy would ever—"

Macy interrupted him. "He had a baby boy; did you know that?"

"Yes."

"He died."

Morgan dropped his coffee cup on the table and was on his feet and across the foyer in record time.

"I know," Jeff said slowly.

"I've heard them talking about him ... there's a picture of him on our wall."

"Hey Macy!" The foyer was like a tunnel and Morgan's voice boomed.

They were sitting halfway down the staircase. Jeff had his arm around Macy's shoulders. Slowly Morgan made his way up to where they sat. "What have you been doing up there? I've missed you."

Her sparkling blue eyes looked at him, innocent, happy to see him, and his two-hundred-pound body melted, becoming rubber.

"You missed me? But I'm just here, Daddy."

"I miss you all the time." He held out his arms and she jumped into them. Macy loved stories that she was the star in; he smiled down at her.

"When?"

Morgan walked back down the stairs. Jeff had politely left them alone. "When you go to sleep at night, I miss you; when you go to school; when I'm out of town. Sometimes I'll be in a meeting and everyone's talking and I'll remember something you said that made me laugh, and I'd laugh right there in the middle of my meeting."

"What makes you laugh?"

"Like the day you told me it's not a good idea for Grandma to comb your hair after she's had a *serious conversation* with Grandpa. Or that Uncle Jason should ask the doctor if he could grow breasts so his hands aren't always up Auntie Carrie's shirt."

His little girl giggled. "I think Grandma is gonna make me bald like Uncle Rutherford." She giggled again and wrapped her soft little girl arms around his neck, looking at him shyly. "Daddy?"

"Yes pumpkin?"

She whispered in his ear. "Is Auntie Rachel your girlfriend?"

Startled, Morgan looked at his little girl. "Why do you say that?"

"Me and Cassandra Lake ... we spied on you and Auntie Rachel. We saw ya kiss. Cassandra says that makes Auntie Rachel your girlfriend. Cassandra knows lots and lots of stuff, Daddy—lots of stuff."

***

Morgan tapped the steering wheel in agitation. Hearing his little girl's words, her worries that she wasn't enough, haunted him. He needed to pay closer attention to what he was doing. Macy needed to know she was his top priority. No boy babies required. He also made a mental note to pay closer attention to Miss Cassandra Lake and her treasure trove of knowledge. As for his relationship with Rachel, he was becoming careless. If a four-year-old saw it, that didn't make him happy. He was losing his edge. His control. He couldn't discount how much she loved Rachel and what that meant. Having a casual affair with a woman was one thing—that didn't impact Macy's life—but having a casual affair with Rachel? The consequences to his little girl might be damaging if it didn't go the distance. Rachel was the only mother figure she knew. If it didn't work out and Rachel wasn't part of her life, that would mean her mother figure was gone for a second time by the tender age of four. He couldn't let that happen.

There were the two families to consider as well. Long-term relationships are a risk if they end badly. This could get messy if either camp took sides. He was sure speculative discussions had taken place amongst his nosey family members, but at least they were adults and it was contained. Maureen was another matter. Morgan wasn't under any illusion about her feelings. He could feel her angry breath on his neck. Regardless, he didn't want this in the open, especially since he was so unsure of what Rachel wanted. There could be no more mistakes.

***

Morgan drove his SUV through the iron gates of Jeff Gilles house and along the curved driveway, stopping in front of the garage doors. Morgan climbed out of the car and moved to the back of the truck to help Jeff with his luggage.

Rachel watched the two men stand in front of the car talking; Morgan slapped him on the back; Jeff shook his hand.

Jason said, "Rach, sorry if I upset you earlier. I thought maybe you hadn't picked up on the nuances of Rick's job offer. You seemed like a mess before you left. Did I do the right thing?"

Rachel interrupted him. "Don't apologize. You were right to give me the heads up. I *was* naïve. Rick has been angry with me since we broke up. I should have known there was more to it. I thought he was trying to mend fences because Louise and I are friends. I'm sure that is his intention." She turned around to look at Jason, "It never occurred to me that he was interested. Then ..."

"Last weekend?" said Jason.

"Yes," she said, surprised at his astuteness. "Ya know Jason, you're smarter than you let on."

"Yeah, yeah, I'm a marvel. So Summerhill laid his cards on the table, eh?"

"Yes."

"What did you say?"

"Jason ..." Rachel bit her lip. She didn't want to put Jason in the middle. Many times, in her life, Jason had told her hard truths she didn't want to know. He's kept the secrets she couldn't tell anyone else. But Morgan was his brother and she was no longer a child. "I can't ..."

"This is just us, Rach."

She hesitated. "I don't want to put you in the middle."

"I am in the middle though, cause you need someone to tell."

"I told Rick no."

"But you're worried."

She laid her head against Morgan's leather seat; his scent reached her nostrils. "Ottawa has nothing to do with my real life. I work there. My life is here. But I'm worried, that being in Ottawa will hurt ... what I'm trying to build with Morgan."

"Seems to me like you two are as thick as thieves. What was up when Jeff and I got into the car?"

Rachel blushed.

"A private hello?"

She whispered painfully. "I'm so close Jason, it scares me."

Jason's cool hand stroked her hot face affectionately. "Love is a scary thing half-pint." His hand dropped.

"Does Morgan ever say ...?"

Jason looked at her like she had lost her mind.

She smiled half-heartedly. "Ask a silly question."

"I know how badly you want this."

Her voice was thick. "I just don't know if I can survive another separation. I get deeper every time."

"I can tell."

She looked up. "Really?"

He nodded. "You've both have been careful, but since he built the cottage, there's been a change. Last summer, every day after work he drove up there, fighting traffic—highly motivated."

"Well, Macy was there. He adores her."

"He does," Jason said quietly. "He does." Meeting her gaze, he continued, "But things *have* changed between you."

"Yes, but it's still very ..."

"New?"

"Yes."

"Why did you take the job in Ottawa then?"

"It was a good opportunity."

"What did Morgan say?"

"Say?"

"About taking the job?"

"Nothing."

His brows shot up in surprise. "Morgan didn't have an opinion?"

"No, he didn't, not that he shared with me."

"Did you ask for his opinion?"

She stared at Jason for a moment. "No," she paused, then sat back. "I didn't," she said slowly.

"Why? If you love him, want to make a life with him, why didn't you include him?"

Rachel turned to look out the window. *Why indeed?* Jeff and Morgan were still talking. "I don't know."

"Sure, you do."

She hadn't included him. If he hadn't included her, how would she have reacted? Not well. Raked him over the coals no doubt, but Morgan did include her, in every aspect of his life. This whole time, she believed Morgan had pushed her out the door with his congratulations. Was he hurt that she hadn't included him?

"Last summer was the best summer of my life. Morgan was a saint."

Still mentally and physically bruised from Rodney Horvat, when things became sexually charged with Morgan, she'd taken a step back. Put him on hold. So many times, she got lost in him and then boom—fear set in. *God he must have been frustrated.* Men are not boys.

Rachel shook her head. "I didn't include him. I was afraid."

"Of what?"

"That he wanted me to go." *Good God, is that true? Yes, it is.*

"Well, he's been a grumpy fuck since you've been gone. Last weekend everything pissed him off. The only one who isn't feeling the heat is Macy. I think it's safe to say, he didn't want you to go, and you didn't want to go. If I'm confused why you went, then so is he."

Rachel watched Kathy run out of the house to greet her husband, a baby in her arms, and one at her feet. Jeff hustled over to her and Morgan waved before climbing in beside Rachel. Watching them embrace and kiss. A child tucked in their arms and the other one tucked between their legs, a perfect family scene. Her gaze swung to Morgan and their eyes locked. Rachel couldn't breathe. The air was heavy with overcharged emotions and all the things unsaid sat between them. She broke the contact; frightened by her chaotic emotions and no privacy to share them.

***

There was a sea of cars at the Hilliers. Elaine's wedding party included four bridesmaids, four ushers. Rachel was maid-of-honour and Morgan was best-man. Macy was flower girl and Daniel was ring bearer.

Aunt Sarah had lunch catered.

Morgan stood in the centre of the breakfast room, coffee cup in hand. "The weather station is calling for a storm. It's coming from the west. We might miss it, so finish up and get into our carpools. The quicker we get there the more time we'll have to enjoy ourselves." Morgan looked at her. "Rachel you're leaving Sunday, right?"

She looked at him patiently. She wasn't willing to be helpful. "Pardon me?"

"When does your flight leave?" he snapped.

Is he trying to make me mad? It's always the same time. Week in, week out. It amazed her how he could never seem to remember when she was leaving. "It's in my bag but usually it's six or seven in the evening, isn't it?"

"Which is it?"

She wrinkled her nose. "Let's compromise and say 6:30 in the p.m.—Sunday."

Morgan picked up his car convoy organizational list. "The Folks will travel together in Dad's car. Macy, Daniel, and Robby are in Jason and Carrie's car. Car seats are already in there. Elaine and Shawn and two bridesmaids or a bridesmaid and a groomsman— don't care which, just figure out who and be ready to ride with Rachel and me—and the rest of groomsmen will take Jason's van with the extra luggage." He looked at his watch. "We'll leave in fifteen minutes. Any questions?"

Morgan's best planning couldn't control Toronto traffic or Mother Nature. Ten minutes into their journey, a broken-down tractor trailer in the collector lanes had them at a dead stop for almost an hour. It was a snail's pace for another forty-five minutes until they passed the trailer—for everyone who needed a gawk. Rachel never looked. Weekenders packed the 400 highway heading to cottage country before the storm hit. There weren't too many more weekends left before winter set in, and cottagers wanted to squeeze as much time out of the season as possible. Fast moving black clouds from the west were gaining sky space. Rachel watched them with a careful eye. They had been on the road for almost two hours, but had barely made it out of Toronto when the kids needed a bathroom break.

This might be a long haul.

When they came out of the service centre, the atmosphere had changed. Blackness covered the sky and flashes of light cracked across its darkness. Rachel gripped the door handle. She wasn't a fan of electric shows.

"Don't look so worried, sweetie." Morgan's warm hand squeezed her leg. The bright flash of lightening left a jagged mark down the centre of the sky. Rachel gripped Morgan's hand and held it tightly.

"Maybe we'll drive out of it," he said quietly.

"Liar."

"Cynic."

"Morgan's right; we'll drive out of it," said Shawn.

Rachel stuck out her tongue at Morgan and then said, "I hope you're right, Shawn."

"Me, too." Elaine's fear was unmistakable. "How much further, Shawn?"

"Another two and a half hours," he said. "It'll be alright, honey. We aren't in any rush. If we have to stop, we will, okay?"

"Okay," Elaine said, her voice faint, and turned to her bridesmaids tucked in the back. "You guys okay back there?"

They both laughed. "We're storm freaks—no worries Laine."

The further they went the worse it got. Thunder boomed and lightning blinded them. Torrential rains crashed down hard and mean. Brake lights suddenly converged into a sea of red.

Morgan slowed the truck to a snail's pace. "Must be another accident ahead."

For forty minutes, they inched along the highway until they came to a complete stop. Morgan picked up his cell phone.

"Dad? Yeah, it looks bad." Morgan swore. "Shawn says it's another two and a half. At this rate, who knows? I think we should re-route. Yeah ... safer, sounds good. You'll call Jason? Okay, next exit."

"We're taking the next exit. We'll find a spot to take cover and head out when it clears."

The next exit was barren. After ten kilometres, they passed only a few small houses. The blue information signs along the road didn't indicate there was anything ahead. The storm roared around them. GPS and cell service were nil.

"Roll down your window, Rach," said Morgan. "Anything up ahead?"

"I see a white farmhouse," said Rachel as rain lashed her. "On the right."

"We'll go there," decided Morgan. "They'll know the area." He stopped just shy of the wrap-around porch. Rachel slipped on her raincoat, but Morgan stopped her. "Stay here."

Lightning cracked overhead as Morgan hopped out of the truck. He ran to the porch. Before he crossed the porch, a man and woman opened the door wide to admit him. Within minutes, he was back out. Morgan waved everyone to the porch.

"Here?" said Elaine.

Rachel shrugged. "Here." Yanking up her hood, she pushed open the door and ran.

Everyone huddled together on the porch, except for the children who remained in the car with Carrie. The air was suddenly cool and Rachel shivered.

Morgan said, "The storm has taken a turn for the worse and there's an extreme storm watch in effect."

"Tornado?" said Rachel's dad.

Morgan nodded. "Funnel clouds have been spotted northeast of here."

Rachel trembled. Concern marked everyone's face.

"The accident on the 400," said Morgan, "is bad and they're closing it. It's a hundred and forty clicks to the next town with a hotel big enough for us all. I don't think it's a good idea to drive too far off the beaten track. We could take back roads to Barrie and find a place there until it passes, but I'm concerned that we'd be heading into the storm. The other option is to stay put. Mr. and Mrs. Van Os live here and they have offered to let us stay until the storm blows over. What do you want to do?"

The vote to stay was quick and unanimous.

A fire roared in a large stone fireplace that dominated the living room. Rachel kicked off her boots and made a beeline for it. She wrapped her arms more tightly around herself. "I'm cold."

"Take off your jacket," Morgan whispered, prying her arms apart and unzipping her.

"But I'm cold," she whined, cranky. Her many sleepless nights were starting to catch up with her.

"I'll take that, Morgan," her mother snapped.

Rachel watched her mother move to the back of the house. Taking advantage of her retreating form, she put her arms around

Morgan's waist. The steady beat of his heart soothed her.

"Are you tired?" he whispered.

"Exhausted. I haven't had a good night's rest since I left home." She mumbled into his shirt then snuggled closer enjoying his warmth and solid chest. She allowed herself to relax, let her guard down and take the comfort he gave. She smiled at her thoughts. That was the last thing she remembered until Morgan whispered in her ear, "Time to get up."

"No." She smiled. "I want to stay here." She was content.

Morgan's tone was sharp. "Rachel."

She stretched; throwing her arms up over her head then slumped against his body. "Oh Morgan, one minute, you're too comfortable." She blinked, her eyes adjusting to the dark empty room. She looked at Morgan. "Where are we?"

"The farmhouse." Morgan was so still, his blue eyes blank.

She rested casually against the side of his body. His arm along the back of the couch. "Right," she nodded. She heard laughter coming from the back of the house. The fire was happy and large. "Where is everyone?"

"Family room at the back. I haven't seen anyone other than Shawn since they went back there."

"It looks dark outside. How long was I asleep?"

"Almost two hours."

"Is the storm over?"

"No—a tornado hit Barrie."

"Oh my God!"

"I know."

"Those poor people."

"We'll have to do something to help." His stare was vacant. "It hailed earlier. The hail was the size of golf balls. Shawn came in to tell me we're staying the night. He called his parents so Elaine's shower has been rescheduled for lunch tomorrow."

Morgan didn't look at her. Something was wrong. A crack of thunder shook the front windows.

"Morgan?" Concern vibrated in her voice.

"Yes?"

"What's wrong?"

He remained silent.

"You must be uncomfortable with me lying on you." She moved, but his arm quickly moved down her back and cradled her to him. She stared up at him, noticing the fatigue around his eyes, the weary sag of his shoulders.

"Tell me what's wrong,"

Morgan dropped his head back against the couch, staring listlessly at the ceiling. The voices from the back of the house sounded distant—like a door in the hall separated them. They were completely alone. On impulse, she straddled him, looping her arms around his neck and sunk into him, holding him tightly, stroking his hair. He drew her into his arms.

"What is it?" she whispered. He pressed his face into her hair but remained silent.

He trembled, squeezing her tighter. His need intoxicated Rachel.

"It's nothing," he whispered back.

"It's something if you're feeling it," she said, drawing back to see his face, but he wouldn't look at her. His dark hair fell across his forehead and gently she brushed it back. "Is it work?"

"Partly—problems at the Quebec office."

"That's where Jeff and Jason were?"

Morgan nodded.

"What's the other part?"

"I've been thinking about what Jeff said in the car." The eyes he turned to her were deep blue, strangely blank, and yet energy emanated from him. "Jeff and Kathy aren't the only ones who haven't been living in the house they built." He slid his hands under her backside and fit her more snugly into him. Rachel gasped at the feel of his arousal pressing into her, but his face hadn't altered. "I mean, what's the point—why do I work so hard? For what? To get more? Or is it to fill the emptiness?" he paused a minute, "What good is money if it doesn't give me what I want?"

He made her breathless. "What do you want?"

"Time—time with the people I love," he bit out. "I'm tired—" he broke off.

Blood pounded in her head. "Tired of what?"

Morgan caught her face between his lean fingers. There was no gentleness in his touch. "I'm tired of coming home to a dark empty house. Tired of getting into a cold empty bed after a crappy day. Tired of being the strong one, the capable one."

The coolness in his eyes dissolved, and passion replaced it. "Those people in Barrie? What were they doing when that tornado hit? Sitting down to dinner with people they loved? Or sitting alone at an empty table? Or on the phone with some asshole, they don't respect? Where were they when their lives changed? Destruction is all around them. Do they have who and what they want out of their lives?" Their eyes locked and time was suspended. "I know what I want. I want someone to be there when I get home. Someone to share my life. A mother for my daughter. What good is my success if it can't get me that?"

Pain shadowed Morgan's eyes. She saw the mirror of her own emotions in his eyes. Electricity spiral between them, it shot through Rachel's body; her heart hammered. Her lips parted but her words were lost as he kissed her. Aching sensations ripped through Rachel, making her weak and hot. Her hands crept along his arms. She groaned at the power she felt in his tense muscles, in his wide shoulders. Hungry desire consumed her. She wanted him, to share his life; her body begged him.

Morgan's hands slipped beneath her sweater. He cupped her

breasts; her nipples hardened under the insistent brush of his fingers.

"See Daddy, I told you!"

They broke apart to find Macy's cheeky little face within inches of theirs. Colour poured into Rachel's face, her breathing out of control.

Macy stepped back and put her hands on her hips. "I've been sent ta get ya." She giggled. "See Daddy, you have the same decease as Uncle Jason."

Rachel's colour deepened. Guilt made her teeth clamp down hard on her bottom lip. Morgan burst out laughing. "I don't know what you're talking about."

"Daddy," she told him matter-of-factly. "You remember."

"I think I'm allowed to play with Rachel," Morgan whispered, "if she wants me to."

Rachel cringed, hitting Morgan's chest.

Morgan cocked his eyebrows in melodramatic shock. "Now you're indignant?" His lips were close to her ear; his hot breath made her shiver. "*You* seduced *me*!"

Rachel's hands flew to her hot cheeks. "*I never!* You, you—"

"I what? What did I do?" There was a playful light in his eyes, an indulgent smile on his lips.

Rachel twisted off his knee, stepping away from the couch to stand in the hall. She could see an open door in the hallway and a large dining room table set with covered dishes and place settings. Heavy chatter came from the kitchen with shouts of laughter. She was relieved no one had witnessed their passionate exchange—well except Macy, which was, apparently, an inside joke between her and her father. *Good God.* She'd lost her head, obviously so had he. She had to pay better attention. Maureen would have a cow in front of all these people.

Frustrated, Rachel hit Morgan again for lack of a better idea.

"Give us a kiss Rachel," Morgan whispered, his charm at full throttle.

Despite herself, she laughed, pushing at the air when he grabbed her.

"Cassandra Lake's daddy has been divorced two times," Macy, nattered away like an old granny, finding a spot at the large table where everyone had started to assemble. "She knows *everything* about kissing stuff. She says the kissing stuff makes a lot of noise—scary noises."

"Maybe that's why her daddy's been divorced twice," said Jason.

Morgan's eyes narrowed on his daughter's innocent face as he pushed in Rachel's chair before taking the chair beside her. "How old is Cassandra Lake, exactly?"

Macy's round face became reverent. "Oh, she's seven Daddy."

Rachel saw Morgan wasn't pleased with Miss Cassandra's influence; it wasn't the last word on the precocious seven-year-old, Rachel was sure.

"Unlike Cassandra Lake's daddy," said Jason, "I haven't been divorced twice, but *I* heard no scary noises last night." Jason dipped his head to kiss Carrie's lips. "Not much got past me, as I recall."

Rendered speechless at his admission, Carrie jerked back from him, her horror unmistakable as she stared at her husband.

"You weren't so indignant last night." Jason gave her a wicked smile.

"Jason!" Carrie's cheeks burned bright red.

Shawn chuckled. "*You*—are a dangerous man."

Jason stared at his wife's embarrassed face. The intensity Rachel saw there should have made her turn away, but she was riveted to his face.

Jason kissed her ear and her arms looped around his neck.

Sadly, Rachel always thought she would be the best of friends with Jason's wife.

The lady of the house, Mrs. Van Os, a short, round, Dutch woman with a soft cheery face, said in a thick accent. "Hans and I are so glad of the storm so we could share our table this night."

Mr. Van Os lifted his glass. "To warm shelter and good company."

Everyone raised their glasses. "To warm shelter and good company!"

17

THE SLEEPING BAG

Rachel crawled across the cold hardwood floor in the dark to where Morgan lay. Her eyes had adjusted to the darkness long ago. Sleeping bags were scattered around the living room. Mr. and Mrs. Van Os had two extra rooms upstairs, which The Folks took at the insistence of their children. The rest of the wedding party bunked down close to the fire, but it had fizzled out long ago.

"Morgan?" she whispered, touching his shoulder lightly.

He jackknifed up. "What's wrong?"

She went into an unexpected whine. "The radiator beside me leaked on my sleeping bag. My pyjamas are still damp and I'm cold."

"Is it still leaking?"

Rachel blinked. "*No, the rad isn't leaking*. I mopped up the water with my sleeping bag and turned it off. There's nothing more we can do in the middle of the night. But its freezing in here and it was the only rad in this room."

"Take off those wet things before you catch a cold," he insisted.

"I don't have anything else to wear. My overnight bag isn't in the hall with the other twenty thousand bags, I checked. If I go hunting I'll wake everyone up."

"Well, it's not like I have Victoria's Secret fashions hidden in my sleeping bag."

"Are you going to help me or make jokes?"

Morgan sighed, raking his hand through his thick hair. "Take off your clothes and I'll give you my T-shirt."

"I can't take my clothes off here!"

Morgan lost his patience. "Then get in the goddamned bag!"

She whirled away from him. "Forget it."

Morgan swore violently and yanked her back. "I don't have the patience for this, Rachel. I've had a shitty fucking week. I'm tired, and I'm spending my Friday night sleeping on a hard floor, so shut up and do as I tell you and get in the bag for Christ sake."

Rachel was too tired and cold to argue with him.

"Are you taking off those wet things, or am I?"

Secure in his ex-large sleeping bag, she quickly stripped down. She could feel the heat from Morgan's body close beside her, and it accentuated her coldness. She shuddered. Morgan sat up while she undressed and ripped off his T-shirt. He slipped back down into the bag. She rolled her wet clothes in a tight ball and set them on the corner of the area rug a few feet away from where they lay.

"You're freezing," Morgan snapped, pushing her back against the floor. "How long were you lying in that wet bag?"

"I don't know. I woke up cold and found the rad leaking. After I turned it off, I checked the other rads in the kitchen and dining room, but they're fine. I sat by the fire and tried to dry my clothes. There was an afghan on the couch, but I ran out of wood. I didn't want to wake you but it was so cold.

"You're crazy, do you know that?" His anger was tangible when he yanked her into his warmth. She jerked against him, her teeth chattering. She didn't care that she was naked; his warmth was like a magnet. "Put your arms around me," he demanded.

When her frozen fingers touched his back, he sucked in his breath, hissing at her, "Why didn't you wake me up when it happened, and we could have avoided this?" Answering seemed pointless, but he wasn't satisfied with her silence. "What, no smart-aleck reply? This is a first." His sharp tone hurt.

She was so tired and her body was so tense from warding off the cold. "Please Morgan."

***

Tears sparkled in her green eyes. Morgan didn't want to yell at her. Frustration twisted inside him. The scent of her fragrant skin whirled around him. Her body was soft under his, her generous breasts pressed against his chest. Devouring her seemed more in order. He gritted his teeth. Desire held him in a vice.

Rachel softly groaned, "Please Morgan," and he skid over the edge of his better judgment.

Her arms coiled around his neck; her fingers stroked his hair, sending hot shivers through his tense muscles. When she reached up and her lips touched the pulse on his throat in a gentle caress, he needed no road map to her lips, parting them, tasting her.

Morgan dropped his head onto her breasts, rubbing his face in their softness. Unable to resist, his tongue ran over the hard peak of her nipple and she gasped, trembling like a leaf against him. His chest tightened at the passion that threatened to consume him, passion he had to control. For how long, he didn't know. Did he care? Right now, he didn't. Time with her was limited. And what time he did have was under the watchful stare of the family. These moments were rare and couldn't be lost. Soon she would fly out of his grasp back to Ottawa, back to Summerhill.

Morgan spread her legs, pressing his hardness into her pelvis, wanting to be inside her. He sighed with a shudder. When she was home, he thought, she was with him.

Lifting his head, he moved back slightly. "God ... you're beautiful, baby." Their eyes locked, breathing was impossible.

Morgan wanted her to feel his passion, feel how she affected him. He wanted her to touch him. He needed her hands on him.

Taking her hand, he guided it down his body, showing her where to touch him, how to touch him. At the caress of her tiny exploring hand, he sunk himself into her palm, shuddering uncontrollably. His heart hammered in his ears. To stifle his pleasure, his mouth came down, bruising her lips with his. He was ravenous for her. Her mouth moved under his and he felt her hunger too. Her breathing came in harsh gasps. When she wrapped her legs around his, moving against him, he swore in her mouth.

From a distance, Morgan heard coughing. Faint at first, then getting stronger. Male coughs. Warning coughs.

Morgan pressed his face into her throat to regulate the erratic pace of his heart. This wasn't the place for this, he knew, swearing under his breath. He held her tightly, getting himself under control—a harder task each time he touched her. He wanted to crush her to him, make her a permanent part of him; his greed was starting to become endless.

The coughing persisted.

Morgan's head snapped up impatiently. "All right, I get it. I get it! You can stop now."

Bewildered, Rachel whispered, "Get what?"

"My brother being my mother." Morgan pulled away from her and she was suddenly cold. "Put on the damn T-shirt."

***

At his sudden change of mood after the pleasure she felt coming in waves from his body, the passion he took and gave her—gone; her insides collapsed. This wasn't the time or the place, she knew, but the effort to catch up with reality was difficult.

Rachel whipped on his T-shirt and settled down beside him again.

"Turn on your side," he snapped; his hot breath touched her hair. "And for God's sake lie still." His hand went around her waist and yanked her back against him, none too gently.

The tears that threatened to overwhelm her before, silently

tucking into her ear. He was angry when she woke him, then his anger changed to want at her gentle caress, and naked body. She shouldn't have done it, but she just wanted to touch him; she wanted the anger to melt away. She knew he was already upset for a whole host of reasons. She'd made it worse.

Rachel still felt the imprint of his hands, his mouth. She loved the way he touched her and she was excited when he showed her how he wanted to be touched; each passionate exchange they shared went deeper than the last, not just physically, but emotionally. Rachel wiped her tears; careful not to make a sound or move for fear it would make matters even worse and wake up the wedding party. The hurt in her chest was unbelievable. She squeezed her eyes shut. It was official; she had turned into a crying, whiny nutcase.

"Don't cry," he whispered huskily, laying his head on hers, his strong arms cradling her. "I'm not angry with you."

Softly, she asked, "Are you sure?"

"I'm sure. I just woke up on the wrong side of my sleeping bag," he sighed, kissing her ear. "Now you're here I feel better about sleeping on the floor. Go to sleep."

Early the next morning, dressed, with a cup of coffee in hand, Morgan shook her awake.

Mr. and Mrs. Van Os had breakfast for them before they left. For their kindness, Morgan was very generous. He arranged for someone to fix their heating problem and replace their damaged hardwood floor.

Since the hot and heavy petting in his sleeping bag, Morgan and Rachel had said little to each other. It wasn't until she was packing away her bag in the back of his truck, that Morgan startled her with, "Are we friends?"

"Of course." Rachel stepped back to let him throw in his bag.

"The weekend seems short ... you leave tomorrow."

He never failed to bring up her leaving. Couldn't he wait? Here's your hat what's your hurry? "I'm sorry I woke you up. You must get sick of me bugging you."

"I wasn't angry with you."

"Regretful?"

Dumbfounded, he said, "God no." He sat at the edge of the truck's bumper, putting his hands on her waist; he pulled her to stand between his legs. "Having you touch me excited me. I lost my head. It was hardly the place or the time for an intimate moment." He ran his fingers through her hair.

"I ...," She blushed, averting her eyes.

"Tell me, Rach."

"I ... I enjoyed touching you," she admitted, whispering almost guiltily. "It excited me too."

"You're a very passionate woman Rachel. I know you've had reason to be frightened, reasons to bury your sexuality, but you have so much to give. You should enjoy it."

She stepped back from him. "What does that mean?" Morgan didn't stop her and that bugged her—hurt her. "That I should get back in the game? Do the rounds. See who turns me on?"

Morgan's face hardened. "That's not what I meant. You're afraid of risking anything of yourself because of what happened. You've lost your confidence. You're suspicious. But your confidence *will* come back, and in the meantime I'm familiar territory and we enjoy each other—" A hail of goodbyes had his angry eyes look in the direction of the house. "As usual, this isn't the time to discuss this without a truckload of visitors."

"I see," she bit out. The penny dropped. Now she understood. He didn't care about her. He didn't care how she felt. All that stuff he said last night was what he wanted, those were his plans. They didn't include her. She was good for right now, while she gained her sexual confidence. She was nearby. He enjoyed her and he was willing to be helpful. How nice!

Her weakness for him humiliated her.

"You trust me," he said, standing up, his face tight, his jaw clenching and unclenching as he loomed over her. "I'm familiar. You've been using your femininity on me since you were a teenager. That's how you learned how to control your boyfriend collection."

"That's not true!" Shocked, Rachel moved further away from him. "Why is it that the men in my life have such a low opinion of me? I'm surprised you touched me at all." She pivoted away from him when he reached for her.

"Rachel!" he shouted, his tone demanding, angry, but she didn't care.

She hissed at him, "It's good of you to be my sexual stand-in until I get my confidence back, but don't bother, it's not necessary. I've had a better offer so why don't we make a nice clean break right now, and we'll get on just fine."

The last thing she wanted to do was get into the front seat of Morgan's truck and she certainly didn't want to sit at the very back; that would be disastrous, without Gravol. Instead, she insisted Shawn take the front seat with Morgan and she would sit with Elaine in the middle. Twenty minutes later, they were on the road, and Elaine fell asleep. Morgan and Shawn were knee-deep in business and Rachel's thoughts crowded her.

Had she been using her femininity on Morgan over the years as a benchmark?

Of course, I have.

In the last year, their affection for each other had become sexually daring, intoxicating, but she never thought she was a casual … affair.

I know he cares. Last night wasn't casual. He opened up his heart. Told me what was missing, what he wants. I could see it in his eyes. It wasn't casual. Last summer wasn't casual. He can't think I'm using him because he's safe and familiar?

It's been an unwritten agreement between them that their newfound affections be private, but she had to admit, it's getting harder and harder.

***

Elaine snored, evidence that her night's sleep on the Van Os' floor was uncomfortable. The bridesmaids in the back of Morgan's Escalade, chatted incessantly, jumping from business to fashion, to movies, to the buff guy at work. Their voices grated on her. Morgan and Shawn discussed Quebec in a special language that Rachel had no desire to decipher.

The 400 quickly merged into number 11. A narrow highway that curved into the rolling hills on either side. Rachel's eyes darted from side to side trying to light on something stable to focus on. She concentrated on distant fields, but the cars on the other side of the road whipped by, distracting her. Focusing was difficult. She looked down at her entwined hands, gulping, concentrating on her breathing. It was childish to sit back here, she thought. Her head felt heavy. She lifted her hands to her face for support. The movement of the car under her feet jerked her back and forth like she was running beside the car. Her heartbeat accelerated. Her hands trembled. Morgan had bought Gravol for her yesterday, giving her some before they started on their journey north. He didn't offer any this morning and she didn't want to ask, which was completely stupid.

The trapped air in the truck started to make her dizzy. Elaine was breathing too hard. The bridesmaids in the back were taking the breathable air with their senseless yakking. Rachel couldn't catch a breath. Nausea overwhelmed her. The muggy air in the Escalade made her panic for a cool breeze. *I'm going to be sick.* She jerked forward to open the window. It didn't open. She pushed her face against the cool window. She needed to get out. Alarmed, she pushed at the buttons on the door panel to no avail. Her stomach curled.

305

Savagely she banged at it in frustration. She drew the stale air into her lungs; she exhaled a scream. "I need to get out!"

Rachel tried the door latch again. "I need to get out!"

Elaine was at her side. "She's going to be sick—Morgan!"

Rachel kicked at the door. From far away, she could hear Morgan's voice but the words were garbled.

The truck slowed down and moved to the shoulder of the highway. The doors unlatched and Rachel pushed it open and stumbled out. She stepped away from the car. Tires squealed. Screams came from behind her. She was yanked against something hard, but she was single minded in her desperate need for air. She was shoved along the gravel shoulder. She jerked free from the punishing hold on her body, tripping over her feet before getting her footing. She ran out into a vacant field, labouring to suck the air into her lungs. Her heart pounded madly in her chest. She ripped open her coat and peeled it off.

Morgan grabbed her arm and spun her around to face him. "Rachel?" His face swam around, but she couldn't focus.

Gasping she said, "Can't breathe. Going to be sick." Her hands moved wildly around her.

Morgan held her steadily. "Be sick then."

Rachel heard her mother's voice, "Rachel, love …"

"Breathe through your mouth," snapped Morgan. "Get a hold of your breath."

Her father said, "Let's give them some space Maureen."

"I'm her mother, I don't have to give her space."

"Maureen look at her!" her father snapped.

"Suck in the air, now exhale," said Morgan as he walked her over to a maple tree. "Through your mouth, try to get control of your breathing first … in … out … in … out." He took her hand and put it on his chest and breathed with her. "That's it, nice and easy."

Behind the tree, there was a small half-hearted stone wall. Rachel rushed to it throwing herself over the clump of rocks to be sick. She felt Morgan behind her, holding her hair, rubbing her back. When the lurch of her body stopped, embarrassed, Rachel whispered, "I'm better."

"Good girl." Guiding her back to the tree, Morgan said, "Sit down on the grass for a minute. Breathe through your nose now." He shouted across the field. "Anyone have water?"

She crossed her legs, her hands supporting her head; it felt like a thousand pounds. Within minutes, Morgan handed her a bottle. "Rinse," he said. She did as he said. "Drink." She did. "Here's some gum."

"Feel better?" he asked gently.

"Yes," she lied.

Morgan knelt in front of her and tilted her chin up, forcing her wounded eyes to meet his.

"No," she mumbled.

He touched her damp hair. "What goes on in that head of yours, I wonder?"

Rachel searched his brilliant eyes. "I don't even want to know, never mind sharing it with you."

"Is she better?" there was an edge to her mother's question.

"Yes," Morgan said, reassuring Maureen, reaching in his pocket for a handkerchief.

"She was fine this morning," Maureen accused as she looked at Morgan. "She's been out of sorts lately."

"It's just car sickness," Morgan said grimly, helping Rachel to her feet. She clung to him for support. Gently he wiped her tears before handing her his hanky. "I don't think sitting at the back of the truck is best Miss Rachel."

John Wharton held out his hand to Morgan. "Thank you for acting so quickly son. I nearly had heart failure when she walked into traffic."

"You and me both," Morgan laughed, shaking the older man's hand.

Morgan handed her two Gravol tablets and watched her take them.

"Come on." He was close beside her as they all turned back to the car.

The wedding party lined the side of the highway. Trucks and cars swished by as they waited patiently to continue their weekend. Guilt pressed down on her shoulders, making her hunch.

Morgan squeezed her hand and said, "No big deal."

***

At the truck, Morgan secured Rachel's seatbelt in the front seat. "We'll leave your window open a bit, okay?" He stared at her and she nodded. "Would you prefer to drive? I know that's better for you."

A slight shake of her head was all he got; she wasn't herself. Worry etched her beautiful face, prompting him to smooth his fingers along her furrowed brow. "If you need to stop again, we have time. You're more important." He wanted to linger, to scoop her up in his arms and dash into the forest with her, to live quietly, but eyes watched, people waited, obligation beat at his heels.

Morgan gazed into her vulnerable green eyes, large in her beautiful pale face, her skin almost transparent, and his heart seized. He bent his head and kissed her forehead tenderly; his hand cupped her soft cheek and then slid down to her warm curved neck. "Better?"

"Better."

Morgan pulled himself away from her and closed the door. He walked to the back of the truck; Morgan fell back against it and sank down on the bumper. He ground his teeth together, dropping forward to lean his forearms on his legs, his head falling into his hands.

When she jumped out onto the highway, staggering blindly, cars swerving to miss her, fear and panic had him screaming like a lunatic, fighting to get to her.

Christ!

***

Robert Hillier sat in the vehicle behind Morgan's Escalade watching his son struggle for control. He knew the feeling—well. He turned to stare at John. John nodded, understanding.

He looked at Morgan—poor bastard. He sighed. *Morgan has no idea what he's in for. She's her mother's daughter all right and she'll twist that young man in knots before this plays out. To get this girl, he's going to feel the pain.*

Morgan was the man for his daughter, of that John was sure, but his beautiful daughter was confused; he could see it in her. The chemistry between them was undeniable—it had always been there—but there had been a change in the last year. Their history was complicating matters, more complicated than John had realized. Her hesitation—his hesitation said volumes. Having earned his battle scars with Maureen, he could only wish the young man luck. Morgan was a good man, determined. Best to let them figure it out.

Sarah Hillier patted Maureen's hand. "You okay?"

Maureen grasped her hands tightly together, her brow wrinkled. "I thought she was going to get hit."

John reached back to her. "I know honey, but he grabbed her in time."

"Why is Morgan sitting on the bumper?" said Sarah.

"He dropped something," said Robert. "John would you get the map out of the glove box. Let's get our bearings while he looks for his cell. We'll spread it on the dash."

Maureen said quietly, resting her head against the bucket seat. "Rachel has been through so much this past year. I know moving to

Ottawa is hard, but it's a good opportunity."

Sarah offered, "I think it's harder because things have changed between her and Morgan."

"What do you mean?"

"I know it started long before she left for Ottawa," said Sarah, elegantly sliding back against the leather seat. "Since she came back from Paris it's been slow but steady. That trip to Allen Beach when she came back, it was the first time I had seen him smile in years." Sarah remembered the exact moment. "But it started long before then." Sadness filled her face.

"What started?"

Sarah shook her head, whispering to herself. "That awful day— I saw it. Heard what they were trying to say to each other between the hateful words." A sheen of tears gathered in her eyes. "My poor boy, his defences were down. He couldn't stop himself when I slapped her."

Maureen looked at her friend. "Who did you slap? What trip to Allen Beach?"

"Before he bought the cottage ..." Sarah's confusion at the question was evident. "Oh yes, sorry got caught up in ... yes, yes when Rachel came back from Paris ... Morgan and Emily had just got divorced." She lifted her hand, thinking back. "Macy was a newborn."

Maureen sat forward. "Where was I?"

"I don't remem—oh wait you and John went to England to visit your family. Remember, just before the summer ended?"

Robert rustled the map. "This was bound to happen. I agree with Sarah; they've been working toward it for years. We should stay out of it."

"There's nothing really to stay out of. They're very good friends, I understand that, but—"

"Come on Mo," Sarah laughed, "they're in love. Have been for a long time, but her age has been a factor."

Maureen shook her head. "Rachel is very fond of Morgan and she loves Macy but ... she hasn't mentioned that they are dating."

"Certainly not officially. And certainly not to any of us. It *is* Morgan. Even as a boy, he was secretive. He probably doesn't want the newspapers to get a whiff after the Emily fiasco."

"I was asked yesterday if she was back with Rick Summerhill. I haven't had a chance to talk to her yet."

Sarah shrugged. "I know what Stephanie is saying, but it's wishful thinking."

"Rick is a nice man." Robert said wearily. "This is going to get a helluva lot more complicated."

"She didn't want to go to Ottawa, that much was obvious," said Sarah.

Concern marred Maureen's clear complexion as she sat back and turned to her best friend. "Rick is trying to help her adjust to Ottawa and the new job. I know it's difficult, but she'll adjust. She adjusted to Western and Paris. Ended up staying an extra year."

Sarah avoided Maureen's eyes. "She isn't just *very fond* of Morgan. They've been spending as much time together as they can. She comes home every weekend. I must admit Rick does complicate things. He seems quite smitten with her and from what his mother says, never really got over her. Do you know why they broke up?" Sarah looked at Maureen.

"No, the four of us were in Chicago and Gary was on the scene by the time we returned," Maureen said grimly. "One thing *is* for certain; Ottawa is good for Rachel. I know she didn't want to go so soon after she came home, neither did I, but she loves teaching, and this is a great opportunity. She wants to finish what she started. It isn't a mistake accepting a great opportunity." Half to herself she whispered, "It isn't a mistake. I understand she's fond of Morgan, but Morgan is an extremely busy man with many obligations. Rachel is just a girl—still immature and impulsive. Hardly the kind of person Morgan is looking for with his ready-made family."

Sarah's head snapped round to look at Maureen when John said, peeking discreetly around the edge of the map. "Morgan's on his way over here."

"I think we should stay out of it," said Robert.

"She *is* my daughter, Robert," Maureen snapped.

"That hasn't been lost on me, Maureen. I didn't say stop mothering her, but they are both adults and they don't need us meddling in their love lives. The closeness of our families already complicates this. We need to let it be and if they come to us for help—we listen."

"I think you're right, Robert," agreed John. "Best to stay out of it."

"I do, too," said Sarah.

Maureen nodded reluctantly. She rubbed her forehead with cold fingers.

Sarah watched Maureen. "You okay, hon?"

She smiled. "Yes of course ... I'm a little distracted."

Robert opened the window and Morgan said, "Shawn says it's another hour."

"Straight ahead," said Robert showing his son where they were, running his finger along the highway to the cut-off. "Turn right then left into the Gables'."

Morgan nodded, returning to the truck without a word.

***

After eight that morning, the sky bright, the convoy of cars pulled into The Oaks Resort, then veered to the left and drove along a private road to the Gables' house. Rachel gasped at the beauty of the rambling log cabin nestled against six acres of forest. To the right was Rosseau Lake.

The Gables greeted them warmly. The front of the house had a sitting room with a spectacular marble fireplace as the centrepiece. A study was at the far-right corner. At the back of the house, a games room, complete with gadgets, brought cheers from the men, and a generous kitchen connected to a beautiful solarium with a lake view. Separated from the kitchen by carved wooden pillars, was a dining room with the largest harvest table Rachel had ever seen. Everything was elegant but casual. The staircase was in the centre of the room, which led to what the Gables called the loft. The loft had seven bedrooms. The Folks each had a room, the bridesmaids were in one, groomsmen in another, Jason and Carrie had a room, the three kids bunked together in Shawn's room, Morgan and Shawn had the game's room, and Elaine and Rachel requested they share the pull-out couch in the sitting room right beside the fireplace, to leave more room for the bridesmaids.

The Gables had planned a day filled with fun events. While the women were at Elaine's shower, the men entertained themselves with an obstacle course, tug of war, canoe race, and horseshoes. After their luncheon, the women went outside to watch just as Morgan was dubbed star athlete. He received an outstanding achievement award that included a certificate and a very, very tiny silver cup.

Morgan caught Rachel's gaze. She put her hand over her heart and mouthed, "My hero." He gave her a wink and a laugh.

"Does the star athlete want a kiss?" Shawn joked, his arms stretched out to Morgan, but Shawn's cousin Helen, who worked at the resort, a pretty blond with a voluptuous figure who handed out the prizes, took Shawn's remark as a personal invitation. She knocked Shawn out of the way and wrapped herself around Morgan, yanking his head down to her lips.

Rachel froze. From a great distance, she heard male cheering. The mug of hot chocolate she held slipped from her fingers, crashing onto the snow-covered grass, splashing her pants and boots. She was oblivious to the sting of the hot liquid as she watched the woman's long red fingernails working through Morgan black hair. She was tall and her body curved into Morgan's in all the right places.

Needing a distraction, Rachel reached down to wipe the hot chocolate off her pants and boots with her mittens.

"Love," said her mother, taking the mittens out of her hands, "we should soak your slacks before they stain."

Rachel straightened. "Does chocolate stain?"

Maureen Wharton smiled broadly at her daughter. Her mother's strawberry blond hair framed her beautiful complexion, speckled with freckles—the map of Ireland on her face.

She put her arm through Rachel's, steering her in the direction of the house. "It's lovely here," her mother said, pouring on the Irish, that casual yarn-like way she had; saying something, but not quite. "Peaceful, but I don't think I'd fancy being so isolated. I know the resort is full of people, but they are on vacation—just passing through. From what I understand, the closest people outside of the family are quite a bit down and over. The Gables have been here over a hundred years. Quite remarkable, isn't it? The whole family lived within ten kilometres of the resort. Even her side has moved here."

Mother and daughter strolled through the green grass, laced with snow here and there. Rachel liked listening to her mother's soothing tone. "Quite a day, wouldn't you say, Rachel love? The Gables are lovely people. Elaine has made a wonderful choice in Shawn. Such a nice man."

"Isn't Elaine what men look for?" asked Rachel.

"What's that, darling?"

She glanced at her mother. "Elaine isn't just beautiful and smart; when Elaine speaks everyone holds their breath, waiting to hear what she says. She's a woman of repose. Not like me, a headcase bouncing from one unfinished thing to another."

Her mother stopped in her tracks and turned to search her daughter's sad eyes. "You and Elaine have always been very different, maybe that's why you're friends." She framed Rachel's face. "You're a bright star, so full of life and fun, and laughter—and to your father's dismay, you attract men like honey."

"Elaine attracted the right one," said Rachel.

"You never want to attract the right one." Her mother tilted her head slightly. "Has that changed?"

Rachel ignored the question. "I don't understand men."

"Me either, but I sure do like *watching* men." Her mother's musical laughter lifted to the tall trees. "I like watching them strut their stuff to impress the womenfolk. Did you see your father today?" She threw her daughter a fanciful glance. "It does my heart good that he still wants to show me his biceps. And you know what, my darling? I still get a thrill when he does."

"Too much information."

"Don't be silly—I'm not dead."

"Mum … how did you know Dad was the one?"

"I didn't, not a first, but he did. I wanted to have fun, go to the dance, chum around with my mates, travel to exotic places. And then this gorgeous brawny young man with hazel eyes, an easy smile, and a cocky attitude walked into my life. All the girls were after him. Of course, he completely ignored me while he made the rounds. It infuriated me. I attracted the honey in my younger day, too."

Rachel laughed; her mother still attracted the honey. "So, what happened?"

"He taunted me relentlessly. Told me I was shallow and needed a strong hand. I thought he was applying for the job and made a scathing remark that his interest was unwelcome. He calmly told me he wasn't interested in taming a selfish little bitch."

"Daddy said that?"

"That and much, much more, in one of our battles of wills, and there were many battles, but when he finally kissed me, to say he knocked me for six is an understatement."

"Then you knew?"

"Absolutely not. It took me a while to figure things out. I was stubborn. Not intentionally, I was frightened. Mostly, I hated wanting him or needing him. I didn't want to be like my mother."

"You never talk about your mother."

"We weren't close. She wasted her life on a layabout man like my father. But, in her books, he was the cat's meow. She put him ahead of us—she ran herself ragged trying to please him. His drinking and gambling put us in the poor house and put her into an early grave. Poor woman worked three jobs to pay his debts. He was like King Tut, gallivanting about town while she took care of all of us, the house, worked, tended her mother. And she stayed with him to the bitter end. He mellowed as he aged but I didn't care. He was a selfish bastard."

"So, needing Daddy, wanting to be with him was …?"

Maureen paused, nodding to herself. "A sign of weakness." She laughed, but her face twisted. "Good God, what that man has put up with as a result. Even though John is nothing like my father, he's had to pay for everything that old fart ever did. That he stuck around? Most men would have given up." A sad gloom filled her mother's face. "You know that saying—you are what you eat?"

Rachel nodded.

"Be careful, my darling," she whispered. "You are what you hate as well."

For the first time Rachel saw heart-breaking sadness on her mother's face. "I've never seen two people so in love as you and Daddy."

Her mother blinked rapidly. "Loving someone is very scary stuff."

Once upon a time, loving Morgan had been easy.

"Your father told me he knew I was the one the minute he saw me. It was two years before we became an item. I needed to grow up, he said, and he was right, but I could very easily have made a mistake."

"How?"

"I didn't stand still long enough to find out what I wanted before I was moving on to the next thing." Her mother pushed open the Gables' front door. "That's why I'm so proud of you. You're the first person in my family to finish university and teacher's college, and now you're a teacher. I hate that you're so far away." Her mother frowned. "Forget I said that."

Rachel's heart sank. She hugged her mother. "I'm glad you're proud."

Her mother said in her ear. "What's this I hear about Rick Summerhill?"

She frowned. "What do you hear?"

"That you're dating him."

"He's a wonderful man."

"Is there any truth in what I hear?"

"I don't really want to talk about this Mother."

"Oh dear, you said 'Mother.' I haven't heard that in a while. Listen Rachel, you're a grown woman and I don't know what kind of a relationship you have with Rick, but it's not hard to see he's smitten with you. He obviously isn't over your break-up. And you must feel something for him? You went to Ottawa. Why not give it a chance?"

Her mother tucked her hair behind her ears. "You're there; he's there, you haven't dated anyone in a while. I know you and Morgan have always been good friends, but he's a man that comes with baggage—a divorced father with a small child. I know Emily hasn't been involved, but she's still Macy's mother. Losing James dried her up I think, but she could very well return and want to have a relationship with Macy. Or Macy with her. It's hard for a marriage to survive the death of a child, but to leave Macy the way she did, she may regret abandoning her. Things you do when you're young and foolish are regrettable when you've been out in the world a while. It can be exhausting being alone."

It is exhausting being alone, thought Rachel.

Her mother didn't pull any punches. "Are you on birth control?"

Rachel felt heat rise from her neck. "Mother."

Her mother stared at her for a long while and her blush deepened, unable to meet her mother's eyes. "Are you?"

"Yes," she lied, it seemed easier.

"Are you dating Rick?"

"No."

"What about Morgan?"

"I told you I don't want to talk about this," she whispered softly. Knowing how her mother felt, it was impossible to be honest, so it was best to remain silent.

"Men have very fragile egos. It could get messy."

"Mother you obviously want to tell me something, so tell me."

"I don't want you to feel pressured into doing anything you don't want to. There's no rush here, no timetable. And don't," her mother hesitated, "don't let your childhood affection for Morgan misguide you into thinking it's something it's not. You could end up losing ten years and throwing away something wonderful with Rick or with someone else who comes along. Give yourself time."

"You don't like Morgan, do you?"

"Don't be silly, of course I like Morgan." Maureen took off her coat in one fluid movement as always and tossed it over the armchair. "After that nastiness in London, gravitating to him for comfort was natural. He's older, he's familiar, he's the big brother you never had, and more than likely, he's become accustomed to giving you advice, of guiding you along the way, but you are a very capable young woman. Well educated, well-travelled, wealthy in your own right, and his influence is not as necessary as it was when you were younger. He may have difficulty accepting that—possibly jealous of other men having a place in your life. It's natural."

Rachel's heart pounded. She braced herself. "You were very concerned for him when he was married to Emily—empathic even."

"That was a horrible situation," Maureen said coolly, in control. "Not one I would wish on anyone."

"You just don't think I should be involved with him?"

Maureen's stare was direct. "No, I don't think he's the right man for you. You're naive in comparison to a man like Morgan. His baggage is deep—a son that died, a failed marriage, an ex-wife who could show up at any time, a little girl who will want to know her mother at some point; you shouldn't have to deal with that at your age. Childhood issues and learning to cohabitate with a man you love are enough for any young couple to deal with but Morgan has had to deal with very serious issues. And you have no idea the effect that has left on him."

Rachel looked away. Her chest hurt. "I think I'll have a shower."

"You do that darling. Use our bathroom."

18

RECEPTION

The hot spray from the shower felt good. It mingled with her tears. Little miss pretty body wrapping herself around Morgan on the Gables' makeshift podium bothered Rachel—a lot. Morgan was a grown man. He could kiss who he liked. Rachel ran the shower gel down her body, reminding herself how she felt when Morgan touched her. A passionate woman, he called her. Said she should stop burying her sexuality—that she was afraid of risking anything of herself. Sadly, that didn't seem to be the case when it came to Morgan. Rachel abandoned common sense in his presence. She wanted him; she begged him with her body. Was it just because there was no danger with Morgan? He was familiar. Safe. He would never take advantage of her. He would always have affection for the little girl who ran to him crying. But Morgan was a man with needs. He was lonely. Last night, there was no mistake; he wanted a wife and a family in his future. Rachel's heart contracted with pain. Morgan was looking for someone to fill the void in his life. He was ready for something more permanent. Macy was older. More independent. Obviously, he didn't want it to be Rachel or he would have made a move in that direction.

And what if her mother was right? What if Emily came back? Naturally, Macy would want to know her. She would intrigue Macy, a jet-setting journalist who went on fantastic adventures. Emily had certainly become exciting since she and Morgan broke up. Rachel saw her on Global, Newsworld, CNN, and the BBC, standing on war-torn hills, dodging bullets, taking risks. There was no way even the narrow little piece Rachel had carved out with Macy would sustain a cool celebrity mother.

Rachel had to accept the obvious road signs in her life. Morgan's interest was sexual. Casual. How many ways did he need to articulate that? If Rachel were honest with herself, she would see the glaring truth. Morgan was a mature, sophisticated man, a business leader, well respected, intelligent, elegant, sexy, handsome. He made Rachel's heart pound at the very sight of him, what affect did he have on other women? The answer was obvious, the same affect. As her mother was fond of pointing out, Rachel was young, inexperienced, naive in comparison to Morgan. Was an impetuous, immature, pain in the ass girl from next door really what he wanted? Morgan could have his pick. Wasn't she just a leftover obligation from his boyhood? Someone he enjoyed. She was the girl in between wife one and wife two. The girl right now. It was ridiculously obvious.

Her mother could see it. She was just telling it like it is, and that's why she wasn't supportive of Rachel having a relationship with him. She knew Rachel was the in-between girl.

She stopped the shower.

She wasn't going to think about Morgan anymore. She was exhausted; she'd been exhausted for years.

Patting herself dry, she put lotion on her warm skin and combed out her tangled hair. Last night, she completely lost herself in Morgan. She threw herself at him, tried to charm him out of his loneliness. She had charmed him out of his dark moods before; not like yesterday. Yesterday, she pressed herself into him, distracting him with different needs. She wanted him to want her, wanted him to say she could make it better.

She was a *sad sack* who was completely devoted to him. Idiot! Not coming home last weekend made the week an eternity; she missed him. Several times last night, she woke to find herself snuggled in his arms, and she was goofy happy because she wasn't trapped in her other life, away from him.

Maureen sat in the armchair reading a magazine when Rachel came out of the shower; a royal blue outfit lay out on the bed.

"I bought it for you," her mother said brightly, pointing to the sweater and pants. "I saw this in Holts last week and thought it would be perfect for you." She was off the bed and walking to the bathroom. "I'm off for a shower."

A beautiful cashmere sweater and matching fitted virgin wool pants lay on the bed. When Rachel tried them on, immediately, she felt self-conscious. The sweater had a deep rounded neck; the soft fabric clung to her generous breasts and narrow waist. The pants tailored neatly to the curve of her hips; the side zipper accentuated her flat stomach. The outfit was gorgeous. The royal blue colour was flattering against her pale skin and strawberry blond hair, but it displayed every curve and dip of her figure. Rachel liked baggy sweaters and tops of late, loose jeans or track pants; she rarely wore anything so tailored—so revealingly tailored—except for the outfit she'd wore to travel home in yesterday. But the minute she was inside the Hilliers' house and around so many new people, she changed into her bulky white cabled sweater that went to her knees—one of Morgan's old cast offs—and jeans.

"What's wrong?" asked her mother.

Rachel whipped around from the full-length mirror guiltily. "It's beautiful. I love the colour."

"But?" her mother prompted.

Rachel stared back at the full-length mirror. "It's clingy."

"It shows what God gave you. You're always hiding your assets under too many clothes lately," tutted her mother, crossing the room to her daughter.

"But my ..." Rachel's hands moved around the perimeter of her breasts.

"Love, you come from a long line of busty women. Fighting it is senseless. You have a gorgeous figure and the colour is spectacular on you."

Doubtful, Rachel said, "I don't know, Mum."

"I'm your mother," Maureen said, heading back to the bathroom. "I wouldn't steer you wrong. Plus, it's just family. A good time to take it out for a spin."

Morgan had said she buried her sexuality. If she wore this, there would be no room to bury anything. The conservative dress she'd brought didn't hold a candle to this understated but elegant outfit.

Would Morgan like it? She studied herself in the mirror. She smiled, deciding to keep it on. She applied her makeup carefully and slipped on the pearl headband Macy had given her last Christmas to hold back her mass of curls. She had decided not to straighten her hair. Morgan had given her a short strand of pearls to match Macy's gift, which she secured around her neck, then stepped back to have a look.

Rachel's father came into the room. "Hello, my beauty."

Her mother emerged from the bathroom dressed to kill. John Wharton threw down his suit on the bed and let out a long whistle, grabbing his wife around the waist. Rachel saw her father whisper something to her mother, which brought a pretty blush to her cheeks. She wanted what her parents had. The rhythm, the need for each other, the warm tenderness—that's what it's like with Morgan, thought Rachel.

"Okay, okay, I'm leaving," she laughed.

Maureen Wharton said over her father's shoulder, "You look beautiful love."

"Like anyone will notice with you in the room," Rachel shouted back, envying the easy, graceful moves of her mother in the green silk dress that wrapped lovingly around her still girlish figure.

Maureen Wharton waved her hand like Rachel was talking nonsense.

Tiredness overwhelmed her as she quietly shut the door and briefly leaned against it. All her pent-up emotions had nowhere to go. She missed her girlhood bull sessions. Everything was talked out in those days. At great length. Problems solved. The unsolvable went into the laughing zone, but friendships were changing. Since Elaine's engagement to Shawn, her friend had drifted away; conversations were weak, unfulfilling. They used to talk about everything, anything. If their families weren't so close, Rachel doubted she would see much of Elaine. Her relationship with Louise Summerhill had changed. The Summerhills had a cottage about five kilometres down from Morgan's place on River Road, but she hadn't seen Louise since she had her baby. Girlish traditions, like so many of Rachel's friends, had changed.

Everyone was to meet in the great room, but when she reached the bottom of the stairs, there was only Macy, sitting primly on a cushioned stool. She was dressed in a red velvet dress, white leotards and patent leather black shoes, with a silk red ribbon in her beautiful black curly hair. Her little legs were crossed and her hands sat folded on her knee. Rachel's heart stopped. A pain ripped through her chest knocking the breath from her. Love and pain overwhelmed her at once as she stared at the beautiful little girl. Rachel sat down on the top step of the small landing at the bottom of the stairs.

"My baby girl is so grown up," Rachel cried in a soft whisper. "You're so beautiful." She held out her arms and Macy eagerly jumped into them, knocking Rachel back.

Rachel held Macy tightly, kissing her incessantly, afraid to let her go. "I remember the first time I held you. You were two days old and fresh to the world. I had never seen such a beautiful baby. Now you're a beautiful young lady."

"Auntie Rachel!" laughed Macy.

"I'm allowed to gush." Rachel framed her little face, capturing every detail to memory. Macy's steady, deep, blue eyes stared back at her. Long black lashes fluttered up at her, the kind women kill for. She looked like Morgan. Macy was so familiar, so peaceful. Rachel could feel Macy's peace reach out to her and heal the hurt inside her body. "You're the image of your father," Rachel whispered, tears misting her eyes, and she yanked her into her arms again.

Macy's little arms wrapped around her neck and held her tightly. "Don't be sad, Auntie Rachel." Macy loosened her grip on Rachel and sat down on her knee. "Why don't you tell me a story about when I was a baby?"

Rachel laughed. Macy loved baby stories.

"A funny one," insisted Macy.

"Let me see, my favourite funny Macy story is ..." Rachel smiled. "Daddy decided to take us out to dinner." Rachel wrapped her arms around Macy, resting her head against the little girl's for a minute before continuing. "We bought you this cute white tuxedo with feet for the occasion. You looked precious."

Rachel played with Macy's curls with a loving hand. "Daddy and I had this routine where I would hold you so he could eat half his dinner then we would switch. I think you were one before we had a hot meal."

"How old am I in this story?" asked Macy.

"Eight months," said Morgan. Both Rachel and Macy looked up at him standing in front of them. He devastated Rachel in his dark suit.

"Sit with us, Daddy," encouraged Macy, a happy smile on her face, and he sat down beside Rachel.

"It was Daddy's turn to hold you first, but you were having a fussy day, so to amuse you, Daddy ..." Rachel concentrated with difficulty on the story. Memories flood her mind. Morgan's enthusiastic face as he bounced his baby girl. Unable to resist, Rachel glanced up at him.

Morgan smiled down at her and her heart fluttered. He bent his head and kissed her forehead; his hand smoothed down her back to stop at the curve of her hip where it met with the stairs landing and stayed there.

"Daddy bounced you up and down on his leg." Rachel turned back to Macy so she could focus. "You loved it, squealed with glee. Then it happened." She jostled the little girl from side to side, then stopped, and held her tightly, "Daddy stopped bouncing—only to discover you had done a huge constitution for Canada in your diaper."

"What's a huge constinewsion for Canada?"

"A big fat pooh," said Morgan.

"And it was all over Daddy's pant leg. And the smell! It was terrible. We washed you down in the bathroom, but we hadn't packed you a change of clothes, so we took you home in a blanket."

Macy and Rachel giggled together. "Daddy didn't take kindly to my laughing, but every time I saw that big, brown, wet spot on his pants, I couldn't help myself. Imagine Morgan Hillier with pooh pants. If the papers had got a hold of it!"

"What about my tuxsneedo?" asked a laughing Macy.

Regretfully, Rachel said, "It went into the bin, my darling, with Daddy's pants. Neither of us wanted that job."

Daniel burst into the room. "Hey Macy, come on," he said, his face animated. "The man gots a train. Come on." He dashed away.

Macy looked up at Rachel and Morgan, a plea in her eyes. "I promise not ta get messed up."

Rachel was sceptical. When she glanced at Morgan, the same charming plea was in his eyes. "She did promise," he said.

"Away you go," said Rachel, setting Macy on her feet, watching her scurry away.

"I had forgotten the diaper gush story," said Morgan's mother, walking further into the room with a glass of wine in her hand, a soft smile on her face.

Out of the corner of her eye, Rachel saw Morgan's long legs stretch out in front of him. Her hand itched to touch him. She was acutely aware of the powerful lean line of his muscular thigh pressed into hers, aware of his closeness, of his arm along her back, his hand sitting at her bum.

"Did you put it in her book, Rachel?" Aunt Sarah's quiet question made Rachel startle.

She licked her dry lips. "How could I not?" Rachel collected snippets of Macy's life in a mother's diary—a shower gift for Emily that she would never use. So, Rachel wrote the little girl letters in the diary, put in photographs. Rachel went a little crazy; obsessive you might say, with the pictures.

"You are wonderful with Macy," said Sarah thoughtfully. Her husband came in and sat down close to her on the sofa. "Whenever I think of the time you've spent with her, the summer vacations you gave up—just barely a baby yourself when you took to caring for her. It's the little things, the baby books, the tent parties that make the difference." Then she laughed. "Remember when you and Macy tried to bake cookies and nearly burnt Morgan's house to the ground."

Rachel and Morgan responded in unison. "Yes!"

"So many wonderful memories," said Sarah, her happiness suddenly replaced with harsh disapproval. "Thank God Macy's nothing like Emily."

The minute the words were out, Aunt Sarah regretted them and threw an apologetic look at Morgan, but he remained silent.

Rachel looked up at Morgan. "She could have been spiteful. She could have made things difficult for you." He filled her gaze. Her body naturally leaned into his. "Instead she did the right thing for Macy. She knew Macy was better off with you. She was gracious, there's something to be said for her being gracious."

Staring deeply into his eyes, Rachel held her breath when Morgan reached out; his finger twisted in one of her curls, and brought her face within inches of his. Their lips close, their breaths mingled, Rachel was locked into his tender intensity; it was unbearable.

Her mother rushing along the landing broke the spell. "Oh dear, are we the last one's?" Maureen Wharton hurried down the stairs with elegant grace. Her face flushed. "John's fault, of course,"

Rachel jerked back from Morgan and his hand fell from her hair. She wanted to avoid any further mother-daughter talks; finding Rachel in a passionate clinch with Morgan would spur that on. Rachel stood and moved away from the stairs, smoothing her immaculate pants, plucking at non-existent lint—desperate for something to do.

If Rachel did pursue a relationship with Morgan, even a casual one, her insecurities about Morgan coupled with her mother's disapproval would mean no chance of a happy conclusion. A rift between her and her mother was definite. Rachel's speculations that Morgan was only interested in a casual affair remain unconfirmed, so until she was sure, she should keep her distance. The problem was living up to her good sense. Anytime he was near her, she lost her judgment, and became liquid glow.

Mr. Gable strutted into the living room in a grey suit; a charming, handsome man was Mr. Gable. His guests gathered round. "It's time ladies and gents."

***

The Gables' resort was rich with dark wood panelling, heavy furniture, and the stiff quiet air that comes with tradition. Under the assumption that dinner included the wedding party and Shawn's immediate family, Rachel was disturbed when she walked through the double doors to find a champagne reception in full swing. The room was elegant but casual; deep comfortable armchairs and couches were scattered around the room. The adjacent ballroom was decorated with wedding trimmings, balloons, white rose centrepieces; none of which did anything to assuage her sudden claustrophobic feeling or how out of place she felt amongst the formally dressed crowd of a hundred or so of the Gables' family and friends. The minute the Hilliers were in the room, the guests pressed in on them. She let go of Morgan's hand as he greeted a strange man with a beard and cold eyes.

She stepped back.

She let go of Macy's hand, and Macy was pulled into the clutches of Mrs. Gable, "This is Elaine's niece Macy."

She heard Morgan say, "This is Rachel—" and then stopped when she was no longer at his side. He turned, but she couldn't look him in the eye.

She stepped back again.

Morgan was at her side, "Rachel?"

Her words rushed out as she concentrated on his blue tie. "I thought this was a small dinner party. No one told me. I'm not prepared. Why didn't you tell me?"

"I didn't know."

Something in his cavalier tone made her feel inadequate. "And yet you handle it so well," her gaze shot out to the crowd, watched The Folks be swallowed up, watched the wedding party mingle, taking it in stride. Rachel couldn't. Frightened by all the things she didn't know about the room, all the things she didn't know about the people in the room. *I guess I'm the only defective one here, then.* She started to shake. *I'm so sick of feeling this way! Like I'm some kind of mental case.* She walked away.

He fell in step with her. "If I could take the burden for you I would, but I can't, so you're going to have to be patient with yourself. Dr. Soldone told you it would take time, but you have to use the strategies she gave you. It might feel like it but the Gables didn't do this to hurt you or piss you off, they're excited that their only son is getting married and wanted to surprise us with this weekend and this party. I'm sorry you're upset, but she's my sister and he's my friend and I'm not going to miss it because you took on more than you can handle."

Affronted, she stopped to look up at him. "Go then."

Morgan's face was blank, remote. He turned and walked away. She watched him until he disappeared into the well-wishers. Everything he said was true, but it didn't change anything. She sighed, her head falling back on her shoulders. Dr. Soldone said it would take time. That Rachel needed to concentrate on doing her visualizations daily, the affirmations, stay away from news media for a while, do her breathing meditations ... all to cope. She had never been a person who was easily overwhelmed. Now the simplest things overwhelmed her. Adding to the difficulty, she never knew what triggered her. Getting on a plane was not a problem, but going to a grocery store with all its nooks and crannies was not possible. Too many things to do in a short time used to energize her. Now it made her want to go to bed. She never was an analytical type. Now she analyses everything and everyone, trying to decipher what their motives were, what it meant. Her thoughts altered. Rodney Horvat never did anything physical to her, but he changed her life. She felt exposed, as if a part of her had been taken from her, again, without permission.

"What ifs" drove her crazy. Oddly, the question wasn't—what if he had broken into the apartment and ... She didn't want to think about that. It was the what ifs of her daily life. What if I fall down the stairs? Crack my head and die? What if Morgan marries another woman that's not me, again? What if Macy loves this woman more than me? What if Emily comes back and wants to be Macy's mother? What if my parents die? What if I have a panic attack, walk out into the street, and get hit by a car? What if I take my eyes off Macy for a second and she's gone? Crazy things. Obsessive things. Dr. Soldone said it was normal to have fears and mortality issues.

Why doesn't it feel normal?

She slipped into a lobby chair and breathed deeply. She did have an obligation to Elaine. She could have backed out. Elaine asked her if she was up for it. And now the wedding was two weeks away. *Breathe deeply.* What did Morgan mean—"a fact I can't seem to get through my thick head?" He was complaining that she gave him a way out? She didn't want to drag him down with her. If anyone needed to have fun it was Morgan. He worked hard. His free time was with Macy and his family—her family too. Her heart started to race. *Breathe. In and out.* Morgan didn't want strings. Rachel wanted strings. But was it fair to expect him to deal with everything on his plate and her problems? *Breathe. In and out.* It wasn't fair. She loved him, but he didn't love her, rather, he didn't love her the way she loved him. *Breathe. Clear the mind. Breathe. In and out. In and out. Slowly. In and out.*

The buzz of the resort died away and her mind relaxed into quietness.

She dreamed her movie. Morgan was laughing, waving to her, "The water's great. Come in." She dove in off the raft and spouted up beside him. He kissed her, wrapping his arms around her, he twirled her quickly in the water and she squealed with laughter.

"Are you all right, Miss?"

Her eyes snapped open, staring up at a man who loomed over her, making her uncomfortable. "Ye—yes, thank you." *Breathe.* "Just getting a breather."

He stepped back and smiled. "Enjoy your evening."

"You too."

***

Rachel stepped cautiously into the crowded room breathing deeply. She slid passed the door to the panelled wall.

"There you are," said her mother as she put her arm around her shoulder. "This is my daughter Rachel," she said to the group she was chatting with.

Rachel didn't pay attention to their names just smiled appropriately and shook whatever hand her mother said to, while she breathed deeply. She glanced around the room for Morgan. He stood at the far side, the trophy giving blond in a black strapless cocktail dress chatted happily to him. Her hand managed to find its way onto his forearm with great regularity. They looked good together. He was dark, she was fair. Both tall. Her breasts were perfect—not too big, not too small. Small waist. Her hips were round, but not ill portioned to the rest of her body. Older. Early thirties like Morgan. No rings, she noticed—perfect. Stupidly, tears clouded her vision and she turned away, leaving her mother to charm the small crowd gathered around her.

"May I offer you some champagne?" asked a waiter.

"No, thank you." The last thing she needed was alcohol.

"If you don't like champagne, I can get you something else?"

She smiled at him. "I'm afraid I don't like the taste of alcohol, cabbage, or smelts."

He laughed. "Cabbage and smelts? I agree."

An elderly lady with a cane said, "I have no such trouble young man, or do you only serve the pretty ones."

He smiled at Rachel. "Excuse me."

She moved closer to the windows that ran the length of the wall. It was a lake view. The Gables had built a pier that stretched one hundred metres into the water. Lantern-like street lights were paced a metre apart, illuminating the pier with the help of a harvest moon.

"I could get you a Coke?"

Rachel turned to the waiter. "You are very kind. I'm fine, but I promise the minute I'm thirsty I'll track you down like a bloodhound."

He tapped his nameplate. "Gordie. You are?"

She smiled. "Rachel."

She turned back to the water; it looked black.

"Rachel love, we're going into dinner now." She saw her mother in the window. "Everything all right?"

She forced a smile. "Of course."

The wedding party sat near the family. Rachel was the first member to arrive at their table. She didn't know where Morgan was until he whispered in her ear. "I missed you."

"Really? That's a surprise." She slipped into the chair he held out for her.

"I'm sure you'll tell me why." He sat beside her. They were alone.

"It didn't look like you were wasting your time missing me, that's all."

Morgan slid his arm along the back of her chair, his other arm across the table in front of her. He faced her. Relaxed. He wasn't drunk but he'd had a few drinks. Whisky.

He smiled. "You don't think so? Why?"

She briefly glanced over at her mother. Maureen's back was to Rachel, so was her father's. None of the guests at the party were from the Hillier family. She threw a dismissive glare at Morgan. "You seemed quite enamoured with the trophy-giving blond. Since you're in the market for a woman to fill your empty house, she looks like a good candidate. Has all the right parts: beautiful, legs up to her armpits, blond, perfect figure, right age, spontaneous, and she's very interested in you."

"Jealous?" His breath was hot on her neck and her legs jittered as she watched the crowd settle into their seats.

"Would it matter if I was?"

"*Yes.*"

Rachel turned at his tone. His face twisted, like he hurt; his eyes were so blue they were dive-able. She couldn't look away. She sucked in her breath, exhaling with a tremble. Morgan was so close she felt his breath mingle with hers, so close but not touching, so close an electric charge hummed around them. She whispered, "Not jealous darling—envious."

"Jesus Christ," Morgan hissed, his head dropped slightly, drawing him closer to her.

She felt him tremble.

A groomsman joined them at the table. "I'm starting to feel sorry for you two."

The yakky bridesmaid from the drive up agreed. "Me too, but kudos, you manage to steal your moments and get it all in, even with the ancient bedroom arrangements."

Rachel and Morgan remained silent. Her eyes darted back to her mother as the rest of the wedding party sat down. Maureen was in deep conversation with a distinguished looking man at her table. Rachel turned to Morgan, grabbing the lapel of his jacket. "Morgan …"

His voice was heavy. "Yes."

"I'm sorry—about before," she whispered, moving her hand to his chest. He felt hot to her touch. "I *do* want your help. I just don't want you to feel like you don't have a choice. I don't want you to feel obligated to me out of some sense of—guilt."

"Never." His hand covered hers, lifting it to his lips.

"May I have everyone's attention …?"

Rachel reluctantly moved away from him and was glad that he too was reluctant to let her go.

The festivities began. But the evening was a blur of dinner, old movies, family speeches, and toasts.

***

Morgan laughed beside her; his full attention on the podium as Shawn retold the story of how he met Elaine. Rachel revelled in

Morgan's proximity. If Gary Kurfont was movie star material, Morgan was in a class by himself. She had never seen such a beautiful man. Now, when she thought of the games she had played with him, unwittingly, it seemed at the time, or rather, she'd never allowed herself to see how manipulative she was, but it made her cringe in her seat. Truth is a hard mistress because it has no relationship to what is *just* or *right*.

Everyone lifted their champagne glasses as Shawn toasted his bride to be. There was so much love in the room. Elaine elegantly crossed the space to him. Silent tears rolled down her pink cheeks. Shawn embraced her and her head fell softly onto his shoulder; her body curved into his. He whispered something in her ear. She lifted her head, her tears intensified and she pressed her lips to his jaw. The purity of their love was so evident, but then, this was the easy part.

Morgan looked at her. She smiled, clinking her glass with his.

School age tales and toasts to the bride and groom dominated the evening. Halfway through, Macy and her peeved little face made her way over to Rachel and perched on her knee. "When is it over?" She whispered. "Very soon."

Uncle Robert gave a special toast to his daughter and Jason had the entire room sniffling when he relived his own wedding day; ending with, "We've had our arguments," said Jason, and raised his glass to Shawn, "but makeup sex is well worth it."

Laughter broke out. Macy glanced up at Rachel, a confused look on her little face. "What's makeup sex Auntie Rachel?"

Rachel heard a few men around the table choke on their wine. Unflustered, she said, "Kissing." Satisfied, Macy ate her ice cream.

Morgan declared his deep abiding love for his sister and Shawn. The two men's long-time friendship had turned them into brothers; now it was official. From their university days to when Shawn went to work for Morgan the second year he was in business.

It was a happy evening. Elaine was radiant. Shawn couldn't keep his eyes off her. Mrs. Gable cried, which started Aunt Sarah off, and when Aunt Sarah was off to the races Rachel's mum was close behind. When the last anecdote for a happy marriage was given, the party dispersed into the lobby where everyone recited what a lovely time they'd had. At the far end of the lobby was a large, half-moon, mahogany bar with a lounge area. Comfortable overstuffed camel coloured leather chairs, love seats, and small round tables, sorted into large and small conversational clusters curved the bar. Through the exuberant goodbyes and promises to see everyone again at the wedding, Rachel didn't notice him at the bar, or the woman at his side.

"Hello, Rachel."

She whipped round at the sound of his voice. Shocked, she stared as he slowly made his way across the room, giving her time to pull herself together. "Fancy meeting you here?"

"Fancy indeed." He kissed her cheek.

"Rick!" bellowed Mr. Gable as he smacked Rick on the back.

"Hello, Mr. Gable." The two men shared a hardy handshake.

Rachel raised her eyebrows at Rick.

"The Gables," Rick explained, "are friends with my parents. I spent many summers here as a child."

"Even worked him during the summer," said Mr. Gable and then sighed. "What a small world. Obviously, you know Rachel. Do you know the Hilliers?"

"Yes sir."

"Are you're parents here?"

Rick said, "In the atrium."

"In the atrium? Well I must go and say hello."

"They will be pleased sir." The men shook hands again. Rachel finally noticed the woman standing quietly beside Rick; tall, dark, large brown eyes with the most exquisite lashes. A very pretty peaches and cream girl. And familiar.

Rick said, "This is Siobhan Reilly. Siobhan, Rachel Wharton."

Siobhan's brow was furrowed. "Have we met before?"

"I was just about to ask you the same question."

Morgan joined them; he slipped his arm around Rachel's waist. When he looked down at her, she could see he was feeling no pain. "Are you ready to go, Dollface?"

"Morgan Hillier!"

Morgan and Rachel both looked at the shocked pretty peaches and cream girl.

"Siobhan Reilly?" she said excitedly, pointing to herself.

"Siobhan Reilly." He smiled that winning smile. His arm slipped away from Rachel and moved toward the other woman. He kissed her cheek. Rachel noticed Rick's indulgent smile, and she wished she was that sophisticated.

Siobhan turned to Rick and laughed. "Morgan and I dated in university." Before giving Morgan her full attention. "What on earth are you doing here?"

"A party—my sister's getting married. And you?"

Rachel remembered her. She hadn't taken the break-up well. She always seemed to be around—not in a creepy way—she always managed to have a good reason to *be* around. It was as if she had an army monitoring Morgan's movements. She showed up wherever he was, in a casual, no pressure kind of way. She was very good at it.

"The Summerhills invited me and the kids up for the weekend."

"How many children do you have?" asked Rachel.

"Two—a boy who's seven and a girl who's five."

"Isn't your daughter five?" asked Rick.

"Just turned four," Morgan said politely.

Rachel was impressed with how civil they all sounded. "Your husband didn't come with you?"

"We're divorced." She shrugged. "You try and sometimes it doesn't work out. My children are the best thing that came out of my terrible marriage, without a doubt."

Morgan nodded. "I have to agree."

"You're divorced?" asked Siobhan.

Rachel could almost hear the other woman's mantra—*I wish, I wish, I wish.*

He nodded. "Four years ago."

Siobhan nodded in Rachel's direction. "How do you two know each other again?"

"They're best friends," Rick said, moving his hand to the small of Siobhan's back. "And we need to get going; the kids are going to hit the wall very shortly."

"Speaking of which …" Morgan said as his father came over to them, a limp Macy in his arms. "I'll take her, Dad."

"No … no … I've lost my little girl for sure—she's definitely marrying him after tonight. Can't you at least let me borrow yours?"

Morgan held up his hands. "She's all yours."

Maureen appeared out of nowhere, smiling prettily. "Hello, Rick."

"Mrs. Wharton."

"I'm heading back darling." Maureen manoeuvred herself between Rachel and Morgan and kissed her daughter goodnight.

Aunt Sarah joined them. "It's been a long day. I'm exhausted." She kissed Rachel and then turned to her son. He kissed her cheek. "I'll put Macy to bed sweetheart. Don't stay up too late."

"We'll be right behind you."

And the two older women left.

Morgan grabbed Rachel's hand.

"We're going too." Siobhan tucked her hand through Rick's arm.

Outside the manor house, they said their goodbyes. Rick and Siobhan headed for the garden where Mr. Gable was laughing with Mr. Summerhill and their two wives sat sedately on a nearby bench deep in conversation. Siobhan's two children tumbled and jumped in the moonlight—not a care in the world.

Rachel looked up at Morgan. "Imagine meeting Siobhan Reilly here? On the same night as Elaine's party? With Rick Summerhill no less? And his parents? And the Summerhills know the Gables to boot?"

Morgan walked backward, tugging at her hand to follow him. "A little too fantastic wouldn't you say?"

"Yes, I would."

19

UNSAID

Elaine and Rachel lay facing each other on the pull-out couch. Morgan and Shawn had taken the Gables' two Labrador retrievers for a walk.

"What a great evening," said Rachel.

Elaine smiled. "I never dreamed it could be this wonderful, Rachel. I want it to be this way for everyone." It was like they were little girls again, huddled together, sharing secrets. "It's like something you read in a book," she laughed.

"True love," said Rachel.

Elaine's eyes sparkled in the darkness. "True love."

"Have you slept with him?"

"Yes."

"Good, because you should never marry a man you haven't slept with."

Elaine laughed. "That's good advice."

"Do you remember Sonny Reeves?"

"Oh God!" Elaine hid her face.

"Oh God, is right," Rachel pushed her shoulder. "Aren't you glad you're not marrying him?"

"Can you imagine?"

"I wonder whatever happened to *the wild child*."

"Six years for drug dealing and a myriad of other charges," Elaine said.

"No!"

"Lived with Ariel Sental."

"The beauty queen?"

"She's not a beauty queen anymore," Elaine said in a singsong voice.

"What happened?"

"She had a couple of babies with Sonny; he dumped her, and then she let herself really go skid row, or so I hear."

They both howled with wicked glee.

Rachel flopped back on the bed. "She was *such* a bitch!"

"What goes around comes around."

Rachel looked at Elaine. "Do you believe in karma?"

"I've never really thought about it—but yeah, I guess I do. Why?"

Regret was in Rachel's voice. "You know, regrets, things I'm not proud of."

"We've all done things we're not proud of, but I think there's a vast difference between adolescent stupidity and intentional harm. Ariel tried to ruin lives. She was too shallow to even be selfish. She was just mean. There's no comparative study."

Rachel rolled onto her side. "What do you regret?"

"Sonny Reeves."

"Really?"

"He was my first. Talk about adolescent stupidity. He may have looked good on the outside, but he was a controlling, abusive bastard."

"I remember you telling me you loved him." Rachel shook her head. "I never liked him."

Elaine's face twisted in remembered pain. "You have good instincts. Make sure you listen to them. I was stupid. I believed he was the one. Convinced myself. I excused his bad behaviour when he called me a whore because he was really, really sorry afterward. I told myself—it's not like he *hits* me; everything *else* is so wonderful—

at least when he's not accusing me *of fucking every guy I meet* and calling me a *liar* and a *slut*."

She put her hand over her eyes. "God how stupid was I? Well, he didn't hit me, but mental abuse is okay, right? I kept telling myself—we have so much in common, but we didn't, we had geography in common."

"I'm so sorry Laine, I had no idea."

"No one did. That was part of the plan." She looked at Rachel. "I always admired you, Rachel."

"*You* admired *me*?"

Elaine's expression was earnest. "You never took shit from anyone. You had all these dating rules and if anyone stepped out of line, you cut them from your list. Guys you cut would beg me to talk to you—to give them another chance." Elaine laughed. "You had a book. Do you remember Stance Makin?"

"*Oh yes.*"

"He begged me and begged me to talk to you. I knew he was spreading rumours and choking you out of parties, so I refused, but he hounded me. Said it was all a misunderstanding, that he wasn't behind the rumours and the social suicide plan ... I relented and agreed to at least talk to you."

Elaine looked solemn. "I remember going to your room. You were lying on your bed doing homework. I'd even prepared a speech. You listened, and then pulled out this blue book and flipped to his name. You told me you couldn't reinstate him. He was cut from the list for archaic male bullshit. When I looked down at the book, right beside his name was possessive/obsessive, drama queen, forceful/violent, archaic male bullshit. It's imprinted in my mind. I couldn't believe it," laughed Elaine. "When I asked how you were doing with the rumours and stuff—I will never forget it—you said, 'Sorry Laine, I don't do insecurity,' and gave me a big smile."

"Oh God, what a liar I am. I was so insecure."

"Then I want your kind of insecurity."

"Oh, stop it."

"It *inspired* me to break up with Sonny the next day."

"You made the right decision and soon you will marry the love of your life, so it all worked out."

She nodded, her face sad. "But the insecurities never seem to go away, do they?"

"What do you mean?"

Elaine's eyes sparkled in the gloom. "Shawn is my soul mate. I know people make fun of that stuff, but I've dated enough to know that finding someone who fits in all the right ways is—a magical find. It's easy to make a mistake." Sadness assaulted her radiance. "I've never loved anyone the way I love him. I wish we had met earlier. I wish he had been my first love, my first time, then she—"

"She?"

"She wouldn't be his first love."

Rachel reached out for her hand and Laine grabbed on. Obviously, this weighed heavily on her mind, so Rachel waited.

"She's a doctor. Beautiful." Laine shuttered. "Macy had just been born and I went to see her at the hospital. Doctor Beautiful was in the lobby having a very deep conversation with a very attractive man. I noticed them because they were noticeable. It wasn't until Shawn sauntered into Emily's room twenty minutes later, and Morgan introduced him, that I recognized him from Morgan's grad days, and it took me off guard."

"Why?"

"He definitely caught my attention in the lobby—heart-stopping attention. That had never happened to me before, and then he walked into my niece's room? It was a *wow* moment."

She shrugged, shaking her head. "But he was unavailable. I could see that in the lobby. They looked good together. They didn't touch or yell or anything, but it was intimate between them—deep. They moved in unison or something—like dancing partners."

Elaine's story was very different from the one Shawn had told this evening. "And?"

"After I finished at Western, I went to work for Morgan. By then, Shawn worked there too. He asked me out, but I said no."

Rachel was hooked. "Why?"

Elaine pushed back her hair, melancholy on her pale face. "Getting involved with a man who is in love with another woman …" Her words lingered in the air.

"Did you tell Shawn why you refused to go out with him?"

Elaine nodded. "With a great deal of pleasure. Of course, he said I was wrong, that when I saw them together, they had just broken up and she was holding his stuff hostage. He said she was controlling and selfish. But I saw them together Rach—there was unfinished business."

"Did he keep asking you out?"

"Yes."

"And he didn't ask the doctor to marry him, he asked you, right?"

Rachel could feel her old friend holding her breath, hoping her worse fear, would never become known. She nodded. "No guts no glory, right."

"Right."

"So, Miss Rachel … What have you done that you're not proud of?"

"Good Lord, you'd get bed sores listening to my regrets."

"I just spilled my guts. Give me something."

"Okay, okay, you gut spew-er you … Well, my first regret was my first *time*—big mistake. Terrible. I'm surprised I didn't become celibate."

"That's your regret?"

"I see you want a whopper regret. My bag of regrets is deep and long. My big regret is, while I was dating Rick Summerhill, I cheated on him with Gary Kurfont."

"*No!*"

"I don't want to make excuses for myself but—I was eighteen, away from home for the first time, and Rick and I had a terrible relationship. I broke all my own rules with him. We fought all the time. He was jealous of Morgan and he didn't want us to be friends. It was a pressurized situation and I couldn't lie, pretend everything was okay, and have sex with him. My first sexual relationship was so terrible I promised myself, if the orchestra wasn't playing, there was no vagina penetration."

Elaine howled. "You kill me, Rach."

"Killing was definitely on Rick's mind when he found me with Gary, naked on his couch."

"*Oh my God!* You cheated on him in his apartment?"

"Yeah, that was a bad idea too," she sighed.

"On his couch?"

"Well kind of all over the apartment."

"You've got balls, I'll give you that."

"Adolescent stupidity."

"What did Rick say? Do?"

"He didn't say anything. He just beat the shit out of Gary. Regret 347."

"Is that when you went to Paris?"

"Shortly after." She bent her head. Shame overwhelmed her. "And we come to regret number one—hurting Gary." She bent your head. "He came into my life exactly when I needed him. Everything was falling apart and he showed up. He was a wonderful lover, a wonderful friend and I did love him; I will always love him, but when I left, I was gutless. He told me he loved me and I ran. I know I hurt him. What makes it all so horrible and seedy is I know he forgave me because he loved me, too."

"If you loved him, why did you leave?"

"It's complicated," she whispered. "Trust me Laine, there's nothing about me for to you to admire."

The grandfather clock behind them ticked loudly.

"Rachel, I know something's been troubling you these days. Ever since you took the job in Ottawa ... even before."

Rachel flipped onto her back. "I'm just tired."

Elaine sighed deeply. "I know I've been distracted with Shawn and the wedding ..."

Remorse prompted Rachel to interrupt her friend's apology. "This is an important time for you. You *should* be distracted with Shawn and the wedding."

"That doesn't mean you're less important." Elaine sat up on her elbow, reluctance in her voice. "This is none of my business, so tell me to shut up if you want, but what about Morgan? I see how it is between—"

Rachel shook her head. "I can't talk about Morgan." She didn't want to hear Elaine's observations. As it was, Rachel could barely think coherently about Morgan never mind *talk* coherently about him.

Elaine whispered in the darkness, reaching for Rachel's hand and holding it tightly. "You seem unhappy in Ottawa."

Rachel pushed herself into a sitting position, restless. "It's tough being away, but I can't quit. Besides, I always check out when things get tough. I'm trying something new."

"That's not true. You're always trying new things. I wish I were half as brave as you. If taking the safe way was an Olympic sport, I'm gold metal material—I mean come on, I work for my brother."

Rachel wrapped her arms around her legs, her eyes clouded as she stared at the dark fireplace. It struck her how incomplete a field of vision is. "I'm not brave, Laine."

"How can you say that? You've been—"

Rachel stopped her. "I'm not; I feel like I'm back where I started six years ago—caught in circumstances beyond my control."

Elaine ran her arm along Rachel's shoulder. "What circumstances?"

Rachel rubbed her forehead against her knees. "God, nothing changes while everything changes constantly."

"Rachel, I've wanted to—" Elaine pulled Rachel's head up so she could see her face.

Rachel smiled weakly. "I'm grumpy ... don't pay any attention. I haven't been sleeping very well."

"And it's my fault you're flying back and forth between Toronto and Ottawa."

Rachel patted her hand. "That's not true. You're getting married. You're starting a new life with Shawn, and I wouldn't miss this for the world. Besides, new starts seem to be in the air. Morgan tells me he wants to start a new life, too ... wants to get married again, find a mother for Macy." Bitterness cut through her good intentions. "And I'm starting a new life in Ottawa. Morgan said I should enjoy it, enjoy my youth. Maybe I should follow his advice."

Elaine's tone was soft, pleading. "Rachel."

"I'll be out of everyone's way." She felt quite sorry for herself. "Really, it's worked out well; I would never have applied for the job in Ottawa if Rick hadn't suggested it, but it seems it was for the best. Maybe there *is* a reason for everything," Rachel shrugged. "With Morgan scouting around for new talent, I'd just be in the way. None of his girlfriends ever like me."

"I think you should come home." Elaine grabbed her hand.

"I've made commitments, Lainey," said Rachel, "to the school, to the kids, to Rick. I promised him after your wedding I would at least give Ottawa a chance. This teaching position is a wonderful opportunity for me. Plus ..." *Don't say it; don't say it*, "Rick wants me in his life."

"*Honey,*" there was urgency in Elaine's tone, "do what's right for *you*. Whatever you want, whatever you decide we'll support you. We don't want you to be away. We love you! Regardless what is going on in our lives. We love you!"

The front door clicked and Morgan and Shawn came in. The two men stood in the front hall to finish their conversation; it ended in suppressed laughter.

"This is just between us, right?" Rachel whispered, regretting her words.

"Of course."

Rachel flopped down on the bed and buried her face in her pillow, wrenching the duvet up to her chin, and tucking her head in as much as possible.

A lamp snapped on.

"I can grab the couch in my dad's study," said Shawn. "Morgan take the games room."

"What? You don't want to share with me? I'm hurt. And me being athlete of the day and everything."

Shawn's soft laughter carried him to Laine's side of the bed. "Hey, you sleeping, sweetie?" whispered Shawn, the bed shifting with his weight.

"No," Elaine whispered back.

Rachel squeezed her eyes shut. Concentrating on not moving, concentrating on not making a sound. A hand ran down her tense back and she jumped, holding the sheet tighter.

"Rachel?" Morgan sounded concerned.

"Yes?"

Morgan tugged at the covers but she wouldn't let go and he didn't fight her for them, and her grip loosened. "What's wrong?"

Her insides collapsed at his soft, tender tone. "I don't feel so good. My stomach hurts. It must be that onion sauce at dinner."

Morgan yanked down the covers. Rachel hid her face with her

hand, looking through the spaces between her fingers. "It's too bright."

"Why don't you two take the game room," Morgan said.

Shawn said to Elaine. "Come on, my beauty, I can show you my big screen TV."

Morgan sat down on the bed. "What's up?"

"Just girl talk." Rachel shrugged. "How everything is going to be different with Laine and me."

"They are going to be different, but different isn't bad, is it?"

"It's just sad."

"It is sad. You still have me, but I'd make a terrible girlfriend."

Rachel laughed. "I can't imagine you discussing the perils of womanhood."

He laughed and slapped her bum. "Just remember that." He walked to the other side of the bed and dropped his duffel bag down. She watched him strip down to his boxers, pull-on track pants, tuck the bag under the pull-out, and snap off the light.

When he slipped into bed beside her, she said, "This is a bad idea."

"Tell me about it." His arm snaked out and pulled her into his chest. "Turn over."

She did and snuggled into him, spoon style. His arm casually hugged her waist, his chin rested on the top of her head.

"I'll wake up early tomorrow," said Morgan. "I sleep better when you're near."

"Me too," she whispered, "but we don't have an alarm clock."

"I haven't slept past six in my life."

The tight anxiety in her chest eased. Morgan's steady breathing quieted her chaotic emotions; the warmth of his body slowly eased the tension out of her tight limbs. *God this feels good, so so good. Tomorrow night, I sleep alone.*

"Morgan?" she whispered.

"Hmm?"

The Gables' house was dark, bar a dim light in the upstairs hall. "Will you kiss me good night?"

Morgan sat up on his elbow and turned her to face him. His eyes searched hers as he bent his head. His lips played with hers, going close then pulling away, his eyes steadily staring at her. He held her in a strange electric force field and her body clenched with sexual awareness. His hand caressed her breast, playing with the nipple, and her eyes fluttered closed. A moan escaped her as he brushed her lips apart with a tenderness that made her stomach dive. Rachel's hands ran up his chest to his neck, her fingers tangling in his black hair to bring him down more forcefully.

A raw, out of control passion flared between them as Morgan's hands moulded her to him. Using his arms to support his weight, he lifted himself above her, letting his narrow hips settle on her flat belly. She tensed at the intimate feel of him. She trembled. With a free hand, he caressed the length of her body until he got to her hips; he urged them upward, moving them against his. This was passion; she was starved for it, for him.

Morgan pushed her nightdress to her waist. He leaned down to her ear, his hot breath making her tingle; he whispered, "Take it off." Morgan pressed his palms into the mattress on either side of Rachel's head and lifted himself away from her body as if he was doing a push-up.

She stared up at him for a moment. She saw his eyes, saw his desire.

"Take it off," he said.

Under his ardent gaze, she reached down to her waist and slowly wiggled out of the gown—wiggling a little more than necessary.

Morgan stared at her in the moonlight, his midnight gaze touching her pale body in a slow appraisal, taking his time over the softness of her breasts, stopping at her hips.

Rachel could barely breathe as her body responded to his lingering gaze. Her hips quivered and lifted in agitation. Her breasts ached. His passionate stare returned to her hot face, and he lowered himself onto her again. His lips came down on hers, hungry and hard, and Rachel shuddered violently against him. He bruised her lips, devouring her with an intensity that yanked her into another world.

Rachel didn't fight the sensations that ripped through her like a hurricane.

"Daddy?"

A dull light came from the upstairs landing. Rachel could see Macy standing halfway down the stairs. She felt the tremble in Morgan's body and held him tightly, kissing the side of his head.

Finding her voice, Rachel said, "Macy darling, are you alright? Did you have a bad dream?"

"No. I'm thirsty," she said. "Where are you, Auntie Rachel? I can't see."

"Why don't I help you," said Elaine, as she quietly emerged from the TV room. "Auntie Rachel is way over on the other side."

"Where's Daddy?" said Macy, suddenly frightened.

"He's sleeping honey. It's very late." Elaine crossed the room and stood at the bottom of the stairs. She held her hand out to Macy. "You don't mind if I help you, do you?"

"No."

"Let's see what the Gables have in their fridge, shall we?"

Rachel stroked Morgan's dark head. After a few minutes, he looked down at her. He kissed her hard on the lips, hoisted himself away from her and off the bed, making sure the covers were over her naked body.

"I'll be right back."

Rachel heard him say, "Who's in this kitchen making so much racket? How is a tired man supposed to sleep?"

Minutes later, Morgan came into the living room with Macy on his shoulders. "Off to bed with you." Rachel turned on her side to watch them. Morgan was about to go upstairs when he turned to his sister and said, "Thanks Laine."

Elaine patted his cheek and went back to the game room. Rachel watched until Morgan and Macy disappeared up the wide staircase. She flopped onto her back.

Well, that got out of control fast. She wanted him so badly. He wanted her; she could feel it. If Jason was right and he was as miserable as her, why hadn't he broached the subject with her? Honestly, would it make a difference now that she was there? He probably thought it was a moot point. She was there. She had to finish her contract. He knew she did. She knew he cared about her, cared about what happened to her, beyond desiring her. If Macy hadn't come down, regardless that Elaine and Shawn were in the next room; she would have given him whatever he wanted in the middle of the Gables' great room. It was impossible to keep the tidal wave of sensations he created inside her within the perimeter of decency.

Then again, what man wouldn't take what Rachel was offering? She'd asked him to kiss her. He kissed her only because she asked him. Did that mean something? *God, he is a great kisser.*

What about her pride? Could you have pride when the excess of want consumed your body? Wanting his affection. Wanting his body.

Had she misconstrued his want into a romantic tale? Facing facts was not Rachel's strong suit. But there appeared to be a clear indicator that he was interested in the gratification her body could provide. Reaching an orgasm would satisfy both their bodies, but she wanted more than that, she wanted melding of body and soul. That switch on connection. Her parents, the Hilliers—definitely had it, so it exists. Rachel could see it when they looked at each other.

Should she resist Morgan and keep her pride intact?

Rachel rolled over and faced the dark fireplace, imagine seeing Rick tonight—a fantastic coincidence? Why had he never mentioned that he knew the Gables? Knew their resort? Worked here as a teenager? Showing up with Morgan's ex-girlfriend Siobhan at Elaine's party? Seemed like opportunity and orchestration blended into an elaborate concoction, but for whose benefit? She tossed her head back and forth—impossible. Rick's plans had to be about Morgan—getting back at him in some way. Being suspicious didn't come naturally to Rachel. She'd learned by error. Unfortunately, when her guard was down and the methods of gain were subtle, her suspicion tentacles lost their sensitivity. Was she a pawn? Rick was in love with something—beating Morgan most likely—and Rachel was crossfire debris.

Rachel looked up at the Gables' staircase. Morgan must be reading Macy a story. She pulled the covers up to her chin. Rachel sighed, staring at the high ceiling of the great room. Every so often, she heard Elaine and Shawn whispering, sometimes in the kitchen, sometimes in the game room.

Rachel never missed an opportunity to kiss Morgan, to touch him. Not after waiting so long for the privilege. There was definitely no pride in love. Good God, she'd lost her sense of time and space, not to mention her decorum. They are both adults and while she doesn't want their first time to be in the Gables' great room—she could have little fun in the meantime, why fight it?

Rachel threw on her nightdress and went to the linen closet in the laundry room where Mrs. Gable kept her towels for the downstairs bathroom. She took a towel and returned to the pull-out couch, slipped off her nightdress, tucked the towel under her pillow and waited for Morgan.

She heard Morgan coming downstairs and her heart beat a little harder, a little faster. She felt him slip into bed. Morgan immediately pulled her over to his side and wrapped his arms around her. She kissed his chest at the same time he kissed the top of her head. He sighed deeply, running his hand down her spine, then up again. "I like this—no barriers."

"Really?" she whispered. "Does that work both ways?"

"What's that?"

Rachel tugged at his pants. "No barriers."

He threw his arms out wide. "Take them off."

She saw the challenge in his dark blue eyes, his cheeky expression; it delighted her. This is what she wanted. Morgan disarmed. No thinking allowed. She wanted to snatch her moments with him and throw caution to the wind.

Throwing back the covers, Rachel climbed to the bottom of the bed. Slipping in between his legs, she reached for the waistband of his track pants and yanked them roughly down his body, throwing them aside. She put her hands on either side of his body and rubbed her breasts along his abdomen. She smiled when he swore.

Morgan went to grab her but she quickly moved out of his way. "Sit still or I'll stop," she whispered her warning softly. "Do you want me to stop?" she breathed onto the lower half of his body.

"No," he growled.

Rachel ran her hands under his thighs until she reached the top of his boxers, slowly, very, very slowly, peeled them down, her breasts brushing against him. She watched him clench his teeth, his body jerking.

When the boxers were off, she tossed them. She stuck her tongue in his navel then slithered up and over the muscled planes of his body so he could feel every dip and curve of her softness against his hardness. Her lips kissed his hard nipple then the other one and he sucked in his breath.

Rachel settled against him, flattening her breasts against his chest. Then slowly and with great pleasure, she moved down his body, taking her time, lingering over his favourite spots, tangling her legs suggestively with his. He bent his head, his mouth opened as he pushed his face into hers, his breath coming fast and hard.

"Now," she pushed herself up and whispered into his opened mouth, "there are no barriers."

Morgan crushed her to him, shifting her more intimately against him; his fingers tangled in her hair. His breathing was harsh. He held her tightly. She realized he was fighting his desire. She reached under her pillow and yanked out the towel, placing it beside her. Remembering how he liked to be touched, she pulled out of his grasp and moved down his body again. With a light touch, she played with his hardness, circling and rubbing before taking him into her mouth. He tensed, grabbing the bedsheets.

Morgan reached down, his hands guiding her. Sweat broke out across his body as she relentlessly fondled, licked, and sucked at him.

"*Rach,*" he gasped. "Now," he moaned. His body jerked, his face twisted, a stifled cry tore out of him. She enjoyed watching him have his release. His breathing out of control.

Tenderly, she wiped him clean, taking her time, and when she was done, Morgan jack-knifed up, his hands cradled her face. His eyes were brilliant in the dimness. Softly he kissed her, pulling her down to lie with him.

Rachel stroked his face, pushing back his damp hair. "Did you enjoy that darling?"

Morgan was still as he stared at her, his eyes haunting, but he remained silent.

"You've given me so much I wanted to give you—"

His mouth caught hers, his tongue aggressive, wet, demanding; she could barely breathe. Her heart jumped wildly in her chest. His arms gathered her close melding her into him, and then he buried his face in her neck. Rachel held him, not sure what else to do, not sure what his reaction meant.

"*Shh...shh,*" she cooed, stroking his hair. She shivered. Keeping his arm around her, he reached down and brought the covers over them. Wrapped tightly around each other, they slept.

20
DAWN

Rachel moved. She felt a strange, delightful weight around her, like a warm cocoon. She inhaled. Morgan, she thought and sighed. She pressed her nose into his hairy chest, and breathed him in, getting drunk on his scent. She kissed him, taking the kinky hair on his chest into her mouth. She ran her hand up his muscled arm to his shoulder and a weak sigh escaped her. She felt him move, felt his hardness sink into her abdomen. She laughed; he pressed her back onto the mattress, his head nestling on her chest, throwing his leg over hers.

From a great distance, Rachel heard her mother. She was angry. How could anyone be angry, thought Rachel, on such a beautiful day?

"Morgan, honey." Aunt Sarah sounded so peaceful, but what is Aunt Sarah doing here?

Morgan's head jerked up, waking Rachel out of her reverie with his sharp movement. She opened her eyes slowly; Morgan above her. He twisted around, looking over his shoulder, careful to cover Rachel's nakedness with his body.

Their mother's voices came from the foot of the bed. Maureen *was* angry.

"Breakfast is almost ready," his mother said casually.

"Have you lost your mind, Rachel?" Maureen said sharply. "In the middle of the living room? You're joking, right? And Morgan, don't you have any sense of decorum?"

With equal sharpness, Morgan said, "This is none of your business."

"This is *very much* my business, Morgan."

Rachel dropped her head back against the pillow and closed her eyes.

"Rachel Wharton, hiding behind Morgan won't protect you," her mother snapped. "I'm so annoyed that you would do this—here. Get out of that bed and get dressed before you gain an audience."

"I suggest you both leave," Morgan said angrily.

Aunt Sarah ushered Maureen to the kitchen. "Why don't we give them some privacy."

"I think they gave that up some time ago," snapped Maureen.

"I smell coffee," said Sarah.

Morgan held the sheet over her and jerked away. He climbed out of the bed naked. Rachel couldn't help noticing his beautiful body in the stark light of morning. Anger in every muscle, Morgan yanked on his track pants and his dress shirt from last night.

Rachel lay there, watching him. She couldn't think what she should do. Morgan stomped over to the armchair where she'd left her housecoat. Standing by the bed he said, "Sit up, sweetie." He seemed to know she was incapable of thinking. Holding the sheet across her breasts, she sat up, and he helped her out of the bed and into the housecoat.

Cautiously she peeked up at him and he smiled. He pushed her hair back from her face. "You are one exciting woman, Rachel Wharton. You can get me from zero to a hundred and twenty in less than a minute."

She blushed and buried her face in his chest.

Morgan laughed softly. He tugged lightly at her hair and she stared up at him. He traced her mouth with his finger. "I haven't slept that well in years." He searched her eyes. "So much for never sleeping past six."

Rachel put her finger over his lips. "Best laid plans," she whispered, stepping back from him slightly. "Even with the rude awakening," she looked away, "I enjoyed being with you last night. I hope *you* … "

Morgan ducked down to be on level with her eyes, his hands cradled her face. "*Oh baby,* I enjoyed it, *I enjoyed it.*" His voice was deep, a husk in it, his thumb ran over her lips, then his lips followed, kissing her tenderly. "I love waking up with you."

Rachel loved waking up with him. She loved smelling him, feeling him close. She loved that he went from zero to a hundred and twenty. She loved that he found her exciting. She loved many things, but she said nothing, she stood and watched him, still and silent. She knew better than anyone—how the light changes everything.

She heard the groomsmen in the upstairs hall—Jason laughing—and Morgan dropped his hands and stepped back.

Morgan patted her backside. "Go get ready."

Rachel did as he told her, passing the wedding entourage on the stairs, her bag on her shoulder. Rachel concentrated on her movements, her morning rituals. Her mind was blank.

When she finished dressing, she stared in the mirror. Her cheeks were rosy; her green eyes were bright. She smiled at her reflection. She felt wonderful. Who was this young girl with stars in her eyes?

From the top of the stairs Rachel heard angry voices in the kitchen. Her heart pounded a little faster as she made her way to the kitchen. She heard her mother's voice.

When she reached the bottom landing, Jason said, "What's the big deal? So, she shared his sleeping bag?"

"Sleeping bag?" said Aunt Sarah.

"The other night, at the farmhouse," said one of the helpful bridesmaids. "The rad beside her leaked and her bag got soaked, so Morgan gave her," her voice faded, "his T-shirt."

Rachel closed her eyes.

"There was some difficulty getting that T-shirt on as I recall," Jason smirked.

"Shut up, Jason," snapped Morgan.

"Come on," laughed Jason. "What's the big deal? Why so bent? They're both adults."

"I agree," said Elaine, her tone sharp and irritated. "This is between Morgan and Rachel."

"This is definitely *my* business. She's *my* daughter. Finding my daughter in bed with you isn't the way I usually start my day, Morgan."

Jason whistled. "Last night too? Clearly it runs in the family."

"Jason! Oh my God is nothing sacred?" said Carrie.

Rachel's mother ignored Jason. "You're confusing her. You're older; you should have more sense. You know how vulnerable she is right now and you're taking advantage of that vulnerability," said Maureen Wharton.

Mechanically, Rachel walked down the rest of the steps.

"You've been interfering in her life since she was a child without even realizing it." Maureen moved further into the room. "If you care anything about her, you'll give her space."

"Maureen—" her father tried to interrupt, but her mother ignored him too.

Rachel's legs were wobbly but she let go of the banister. Her mother had her back to her; she was stiff with anger, her fists clenched at her sides. Rachel knew her mother disapproved of Morgan. She thought Rachel could do better; be with a man with a clean slate, but listening to her words and tone, she realized for the first time, Maureen sounded bitter.

"She reveres you. She hangs on your every word, looks for your approval before she even looks to us." She pointed to Rachel's father. "The little girl who adores you is still there, and I think you've crossed a line here, Morgan."

"She's irritable and emotional. You can see that. Why do you think that is?" Her mother paced. "I know you helped her through that awful ordeal in London, and for that, I will always be eternally grateful, but there is fallout from that ordeal. I'm concerned for her mental and emotional well-being. Taking on a new city, a new job is enough to deal with, but asking her to take on your emotional baggage—it's too much! She's young and she's unattached. She shouldn't be picking out houses in good school districts. She should be enjoying herself. Testing the waters. She deserves *what you* had."

The wonderful feeling Rachel woke with was gone. The colour drained from her face.

Robert Hillier was the voice of reason. "I think we need to calm down. First Maureen, she *is* your daughter and I can understand finding Rachel this morning was unexpected, however, there are a few realities here." His gaze never left Maureen's distraught face. "We agreed yesterday we were going to stay out this."

Her mother's hands went to her waist. "We are guests here, Robert," she pointed out, "for your daughter's impending wedding, and Morgan could have shown better judgment—God knows a bit of restraint goes a long way. This is hardly the time or place to be—"

Uncle Robert closed his eyes before looking at Maureen. "The fact remains, Rachel isn't a child, she's a twenty-four-year-old woman. She wasn't held against her will. You were right upstairs if she needed your assistance. The fact is, she didn't need your help, did she Maureen? And while the timing is not the best, the problem is, Rachel lives in Ottawa, and the weekend is the only time they have together—which is not news, they've always spent their free time together," he cocked his eyebrow, and held up his index finger briefly. "I'm not making excuses Maureen, but I still remember what it's like being young. He's thirty-one and she's twenty-four. I think we need to stay out of this. It's none of our business."

Robert sighed deeply and turned to his son. Father and son stared at each other; a silent communication passed between them. Uncle Robert said, "Now let's have a pleasant breakfast." There was finality in his voice as he turned to leave.

That's when Uncle Robert saw her and stopped where he stood. The kitchen was full: her parents, the Hilliers, the Gables, the wedding party, listening in on the private moments of Rachel and Morgan's life. She could see Macy and Daniel playing outside.

It had been between the four of them this morning, and her mother had turned it into a free for all. *Why would she do that? Why would she deliberately embarrass me?*

Morgan stood apart from everyone, a coffee mug in his hand, still wearing his track pants and dress shirt. His face was blank, frighteningly blank, as he stared back at her. She could feel his anger, his frustration, the sting her mother's words had left. Maureen had made an impact on him; she could feel it, and it terrified her. She didn't want him to stop being a part of her life. He stood there, amongst these people: people he knew, people he didn't know and handled her mother's accusations alone. He had sent her upstairs to get ready on purpose, she realized, in case this happened.

Morgan had handled many things to protect her in the past. Today was no exception. He had exposed his private life— something Morgan cherished—to these people, because of her. The family always loomed so closely. They never really had any time together away from everyone these days.

Rachel told her mother, "He didn't deserve what you said to him."

Her mother spun round. "Rachel."

"He listened while you questioned his motives and his integrity. He doesn't deserve it. Last night was my doing, not his."

Rachel took a step toward her mother.

"Rachel—" started Morgan.

"I know what you think," she told her mother, "but you're wrong."

Rachel wanted her mother to understand, but she could see it in her eyes; they weren't going to agree. It hurt Rachel. She felt abandoned. How often had she needed her mother, and she hadn't been there? Too many to make up for. Maureen was either absent when needed or disapproving when Rachel chose what she wanted. The most important person—the most important relationship she had ever had—was with Morgan, and she disapproved, again and again. She closed her eyes and shook her head. She wanted to run over to Morgan and tell him how much this hurt. She wanted to smooth out the doubt her mother had left him with; she wanted to fill up with her love. She could feel him; he crowded her mind.

"Morgan understands what I'm saying."

Rachel looked at her mother. "You know him better than I do, mother?" Her voice slowly rising. "Because his thoughts are *deafening* me right now, I can barely think." Pain flickered in her mother's face and Rachel's heart turned over. She grasped her mother's hands and desperately she whispered, trying to get Maureen to her side "I love you. I know you're concerned, but you have to trust me."

Air suspended as mother and daughter stared at each other.

Maureen Wharton looked at her daughter blankly. Rachel could feel the rigidity in her body. "I think you showed poor judgment here Rachel, but as Robert said, you're a grown woman, capable of making your own decisions. Even if those decisions are mistakes." She let go of Rachel's hands and Rachel's heart sunk. "You need to eat."

There was a silent awkwardness in the kitchen. Aunt Sarah took over. Patting Rachel's cheek, she said, "Your mother's right, you need something to eat."

Muffins, bagels, ham, croissants, toast, sat out on the kitchen table. She glanced at Morgan as he watched her intently.

"There are eggs in the fridge," said Mrs. Gable.

"Are you hungry for an egg?" Morgan asked politely. "I could make you an omelette?"

Rachel's eyes met his. "Thank you." Sadness pulsed through her; sad to be here, sad to be in this crowded room with him, sad that it was Sunday and their days had thinned out into hours, saddened that her mother had abandoned her in front of witnesses.

"We haven't had a chance to walk around the grounds," John Wharton said to his wife. "Will you join me?"

Rachel saw her father take her mother's hand as she nodded. "Excuse us," he said.

Morgan took eggs out of the fridge. Rachel went to stand beside him as he cracked them into a bowl; he nudged her childishly with his arm. "You okay?" he whispered.

"No," she whispered back buttering toast. She was careful not to touch him.

Morgan made her a western omelette with strawberries on the side and a hot cup of tea. She nibbled at it. Something broke between her and her mother today. If only she had woken up earlier.

Would that fix it? Or was this bound to happen? Maureen had to find out sometime. Rachel had hoped when she did find out, she would be sure of Morgan, sure of their direction, instead of this limbo she lived in with him. Considering the closeness of their families—if this didn't work out, it could be devastating to their long-time friendships. Rachel supported her heavy head with a hand under her chin. Maybe it's better this way, she thought. Her mother knew now just how serious this was for *Rachel*. There was no turning back now.

Macy and Daniel came in with rosy cheeks and a tale to tell. Of course, Daniel, who was a year older, didn't feel his age gave him the advantage it should. "Macy makes me do all the yucky stuff she doesn't wanna do," he said.

"When are we leaving?" Elaine asked Morgan. The family sat around the large dining room table, each at different stages of eating breakfast.

"It depends on Rachel's flight," said Morgan looking at her. "When does your plane leave?"

How many times have I told him? Does he do this deliberately? I take the same damn flight here and the same damn flight back every weekend. How many times has he asked me this question? Fifty? A hundred? When do you go? When does the plane leave? A man who runs a conglomerate and he can't remember one measly flight time?

Or was he just anxious to get rid of me? I had served my purpose so it's time to move on. Everyone was probably anxious to get rid of me—I'm sure I've ruined Elaine's special weekend with my wet sleeping bag, my car sickness, giving her brother head in the living room. Elaine is not alone—my mother will be glad to see the back end of me today. Embarrassing her. Loose morals—a daughter of hers. Maureen was mortified to find me naked, under Morgan this morning. That's probably really what's she's pissed about. What must the Gables think? I can hear her saying it to her father right now.

Clearly, I'm living in some crazy alternate universe from everyone else—a universe where having common sense is completely foreign. I can take it that everyone thinks I'm an overwrought airhead. I can take that they are probably thinking, what does Morgan Hillier see in her anyway? But Morgan? I can't take the idea of him wanting me gone. Did I embarrass him, too? Am I just a liability? Emily wasn't a liability. Even Jason said that. Emily hated one person—me. And why wouldn't she? I sucked up to her husband whenever I could. At least Emily had reason to go squirrelly—her marriage broke up and her son died. I'm just nuts!

Obviously, Morgan has had time to think. Time to decipher what my mother said. I know I'm not worth all this aggravation—maybe he knows it, too. He doesn't want his life exposed, or to be chastised by my mother in front of his little sister's friends—his parents. If he had brought a girlfriend this weekend, Morgan would have arranged for a room at the resort—no recrimination.

Oh God ... there it is, the worthy factor. Why would a man like Morgan, a man who could have anyone, want me? The pocketbook answer? He doesn't. He never has called me his girlfriend, not even declared we were going out together, and there I am making a stand with Maureen like an idiot over a man who wants me gone. Everyone else's silence, probably was an indicator, too. Embarrassed for me?

He wasn't being coy when he said he wants a wife. And I can't be that! I'm too busy being the in-between girl—now that's embarrassing!

"Rachel?" Morgan's brow furrowed when she lifted her eyes to his. "What's wrong?"

Her eyes probably told the sad, pathetic tale of her thoughts. Quickly, she covered her eyes, and stood, whirling away from the table. She laughed. "Well I don't know," she said slowly.

"Don't know what?" He moved around the table, but she stopped him with her hand.

"No, no, nothing to worry about, just being an airhead. I just meant—Ottawa, the plane."

"Did you forget, Auntie Rachel?" asked Macy.

She looked at the little girl and whispered conspiratorially, "You know what? I did." She shook her left hand and snapped her fingernails with the right. "I guess I forgot I was leaving for a second. I don't even know when I leave," she said quietly, "but I'm sure it can't be soon enough." She shook her head and laughed again. "I better go look at my ticket." She turned to leave.

"Forget it," Morgan snapped, "finish your breakfast first."

She spun around. "Is that an order or a request?"

His head jerked up from his coffee at her tone.

"Well," she took a breath and turned away, "since your whole day is predicated on what time *I go back to Ottawa*, I think I better find that ticket."

"Rachel—" Morgan's voice had an edge.

She swung around, agitated, hurt, frustrated. "What?" she threw her arms out wide. *"What?* Do you want to know when I'm leaving? I'm going to get the *ticket* so I can tell you. I mean," she laughed, glancing down at her watch-less arm with exaggeration, "look at the time; it's barely eight o'clock in the morning. We need a plan. We need organization. A *precise* guy needs a *precise* answer."

Rachel raced up the stairs two at a time. She'd left her bag in her parent's room. She flung open the door and it crashed against the wall stopper and she slammed it shut. She raced to her bag and dumped it like a crazy woman. The e-ticket flew out. With shaking hands, she yanked open the folded paper—flight 147 Air Canada, 18:32, arriving in Ottawa ... *Who the hell cares!* She swung open the bedroom door to scream the information down the stairs, but she stopped herself.

Rachel turned on her heel and went back into the room. She gritted her teeth and threw the ticket she held so tightly on the floor and tore her clothes roughly off, stumbling into the bathroom. She put the shower on cold; the jet of water was hard when she stepped under it. The cold water felt good, like tiny needles hitting her skin.

I hate him, she hiccupped, *I hate him so much.* And she hated herself more for giving him the power he had over her.

Rachel slipped down onto the tiles and cried softly until there were no more tears to cry. Then she put her hurt away where the sting lost its impact.

***

Lunch was early. A lovely spread of meats, cheese, breads, and fruits, but Rachel had no interest. Instead, she talked to one of the groomsmen, an emergency room doctor called Kevin. He told Rachel harrowing tales.

"How on earth do you handle the sorrow?" she said, astonished and awed.

Kevin shrugged. "It's bad when it's a child. I like them to come in loud—screaming if possible, and moving around like crazy."

"A screaming child?" Rachel shuddered at the thought.

The young man became thoughtful, staring at his plate before turning his intense brown eyes to her. "It's worse when they're quiet. Trust me, it's worse when they're quiet."

Rachel gazed into his dark eyes and saw the burden he carried, willingly, and it humbled her. She loved children. That's why she became a teacher, but since she started working—she saw things that disturbed her.

"There's this little girl who walks to school every day. I don't know where she lives. Her name is Mary. She goes to the elementary school down the street from the high school where I teach," Rachel told him. "She's the most beautiful child: curly brown hair and big blue eyes."

Rachel put the strawberry she held on her plate. "I met Mary walking to school one day. It was cold and she had on a spring jacket, no hat, no gloves, and running shoes," she paused, and she swallowed hard.

"She had a plastic bag in her hand and she was so excited to show me her treat. It was her lunch—two pieces of pizza. It wasn't even wrapped up, just carelessly thrown in a plastic shopping bag." Rachel put an unsteady hand to her forehead. "I can't imagine the kind of world little Mary lives in." Rachel shook her head. "She's is a little star, so accepting, so thankful for her lunch treat. She never complains. She always has a happy story to tell me as we walk to school."

Rachel looked at the young doctor. "You're right, it's worse when they're quiet."

Kevin smiled at her. "Mary's lucky. She met you. I guarantee little Mary has a new designer snowsuit with all the trimmings." Rachel couldn't keep the surprise out of her face. She *had* bought

Mary a Columbia snowsuit.

Kevin popped a grape in his mouth, nudging her with his shoulder. "You high strung, sensitive types, are all the same; you light up a room, and then you leave, taking the sun with you."

Rachel's troubled gaze met Morgan's narrowed blue eyes, and she felt sucked into a vacuum of emotions. She jerked away.

***

After lunch everyone went to the games room; the men played billiards, the ladies were laughing at Mrs. Gable's resort stories. Shawn sat on a stool near the window—Morgan was taking a shot.

Rachel walked over to Shawn. "Shawn?"

He straightened in his stool when he saw her. "Hey, Rach."

"I was wondering … it looks like it's going to be a lovely day, it seems a shame for everyone to head back early when it's just me who has to leave. I was wondering if there was a car rental place or something near here or maybe Gravenhurst?"

"Well, there is …" He looked uncomfortable.

Mrs. Gable said to her son, "If you don't have to leave so early that would be wonderful. We could have dinner at the lodge."

Rachel didn't turn around, but she could hear the older woman's contained excitement. "Do you have a shuttle at the resort that goes into town?"

"Pete picks up our fresh fruit for the week on Sundays." Mrs. Gable stopped abruptly when Shawn looked over in her direction.

"Actually Rachel," said Shawn, "you could do me a favour. I bought Elaine a car for her birthday, but she's too nervous to drive it on the highway because it's a small car. I'm not familiar enough with a standard transmission to drive it back to Toronto. Elaine tells me you love cars and can drive a standard. Would you be comfortable taking it to TO?

She shrugged. "Sure. What kind of car?"

"Really?" he said brightly. "That would be great. It's a Mazda RX8."

Rachel's eyes sparkled. "Six-speed?"

"Yup."

"What colour is it?"

"Red."

Rachel laughed. "And you bought this for Elaine?"

Shawn gave her a lopsided grin. "Don't *you* start."

"Should I drive it to the Hilliers' or should I just park it in my parents' driveway and she can just keep my Mercedes? She's been driving it since last July. Sorry, she *borrowed* it to go to lunch and it's been a missing person ever since."

"You would do that?" Shawn stood; his relief was evident. "I was going to ask you…"

She smiled. "You picked the right car for me—sleek and fast enough to be dangerous." She went to move away and stopped. "I'll get my things. Can I have a test drive before I head out?"

"Sure."

"Great."

Out of her peripheral vision, she saw her mother stand up but Rachel ignored her and left the room quickly and efficiently. She didn't think while she pulled her stuff together. She just knew she needed to be gone. Driving a beautiful sports car into good humour seemed a perfect way to get where she was going, which was anywhere but there.

She came downstairs and said a cool goodbye to the family, but thanked the Gables for their hospitality. Elaine and the children saw her out and Shawn yelled, "I'll pull the car out."

The bridal party shouted their goodbyes and she didn't wait for a reply from Morgan; she left. Once outside, one of the doors of the five-bay garage opened.

Shawn drove the beautiful car into the sunshine badly. It

sparkled. Rachel jumped up and down, clapping.

Shawn gave her a quick study of the car before she took it for a spin. It was a dream. *This is going to work out just fine!* When she returned, Macy and Daniel wanted a fish swing. Morgan and Jason had joined them outside.

Macy cuddled into her arms. "Do you have to go?"

Rachel tried not to cry. "I wish I didn't have too."

"I wish you never left." Rachel saw the tears in her eyes.

"I wish that, too. I won't make that mistake again."

"You promise?" She looked up at Rachel, her huge, sad, blue eyes made her heart hurt.

Rachel wrapped her arms around the tiny body. "I promise."

"I love you."

She struggled to get out the words, "I love you so much." Going back to Ottawa was such an effort; this made it a gut wrench. Being strong was Rachel's job—for Macy. She looked at her. "Don't forget to save all your stories for me when I call. You know I hate to miss any stories."

She nodded. "I will." Tears silently ran down her face.

Morgan's hand grasped Macy's shoulder. Macy fell back against his legs. He picked her up. Immediately she tucked her face into his throat and wrapped her little arms around his neck. Rachel stood; her head bent. She pressed her fingers to her lips.

Morgan said tersely, "Take care of yourself."

"You too." Unable to look at him, she stood there, awkwardly, waiting—for what? A reason not to leave? Or at the very least: "I'll miss you. Can't wait to see you again. I don't want you to go." None of those words came. Not because he didn't say them now, because he rarely said them, and if he did, it was usually over the phone or in the throes of passion.

Morgan ran his hand down her back and pulled her into his side. He kissed her forehead. "Drive safe. Take your time."

She nodded into his chest. Her arm went around his waist and held tight, while her other hand fell to Macy's back.

The front door opened. "How did the car work out?" asked Mrs. Gable.

"Err … good, Mum, good," said Shawn

Rachel stepped back from Morgan. "I better head out." She reached up and kissed his jaw and then Macy's back. The walk to the car seemed long and shaky.

She fired up the engine and put it in first. She couldn't look over to where they stood. It would delay the inevitable.

Rachel hit the gas and lifted her foot off the clutch. She pumped the horn as she drove down the narrow road. When she was poised at the corner stop sign, she looked back. Morgan stood in the driveway still, Jason and Elaine stood behind him, Shawn was turning away to go back into the house. Morgan looked small and lonely against the big sky. Snow scattered across the fields. Colourful leaves still hung on a few maples. There was a cold snap in the air. Winter was moving into second gear this far north. Rachel turned away; her heart felt like it was bleeding. Fiercely, she pushed the stick into first and zoomed onto the highway, changing gears and driving as fast as the wind could take her.

21

MORGAN STRUGGLES
FOR CLARITY

Morgan stood outside the Gable's house watching Rachel drive away. She changed gears like a pro, taking the corner at the bottom of the driveway fast, hugging the road in her shiny little red death trap. He looked at Shawn.

"Take it up with your sister." Shawn held up his hand and walked back into the house. Morgan watched Rachel burn rubber at the stop sign. He winced; heard her speed onto the highway. He counted her gear changes. She was in sixth within sixty seconds. She flew.

"It just seemed more like her kind of car," Elaine said sheepishly.

"Do ya think?" laughed Jason.

Morgan nodded. "Yes—it's does."

"I'm sorry," Elaine explained, "I like *her* car, and Shawn bought me that one."

"There's no need to apologize. Rachel is a grown woman. As you said, it's her kind of car." Morgan put Macy on her feet.

"Hey Macy, wanna play checkers?" said Daniel.

She looked up at Morgan. "Okay, Daddy?"

"Sure." He stroked her hair. "You okay?"

Macy shrugged. "She'll be home soon."

He nodded. "She will."

Once the front door shut, Elaine said, "Morgan, I can see you're not happy about this, but—"

"I don't think I'm supposed to be." Morgan moved away from

his brother and sister.

"She's a good driver," said Jason.

"Yes, she is," Morgan conceded, pacing around the Gables' circular driveway. "It's the other five million people on the road that I'm concerned about. The semis, the trucks, the vans, the U-Hauls that are thousands of pounds heavier than her little sardine can of a car!" He stuffed his hands in his pockets. "And giving a dangerous woman a weapon isn't what I would call prudent behaviour—good driver or not."

"Rachel's not dangerous, that's a bit melodramatic," said Elaine.

Cocking his brow, sarcasm oozed from Morgan's tense mouth. "And you know her so much better than I do, is that it, Elaine? Are we talking about the same girl?" He laughed. "She's so fucking dangerous I'm turning grey prematurely." Anger bubbled up in him, taking control.

Morgan pointed to the highway. "Because that girl—is impulsive, careless, irresponsible, a speed freak, and bad tempered! —the same girl who just drove away, pissed off at me, for God knows fucking what!" he shouted. "That's the girl I'm talking about!"

Morgan clenched his teeth to control his panic, to squelch the flash photos of her mangled body in that red tin cup. He sucked in a deep breath. *I'm losing my mind.* He turned his overheated body into the path of the cool breeze. "I'm going for a walk."

"Do you want company?" asked Jason.

"No!"

***

Morgan walked the back forest of the Gables' property. With every step, he pounded out what was bouncing around in his head. When she returned from Paris, they had been doing so well, moving forward in the right direction, thought Morgan, not that they didn't have their issues, they did. Their communication sucked since their relationship became more sexual, but Rodney Horvat made a significant change. After seeing his darkroom—Morgan gritted his teeth—she started having panic attacks.

Morgan kicked a random rock in agitation.

Fear paralyzed her last summer. Her panic attacks were out of control. Her friendliness disappeared. She fidgeted constantly; jumped if anyone came near her; crowds disturbed her, music. She stopped going out, seeing her friends. She tried covering her beauty. Wore dresses the size of tents and sweaters in thirty-Celsius heat. Her protection consumed her. School had been coming to an end. She was scared. She needed help. She needed to be distracted. She needed to be needed. She needed something to catch her interest and fill her up. That's when Morgan suggested the beach house project.

Rachel and Morgan had been at his parents. May was hot so they opened the pool early. Rachel had on a sun hat the size of Jupiter and a white sundress that went from her shoulders to her sandals. She was sitting at the kids' table doing a puzzle with them.

From behind his dark sunglasses, Morgan watched for her reaction. "I want to tear down that old cottage I bought ... I think I should build—" Rachel was up like a shot from the tiny table.

"A new one."

"Demolish it?" Robert Hillier said. "There's nothing retrievable?"

Morgan shook his head. "It was an elderly lady who lived there and frankly she wasn't able to keep it up. I think it would be more economical just to tear it down and start again."

Rachel stepped away from the children's small table, listening intently.

"It's a beautiful piece of property," said his mother. "I was wondering what you were going to do with it."

Morgan was listening to them with half an ear. Rachel had moved to the middle of the patio, her hands tucked behind her back.

He smiled. She was pretending she wasn't listening and turned sideways to look back at the children, throwing out words of encouragement, "Good one Daniel. Macy you're a star." The sun beat down on the patio and he could see the outline of her curvaceous figure under the tent dress. Her breasts were more than a generous size for such a small woman, narrow waist; she turned back to him, her slim, beautifully round hips; her little ass fit into the palms of his hands perfectly. His dad broke his concentration.

"With everything that's going on with the business, do you think this is the right time to take on a building project?"

Morgan shrugged. "When is perfect? If I wait until all the circumstances are perfect or when I have time, I'll be an old man and my little girl will be away at university."

"I think it's a marvellous idea, Morgan," said his mother and then exchanged a glance with his father, reaching out to touch his hand. "I was thinking of going to St. Lawrence Market."

Robert smiled. "Can I be your driver?"

Once his parents left, his attention trained on Rachel. She lifted her leg into that ballerina pose she always did. He could see her calculating. "What do you think, Rachel?"

The old bubbly Rachel surfaced. His heart beat faster when she smiled at him "That sounds exciting." She was immediately in front of him, standing between his outstretched legs. "When do you want to do it?"

What a question!

She put her hands on his legs to balance herself while she gracefully slipped to the ground, sitting on her knees. Her sunny face looked up at him. *She is the most beautiful woman I have ever seen.*

He sat forward slightly. "I want to do it now. I've been thinking about it for a while. I met with an architect; he has a construction crew ready to go. There are a few logistical problems."

"Like what?"

"My dad's right, I don't have a lot of time and there will be details that need to be decided: choosing floors, windows, tile, bathrooms, fixtures, lighting, the list is long so I'll have to hire someone."

Morgan heard Rachel swear under her breath when Jason yelled his hellos, arriving to pick up Daniel, and he smiled.

"Hey buddy." Jason ruffled his son's hair.

"Hey Dad, can Macy come over?"

Macy nodded enthusiastically.

His brother looked at Morgan. "Okay with you?"

Morgan looked at his watch. "We're taking Macy for an early dinner and a movie—a couple of hours?"

Jason nodded. "I saw Mum and Dad leave."

"They went to the market."

With goodbyes said, and the patio doors closed, Rachel turned to him. "I could do it. I'm finished for the year. Teacher's college doesn't start until September."

He shook his head. "I can't ask you to do that—give up your summer. I thought you and Louise were going to Italy before you come back to look after—?"

"No!" Annoyed, she sat back on her legs. "Morgan I seriously wonder if you listen to anything I say. *Louise* is going to Italy—*on her honeymoon*. I don't think Stephen would be too happy if I tagged along. Her wedding is in June. She's one of my dearest friends and of course, I want to be helpful in any way possible, and there'll be plenty of girl stuff going on that I don't want to miss, and I won't." She blushed; her green eyes sparkled brilliantly. "If you don't want my help you just have to say. You don't have to make excuses."

She pushed away from him, but he grabbed her tent dress and pulled her onto his knee. He yanked off her floppy hat, holding her close, her arms sandwiched between them; her soft floral scent filled his nostrils. She was breathing heavily; her eyes averted, her jaw tight.

"I'm not making excuses. It couldn't be that I'm concerned about you? That you've been under a great deal of stress lately and asking you to take on one of my projects might add to your stress level? Or could it be that you've already signed yourself up for taking care of Macy for me this summer, and to ask anything further might be a little fucking selfish?

"Nothing would please me more Rachel than having your help with this project, but only if that's what you want, only if that's what you're ready to give. This is a big job. I was thinking of hiring someone to handle it; it's that big."

Her face was tense.

"Rachel ..." He sighed deeply; he dug his elbow into his knee as he put his forehead in his wet palm. This wasn't going the way he had hoped. In the process of being coy he'd managed to hurt her. *Fuck!*

She slid her arm along his shoulders and his muscles tensed. It was the first time she had touched him since she was in Horvat's darkroom. The affection between them had been tempered since Leah's wedding and then further tempered by Horvat. "I'm sorry Morgan," she whispered, shaking him gently. "I've been such a bitch lately, and you've been so patient with me."

She spoke softly and his chest tightened. "I'm so sorry. I'm driving myself crazy. I need to get out of my head."

Rodney Horvat took her sweetness and love for life and remade her into a frightened and hesitant woman. He wanted to suck it out of her and take it into his own body. It could be worse; the fucker could have—Morgan didn't want to think about what the bastard had written on his wall. He didn't want to think what could have happened. She was here, in his arms, safe, close.

"Rach—"

"Don't be mad."

"I'm not mad."

"I want to help. I think it might be what I need."

He pulled back and gave her a lopsided smile. "If I said I think so, too, does that make me sound like a selfish bastard?"

She smiled weakly. "Yes."

"Good, that's what I was going for."

She laughed. Morgan stood, swung her up into his arms, and threw her into the pool's deep end. She screamed as she flew through the air, "You dirty bastard!"

***

Once Rachel immersed herself in building and decorating the cottage, the frequency of her panic attacks reduced. Her exuberance and her confidence started to remake their appearance. The cottage filled a hole in her and it became a retreat, a protective cove. Morgan's good intentions paid off; even his ulterior motives basked in the sun. When Rachel was away at school, his time with her was limited. The cottage would change that. But there were concessions he had to make. First, everyone was excited about the cottage. That meant the family was going to be spending time there whether he liked it or not, so he had to make it larger than he originally intended. He wanted to ensure that Macy had her own space and that he had privacy to be with Rachel. To get that, he had to house his parents, her parents, his brother, and sister, and their significant others. If he didn't, everyone would be on top of him, and that would drive him nuts.

While building the place, Morgan had a trailer delivered to the property. At first, it was rarely used, Rachel and Macy went to the site three times a week. Having the trailer on-site ensured both Rachel and Macy had a safe place to stay during the day. His plan was underway.

When Rachel called him one afternoon to say she and Macy were exhausted, that it had been a busy day and she wanted to stay at the trailer, but was uneasy, Morgan rubbed his hands together in anticipation. He drove to the trailer after work and spent the night with them. Renting the trailer had been a subtle plan that snuck under the radar undetected. The occasional weekday sleepover gained momentum and spilled into the occasional weekend, which soon became every day and every weekend as the project became a flurry of activity.

The trailer was luxurious by trailer standards, but it was confining for Morgan. Listening to her sing in the shower, seeing her in close quarters, braless, in a tank top and shorts, watching her sleep—was challenging. His bunk bed was across from hers and he would get a good look at her beautiful breasts when her tank top would twist around her. He remembered how they felt in his hands, in his mouth, and he would have to take a running leap into the lake. It was pure torture. Rachel was blissfully unaware. It was the worst and best summer of his life.

It would have been so easy to coax her over to his side of the trailer, but he couldn't. Her panic attacks were under control, her confidence was slowly coming back, and the physical contact between them was comfortable, familiar; he didn't want to fuck it up. The doctor said relapses were inevitable. Her fears, at times, overwhelmed her and triggered an attack any time she felt pressured or trapped. He didn't push it. Time was on his side.

By the end of May, the cottage was enclosed and by the third week of June, she was moving in furniture and decorating walls. They had a big Canada Day Party on July 1st complete with fireworks. For the rest of the summer, the two families were permanent fixtures at the harvest table that he and Rachel designed and had a local carpenter build. In the trailer, he slept two feet away from her. In the cottage he was on the main floor at the far end of the house; she was on the top floor at the opposite side of the house sharing a room with his sister. The placement of his room was strategic. It was apart from the family. A generous bedroom and ensuite, a small living room with an attached study, a bedroom for Macy, and an exercise room down the hall. The green room was the campout room. It was upstairs on the far side of the house, completely designed around children with an outdoor theme. It was huge. The children all slept there when they had a house full, which was more often than not.

When they were designing the master bedroom ensuite together, he told Rachel to spare no expense. "Build your dream bathroom." Having a bath was one of Rachel's favourite things, so she spared no expense. Once it was complete, he knew it would be difficult for her to stay out. It was just a matter of time before she made it her own. He was counting the days.

Payday came.

Morgan had been away on business and raced to the cottage as soon as he landed. The cottage was vacant when he arrived, but there was evidence of life. Deciding to take a shower, he went to the bedroom, pushed open the bathroom door, and there, immersed in bubbles, was Rachel. A soft concerto played in the background, candles, a wine glass, hair piled on her head, she astounded him. Morgan could only stare.

She smiled impishly at him. "Sorry." She lifted her wine glass in salute.

He tried to act casual and disassociate himself from his hard-on. "Is that wine?"

"Your mother made it for me. Half ginger ale and half wine. Well, more like three quarters of ginger ale and a quarter wine. It's very delicious." She giggled.

Clearly the quarter cup of wine was affecting my poor little lightweight. "Where is everyone?" he asked.

"At the beach." She lifted her small shoulders, "I thought it would be a great opportunity to enjoy this wonderful bathroom." She laughed, dipping her head back, giving him a full view of breasts.

"I think you knew it was just a matter of time before I gave it a whirl, but I must admit, this isn't my first time. Hey," she pointed, "you're not supposed to be back until tomorrow?"

"You sound regretful."

Her eyes were huge in her small face. Her desire very readable. "Oh no, tall man," she whispered, "far from regretful."

Morgan leaned down, unable to resist her, his hands on either side of the bath rim; he kissed her, a soft, coaxing kiss. Her warm, wet body was soon out of the bath and plastered against him, his suit soaked. She pushed off his jacket and yanked at his tie.

Her hot breath was in his mouth. "I've missed you."

Sitting on the edge of the bath, his hands ran down her white skin and around her backside, lifting her to straddle him. He tasted her neck. Supporting her shoulder blades with his hands he pushed her back, his mouth taking in her nipple, sucking greedily on her. Her trembling sighs and her jerks of passion answered a calling in his body.

Morgan didn't hear them coming up from the beach. Didn't hear Macy shout for Rachel.

It was her groan, "No, no, not now, please go away," that forced him to lift his head.

He stroked her twisted face. "What babe?"

"They're back. Macy is calling me."

Then he heard it. "Rachel, honey?" shouted his mother, "Where are you? We're back."

Morgan stood and put Rachel on the floor. He kissed her hard on the lips. He hated saying obvious things. "They'll be coming here."

She nodded.

Standing naked in front of him, her arms across her breasts, he whispered, "You're beautiful." He handed her his bathrobe off the back of the door.

She blushed. "So are you," she whispered.

With great effort, he turned away from her. He hated to leave, but he knew it was necessary. He wasn't ready for the meddling questions that would come if the family knew how deep this went; specifically, Jason and his big mouth, and specifically because they have never discussed their status as a couple. He wanted her, to be with her, love her, live with her. He moved them along in that direction. He took liberties; she let him. Healthy signs. In his mind, it didn't require clarification. It was good enough for him right now. His father knew this wasn't a casual affection, so that meant his mother knew. Morgan was less than careful in their presence, but they had read the obvious indicators that things had changed. Taking her to New York, Leah's wedding bullshit, letting her have so much say in raising Macy, his maniac behaviour when the police told him what Horvat was up to, and how much time he spent at the trailer with her alone. On a few occasions, his mother had interrupted an intimate exchange. He thought it would be his mother to broach the subject. When it finally came, it was his father. They were having coffee in the kitchen. Robert invited him to dinner. Morgan refused.

"Off to the site?" his father had said.

Morgan smiled absently. "We have walls."

His father moved to the table and picked up the *Globe*, flipping carelessly through the pages. "The trailer is bigger than it looks, but still ... close quarters."

Morgan looked at the shine on his shoes. "Close."

"A happy close or a torturous close?"

Morgan laughed. "Both."

His father said, "In deep?"

There was no point in belabouring what was so obvious. Morgan met his father's stare, inhaled deeply and nodded. "Pretty fucking deep."

Morgan closed the bathroom door; he could hear her

humming—a few giggles. Smiling, he was ripping off his wet shirt when a brief knock came to the door and his mother walked into his bedroom. "Rachel honey?"

Morgan's tone was clipped. "She's in the bath." He didn't look at his mother.

There was a pause. "We weren't expecting you."

"No."

"Wrapped up early?"

"Yes." He yanked a T-shirt on.

"Good. Rachel will be pleased."

He glanced at her. "Really?"

"Don't be coy Morgan, it's unattractive in such a capable man."

Morgan undid his belt and pants, stripping them off. His mother refrained from asking why he was so wet. He grabbed a pair of Bermuda shorts Rachel had bought him a couple of weeks ago. "Mother, you can see I'm dressing and I'm no longer five?"

"Did you stop at the house; is your father on his way?"

"Didn't stop at the house."

"Jason and Shawn?"

"Didn't stop at the office."

"Just raced here as fast as your car could take you? Hmm."

Forcefully, he pushed his legs into the Bermuda shorts. "Who's being coy? If you have something to say, Mother, say it."

The bathroom door opened and Rachel came out in his bathrobe, looking very pink and young. She stumbled over her words when she saw his mother, her face going beet red.

"Au ... Aunt Sa ... Sarah, you're back. That's ... that's good."

"Is it?" she smiled.

"No, Mother," snapped Morgan, "it isn't good. She's being polite. Your timing sucks."

Mutely, Rachel stared at him, like a doe in high beams, and he spoke gently to her. "Did you bring clothes down with you, babe?"

She nodded, rooted to her spot.

He did a quick study of the room; her clothes were haphazardly thrown on the armchair near the sliding doors. "Mother, will you excuse us please?"

"Of course, darling. I'll give Macy a snack while you get organized."

When she was gone, Rachel said, "I feel like my hand got caught in the candy jar."

"Then its official, you're my favourite candy."

Torturous, his father had said—an unmitigated understatement. Leah Wharton's wedding and the Horvat fiasco may have set him back, but after that day in the bath, she had started to feel good, comfortable. He'd started to gain ground with her again, but it was a slow torture. Their walks on the beach ended with long wet kisses and it was starting to take a physical toll on him. Heavy petting had lost its charm at fifteen. He was a walking ball of frustration. To add to that frustration, on the nights she had a nightmare about Horvat, she would come to his room, crying, shaking, scared, looking for his comfort, his protection. He would move over in bed to let her in. His frustrations lessened when he watched her sleep curled up to him, looking young and vulnerable.

The wait would be a bit longer.

Her parents weren't around much her last year at school. It made the new dimension in their *friendship* easier to transition. Maureen was travelling a great deal; working excessive hours at Clambour Wealth Management. A new CEO had taken over—Matt Hooper. Morgan knew him. Shiny faced guy—tried to be tricky. Morgan appreciated shrewd, not tricky. Hooper didn't impress Morgan. Maureen, however, was working both ends of the stick trying to dazzle him. John's Foundation went international and he was a liaison with the federal government for a national education plan; his time was limited with the amount of travelling he was doing.

When August arrived, it was time to return to London for her graduate studies, the torture kicked into high gear. Studious by nature, she immersed herself in the mission to finish school. When she came to town, Rachel went to the cottage with him; otherwise, she stayed at his parent's place. Their time together had altered, but their friendship deepened. The sexual tension was still there, but since his bathroom feel, he wasn't given *that* same liberty. She had pulled back again. He didn't press her to move forward. When she asked for his help or advice, he gave it. He read her essays, impressed how easily she conveyed her thoughtful intelligence onto paper. When he caught her kiss-me-gaze, if they were alone, he did. At times of stress and insecurity, he held her until the tension left her body. And when she made it to the end—top in her class—he was proud.

Rachel finished school in May and they had a party at the cottage. Her parents attended. They were not themselves; they seemed tired, stressed, but they were proud of their only child. Morgan bought her a diamond bracelet. Maureen and John gave her a Mercedes. With her mind no longer focused on school, her focus shifted to Morgan. Like last summer, she lived at the cottage with Macy, his mother, and sister. He drove back and forth every day. A gruelling commute by any standards, but at the end of his frustrating journey, she was there, his daughter in her arms. At the weekend, the rest of the family joined them.

Summerhill threw a spanner in the works. Behind the scenes, he had been working on getting Rachel a job at his school in Ottawa. Maureen grandly announced Rachel's great news; Summerhill had secured her a position. And like a flash of lightning, by late July, Maureen had swished Rachel home to prepare for her new adventure. Every instinct told him she didn't want to go, but he remained silent. He didn't broach the subject with her because she didn't discuss her options with him or ask his opinion. Analytically, he reasoned if she was unable to stop what she didn't want, she wasn't ready for a place in his life. The question that begged to be answered: would she ever be ready? She was young. She was impulsive. When would the time be right? Was he deluding himself into thinking that their friendship and chemistry could be sustained in a long-term relationship? The easy answer for him—yes. Her answer might be different. Questions plagued Morgan and exposed him once again to pubescent insecurities.

Rachel's panic attacks returned once she confirmed her employment in Ottawa. His suspicions grew. Maureen did her level best to keep Morgan out of the picture. A curious vigilance that surprised and irritated him; a departure from Maureen's customary mothering skills. Maureen loved her daughter, but she had a curious dance that integrated her detachment with her involvement.

Rachel left for Ottawa. Within a week, she called home crying, lonely, insecure, and needing a way out. Missing her, pissed off that she hadn't included him in her decision, lonely, tired of living like a monk, tired of their hot and cold relationship—even how they parted at the airport was one more thing to be pissed about—so when she called for comfort, he lost his temper. He did manage to regroup, which resulted in their agreement that he would finance her trips home because Maureen had cut her off. Rachel was to live on her teacher's salary. With his sister's wedding, the expense of flying, and all the trimmings that went with being the maid of honour, it made it impossible for her to come home. He didn't want that for her or himself.

It was during that conversation that Rick Summerhill re-entered Morgan's life after many years.

Rachel told Morgan, "There's someone at the door."

Circumstances had intervened again. "Are you on a portable?" Morgan said.

"Yes."

"Let's see who it is?" He was relieved when she laughed.

The voice sounded far away. "Hello Rick." She said into the phone.

"He called me the other day. Would you put him on the phone?" He heard her say, "Morgan wants to talk to you."

"Hillier—you barked?"

"Where is she?" He wasn't up for Summerhill's wit.

"She went to the bedroom."

"When she comes back give her a job to do, like make tea or coffee."

Silence.

"Summerhill!" he snapped. "Do you understand?"

"Yes."

"I'll come straight to the point. She's upset and not adjusting to Ottawa. I'm sure she'll be fine, but right now she needs a friend and she needs to get out of that apartment. Take her to a movie, dinner, anything. And be charming Summerhill. Keep it casual and simple. I'm trusting you with this information because I need your help and if I've made a bad choice here and you hurt her while she's vulnerable? Not only will I beat the shit out of you, but I will personally see to it that your life is permanently altered negatively. And before you give me your indignation, let me make myself clear, *I don't give a fuck what you think.* All I am interested in is her and whether or not you are part of the solution or the problem. What will it be?"

The pause was long. "She's coming back … I just stopped by to see how she was getting along in our fair city, and hoping I could get a cup of coffee for my concern."

Morgan heard her say, "Wait and I'll get out from underneath this brick house I'm under and make you a cup of coffee."

"She's in the kitchen," said Summerhill, "and just for the record—the solution."

Hearing Summerhill say the words made Morgan cringe. "Good.

Let me talk to her."

"He wants to say goodbye."

Her voice was faint but happier than it had been. "Morgan, thanks for everything."

"You sound better."

"I feel better."

"I'll see you next weekend?"

"Next weekend."

***

Bringing Summerhill into his confidence complicated Morgan's plan of action. Summerhill had seen the opportunity Morgan gave him, and the bastard took it.

Morgan's relationship with Rachel was always at a crossroads these days. They had always been close. She had looked up to him since childhood, relied on him, but now their relationship had advanced well beyond childhood friends. It had been building steadily. The kiss at the train station had blown his mind. It had moved their relationship to new intimacies. He had difficulty keeping his hands to himself. The night of Leah Wharton's wedding, he pushed the envelope. One minute he was trying to comfort her, give her a soft kiss to reassure her, and to take the sting out of her hurt. But her big green eyes, her pale skin in the dark Escalade, the warmth of her body, her drugging sweet scent were hard enough to fight on their own, but when she took charge of their soft kiss? It pushed him over the edge. Not only was she a beautiful woman, her sexy innocence was hard to resist. Within seconds he had her trapped under him. Relentlessly, he demanded her response until her body bowed like an exquisite instrument as she quaked in his arms. He couldn't stop touching her, tasting her.

Ishmael had interrupted them. Morgan had been pissed. In retrospect, it had brought him to his senses. "Excuse me sir … we are almost at Miss Rachel's." Those words had hammered against his brain. *I'm returning little Rachel Wharton to her parents within moments, with the smell of her on my skin, the taste of her on my lips.* Childhood pictures flashed through his mind in that moment. Rachel as a baby. Rachel in a Christmas pageant. Her innocence. The childish focus of her green eyes when he explained what she couldn't understand. Rachel on the swings outside their back door. The first time she got drunk and he was a complete asshole and unable to think sanely. Rachel's saucy face when she told him that she'd had sex with Jessup Former. Her brand of grace had attracted his attention, since forever. Morgan couldn't reconcile these pictures with the pictures of her beautiful body pressed intimately into his, her breathy voice begging, demanding, laying bare her wants.

Morgan had struggled to gain control, struggled to squelch his desire to take her home with him, and carry out his epic fantasies. His control was further challenged when she retreated into tears. His body was painfully withdrawing from the pleasure of watching her beautiful face twist in pleasure, her body shaking and contracting; listening to her moan his name as she climaxed. Had she been any other woman—wanting her to the point of distraction as he did— he would have taken her home. But she wasn't any other woman; she was Rachel. Her status required pause. Elaine never broached the subject with him, but Morgan was sure the back of the Escalade had had an earthy scent when she opened the car door, and Rachel had the appearance and gaze of a woman who had—been had. His sister hadn't questioned him. She'd enveloped Rachel into her arms and whisked her upstairs before his parents greeted them.

Unfortunately, when Rachel came downstairs alone after her shower, his nerves were stretched to their outer limit. She looked insecure and embarrassed. Regret in her cool disdain. It was the second time within months that his parents had been forced to read between the lines and draw conclusions he was incapable of discussing. The air had been charged. Rachel's hurt, frustration, contempt shot out of her eyes like rays of light at him, and Morgan lost his temper. He punched the wall. He saw her fear. When he told her to get out, fearing he would hurt her, the harmony they had shared went with her. Distance and loneliness were on the menu again until Rachel called, frightened. Her mysterious caller had changed his strategy. Her fears prompted him to step back. It seemed he was always weaving his way back into her good graces and then moving with more caution until she signalled him that she was ready to move forward.

When he picked her up two days ago at the airport, it took every ounce of his control not to feel her up in the middle of airport Arrivals. The sleeping bag feel at the Van Os' just made it worse, but the Gables' living room was the winner. Morgan shook his head. *Christ Almighty,* his hands had touched every inch of her body without reserve, easing the long and unsatisfied need inside him. He was wild for her. Wild for the way she reached for him, drunk on the soft little cries she made in her throat. He watched her pale, slender, body respond to every stroke of his hand; his breath came rapid and rough.

Macy whispered in the darkness, "Daddy?"

Jesus—when I came back—Rachel was on fire. Aggressive. Dangerous. Her teasing, her hot skin. Holy shit! I couldn't believe it. I was pubescent the last time it was that good—and then I lost her again. Just like that. Gone. I'm losing my fucking mind. That's the problem!

22

QUEBEC

Following the weekend at the Gables', Rachel went to Quebec. The Grade 11 students were spending the week soaking up Montreal's culture, while Rachel and four other teachers chaperoned.

Still tender from her goodbye with Macy, she called the child often, but she made sure to speak to her when she was at either Carrie's or Aunt Sarah's. She didn't want to talk to Morgan, and he felt the same way. There were no messages left on her apartment phone. He was quite content to sit on the outskirts of their relationship, then so would she. She spoke to her mother on Thursday, as usual. They didn't speak of the weekend. Surface conversation. Maureen was quick to remind her that her cousin's-husband's-graduation-from-medical-school-dinner-celebration was the following night. Her mother had reminded her umpteen times, only because she knew Rachel would rather eat dirt than go to cousin-Polly's-husband's-medical-graduation-dinner. Polly belonged to her father's great Aunt Adele, an affected piece of work who lived vicariously through her children and her children's spouses. The stunner was that Rachel's refined father was related to such a narcissist woman who completely lacked a personality.

Teachers and students returned to school early Friday afternoon, and Rachel was glad to say goodbye to the eighty students and their rushing hormones and rampant dramas. Rachel had enough trouble trying to keep herself close to centre without trying to be the voice of reason—*Rachel*, the voice of reason? It was exhausting.

Students filed out of the coach to waiting parents. Watching parents reunite with their children, husbands, and wives, reminded her how singular her life was, how much she missed Morgan. The week had been long and arduous without contact with him. The way she left the resort early, in retrospect—was a bad decision. He hurt her feelings but to the point of completely ignoring him? And for what? Because he kept asking when she was leaving? The truth was, she was anger with her mother and she took it out on Morgan. He did so many things right. He was so kind and good to her. She was embarrassed that her personal life was skewed around the Gables' kitchen, and she was so bloody frustrated at not having the time to just—be with Morgan. Without interference. He was the one that took all the blows and she treated him so badly. When she got to Toronto she'd apologize for her childish behaviour and beg him to go to her cousin's-husband's-graduation-from-medical-school-dinner-celebration.

Would he want to be under Maureen's watchful stare? Probably not. At least Saturday night would be fun. Louise had invited her to dinner, to see her new house. She wanted to ask Morgan to go with her to that as well.

That evening, the airport taxi dropped her off at her parents' house. The usual convoy of cars were in the Hilliers' driveway. Rachel left her bags on the porch and walked over. Every door on every vehicle was open. Elaine and Shawn were arguing, a piece of luggage between them. Rachel didn't pay any attention. Jason was convincing Daniel that the five-foot dog he wanted to stuff in the van was too big.

"Hey," said Rachel.

Jason turned to her. "Tell him this isn't going to fit."

Promptly she said, "Daniel darling, it isn't going to fit. And even if it did, your dad wouldn't be able to see out the back window. And if he can't see out the back window someone could get hurt."

Daniel saw the sense in her argument and said, "Okay," and ran across the lawn to his own house next door, dragging the big dog by the ear.

"Thank you," smiled Jason. "I heard you have to suffer through dinner with irritating Pollyanna tonight?"

"Don't rub it in." She pulled her trench coat closer.

Carrie yelled from their porch at Jason. "Why did you let him drag that bloody dog through the muck?"

"I did no such thing. Rachel told him he couldn't take it to the cottage and he ran away like a scared rabbit."

"Bastard," Rachel whispered.

Carrie looked peeved. "That figures somehow. I thought Rachel wasn't coming tonight?"

"Don't worry, Carrie," she yelled back, "I'm not."

Jason's head swung round. "She didn't mean it like that."

Rachel shrugged. "Does it matter how she meant it?"

"Yes, it does."

"Then where have you been, Jason?"

He walked to her but stopped mid-stream when Siobhan Reilly came skipping out of the Hilliers' house with her two kids.

"Rachel—wow! We keep bumping into each other," said an energetic Siobhan Reilly. It took a minute for the image of Siobhan walking out of the Hilliers' door to penetrate, and for Rachel to adequately recover. She had been gone a week—wow! A lot had happened in a week.

The man himself walked out. She could feel his eyes on her but she was far more interested in his date for the weekend.

Rachel gave a soft laugh. "We'll I guess that's easy to do since I live right across the street."

"*Do you really?*" She handed a cooler to Jason. "Your mother wants you to take this."

Rachel's laughter formed into a permanent smile. "Small world isn't it?"

"We're just off to Morgan's cottage. Have you been there Rachel?" asked Siobhan.

"A few times."

Jason leaned against his van and folded his arms. Silent. Rachel hoped he would continue in the same vein. She didn't want to fall apart in front of this woman because one of his witty snipes found a target.

"Rick showed it to me last weekend. It's quite a place, wouldn't you say?"

Elaine and Shawn stopped fighting.

Rachel's eyes trained on Siobhan. "It's lovely. I'm sure you will enjoy yourself."

She pouted at Rachel. "Too bad you have that family thing."

Divorced women with two children certainly don't waste time getting the lay of the land. "Well I better get moving or my mother will start yelling from the second-floor bedroom like a back-entry maid."

"Are you driving up with your parents tomorrow?" asked Morgan. Aunt Sarah and Uncle Robert joined them on the driveway.

She glanced over at her house and pulled her belt tighter. "No. I didn't realize you were all going to the cottage this weekend. I've been in Quebec all week on a school trip. My mum told me your parents are coming with us tonight and then tomorrow night The Folks go to the opera." Rachel sighed; sick of herself, sick of him. "I guess I assumed with The Folks in town ..." She looked over at Aunt Sarah, who opened her mouth, but Siobhan beat her.

"That's why we're having a big party. We have the extra room. The place will be jumping." Rachel wondered how much of Siobhan's excitement was delight, and how much was bravado. Even in her funk though, she didn't miss—*we.*

"It's good to be in the know," Rachel said. "Sorry I'll miss it, but

Louise invited me over for dinner tomorrow night. I haven't seen her new house yet and Adam is crawling—very exciting."

I thought you would come with me Morgan. Maybe give me a chance to make it up to you for childishly running away last weekend, but then, I'm just stupid. I shouldn't have made assumptions. I can't expect to spring plans on Morgan Hillier. He's a busy guy. What can I expect? I had deliberately avoided you all week and now, you have plans. Did I expect you to be a wallflower? Why should you? You're single. Do I need a house to fall on me?

"Well …," Rachel was tired. "It's been a long day. We left Montreal this morning at four, and then the plane here, so I'm running a bit behind."

Siobhan put her arm around Morgan's waist and smiled prettily at her. "Give Rick my love."

Rachel noticed Morgan step out of Siobhan's hold, and Rachel smiled. "I'll be sure to when I get back to Ottawa."

"I thought Rick was going with you to Louise's?" she asked.

I just bet you did. "I don't know why you would think that, but I admit I did think I *might* have a date for tomorrow, but …," she shrugged, "I'm out of luck. I'll just have to fly solo."

It was Siobhan's turn to laugh. "I didn't think flying solo was your thing."

"That doesn't really surprise me somehow." Rachel started walking backward slowly, away from them. "Have a great time." She whirled around and was walking quickly down the long driveway when she heard a squeal of delight.

She turned and saw Macy running toward her. Rachel's spirits lifted immediately. "*Macy* …" she breathed. She held out her arms and Macy jumped into them, wrapping her spindly little legs around Rachel's waist.

"You're home, home, home." Macy bounced in her arms. "I went to kinder gym today with Auntie Carrie, and guess what?"

Rachel looked up in the sky and then at Macy. "You're going to the Olympics?"

Macy had a shocked, silent awed look on her face. "How did you know?"

Rachel laughed. "You *are* going to the Olympics?"

"Yes!"

"Good enough to *one day* go to the Olympics." Morgan stood beside them. His arm reached out to stroke his daughter's hair.

Rachel looked at Macy. "Aren't you the little talent."

Macy giggled, running her hands from the top of Rachel's head and down her hair repeatedly until a serious looked filled her face. "Why are you leaving?"

"Leaving?"

"You were walking away. Did you forget your stuff?"

Rachel licked her lips. "No, I have to go out with my mum and dad tonight."

Macy's eyes clouded. "Are you coming to the cottage later?"

"No Dollie, I didn't—I thought," Rachel struggled to find the words, watching Macy's sweet face, hanging on her words, waiting for a decent explanation.

"Would you like to go with Rachel tonight, Macy?" At Morgan's suggestion, Macy and Rachel's heads swung up to look at him. His eyes fell to Rachel. "You could take her tonight, couldn't you?"

"Yes, yes of course. You wouldn't mind?"

"If Macy doesn't." Morgan looked at his daughter. "Sometimes it's hard with Rachel living so far away. Sometimes things get mixed up. This time things got mixed up. I know how much you've missed her, so if you want to go with her tonight with Aunt Maureen and Uncle John, you can. Grandma and Grandpa will be there, too."

"For a sleepover, too?"

"Yes, if it's okay with Rachel," he agreed before looking at her. "I could drive back tomorrow to pick her up or you could drop her off at the cottage. I know you have plans tomorrow night, but you could come early and have lunch, spend part of the afternoon before you head back to the city. Which one?"'

His suggestion pissed her off. Did he just want *time alone* with *Siobhan* or did he want her to come to the cottage because things just got *mixed up*? She didn't look at him. "That's such a charming invitation."

His voice was even and deep like he was reading a silly tale about Amelia Bedelia. "As much as I would love to battle this out with you, as you may well notice, the family is watching—as usual. I realize you're hurt. That was not my intention, but it does seem like that is all I *ever* do. I *never* get it right. The bottom line is, poor choices were made, mistakes happen. I'm trying my best here."

"Well if this is your best, then I should be grateful." There was no expression in her voice. Macy still bounced gently in her arms. "I appreciate you letting me take Macy for the night. As to which option? I'll drop her off at the cottage tomorrow, but I won't stay. You have a party to get ready for and I don't want to be in your way. *It seems* that's all *I* ever do." She smiled at Macy. "You want to come with me tonight?"

"Yes," she bounced.

"Then give Daddy a kiss bye-bye." Macy turned her face up to Morgan and he leaned down to kiss her, his arms reached around and embraced them both. Rachel stiffened.

"Macy," said Morgan, "go ask Uncle Jason to unpack your overnight bag and put it in Grandma's mudroom, okay? And ask Grandpa to give Daddy a minute?" He lifted her out of Rachel's arms and put her on the ground."

"Okay, Daddy." She raced away.

They both watched the little girl run up the driveway yelling to Jason and then turning to Grandpa. Uncle Robert looked down at Morgan and then nodded. He filed everyone into the house. Rachel was unprepared when his arms went around her, lifting her off the ground. He stared at her and she saw the ache in his eyes. It matched her ache.

Why can't we make this work? Why can't I stop being afraid to tell him how much I love him? Unadulterated fear.

She stared at him. His lips found hers easily. When his tongue ran over her mouth, she shivered, and her mouth opened to his, her head tucked into his shoulder.

When he lifted his head, he whispered against her lips. "Have dinner with me and Macy, we'll spend the evening together."

Their breath mingled. "What about Siobhan?"

"*Rachel.*"

Tearfully, she whispered, looking up at him. "I can't keep doing this Morgan."

"I don't want to discuss this here." He set her down, stepped back, and his hands dropped away from her. "Aren't you getting sick of our personal lives being public domain?"

"And you think that's my fault?"

"Jesus Christ, Rachel." His hands went through his hair with a controlled violence. "I don't want to fight with you."

"I know what you want to do with me. And because I'm a complete idiot I've made it bloody easy."

"Then we're both fools. Because I've taken more shit, for longer, from you than I've ever taken from any other woman—including my wife."

Including my wife. The words were like daggers. She lost her breath. She stepped back from him. Her fingers pressed hard into her lips. She felt the tears building in her eyes. Why did this bother her? But it did.

"Babe—please don't. No running, please, I can't take it." He reached for her and she moved away from him, but he held her firmly. "No running, stay. I'm asking you to stay."

Hurt bubbled up inside her. Tears stung her eyes. It was too much. Last weekend her self-confidence took a shit-kicking. If Rachel were in Elaine's shoes, she would have wanted Rachel gone— "Get that crazy ass bitch out of here!" She'd ruined Elaine's weekend. It wasn't intentional, but she had. Something more to add to her regret list. Spending a horrible week in Quebec hadn't helped. They'd hit an ice storm that rendered them immobile. Power was lost in more than three-quarters of the city. Loss of mobility and power on a school trip with a bunch of teenagers who lived off drama, while trapped in a community centre with two hundred other people, made the week long and emotionally draining.

"I'm sorry Rachel, please don't run."

Rachel wiped her face and tried to control her breathing. His hands were gentle, caressing. It calmed the white noise in her head.

She was so weak. He held her and she couldn't resist him. She slid her arms to his waist before she stepped back, but only slightly. His arms ran down her back and pulled her into the side of his body, shielding her from the cool wind. Rachel's arm slid under his leather coat and around his waist, her head down.

"Rachel?" prompted Morgan quietly, stroking her hair back from her face. "Can I take you to this graduation dinner tonight?"

She held her questions, not wanting to lose the moment. "Please."

She looked at Morgan. His face was remote.

"Let's go." His hand ran down her arm and entwined his fingers with hers.

His knuckles were bandaged. "What happened to your hand?"

"A stubborn hedge." He tugged her and they walked across the street in silence. Morgan was many things; a hedge trimmer was not on that list.

Her mother was running down the staircase when they came in. "Rachel darling, thank goodness, I thought— Hello, Morgan." Her mother stopped halfway down the steps, her gaze jumping from one to the other. "What's wrong?"

Morgan spoke. "Nothing. Rachel has asked me to come with her tonight."

"I see."

Rachel could hear a controlled sharpness in her mother's voice.

"Will that be a problem?" he asked politely. "Macy will be with us, too."

"No, of course not. I thought Rachel would bring a date, and one more place setting for Macy isn't a problem."

"Good." He had picked up her suitcase from the porch and it was still in his hand. He looked at Rachel. "I'll take this up for you, lead the way." He knew the way but she remained silent.

Morgan put the case down on her bed. His back was to her. She closed the door. His voice was quiet when he spoke. "I was going out to lunch with Jeff and Jason one day last week; we bumped into Siobhan. She works around the corner in the Scotia Plaza, apparently. She joined us. I wasn't paying attention to what they were saying—I kept thinking about last weekend. The sleeping bag, the Gables' pull-out. The next thing I knew the party was happening. I didn't know you were in Quebec. You didn't tell me. When you didn't return my calls—"

"You didn't call me."

"Still haven't figured out voice mail on your cell?"

She blushed.

His voice was quiet. "I thought I was still on your shit list because you were calling Macy anywhere I wasn't. Siobhan said you were going to Louise's for dinner with Rick. I know you're pissed off about something I did last weekend, but I don't have any fucking idea what it is. And frankly, this is beginning to seem like work."

He turned around to look at her. "We never used to fight; we could talk about anything and now, anything I say can set you off and you freeze me out. Every time I think we're in a good place, something happens. What's making you so unhappy? Tell me, for Christ sake, Rachel, tell me!"

She shook her head. Her emotions were sitting too close to the surface. Everything would gush out and she was vulnerable enough when it came to Morgan, but to be completely exposed? To hand over her heart in the defenceless state it was in? Without knowing how he felt about her? And what about her mother? She just said she thought Rachel would bring a date, but she thought it would be Rick. Why? Rick did ask her what she was up to this weekend, asked if she wanted company. She said no. Who told Siobhan that Rick was her date? Was her mother working against her? She'd made herself clear that it was a mistake getting involved with Morgan. What if she wanted to prove it? After Rachel's declaration last weekend that Morgan was the man in her life, why would she do that? Why would her mother think she would take Rick to the dinner after finding her in bed with Morgan last week?

"You can't tell me?"

She shook her head again.

"Babe ..." He walked toward her with his arms out and she gladly went to him. "I'm here for you—always. Maybe we're putting too much pressure on this. You're only here on the weekends. We should enjoy our time together—stress free. No pressure. And when you are finished your contract and we're both in the same city, we'll figure it out, okay?

"Okay. You're right, it's hard to figure all this out long distance."

"Agreed."

"Agreed."

"Just remember, I'm here for you, sweetie. Whenever you're ready to tell me what's worrying you, you know I'll listen. I hate when you are upset but I don't want to push you into saying what you're not ready to say. *Nothing* is as important as *you*. As long as I have a breath, I'm your bitch."

Rachel laughed into his chest.

"You tell anyone I said that—I'll have to kill you."

I love you so much Morgan. "It's the only way."

Morgan laughed, kissing the top of her head. "There's my girl."

"Let's have a nice weekend?"

"Let's have a nice weekend."

***

They did have a nice weekend. No deep conversation. They kept it light. The graduation dinner turned out to be fun. Morgan overshadowed the guest of honour with his polite attentiveness and his willingness to join in silly round table games. Even Macy stole their hearts when she sang *Tiny Bubbles* while everyone cheered her on. Aunt Adele wasn't pleased. Best of all, her dad's brother and his family were absent.

At the end of the evening, they all went back to the Hilliers' for tea and dessert. Macy reminded her father she was sleeping at Rachel's.

"I remember," said Morgan.

"We'll meet you two over at the house," said Maureen Wharton to Rachel and Macy.

Once they retrieved Macy's bag from the Hilliers' mudroom, Morgan walked them across the street, kissing them each on the cheek.

At the door, Morgan said, "Tomorrow, why don't I take you, two lovely ladies, out to lunch, and then we can go to the Science Centre?"

"Yes!" agreed Macy.

"Lovely," said Rachel.

"Auntie Rachel, do you think your Mum baked cookies?"

"She always has cookies for you, Macy."

Macy giggled and opened the front door. "You guys can kiss now."

The minute the front door closed, Morgan said, "I have to find out what this Cassandra Lake is telling my daughter." He lightly touched her lips with his; teasing her with the promise of a kiss.

"This date you wanted to take to Louise Summerhill's place, do I know him?"

Rachel reached up, wrapping her arms around his neck, she whispered, "Maybe," and pulled his head down to her.

23

LOST IN LOVE

Rachel stood at the altar of St. Paul's Church, watching Macy and Daniel make their way down the centre aisle to a soft lilting instrumental. When they reached their pews and sat down, music boomed, filling the church. The congregation was on their feet. Elaine, on Uncle Robert's arm, stood at the threshold of the church foyer. Prisms of lights ran down like spears from the stained-glass windows sitting high on the church walls. As Elaine moved, a rainbow of light fell across her porcelain skin.

Her beautiful Arctic white dress was off the shoulders with a neckline that curved around the swell of her breasts. The bodice was white satin, tailored to her waist, coming to a vee, and the skirt billowed out. The sleeves were three-quarter length, and sheer. It was simple and elegant. The veil Elaine wore could not hide her radiance. It beamed through the sheer fabric. Her large blue eyes sparkled like sapphires.

"*Oh, God,*" Shawn whispered hoarsely.

Rachel saw his rapt gaze as he watched Elaine. Morgan put a steady hand on Shawn's shoulder, and he caught Rachel's stare. Their eyes locked. Morgan was knee knocking gorgeous. Dressed in a black tuxedo, superbly tailored to his wide shoulders; his black hair gleamed in the brightness of the airy cathedral. He was a striking man who wore his strength casually. His eyes darkened with intensity as he stared at her, and Rachel swallowed the tears that threatened to consume her. She trembled, a current of electricity passing between them. Nervously, she looked at the flowers she held stiffly, blinking furiously to gain her composure.

Elaine was a few feet from the altar. Her father stopped, lifted her veil. "I love you, Daddy," she said tearfully, and Uncle Robert hugged and kissed her.

"I love you, too, sweetie," he said, and passed his little girl to Shawn. Uncle Robert shook Shawn's hand. "Take care of her."

"I will, sir," Shawn said gruffly, and Rachel's heart contracted.

Shawn took Elaine's hand. They couldn't tear their eyes away from each other. Rachel stood behind Elaine, off to the side, as did Morgan behind Shawn. From the corner of her eye, she greedily watched Morgan's every gesture, his every expression, his every smile.

Elaine and Shawn were asked to face each other to exchange their vows. Shaking badly, Rachel turned to face Morgan. Her eyes wandered to his. His steady gaze met hers. There was confidence in his stare, tenderness, and she was yanked into him like a whirlpool and transported. Her stomach flipped. It was Morgan's strong and sure voice she heard saying, "I will honour you with my body and my life, until death do us part." Her eyes stung with tears. She wanted it to be them standing here exchanging vows before God and family.

"Rachel?" she heard Elaine say from far away, "I need the ring, honey."

Rachel startled violently. "The ring ... Yes, yes, I'm sorry." She fumbled with the ring, and it flew out of her hand, but Morgan reacted quickly, grabbing it mid-air and handing it back to her, bringing a ripple of laughter from the congregation. She gave it to Elaine mumbling another apology. She wanted to sink onto the floor with the strain. Instead, she stood and watched Elaine recite her promise to Shawn and slip the ring on his finger. Rachel's tears came down fast.

The priest ushered the four of them to the side of the altar where

Elaine sat to sign the registry. Morgan put his arm around Rachel's waist and drew her into his side, shielding her from the guests with his body, handing her his handkerchief.

Pressing his hanky into her mouth, she turned her face into his chest, gripping his tuxedo jacket, letting her tempered sentiment find refuge in the strength of his arms, in the steady pound of his heart.

What is wrong with me? she thought. She was falling apart; she felt like she was sinking into a black hole—no light, no way out, no pride to carry her through what was becoming an ordeal. A terrible weight pressed down on her, wrapping her in a draining melancholy. It gripped her with tension before moving down her body until she was numb. Her tears froze on her face and she loosened her grip on Morgan's jacket.

Rachel saw Morgan's hand move to her face. She couldn't feel his touch but she knew it was gentle. His voice was soft as he spoke to her trying to calm her but she didn't know what he said. He guided her to the seat where Elaine had been and pointed where she was to sign, and dutifully, she did.

In a fog, Rachel propelled herself through the rest of the day. She stood where the photographer said, smiled when she was told to, had conversation with other members of the wedding party, but mostly, thank goodness, she was only required to nod her head in agreement, laugh at the appropriate conversation break, and the rest was a blur.

***

At the reception, Rachel shook hands with each guest that passed through the receiving line: aunts, uncles, cousins, long-lost friends from high school, university friends, new friends from the Hillier conglomerate. It wasn't until the trophy award-giving blond cousin, who had kissed Morgan at the Gables, stepped in front of them, that the blur of the day's events started to clear. She looked ravishing with her hair piled on her head in a sleek chignon. Her royal blue dress clung lovingly to her willowy figure. She ignored Rachel, passing over her, gracefully reaching for Morgan with a throaty laugh.

"Morgan don't you look handsome." Appreciation was in her bright eyes as she stared at him, her hand pressing down on his arm, her hip moving close to his.

"You look stunning, Helen," Morgan smiled, a mocking curve on his mouth. It held sensuality, an amused sexual awareness.

Helen kissed his cheek then made a production out of wiping her red lipstick off his skin. Helen was a tall woman, but the four-inch spiked heels, still brought her a few inches shorter than him, making Rachel feel twelve. Helen was last in the line and wasn't in any hurry to move into the dining room.

Rude, thought Rachel, *that's what she is, not even decent enough to acknowledge my existence.* Obviously, little Miss Helen was one of those women who was a man's woman, despising her sex. Her large, almond-shaped eyes only trained on the male species. Rachel stood patiently while they spoke, pretending not to watch.

Morgan's hand touched Rachel's waist and she jumped. She wanted to jerk away from him but pride kept her where she was. "This is Rachel Wharton." Morgan stared down at her. "This is Helen Fielding, Shawn's cousin."

"Hello," Rachel said politely. "I don't think we've met."

"I'm sure we have, you look familiar. Didn't we meet at my Aunt and Uncle's Resort a couple of weeks ago?" Helen Fielding had one of those deep, sophisticated voices, a hint of humour in every inflection.

"Yes, I was there, but I don't think we were introduced."

"You didn't go to the dinner on Sunday night at my aunt and uncle's resort, The Maple Grove, did you?"

"No, I had to fly back to Ottawa."

"Oh yes," she said, her hand flying to her forehead. "The Ottawa girl. Now I remember. Too bad you missed the dinner. We ended up having a helluva party, didn't we Morgan? No one left for home until Monday morning."

This is a new development. My leaving early was *the best decision for everyone.* Rachel glanced around the foyer of the reception hall, only the wedding party remained. "It looks like you're the last one. Why don't I leave you two to chat?"

How many women do I have to beat off him, exactly? Helen Fielding laying an intimate kiss on him at the Gables' house and then he partied the night away at the resort with Helen. Then last week I go home to find Siobhan Reilly hanging off his arm.

The wedding party stood in the foyer. Once their names were called, each couple was to go through the double doors, smile, and take their seats at the head table. Rachel waited in a corner by herself. She had no desire to talk to Morgan. He was right about one thing—this was beginning to feel like work.

Last night Elaine and Shawn had a casual dinner at the Hilliers', just for the wedding party, giving out personal, but comical gifts, for everyone. Rachel sat with Morgan, dopey with love, fawning over him like a lovesick fool—a humiliating display in the brightness of day, now that little chickadee had come along. "What a helluva party you missed. Isn't that right Morgan?" If Morgan wanted to make eyes at Helen, there was nothing Rachel could do about it. If Siobhan Reilly was more to his taste with her built-in family, *fine!* Morgan was a grown man. Helen was more his style, and Rachel's adolescent reverence was a charming distraction—ego feeding.

Elaine and Shawn were in a breathy exchange. The groomsmen were in a circle laughing and the bridesmaids had broken off into groups of two. Morgan finally pulled away from Helen and made his way over to Rachel, an amused glint in his eye. She turned away.

Morgan whispered in her ear, "Is something wrong?"

"Nope," Rachel said, finality in her voice, and stepped away from him.

The master of ceremonies announced the first couple at the head table.

"Liar," he chuckled.

"Why do you care, Morgan?" she snapped, her head turned sharply to look at him.

"What makes you think I don't care?" He cocked his eyebrow, a stern expression on his face.

Couple two was introduced

"Actions speak louder than words, Morgan, or haven't you heard that? A big smart fella like you, not knowing a fundamental about life?" she said.

Morgan grabbed her hand tightly in his. "You need a good crack on the ass," he said.

Her jaw was tight in a smile as the double doors opened. "And who would do that Morgan? You?"

"As I've had the pleasure of fondling your ass, who better? Or has Summerhill had the same pleasure? You like to keep two at a time if memory serves?" he said.

Couple three was called into the dining room

Rachel's cheeks stung with heat. She smiled brightly. "How dare you judge me."

The face that stared down at her was blank, but his eyes flared with anger. "I *have* dared and you begged me to be *more* daring. I have vivid memories of you rubbing against me, of pressing yourself into me, pleading with me, so spare me the indignation. What I want to know is did you go from my bed to his? We've had a great time but you haven't had sex with me."

Couple four.

"Wasn't it your suggestion to experiment? To enjoy my sexuality? Now that I've found it again, I am to enjoy it, am I not?"

she muttered, immediately sorry for what she implied, and yanked her eyes from the dangerous ferocity in his.

The master of ceremonies voice boomed in the foyer. "We have the coolest couple I've ever met: Rachel Wharton and Morgan Hillier.

"Smile Morgan, it's showtime," she said, then waved to Elaine. "See you on the other side." Elaine laughed.

The head table was at the front of the massive hall in the shape of a half-moon. Morgan and Rachel walked across the room and took their seats. Rachel clutched her napkin, twisting it, torturing it. Trying to keep her chaotic emotions out of her face, she concentrated on the room. A large chandelier hung from the centre at a low light, sconces were evenly spaced along the wall, and matched the chandelier. The room held three hundred guests easily. The tables were dressed in white linen, a centrepiece of white roses, and white china.

Elaine and Shawn entered the room to thunderous clapping. The new Mr. and Mrs. Gable held hands, their faces a testament to their happiness. Rachel's heart contracted in her chest, envious of their rapture, the clearness in their eyes. Love spun a web around them.

Rachel hoped the conversation with Morgan was over, but once Elaine and Shawn took their seats, the wait staff moved around the room with bottles of wine and champagne, and he turned his attention back to her. "I want an answer."

"You're not my keeper Morgan. Who I sleep with is none of your business."

Morgan leaned forward, his fingertips brushed her shoulder and she shivered. There was something in his manner—seemed dangerous. "I'm sick of being your fucking puppet—I strongly suggest you tell me what I want to know."

She wished he would stop staring at her, stop touching her. She wasn't going to be able to keep him at bay if he kept—kept bugging her, and in front of three hundred pair of eyes. Wasn't he the one who didn't want their personal lives to be public domain? Or was knowing if she had sex with Rick more important than privacy? And why did he want to know? Male ego? He was just flirting with *Helen* for heaven's sake. Fuck him. Short of drawing a picture, he made it clear he wasn't taking her seriously.

Morgan grabbed her hand and yanked her up from her chair.

"Where are we going?" Before she realized his intention, he pushed her through the exit door right beside them, and out into a corridor. His long strides took them down the hall.

"You suck up to Helen Fielding and you're lecturing me about who I sleep with?"

"No!" He stopped, his face pushed into hers, he growled. "This is about you and me. This is about me being sick of your fucking games Rachel. I'm not a fucking teenager. We're getting to the bottom of this once and for all."

Rachel had never seen Morgan like this; he was in an icy fury. He opened a door and dragged her in behind him. The door snapped shut and he pushed her against the door and pressed his body against hers.

"You think I was sucking up to Helen?" He ran his finger along the top of her breast.

"Yes."

"What a child you are."

"A child that drives you nuts."

"You've got that right, cupcake; you drive me fucking nuts." His lips came down on hers. She felt his hand on her zipper, heard it slowly move down her back. His lips were wet and hot on her neck; his hardness pressed deeply into her. Her dress was gone and she felt the coolness of the room. She hadn't bothered with a bra that morning, the cut of the dress made it unnecess—

His lips parted hers, his hands caressing, rubbing, gently playing and pinching at her breasts and she trembled violently. Her breath came in hard gulps; his hands were seducing. Without a word he picked her up and carried her across the room to the couch. His body settled over hers. Morgan's eyes glittered down at her. He moved slightly, and his eyes roved over her with undisguised desire. With his long index finger and thumb, he played with her nipple and she bit her lip at the hunger that ripped through her. It made her weak.

"Don't hold it in, baby," he whispered huskily. "I love hearing you."

She ran her hand up his chest. Her stomach plunged as his lips caught hers roughly. Sighing, her lips parted wide and invitingly to meet the bruising demand of his mouth. His hands wandered over her flesh; her belly, her hips, pushing her slip up to her waist, he stroked her inner thighs, and she gasped, arching into him.

Rachel looped her arms around his neck, kissing him back with a wildness that held her in a vice, making her dizzy. Her hands ran over and around his body, down his back to his hips, grounded them down into hers as she twitched and bucked against him.

His lips slid to her neck. He coiled his hand around the bun in her hair. "Does it feel good?"

"Yes ... yes," she whispered.

His tongue licked her hard nipple then pulled it into his mouth and sucked it with a rhythm that made her groan, driving her crazy. He rubbed his face in her breasts and then pulled the other nipple into his hot mouth. Her thighs gripped him, her body writhing underneath his, only aware of the hot pressure of his hard flesh crushed against her.

"Did you go from my bed to his Rachel?" There was venom in Morgan's voice. His grip on the bun in her hair tightened, and he yanked on it, "Did he touch you like this? Have you seduced him like you've seduced me? Have you used this beautiful body of yours to drive him crazy? ... Now that you know what to do with it ... You've come a long way since you were a little green teenager, haven't you sweetheart?"

She went cold. Still. The passion, the excitement of being in his arms drained away. Tears sparkled in her eyes as she looked at him. Hurt and disbelief clouded her vision. Tears squeezed out of the corner of her eyes.

"You ... bastard ..."

"Do you go to him when you leave me? Or are you trying to tell me Rick never tries to get into your pants? Because *I'm sick* of hearing *how he's fucking you*." Morgan ran his hand down to the waistband of her underpants, his face a tight mass of desire, which didn't reach his eyes. His hands were bold and lacked tenderness.

For the first time in her life, she was frightened of Morgan. She didn't recognize him; he was a stranger. "Tell me! Has he?" he shouted, tugging at her underpants, the grip on her hair painful.

"You're hurting me, Morgan," There was violence in his rough hands; her underpants were now down to her knees. She cried. He yanked her underwear off, and her cries became uncontrollable.

"I want the truth! No fucking games Rachel! I'm a patient man but I'm fucking frustrated beyond belief and if I have to listen to one more person tell me you're fucking Summerhill, I'm going to lose my fucking mind! I haven't been with anyone else but you and I don't want anyone else but you, so I want the fucking truth!"

"No!" she shouted. "No!"

Morgan was still. "No what?"

Rachel put her hands over her eyes. She was trembling violently. "I haven't slept with Rick. There is nothing between us. I told you the rumours aren't true. I don't know what people are saying to you, but its lies." Her cries were full of sorrow. "I haven't slept with him or anyone since Paris. You're the only one I've been with—the only one I want to be with—just you. Please Morgan—you're hurting me. Please stop."

Suddenly, the painful hold he had on her was gone and he moved away. Wrapping her arms defensively around her breasts, she turned into the back of the couch and hid her face, crying, struggling to breathe.

Rachel heard Morgan swear violently and she pressed herself further into the soft fabric of the sofa. Dejected.

He wanted to force it out of her, and he did. She had never felt so ashamed at how easily he could arouse her, and how, without conscience, he had used how she felt about him against her. She had never seen Morgan so angry, never thought she would ever be afraid of him.

"Rachel?" He touched her bare shoulder.

"Please leave me alone. You got what you wanted, now go away. Haven't you humiliated me enough?" He laid her dress over her nakedness and she snatched at it and sat up. He had the decency to turn away while she dressed. "Please leave me alone."

"I'm not leaving, Rachel," he said softly. At his gentle tone, she looked at him. She saw remorse there but she didn't care. He had deliberately degraded her. Used her.

She sat on the couch, she didn't know how long, but a calmness she didn't feel, took over. It was Elaine's wedding and she had a job to do. She needed to pull herself together. "Elaine has a change room somewhere here. She has a grey floral makeup case. It has her name on it. Could you bring it to me?"

Without a word, he left and Rachel flopped down on the couch again. How was she going to get through this evening? She had a speech to make after dinner.

Minutes later, Morgan returned with the case.

"Will you please wait outside while I collect myself?" she asked without looking at him. She couldn't bear to see him. "I need a minute, Morgan."

Rachel heard the click of the door.

She propped the case against the back of the chair. Opened the lid where the mirror was and knelt in front of the chair. Her hair was a wild mess around her, her face streaked with mascara. A mess was an understatement. Quickly she washed her face in a nearby sink and then lightly reapplied her makeup; Elaine and Rachel had the same skin tone. She redid her hair. She packed the case again and joined Morgan in the hall.

"I need to get through this evening," she said to him, "so the mess between us—I can't deal with it. We have to go out there and pretend everything's okay for Laine's sake. Once we get through the dinner, I don't give a fuck what you do."

Silently they walked to the change room and Morgan replaced the case.

When they returned to the main hall the salad was being served. Morgan pulled out her chair and she accepted his attention without comment.

Rachel ate little. She took a fork full of salad; a spoon full of the curried cream soup, pushed the potatoes and carrots around and didn't touch the beef wellington. It was delicious she was sure but she couldn't work up any enthusiasm. She smiled at everyone. Laughed when appropriate. She felt Morgan's eyes on her, and occasionally she made polite conversation with him.

She didn't want to smash into a million bits in front of all these people. She ate little bits very slowly but it all tasted like metal in her mouth. Dessert was her favourite, cheesecake, but even cheesecake couldn't take away the bad taste in her mouth. She drank tea—lots and lots of tea. The dead feeling in her body stayed with her. There was no tension between her and Morgan. She didn't care what he did or said. She was mechanical. Politely she listened to the master of ceremonies read telegrams, listened to speeches from Uncle Robert and Aunt Sarah, Shawn's parents, a few friends.

Morgan stood to make his speech and give his toast. She

watched him. Again, he was the Morgan she knew, charming. His laughter was easy, a sarcastic undertone in his humour. He had hurt her like she never thought he could and he'd done it deliberately, and watching him, her heart started to thaw, and it broke for him.

Morgan's words rang in her ears: "I want the truth! No fucking games Rachel! I'm a patient man but I'm fucking frustrated beyond belief and if I have to listen to one more person tell me you're fucking Summerhill; I'm going to lose my fucking mind! I haven't been with anyone else but you and I don't want anyone else but you, so I want the fucking truth!" In his words, she felt his insecurities. His pain. Why would someone go to such lengths to make him distrust her? Everything was so twisted. They were just fighting to be together; they were fighting with unseen forces.

Don't think. Don't think. She didn't want to think about his words and their impact, but she could feel his remorse and it brought more sorrow to her heart than her hurt did.

How fucked up is that?

"And now, please give a warm reception to the maid of honour, the *very* beautiful Rachel Wharton." Morgan wasn't supposed to introduce her. He waited at the podium for her to join him. He tenderly put his arm around her waist and kissed her cheek, then whispered, "If you see my friend, will you tell her how sorry I am I hurt her." There was a catch in Morgan's voice.

Rachel glanced up. Morgan stared at her intently and her heart pounded, hard and fast in her chest. His eyes were full of things she didn't quite understand, but she liked that they were there. She closed her eyes and stepped away, which broke the surge of intense emotion that passed between them.

Morgan moved away.

Rachel took a deep breath and looked out at the crowd. "I've had the great fortune of growing up with the Hilliers and it's been a little like living in the land of giants when you have no hope of being anything more than a niblet." A ripple of laughter passed over the crowd and Rachel regained a bit of her confidence.

"Elaine is the kind of woman you aspire to be. She's thoughtful and kind-hearted. She always knows the perfect thing to wear for any occasion; she's a woman of repose, like a gentle sigh. I used to wish for a body transference so that I could be Elaine for a day, just to know what being a woman of repose was like. I am the flaky one with a bad temper. Elaine is the complete opposite—a planner, a thinker, one who weighs consequences. My fly-by-the- seat-of-my-pants mantra for living, I'm sure has frustrated Elaine over the years, although she would never say so. Do you know how hard it is hanging out with perfection? My lack of perfection still has my parents paying for my deep, deep, neurosis. It comes at $350 an hour with Dr. Feinstein."

Laughter filled the room. She heard the screen coming down from the ceiling and picked up the slide projector remote. She noticed Morgan standing casually against the wall, his hands in his pockets, his face remote as he watched her.

Rachel turned to the wedding party. "If you would indulge me and take your chairs around to the front of the table."

As Elaine walked by her, she said, "What have you done, Miss Rachel?"

Rachel only smiled at her. She clicked the first slide that said To Lainey with Love. "When Elaine walked down the aisle today, I thought first, how breathtakingly beautiful she is," Rachel's voice broke and her hands started to shake. "And I thought of the wonderful memories I have growing up. Not everyone has been as lucky as I've been. Not everyone has an Elaine. I love her," she swallowed hard, "so much, for so many reasons." Rachel breathed deeply. "One thing's for certain—Laine is a good sport, and she never made me feel bad about any of my hare-brained ideas. How good a sport—are you wondering?"

Rachel clicked the button. "I thought a kissing booth would be fun and recruited Elaine as the main attraction." Click. "Knife throwing. Yes, that's Elaine as the target." Click. "Sailing. Elaine is looking quite green. At the end of the summer, the yacht club gave her the Miss Gravol Award." Click. "I convinced her to enter the Miss Chocolate May contest because the prize was a new wardrobe and a trip to New York City—of course, she won. Being Elaine, she took me to New York with her, split the wardrobe, and fulfilled her Miss Chocolate May duties without complaint." Click. "I thought belly dancing would be cool. This was our recital—you'll thank me for that one someday, Shawn." Everyone laughed.

"And these ... are my favourite pictures of Elaine." Rachel clicked, showing pictures of Elaine from birth to graduation from university with a soft instrumental in the background, some funny, some goofy, and some at her most beautiful.

The screen went blank and Rachel turned the projector off. Picking up her champagne glass she steadied it on the podium. Rachel looked at Shawn. "Of course, Shawn, you know the adage, if you hurt her, I'll have to track you down like a bloodhound." She gave him a cheeky smile. "You may laugh m'lad but us flaky types are unpredictable." The crowd clapped. The room was light and airy.

Rachel picked up her glass from the podium and stared at Elaine, who was crying. "Thank you for being the best big sister. I love you. Be happy." She raised her glass to her friend and the guests did the same.

"To Elaine," said Rachel.

The guests shouted, "To Elaine."

They drank to the bride.

24
MORGAN'S ROYAL FUCK-UP

The evening remained unsalvageable for Rachel; it deteriorated to the point of numbness. Elaine and Shawn shared their first dance. The wedding party joined them during the second song. Rachel tried to relax in Morgan's arms but couldn't. They didn't speak. When the dance ended, they went their separate ways. The family quickly took over two tables on the main floor and abandoned the head table. Cousin Helen took up residence beside Morgan; all cozy and spice in his face. He was charming and polite with her, but Cousin Helen had other plans, and dragged him onto the dance floor, touching him intimately at every chance. Rachel ignored Morgan like he was dead. Morgan started to drink; not usually a heavy drinker, an occasional indulgence, but nothing like this. At first, Rachel hadn't noticed how much he was putting away. As the evening progressed, she saw he had moved to doubles; the blank dullness that had been in his eyes lifted. Helen threw back shots of whisky without a wince. To get away from the table, she danced with whoever asked her. Her face froze into a polite smile. Her voice held an interested tone of inquiry. When Macy tugged on her dress, the deadness inside Rachel started to fade.

"I'm sad," said Macy.

Rachel turned to the handsome man whose name she couldn't remember. "Will you excuse us?" She didn't wait for an answer. She took Macy's hand. "How about that comfy chair in the corner, and you tell me what's wrong."

With Macy on her lap, she said, "Why are you sad?"

"'Cause—*that lady*."

"What lady?"

Macy looked fierce, pointing to the family table. "She's mean."

Rachel looked over at Morgan and Helen commiserating with each other.

"She keeps touching my daddy—and when he lefts the table, she says 'Stop hanging around kid, get lost. Isn't it bedtime?'"

"Cousin Helen said that?"

"*She's not my cusin.* Daniel and Robby—those're my cusins. Not that mean lady. Do somethin' Auntie Rachel!"

"I should do something?"

"He's you're boyfriend."

"Why do you think he's *my* boyfriend?"

Macy shrugged. 'Cause me and Cassandra were spyin' on ya and Cassandra said ya were kissing like mums and dads, so that means ya're boyfriend and girlfriend."

Rachel nodded. "Ah yes, the wise Cassandra."

"She said it doesn't last long."

"What doesn't?"

"The mums and dads kissin' part. They start fightin' pretty soon. She said, the only time the kissin' didn't stop was with her real mum, but she died."

"Her mum died?"

"Yeah. She was four. She's gets real sad about it sometimes."

"I'm sure she does. I didn't realize—I thought her dad was divorced."

"Does divorced mean they leave without dyin'?"

"Yes, they leave but don't die."

"Maybe one was a mummy and the rest were his girlfriend's 'cause they don't live with them."

"If they don't live with them, they're definitely girlfriends."

"So, go tell her to go home and leave all of us alone."

"Cousin Helen, she means no harm. She hasn't seen Daddy in a long time so they are just getting caught up." She cupped Macy's face. "But I think, for such a little girl, you have a lot of things banging around in that head of yours. You know what I do when I've got a lot of stuff banging about in *my head?*?

"What?"

"I twirl."

Macy sighed and clapped her hands. "Let's twirl!"

With Macy in her arms, her little legs wrapped around Rachel's waist, they twirled around the edge of the dance floor.

"*Whee!*" shouted Rachel and Macy joined in, "*Whee!*" When she twirled them fast, Macy squealed with delight.

"Throw out your arms and feel the wind," said Rachel. As they twirled their arms glided through the air, and they giggled into each other's face.

Macy was soon whisked away by Jason and Daniel for a game of Freeze and Rachel was seized by Samson Hillier for a dance.

When Samson released her, Aunt Sarah quickly grabbed her arm and tucked it into hers. "Hello my love, I haven't had the chance to check in; you've been busy."

"Maid of honour duties. Work the room."

Sarah smiled and nodded to passers-by. "I'm feeling a need for a little walk about the lobby." She manoeuvred her way through the crowds—all wanting a piece of Sarah Hillier, but with style and grace she easily thwarted their advances. Once away from her fan club, they walked arm in arm through the elegant lobby.

"I hope you will indulge an old woman because I find myself in a pensive mood."

"Your youngest just got married; I'm not surprised."

"That's what I love about you, Rachel. You are so astute."

Rachel laughed. "I wish that were true."

"Rachel, I need to tell you—I couldn't love you any more than I do. I've been mothering you for a long time, my darling, and I know when you are hurt or scared or frustrated, and I see how loving my son has taken its toll on you. Morgan is a complicated man. Even as a child he had difficulty trusting those around him—for a lot of very good reasons. He was hurt terribly as a boy—people with ulterior motives. Sadly, he learned that when he was too young. He's not considered a sensitive person, but he is; he hides it. Clings to his hurts like a badge of honour. The only time I see the unspoiled, sweet boy I raised, the only time I see his defences completely down is when he's with you. I don't know what has happened between you two today, but I've never seen Morgan make such a public spectacle of himself, so whatever he's done—" Sarah stopped, grasped Rachel's hand lovingly and looked into her eyes, "He's hurt you very deeply, and in the process hurt himself triple-fold. No, no, don't bother denying it or worrying that your secret has been revealed. You've done an exceptional job of hiding your hurt. But I've watched the love you feel for him grow and I see the pain in your eyes.

"I also see how you are with Macy—you never let what is going on between you and Morgan affect your love for her—I'm in awe at your capacity to love. Your capacity to love my son even when he's being a jackass." She reached out and smoothed Rachel's cheek, soft tears glistened in her eyes.

"I am so proud of the woman you have become," whispered Sarah. "So, so, so very proud. I love mothering you and will continue to mother you until you shout at me to stop, but I want you to know, regardless of what happens between you and Morgan, that will never change. You are my child and I am your mother—forever."

Tears tripped down Rachel's face and she reached out to embrace Sarah. "I love you so much." Her voice was thick with emotion. "You saved my life when I thought I was going to drown— you have no idea how much a need you."

Sarah kissed her temple and held her tight until the tremors in her body calmed.

***

Sarah and Rachel returned to the family table and within minutes Macy climbed up onto her lap and promptly fell asleep lying on her chest. Sadly, this left Rachel to watch Morgan give Helen Fielding more and more of his attention. He gave Helen sexy indulgent smiles, whispered in her ear, having her exclaim for all to hear what a naughty boy he was. It made Rachel sick and heartbroken. All evening she had been listening to disparaging whispers while she danced through the crowd, a smile plastered on her face; with every step, she felt the expansive hall shrivelling up into a tiny ball.

"Hillier is drunk. I've seen everything now."

"Disgusting display."

"He's usually so conservative."

"He looks like Altman, doesn't he?"

"He might look like him but he's more of a gentleman than Altman—he was such a cruel bastard."

"Who's the blond anyway? She's slobbering all over him."

"I thought he was with Rachel Wharton tonight?"

"He's always with Rachel Wharton."

"Rachel looks like she having the time of her life."

"Look at her play with Morgan's little girl."

"Are they an item?"

"Yes."

"No."

"I heard they were cousins."

"The mothers are close."

"She did say Elaine was like a sister."

"Yes, yes—a fourth Hillier. Grew up together."

"I think there's more between them. You'd get an electric shock if you stand too close."

"Hated the ex-wife."

"The ex hated little Miss Rachel with a vengeance."

"Surprised she didn't take a contract out on her."

They all laughed.

"Rachel's lovely—a bit capricious for him though. He's so buttoned-down arrogant."

"Not tonight."

"Maureen Wharton looks like she wants to take a dagger to Hillier's heart."

"I hear she doesn't like her daughter spending too much time with him—blue blood or not."

"I wouldn't mind getting my hands on some of that Hillier money."

"I wouldn't mind getting my hands on that hunk of a man."

***

Relief flooded Rachel when Elaine appeared in her going away outfit, ready to throw her bouquet. It was easy to opt-out with Macy fast asleep on her. Rachel wanted out as far and as fast as she could.

Helen Fielding caught the bouquet.

How perfect is that?

Getting up, Rachel said, "I'll put Macy to bed." They were all staying at the hotel. She said to Morgan without making eye contact, "I'll keep her in my room."

Morgan said, "That's not necessary."

Rachel ignored him and did the rounds with Macy: kisses and hugs for everyone. When she got to Carrie, Daniel was sleeping on her lap. Little Robert was with Carrie's parents for the night. "Do you want me to take him, Carrie? You and Jason can enjoy yourselves?" asked Rachel.

"No."

Jason intervened. "Carrie, Rachel's offering and it would be nice to have a little time—"

Carrie smoothly interrupted. "Thank you, Rachel. I appreciate it, but I'm getting a little tired myself."

"Of course."

Helen was stuck to Morgan like plaster so Rachel passed him without stopping, but he stood. "Am I not allowed to kiss my daughter goodnight?"

Remaining silent, Rachel waited, aware of their families, their friends close by. He reached down and kissed his little girl's cheek. At his closeness, Rachel moved back, rigidity in every line of her body. He smelled of Helen's heavy perfume and too much whisky. Over Macy's head, he stared at her. His gaze was a mixture of raw emotions. Pain, sadness, loneliness; its intensity burned up her chest; her heart felt like it was shattering into a trillion pieces. She looked away, shivering.

"It's cold," he whispered. "Don't you have a jacket?"

"I'll be fine," she said weakly, even though it was cold in the room and Macy's hands were freezing on her neck.

"Macy has goosebumps," he said, rubbing his daughter's back. "So, do you."

Tension emanated from them both. They were like stick people. Morgan stepped closer to her, lightly touching her arm and she stiffened. He sighed deeply; his brows knit together. "You'll catch cold," he said tiredly.

Morgan shrugged out of his tuxedo jacket and wrapped it around her shoulders. She wanted to refuse, but when the warmth of his jacket enveloped her, and his cologne filled her nostrils, she remained silent.

"Don't you have to return this tomorrow?" she said lamely.

"It's mine," he said quietly, instructing her to, "Put your arms in the sleeves." She didn't move.

The jacket drowned her. He took her arm from around Macy and put it in the sleeve, then rolled it back. She didn't flinch this time, but watched him silently; then they switched. This small caring gesture had tears crowding behind Rachel's eyes. She loved him and hated him in that moment.

Her wide green eyes searched his calm, blank face. "Thank you," she whispered.

"No problem." He wrapped the front of the jacket around his sleeping daughter. "Do you want me to carry her?"

"No, I'm fine."

He kissed the side of Macy's head and stuffed his hands in his pockets. They stood so close together; Rachel could feel the heat from his body and desire assaulted her. Unfortunately, the reality was, Morgan was better off with a woman like Helen Fielding. Women who knew the score, women who knew how to play the game fairly. Women, more importantly, who didn't play it like a melodramatic prom queen.

Tonight, Rachel had watched Morgan and Helen together. They had chemistry. But old habits die hard, she guessed. His protective nature—of the little girl he had cared for his whole life—couldn't be denied. Little Rachel, like little Macy, might catch cold in her thin dress walking from the reception room up to the twenty-first floor.

Rachel needed to stop thinking of Morgan in a romantic way. They couldn't seem to get it right. She couldn't keep living like this; it wasn't healthy. She had to let it go. For her own sake. She needed to redirect her thoughts. How? She wasn't sure. Looking up at him, even after everything that had happened tonight, she still loved him, loved him so much it hurt. She wanted to crawl inside him and take refuge.

One kiss.

One last kiss.

Rachel shifted Macy to her right hip and laid her hand on his chest and rolled onto her tiptoes, he bent to meet her lips. It was a sweet, tender kiss, full of regret. His arm hooked around her waist and cradled her to him like he treasured her. Fat tears, trapped deep inside her, silently released, splashing down her hot cheeks. Morgan rested his forehead on hers. His heart hammered against her fingers.

She smoothed her hand down his arm, stepping back, to hold his hand. "Take care of yourself," she said softly, unable to tell him goodbye.

"You, too." Like slow motion, she stepped back, further and further, until her fingers slipped from his. Turning, she wrapped his coat more securely around her, and Macy and the room suddenly lost its gravity. Every step she took, it was an effort for her foot to reach the marble floor. The hair on the back of her neck stood. Goosebumps covered her body—she was being watched. She looked at the dance floor; hundreds of eyes were on her; the brisk music didn't match their slow pace. A loud hum was in the air. People's mouths were moving but she couldn't hear what they were saying. At her stare, their eyes averted. Phones were tucked back into pockets and purses.

Chills took over Rachel's body. Sweat broke out across her brow. She walked to the door, her breathing heavy, a whispering buzz at her heels. She swallowed her relief when the ballroom captain opened the heavy door to let her out.

Rachel tucked Macy in bed beside her, but sleep eluded her. The harder she tried the more she couldn't. Dozing for an hour then waking up. Dozing. Waking. Finally, she gave up. Paced the room. Reviewed the evening. What happened? Who said what? Who did what? Morgan was jealous of Rick. Even though she had told him that she wasn't dating him. Aunt Sarah said Morgan has difficulty with trust—people with ulterior motives had taken advantage in the past. Rachel knew first-hand how disheartening that could be.

The power of the rumour had also reared its ugly head. By who, though? *What* was he hearing? It must have been significant. Morgan didn't do things without a reason. Something happened. Jealousy was not the emotion Rachel wanted to inspire in him. There was no doubt, Morgan was intense, and he had deep emotions were Rachel was concerned. Aunt Sarah was so right—he did try to hide his sensitive side, but he shared it with her. Tonight, his emotions came violently to the surface, revealing a rawness. Knowing Morgan, that's not how he wanted those emotions to surface. Showing weakness was one thing, he had shown her many weaknesses over the years, but his weakness stirred violence, and that wasn't Morgan's style. She knew he felt remorse.

If she was honest with herself, she knew he wasn't interested in Helen Fielding. It took him six doubles to get obnoxious with her. And Siobhan Reilly? Rachel recalled how he pulled away from her in the Hilliers' driveway, how he felt no obligation to go to the cottage last weekend, how quickly he explained her away like she held no interest for him, and how concerned he was about Rachel. The exhausting game of not knowing what was going on between them was killing them. Pulling them further and further apart. Someone had to make the first move. She needed to take the guessing out of this cat and mouse game and tell Morgan how she felt about him. She needed him to know. There was no self-protection in love, no place to hide.

You're a poor slob in love. The end.

Poor slob or not, she needed to know how Morgan felt about her. He said they had always been able to talk about anything. The sexual tension between them, the uncertainty, the guessing, the wanting, the hoping, had complicated what was once so simple. And as much as she wanted to sleep with him, she wanted it to be right. There had been plenty of opportunities over the last couple of years, and it didn't happen. Deep down she wanted it to be just about them, their decision, no interruptions, and she thought Morgan felt the same way. He stopped them when they were in less than ideal circumstances. At the time she wasn't happy, but in retrospect she was glad. She probably would have boiled his bones if he hadn't stopped. Morgan was right about one thing—he could never do anything right. Her overwrought emotions and childhood insecurities wouldn't allow it to be played out any other way. She was mean to him.

Tonight, he made it plain that Rachel was the one he wanted. And that had frustrated him beyond what was reasonable. Rachel agreed with that. She had teased that poor man to shocking levels, and he broke tonight.

As the sun came up, she decided it was worth putting herself on the line and finding out if there was a chance between them, if they could mend the hurts and start again. He'd said, "When you're ready to tell me, I'm here." She was ready to have that hard conversation. She knew they couldn't go on like this.

Keeping her momentum up, she showered and got ready for the day—a new day, a bright day, a happy day.

When Macy woke up, she bathed her and they walked down the hall to Morgan's room together. She would invite him to breakfast and see what the day brought, she thought. She knocked—no answer. She knocked harder. Macy knocked.

A few minutes later, a dishevelled Helen Fielding, who reeked of cigars and booze, answered the door in Morgan's tuxedo shirt. From where Rachel stood, she could see Morgan's bare back. He was lying face down into the pillow, snoring away. The room smelled of booze, sweat, and staleness.

Rachel worked on autopilot. She pushed Macy behind her. "Tell Morgan I have to catch a plane so I'm leaving Macy with Jason and Carrie."

Mascara caked around Helen Fielding's eyes. She bent down. "You can leave the little sweetheart here."

Macy pressed hard into Rachel. The woman is ridiculous. "No, I can't. Just tell him where she is."

"Sure." Helen was still drunk. The door swung closed.

"What is wrong with Daddy?"

Rachel picked the child up in her arms. "He had a little too much fun last night, Dollie, but he'll be fine."

Her face became pensive. "What kind of fun?"

"He stayed up really, really late and he's really, really tired."

Rachel walked quickly to Jason and Carrie's room and banged harder on the door than she meant too. Jason answered. *Thank God.*

"Hey, Rach. That was an urgent knock if I ever ... what's wrong?"

Rachel handed Macy over and he took her. "Nothing, nothing. Morgan is still sleeping and I have a plane to catch."

Macy said, "He was with *that mean lady.* What's her name, Auntie Rachel?"

"What?" Jason looked at Rachel.

Rachel's hands twisted frantically. "He's usually an early riser. We went to his room, but he had a friend over."

"She was wearing *Daddy's shirt and was very, very ugly.* That's what happened ta Cassandra Lake's *second* mummy," said Macy.

"I told Helen Fielding that I would leave Macy with you and Carrie. She suggested taking her, but I thought, no ..." Rachel started to back away from Jason and Macy. "No ... no, I won't do that, I'll take her to Jason and Carrie because Morgan is still asleep, but I have to go because I have to pack my stuff and go to the airport and Macy hasn't eaten breakfast yet, so I thought you and Carrie probably haven't had breakfast, so maybe you could take her with you? The Folks said they would be meeting downstairs at nine-ish, so maybe you could tell them I had to go, to catch the plane, and I'll call my parents later."

Jason put Macy down. "Go on inside, honey," he said to the little girl. "Daniel's up." Jason closed the door and stepped out into the hall, and held his hands up. "Rachel, calm down."

"No! I've *been* calm! I'm sick of being calm! I'm going to get the hell out of this town and I'm going to start a new life—do you hear me? A new life. Away from you Hilliers. You all just wear me down. I'm sick of you bastards. You … pick at me. Morgan's being a prick, your bitchy wife. I want away—away from all this fucking sorrow. And Rick, Rick wants to be with me. And he doesn't care who knows it. He wants to shout it from the highest building and I'll never have to wonder if I'm important or what he wants—he tells me, he begs me to be part of his life. So, I think I'm going to try front and centre for a while. And you tell your brother to stay the fuck away from me. Do you hear me? I'm sick of him playing with my emotions. Sick of it, sick of him, sick of me, sick of my mother, sick of you, sick of Carrie, sick of it all. One thing is for certain—I'm officially emancipated from Morgan Hillier!" She was shouting by the time she got to the end of the corridor.

Carrie came out into the hall. She said, "Thank God I haven't eaten yet or it would be all over this pretty carpet."

"Shut-up Carrie," snapped Jason.

****

Morgan woke up to shouting. It was Jason.

"I said take off his shirt, get your stuff and get the hell out!"

"You can't speak to me like that—I'm family!"

"You're no family of mine. Now get your ass out of here."

Morgan sat up. His head felt like lead and there was a vile taste in his mouth. "Jason—" His voice cracked. "What the hell is going on?"

"You fucked up!" said Jason.

"Morgan, he told me to get out. Are you going to let him speak to me like that?"

Morgan sat forward and threaded his fingers through his hair; his scalp hurt; his hair hurt. He heard a female voice; it wasn't Rachel's he knew every inflection of her voice. It was unfamiliar.

"Morgan, *are you?*"

He lifted his bleary gaze up, rubbed his eyes. Helen Fielding stood a few feet away from the bed. Jason stood in front of her looking very pissed off. "What the hell are you doing here, Helen? And why are you yelling Jason?" He looked beside him in the bed and then around the room. "Where's Rachel?"

"Sorry pal—you dreamed her, and trust me, dreaming about her is as close as you'll ever get to her again." Jason kicked the clothes lying on the floor. "She came here with Macy to pick you up for breakfast, and what did she find? You snoring away and this chick in your shirt." He laughed without humour.

"At dinner on Friday, you were the only one Rachel could see. That stupid little bitch couldn't seem to help herself. The rest of us might as well be mannequins for all she cared." He threw his hands up. "Then last night? *What the fuck were you thinking?* Screwing it up for what? *Helen?* And there's Mama Wharton tallying up her reasons for hating you. Man, you really know how to charm her."

Jason shook his head, his hands on his hips. "Rachel is *so* done with you. She's flying back to Ottawa for good. Starting a new life, she tells me. She going to take Rick Summerhill up on his offer. Oh yeah, and she gave me a message."

"I can't wait."

"Tell your brother to stay the fuck away from me. Eventually, you'll want a blow by blow, but that was the gist."

Morgan fell back on the bed. "Helen, you better leave." He heard clothes rustling and the bathroom door slam. He winced. "Where's Rachel now?"

"She showed up at our door fifteen minutes ago with Macy. She was going to pack and head to the airport. If you were smart, you'd get the fuck out of bed."

Morgan pulled on his tuxedo pants and Jason threw him a grey T-shirt. His head pounded. Helen came out of the bathroom.

"Running after her?" Helen said. "We didn't even do anything. We were both too bloated."

Morgan stuffed his foot into his shoe. "You don't get it."

"I get it. I see the way you look at her. The touching little scene last night when she left."

Morgan stopped to look at her.

"She's young and unstable; I thought maybe someone with a bit of maturity might be of interest." She shrugged. "You're an intelligent, great looking man with impeccable manners. It was worth a try."

Morgan stuffed his other foot viciously into the other shoe. "Are you coming?" he said to his brother.

"Right behind you."

Morgan's chest hurt; his heart raced. He banged on her door. Jason shouted. "Rachel? It's Jason—open up." No response.

"She moves fast," said Jason. "Checking out maybe?"

They took the elevator to the lobby. There was no sign of her. Morgan went to the front desk.

"Good morning Mr. Hillier. Everything to your satisfaction last night? There's a lovely picture of your sister in the *Globe*."

"Thank you, everything was outstanding, Ben. I could use your help. Rachel Wharton just left her room. Has she checked out yet? You wouldn't forget her, beautiful blondish red hair, petite, probably in a hurry."

"She hasn't been here sir. She may be in the dining room."

Jason hit Morgan's arm. "Go check the dining room. Everyone was meeting for breakfast at nine." He turned back to the clerk. "Did she use express checkout? She was in 2101."

Morgan saw the folks, several cousins and their wives, friends, neighbours—no Rachel. His dad waved him over to the huge table they were sitting at. When his father stood, his face changed as he walked quickly over to Morgan. "What's wrong? Where's Macy?"

"Has Rachel been here?" asked Morgan.

He spread his hands. "No. What's wrong son? You look rough."

Jason came to stand beside him. "She's gone."

Morgan dropped his head onto his chest. "*Jesus ...*" He thought he was going to be sick and put his hands on his knees and bent over. His brother squeezed his shoulder.

***

Rachel stuffed her overnight bag aggressively, walked out of the hotel into a waiting taxi, and returned to Ottawa,

Her cell was ringing. She turned it off. Her phone was ringing when she arrived at her apartment. She waited for the machine to kick in. It was her mother.

"Where are you?" said Maureen. "What is going on? You left without a word. Your father and I are sick with worry. Not that I blame you. Morgan put on a disgusting display with that Helen woman. What were you thinking, Rachel—kissing him after what he had done? I told you—"

Rachel picked up the phone and switched off her machine. "It's me, Mum. I'm fine, no need to worry."

"*Rachel!* What's going on? Why did you leave without a word? This is obviously about Morgan's nasty display last night—at his sister's wedding no less. The only good thing is he looks like death. Serves him right. His behaviour last night was appalling. Good God, Rachel, do I have to write it on the wall for you?"

"That won't be necessary. You were *absolutely* right and I was *absolutely* wrong. Is that *really* why you called Mother?"

"I tried to warn you."

"You've said; I've agreed, but I'm not feeling up to a lecture. I'm sorry I worried you and Dad. I just wanted to leave and I didn't want to talk about it. I don't want to talk about it now. The reason I picked up the phone was to tell you I'm fine and there's no need to worry."

"I'm sorry this happened."

"Me too. I'll call you next week."

Rachel threw herself into her new life—her new start. The Morgan fantasy was officially dead.

She called Rick. "Okay, you're tour guide duties take centre stage. Show me Ottawa."

He laughed. "You won't regret moving here."

Every few days her mother called and Rachel prattled on about how great everything was going.

Rachel lived on the surface.

She refused to dig deep.

She ignored her life on a completely new level.

She lived in a state of pretend happiness.

Desperate to convince herself that practice creates belief.

Good as his word, Rick took her to the movies, to dinner, drives in the country, tours of the Musée de la civilisation and Canyon Sainte-Anne. He introduced her to his politically staunch friends. She hadn't realized Rick had political aspirations. His friends were charming people, but Rachel didn't make a connection. Always a social type, able to mingle with any crowd, she felt inadequate suddenly. Even when she was in France, far away from home, out of her depth and element, she mingled, made friends, and became part of the culture. France was a classic: "It was the best of times, it was the worst of times." Ottawa was different; it debilitated her. Good people with delightful anecdotes on life surrounded her. Their easy laughter was infectious, but it didn't sooth what ailed her. Parties, receptions, art shows, basketball—Rick made life alive with activity.

Strange faces greeted her in every room she entered. Happy, excited faces, but Rachel had never felt so alone in her life. She wanted a history with the faces that sheltered her. She wanted to be her mother's daughter; to be the fourth Hillier; to be Morgan's best friend. The usual suspects where gone and she had a new persona—Rick Summerhill's new friend, the high school art and lit teacher. She wasn't part of something bigger than herself, wasn't part of a clan anymore, and she couldn't seem to catch the rhythm of her new life.

The only bright spot was when Rick took her to a hockey game: the Senators vs the Leafs. Rachel was at the concession stand and a gorgeous woman in the line beside her looked oddly familiar, but she couldn't place her.

The woman caught her staring. "Oh my God," said the woman, "Rachel Wharton."

"I'm sorry you look so familiar, but I can't place you?"

She put a hand on her chest. "Stacey Patton."

"Holy shit, Stacey Patton!" Lacy Patton's younger sister. She was older than Rachel by a couple of years. She had always been a bit awkward as a teenager but she had certainly shed that persona. A stunning woman stood before her now.

Stacey laughed. "I hope you meant that in a good way."

"I'm just shocked. Imagine meeting you at a hockey game in Ottawa. I'm here on a work contract. You're the first person I met since I've been here that I know. Not seeing a familiar face—it might sound crazy—but I've felt so disconnected. It's just so good to see you."

"Well, that makes me feel better. People are usually shocked when they see me because I was a fat kid who was socially inept."

"You *do* look gorgeous, don't get me wrong, but I'm so glad you look familiar. I must sound like a nut."

"Actually, your honesty is refreshing."

"I shouldn't complain. I do know one other person in Ottawa. I'm here with a co-worker—do you remember Rick Summerhill? "

Stacey paled and swayed. Immediately, Rachel grabbed her arm.

"Are you okay?"

"I think I need to sit for a minute."

"Of course, of course." Rachel helped her to a bench. "Let me get you some water."

"No, I'm fine. I just need a minute."

Stacey was a professor at McGill but lived in Ottawa. A microbiologist who also did research for the university. They chatted, commiserated, and laughed. Rachel couldn't have been more pleased. She didn't know how long they sat on that bench, but when she heard someone shout her name, she saw Rick looking around for her.

"Rick! Over here!"

He made his way across the crowds, and she stood up. "Everything okay, Rachel? You've been gone a long time.:

Rachel couldn't contain her delight. "You're never going to believe who I bumped into?"

Rick was cautious. "Who?"

She stepped to the left and Stacey stood. "It's—"

Rick didn't need an introduction; he knew who it was immediately. "Stacey Patton." Instantly, he reached out to embrace her. Kissed her cheek and they just stared at each other for a moment and then broke out into laughter. It was the first time Rachel had felt good in weeks.

***

Rachel hadn't been home since Elaine's wedding. Regardless of what she had said to Jason, she was not going to date Rick. She needed his friendship. She'd been honest with him about her feelings, but he continued to wine and dine her. She was knee-deep in wining and dining. At first, she thought the distractions would keep *crazy* at bay; but they didn't.

Tonight, Rick was taking her to a reception at a local gallery.

They had arranged it last week. Rachel pressed cool fingers against her hot face as she looked out from her apartment window. She didn't want to go. Too depressed. Morgan filled her mind; every move he made, every word he said, every look he ever gave her whirled around in her head. She could call Rick. Explain she wasn't up for it. She could have told him at school, but oddly, when she thought about it, she hadn't seen him today. She hadn't seen him all week, in fact. No calls. No stopping by. Maybe he had a new girlfriend? Poor bastard. Maybe she should warn him. *Love sucks! Don't do it!*

Rachel met the love of her life too early. Regardless of the timing, she thought love always made you feel like you'd been stripped down and left for dead.

If she could choose, would she erase her memory so that Morgan didn't exist?

Tears pinched her nose. No. She wouldn't. She had dated enough to know, lightning rarely strikes your heart. Love this deep and strong was rare. The man Morgan was, the good and the bad, was still the love of her life. He always had been. He always would be. He wasn't a hero she carried in her head. She saw him. She knew him. The happiest days had been with him; the most crippling days had been with him—the joy and the pain were excruciating.

There definitely was something more going on the night of Elaine's wedding, but that didn't excuse his behaviour. When his hands caressed her, Rachel's love for him trumped her anger over his flirty exchange with Helen. But that flirty exchange cut something far deeper in her. She felt abandoned and betrayed. She felt inconsequential to him like she didn't deserve to be at the grown-up table. To compound the problem further, he drank too much and sucked up to Helen Fielding in front of his family and hers—at his sister's wedding—in front of half of Toronto.

In front of her mother for God's sake! Maureen's disapproval was tangible. It hovered over their tables. Pressed down on Rachel's shoulders. Rachel had hurt her mother deeply by choosing to be on Morgan's side, to be with him, and then to have him humiliate her twice in a matter of hours for all to see, supported Maureen's belief that he was the wrong man. Rachel was uncertain how deep the damage went from that night. Finding out churned her stomach.

Given all that, she wanted Morgan, ached for him, and the ache drove her crazy.

The dinner hour had passed. Her quaint neighbourhood was quiet. Street lamps had a dim orange, yellowy tinge to them. A hue of light illuminated the sky. Nothing stirred. Already it had snowed twice in Ottawa, but the snow didn't stay. Each day more leaves piled up along the sidewalks. They were quickly turned into baby hills in front gardens and exuberant children jumped into them. Rachel didn't go home for Thanksgiving.

It was hard to believe she had only been in Ottawa for eight weeks. It felt like an eternity.

Morgan's voice dominated her answering machine for the first couple of weeks after the wedding. "We need to talk. Call me." Rachel didn't call. She wasn't ready to have that conversation. She was too needy and vulnerable.

Morgan stopped calling.

25

FROZEN

Rick picked Rachel up promptly at seven-thirty, looking handsome in a navy suit. He was in good spirits. Whistling. Charming. But when they walked into the Brach Gallery, they both received a shock. Gary Kurfont was the featured artist. A politically minded friend had invited Rick to meet a rising conservative MP scheduled to be at the reception.

Both Gary and Rick impressed Rachel with their social etiquette. The memory of how the two men last met was vivid in her mind, but no brawl ensued. Not a harsh word passed between them. Gary remained a perfect gentleman. Rick continued to be charming company. Rick did his rounds, shook hands, told jokes at his own expense. She had never seen Rick so relaxed. While Rick did the rounds, Rachel stuck close to Gary. They hadn't seen Gary since Paris, but old habits die-hard. She basked in his attention. When she stood close to him, he reminded her of Morgan. Sometimes it was a look, or an expression, or their connection to each other's history, but she missed Morgan less when she looked at Gary. It had always been that way. It felt good being near him. He soothed her anxieties. Breathing became possible. Laughter became possible.

"So, what brings you to Ottawa, Miss Rachel?"

"Work. I teach at St. Martin's High School."

"Teacher? Wow. I can totally see you as a teacher."

"Why thank you, kind sir."

"And Summerhill? Are you giving it another try?"

"If only I had a dime every time I heard that one," she laughed. "No—just friends. He has been living here for a few years so he agreed to be my tour guide." She leaned into him, whispering, "Actually, I think there's girl. Look at him. I don't think I've ever seen Rick so relaxed. He can't keep the smile off his face."

Gary glanced Rick's way before smiling down at her. "Oh—he so got laid!"

She nodded. "He *so* did!"

"He hasn't owned it yet?"

"Too new. Too soon. He'll spill soon. I wonder if it's one of the teachers?"

"No love bubble for you?"

His hair had fallen across his forehead. A lopsided smile on his face as he tugged at one of her curls.

Rachel flicked back her hair and dropped her hands to her hips in a defiant pose, her head held high. "No. I think I'm destined to be a Jane Austen spinster, maybe teach in a rural school where I mould young minds, and they love me *so* much they visit for the rest of their lives and tell me at great length how I have inspired them to be the best they can be."

Gary grabbed her around the shoulder and pulled her into his side, barely able to suppress his laughter. "Good God, Rachel I've missed your melodramatic bullshit."

"Don't mess with the stories Gary Kurfont. The creative process has its own set of rules." She punched him good-naturedly in the stomach and he jumped back, his hands up.

"A thousand apologies."

"Then make it up to me. Come to my class. Show them your work. Maybe teach them one of your technics? Because, although it was very kind of you to say I would make a good teacher, the truth is, I suck. I can't seem to engage the little buggers, so I'm willing to peddle your talent and good looks to get them on my side. The way

I see it it's a win-win. The boys will think you're cool, well, because you are, and the girls will fall madly in love with you."

"How can I say no to an offer like that?"

"Good!"

Rachel gave him the details of the school. She marvelled at how carefree their chat was, how the past was mentioned but skirted it at the same time. They found comfortable neutral ground. She didn't look at his pieces though—too afraid she might find a truthful rendition of herself. Gary hadn't changed. His manner, his quick smile, his full attention was trained on her; he looked into her eyes when they spoke, oblivious to the other patrons who were desperate for his attention. Gary didn't seem to care. He made her feel special. He always had.

An hour after they arrived, Rick suggested they leave. Rachel was relieved. He took her for a light supper and she expected to get grief over Gary, but Rick was a delightful dinner companion. His whole demeanour had changed over the last month. He seemed lighter. She couldn't help notice how often he checked his watch.

Rachel smiled. "Somewhere to be?"

He laughed—a bit bashful. "I'm sorry, how rude, it's just—"

"Whatever it is, it looks good on you."

Rick dropped her off in front of her building. She kissed his cheek and waved him away. Once inside her apartment, she threw her coat on the couch, kicked off her high heels, and sank thankfully into the armchair.

There was a sharp knock at the door. Rachel smiled and grabbed Rick's satchel in the front hall, crammed with his Grade 12 students' calculus test, that he had left earlier in the week.

Rachel swung the door open, her laughter easy and her saucy line ready, but her composure faltered when she saw Morgan. His hands were on either side of the door. His stare was direct. "We need to talk."

She stepped back without argument to let him pass. "Would you like something to drink?"

"No, unless you're making coffee?"

"I can make coffee." She went to the kitchen. With a shaky hand, she filled the pot with water. Her heart pounded in her head as she pulled out the mugs, got the sugar, set the tray, and poured the cream before returning to the living room.

He was standing when she came into the room. His hands were in his pockets, defining his legs. She looked away.

"Out somewhere special this evening? You look beautiful."

Rachel looked down at her black strapless cocktail dress. It was pretty with its pink chiffon bodice and satin trim, but she suddenly felt hot and sticky. Her hands nervously held the folds of the dress. "Thank ... you; I got it at a thrift store for a wine and cheese reception at the Brach Gallery. I'll get the tray."

Breathe, breathe, breathe.

Rachel filled the cups and returned to the living room. She left the tray on the coffee table not trusting her capacity to be a good hostess. She perched on the armchair near the bay window and waited, not knowing what else to do.

Morgan picked up a cup and poured. "Coffee?" he said.

"No, thank you."

He sat on the couch and looked into his coffee. "My behaviour at Elaine's wedding was unacceptable. I never meant to hurt you. I was angry and frustrated." He looked at her. "It's no excuse. I was cruel and I hurt and embarrassed you. I am sorry, Rachel. I can't find the words to tell you how sorry I am."

Rachel's eyes sparkled with unshed tears.

He rubbed his forehead. "Helen Fielding—again extremely bad judgment—and I compounded the problem with drinking way too much. I can't remember the last time I was that drunk. I didn't sleep with her." He put his coffee cup down and motioned to stand, moving closer to her. He moved so quickly Rachel jumped, scrambled to her feet, and moved behind the armchair, not trusting herself.

Morgan stared at her for a moment while she moved further away from him, pressing herself against the wall, and he sat back down. His pain was unmistakeable. "I'm not going to hurt you."

Rachel's tears spilled over, burning her face.

I hate you so much Morgan! Why did you have to do that! I want to beat the shit out of you. You're such a bastard! I don't trust you. You hurt me, I can't believe how much and how easily. The wound is deep. I didn't know how deep until right now, and it scares me.

I have to be my own person! I have to be. You can destroy me. But I love you.

I'm such a feeb! Hating you and loving you. I do love you—but you're such a bastard! I don't want to feel anything! But I can't stop wanting to throw myself into your arms and tell you how glad I am to see you. Tell you how much I've missed you. I ache with it. I want to kiss you and hug you, but I can't seem to move or speak. I'm trapped in this spot.

I've been kidding myself, haven't I? All these years, I've lived in a childish fantasy. This isn't going to work, is it? There's never been any space for us— snatched moments here and there aren't enough. And Maureen never gives me any room to love you, to find out if this could work. She's always pushing me away and putting doubts in my head. Her words keep coming back to me. Keeping me up at night.

I know this isn't all your fault. I know you're frustrated. Good God, I know. Not too many men would have been as patient as you. And you have been—taking hits from my mother, losing your privacy—and I know I've gotten cold feet so many times and kept you at bay. But taking the next step—I don't know if I will survive if it doesn't work out. It's complicated. It's not just about us. It's family and friendships and Macy and a history of hurts and recriminations. Our mothers have been friends for thirty years Morgan. Thirty years!

It's complicated. So, so complicated. It's never just about us.

If I could just stop thinking. I've spent so much time alone, my past haunts me, seeing myself as I am. I've done horrible things. I'm such a hypocrite. How can I judge you when I've done horrible things?

Morgan stared at her.

Rachel wanted the words to come out, but she stood rigidly holding her breath. Tears rolled fast down her face. Morgan just stared at her until his contriteness became detachment.

He nodded slowly to himself. He drained his cup of coffee and it clattered onto the table.

"I came here to tell you the truth. I wanted to see you. Tell you in person what happened." He stood up. "You've started a new life here. Rick is in the picture and if you're happy then that's all I care about." He walked to the door and then turned to her. "If you ever need anything ... you know where to find me. Take care of yourself, beautiful girl."

Morgan opened the door.

Time moved in slow motion. She held her breath. She watched him. He looked over his shoulder at her; there was finality on his face.

Rachel's breath exhaled on a cry.

26

A ROOM OF ITS OWN

Rachel stood at the bay window watching intently. Her eyes bounced from the black Escalade, to the street where neighbours strolled sedately, to children running through the park squeezing the last bit of joy from the twilight, to the last vestiges of her panoramic view of the red sky nestling the falling sun, before her attention swung back to the Escalade. Ishmael waited patiently for Morgan. She gulped down wine.

Ten weeks she has lived in this quaint hamlet. A picturesque diamond with unique charm and an appealing trendy vibe, but even with its scenic delights and cozy small-town atmosphere, Rachel hadn't settled here. It was a canvas of hurtful reminders of everything wrong in her life—a *"Howler"* that had meticulously captured every mistake she had ever made and dispatched it to the world with glee and abandon. She could never love its beauty, not now.

So much had happened in such a short time

Like every other poor slob in love, Rachel had no idea love was an isolation tank—a room of its own, where her secrets lived, where she abandoned her common sense and chose to live inside an optical illusion. She didn't know any better. Love struck her at her first recollection. Her well-intentioned family and friends were left by the wayside. There was nothing to be done; it was impossible for her to see or hear them. She was too busy strapping colourful blinders to the sides of her head, believing her love for Morgan would trump everything. It didn't. It couldn't. But it wasn't from a lack of trying.

Rachel wanted to point fingers and lay blame. Who had brought her to this bitter sad-sackery? But there is no one to blame. On the international scale of tales of misery, Rachel's life's story did not appear. She was an educated woman. She had a family who loved her. She was rich beyond what was polite to discuss. She had never been without life's basic hierarchy of needs. She had never suffered any abuse. She had wanted for nothing. Every advantage that life can give, she had received. Given that, here she was, crying, depleted, hiding in the dark, listening to Sass Jordan's raspy voice singing *You Don't Have to Remind Me*, about unrequited love, on repeat, guzzling a bottle of cabernet-sauvignon like a pro, when she didn't even drink.

Ten minutes ago, he'd stood in this room, asking for her forgiveness, and she'd let him walk out without a word. Why hadn't she said anything? She had no scathing comments. No demands. No gumption.

That's the trouble with love's isolation tank, it only keeps you safe for so long, before it traps you, and I've been trapped for years.

Hot tears stung Rachel's eyes; she squeezed them shut, wincing with embarrassment at her stupidity. When he pushed her through the dressing room door, he wanted to answers. Maureen had warned her that she was playing with fire, that it could get messy, but there was more than fire there—something happened—she was certain; it was out of character for Morgan to behave that way.

Together they had come to an understanding. They were going to remove the stress and doubt; make the most of their weekends together, but it was short lived. What a humiliating crash down a gaping hole. It took the last remnants of her poise when Morgan said, "Did you go from my bed to his, Rachel?" The venom is his voice, the punishing grip on her hair. "Have you seduced him like you've seduced me."

Eleven years of stops and starts. For a while there, she was riding the wave. Possibilities drummed in her veins; her future had design and distinction. For years she'd struggled to climb her life's summit, she thought she had mastered the navigation of its deep gaping holes, but when she reached the top – a humiliating crash down a gaping hole took the last remnants of her poise. And *this* is where she lands. Alone. Stuck in a ratty three-story walkup she despised, living well below par, drinking a bottle of wine out of a brown paper bag, watching the street like a feeb for a last glimpse of him. She held her breath and took a swallow.

If it had ended with him sucking up to Helen, she would have forgiven him—not happily, because she hated watching her touch him. Smacking Helen's hands away kept replaying in her mind, but after she made him feel like total shit, she would have forgiven him. She knew he wasn't interested in Helen. It was finding her in his room that pushed her over the edge.

Trusting him with her vulnerable emotions was a tricky proposition since they crossed the friendship line, but this made it worse. All her insecurities surfaced like magic.

It pissed Rachel off that her mother had anticipated this. That Maureen was right, made Rachel doubt herself even more. Was Morgan a walking time bomb? What other bombs were ready to go off? How astute of her to put doubt into her mind and hammer it home until the time came for Morgan to actually lose it—the first time he'd cracked in all the years she had known him. Rachel had miscalculated Maureen's sheer force of will. It was her fault. She should have known better, given Maureen's drive, ambition, and cryptic brief that "mother knows best." Maybe she orchestrated this ever so cleverly. Nothing would surprise her at this point—who was she kidding? Everything shocked the crap out of her.

It was curious, why Maureen was suddenly interested in Rachel's love life. She'd never had time for it before? Rachel moved to Paris with Gary after knowing him a month. Maureen didn't even bat a lash. Didn't even suggest meeting him. She had too many other pressing matters that needed her attention. Private vacations. Errands to run. Parties to attend. Lists to check. Goals to attain. Glass ceilings to break. Maureen was always absent. Now she's engaged. Giving advice. Guiding.

Out of adolescent loyalty, she'd made concessions for her mother, rationalized her ambition. Maureen was paving the way for others while forging new trails and abandoned Rachel to the kindness of strangers at the age of seven weeks. Abandonment was not the technical word, because she lived in the same house with her mother and father until she left for university, but Rachel was grateful the Hilliers had taken pity on her. If it weren't for them, she would have been dumped long ago into the care of an overzealous nanny.

But no matter how she spun it, there was no denying, Maureen's absence forced Rachel to live on the outside, forced her to find refuge at the Hilliers', and forced her to take on the awkward role of *almost* family. As a result, Rachel never quite fit—anywhere. Speculation fed her childhood fears; they built a fortress leading from her heart to her head. She believed Maureen's love was conditional, and that the choices Rachel made were never going to be good enough.

Money didn't fix anything. People thought it did. It didn't spare you from life's suffering, insecurity, or worry. It provided a different set of circumstances, that's all. It gave you a better house, better clothes, a better car—not loyalty, love, or comfort. When you *did* have money, your loneliness and anguish was marginalized, and maybe that's the way it should be; maybe that's the fair way; maybe life is a trade.

Her eyes kept drifting down to the street. She couldn't help herself. Checking and rechecking. Apart from the Escalade, the road was empty—still no sign of Morgan.

Rachel's not supposed to be upset about her privileged upbringing or being abandoned by her mother. Maureen is a charming, beautiful woman with impeccable manners, whose unbridled ambitions were seeded in her modest Irish childhood; they fed her an edge. Maureen wanted a life outside of Rachel. Her goals absolved her of any motherly accountability. Missed plays, story times, teacher conferences, shopping sprees, mother/daughter tea's; Rachel's first bra, her first period, her first time, were not as important as mergers and acquisitions. Maureen's climb up the corporate ladder, however, did not affect *her love life*. In between her successes, Maureen managed to have a full and private love affair with Rachel's dad and live out her romantic fantasies without censure.

Some people have all the fucking luck!

However, it was counted; Maureen's absences had left a mark.

Rachel was a grown woman. She couldn't be pointing fingers at this stage in her life that she was all fucked up because her mother loved her father, and her ambitions were more important than her daughter. She was proud of her mother's accomplishments and she admired how Maureen had carved out a space of her own. She could have stayed in her husband's shadow, but she made her own way. She was certain Maureen got the shit kicked out of her from the other mothers in her social circle, who criticized her choices. Judged her motherly prowess. Rachel gave Maureen all the credit for all her achievements, but today? Today Rachel was feeling pretty shitty, and not feeling generous enough to give Mo a pass. Especially since Rachel had yet to know the dimension and range of the damage in Maureen's wake.

Rachel had ignored, slighted, and questioned Maureen's guidance when it came to Morgan. Despite her mother's persistence, Rachel had thwarted her best efforts and loved Morgan anyway. Even Maureen's myriad of reasons has mushroomed over the years:

- Morgan's emotional baggage and ready-made family put him out of Rachel's league.
- Rachel wasn't up for the challenge. She was too young and inexperienced for a man like Morgan—far beyond their

actual seven-year age difference.

- Misfortune followed Morgan around like a duty. Lacy's death. His son's death. Emily's mental breakdown. His divorce. Single fatherhood.

- Rachel's attachment to Morgan is normal but misplaced. It's a residual of her adolescent devotion and exuberance.

- Morgan's daughter, Macy, may want to know her estranged mother one day. Did Rachel really want to get into that sordid affair?

- Rachel's immaturity barred her from knowing what Maureen knew; Morgan's calm exterior was mythical. Under his cool exterior was molten lava ready to explode, and she didn't want Rachel near him when the volcano erupted.

- And Morgan's appalling behaviour at his sister's wedding. Getting drunk and cozying up to cousin Helen just gave Maureen the upper hand. Had she to write it on the wall for Rachel? He wasn't the right man. Maureen's list might be limitless

What was at the bottom of Maureen's hatred? Where there's hate, there's fire. So why? Morgan had put her in her place more than once. Maureen was strong, but Morgan's privileged background gave him an edge—a sense of entitlement that he had no problem demanding. Did Maureen want that edge?

Rachel's eyes went to the street. Empty. Morgan should be downstairs by now. She looked at the clock. It had been twenty minutes. She sighed and pressed her nose into the cool window.

The sad complement to this shitty saga was—did it matter? Knowing or understanding the truth didn't always bring comfort. Rachel felt no relief at being liberated from her fears, no relief that she didn't have to struggle with conjecture about her mother's love. Her worries had been gouged out and replaced with the certainty that her fears were *not* a leftover invention from her childish insecurities. The truth was Maureen's love *did* have a price, and it was contingent on whether she approved of Rachel's choices.

Her mother was never going to like Morgan. He was strong. Capable. Maureen was pissed off from the beginning. Rachel saw it and adjusted accordingly—even when Maureen tried to hide it under her manipulative finesse and ladylike subtlety.

For years Maureen had kept her criticisms on reserve. She was careful. Politely insistent that Morgan was a talented man, a successful man, a good father, a good son, but he wasn't the right man for Rachel. Morgan's bad behaviour at his sister's wedding proved Maureen's point. In the process, it shattered the fragile balance between Rachel and Morgan, and played right into Maureen's wheelhouse. She'd abandoned her ladylike manners, destroying what little dignity Rachel had left.

Rachel could feel Maureen's disapproval the second Morgan put his jacket around her and Macy, their gentle kiss, the second their fingers parted; she heard the buzz of wagging tongues and the glare of phones in the darkness. Further embarrassing Maureen, the Wharton name—Rachel had outdone herself. The embarrassment at the Gables was child's play in comparison. She'd embarrassed Maureen Wharton in front of three-hundred pairs of eyes, the most influential people in the blue blood clan, and she was distraught. It wasn't about Rachel's devastation. Not once during the evening did Maureen approach her. Not even to find out if she was having a nice time. She didn't even know that she was upset. Aunt Sarah knew. She let Rachel know how loved she was.

All Maureen could probably think of was how her daughter had committed a social *faux pas*. Rachel and Morgan had finally shown a weakness Maureen could bank on—emotional exposure. The inseparable couple had clearly had a spat. Now Morgan was drinking excessively and flirting with another while Rachel ignored them. A public drama. So, unlike the Hilliers, so unlike the Whartons. Questions hung in the air. The story of Rachel and Morgan, it's beginning, its conflicts, its murky middle, confusion about their status—it became a source of great speculation. With exposure came embellishments, and conjecture always came with the territory. Anxiously, their audience would want the tale's conclusion, quickly so everyone could chat about it over cocktails at the next charity event, and in its absence, they would write it themselves.

Rachel stood on her tippy toes and leaned her head against the window; she looked down at the front entrance. Still no sign of him. She wobbled back. *Where was he?* Her breath fogged up the glass.

Why did getting drunk make you feel sad and pathetic?

Rachel looked down at her hands. Her tears had turned the paper LCBO bag a deeper shade of brown. *Brown really is a shitty colour.* The neck of the bottle stuck out encouragingly and she ripped at the paper viciously and threw it around the room. She was so *fucking* disappointed in herself. She'd let her love story fall through her fingers tonight, like words you can't remember, like moments eaten so quickly you can't recall how they tasted. She was horrified by how she had hidden behind the chair like a feeb when he moved. She stood there like an idiot. No fight in her. Weak. She couldn't prevent it from happening. She agreed by default. She let Morgan leave without saying what needed to be said, too hurt, to tell the truth, too afraid to love him.

Earlier tonight, when she opened the door to find Morgan standing there, she squashed her impulses. Fear consumed her. She was afraid to feel the heat from his body, afraid that the tiniest of breezes would carry his scent, so she kept her distance. She was too close to the edge of the world; too close to falling off to give in to her natural instincts. She was polite instead. She slid into self-protection mode without thinking. She offered him a chair. Offered him coffee. Maureen would have been proud. He sat on the couch.

She listened. She said nothing. She did nothing.

The briarwood box was in her view when she sat across from Morgan. Their childhood memories—where they came from, how they started, what they meant to each other—were neatly separated, wrapped in ribbon, and tucked in that box. Those memories had led them here.

But Elaine's wedding changed everything. Rachel saw herself. She saw Morgan. She hated everything she saw.

Rachel unsteadily lifted the bottle of wine to get a better look. She didn't like wine; she never liked wine; it always tasted sour to her, but someone gave it to her, and it was blurring the sharp edges of her pathetic existence, so she was gaining an understanding of its charm. She took another slug.

The orange clock above the door was loud. It bounced off the walls—stupid clock! *I hate that clock. Before I leave here, I'm going to smash that bloody clock.* She turned to see the time but couldn't make it out. She walked to the middle of the room but her legs were a bit shaky. Squinting, she saw it—thirty minutes since he left. "What's *keeping* him? *Where* he?" She turned up Sass and went back to the window, losing her footing on the way, and had a small collision with the window.

Morgan wanted to explain what happened. Rachel didn't care what happened. The damage had been done to both of them. He apologized, said humiliation had been the last thing on his mind.

Two loves. Crucial. Central. Morgan Hillier and her mother. Her life pivoted around them and both loves were frothed with pain and uncertainty. Her dad, Aunt Sarah, Uncle Robert—so easy to love.

"But not *themmm* guys—nope!"

It doesn't matter who you love. Love is love. The ache. The loss. It stings with the same wallop, regardless of genus. For years, Rachel had twisted herself in knots because she wasn't enough for Maureen, and she'd twisted herself in knots at the unfairness of her unrequited love for Morgan—but really, she wasn't enough for him either. They just couldn't seem to get it together. Their timing always sucked.

Rachel looked down at the deserted street, then jerked back when she saw Morgan walk down the narrow path of the small building. "Oooopsssey ... there hee issss."

Rachel stumbled to the corner of the window to watch him.

The Tall Man. His long strides carried him with efficient purpose. His dark hair caught in the breeze. Even from the back, he was the *sexiest* man she had ever met. Ishmael was out of the car in a flash and held open the passenger door. Morgan took no lingering looks back. There was no hesitation as he got into the waiting car. Ishmael closed the door and looked up at her window. Rachel froze. Ishmael's brow was furrowed, his face sad.

Tears suddenly stung her eyes. "Awwwwww ... Ishshmmael isss a poorrr sloooob toooo." The car was a watery blur of black as it pulled away from the curb and sped down the road. "I guessss thissss isss it? Thisss isss howww 't endssss?"

It was impossible to wipe her tears. She couldn't feel her fingers.

It's like Sass Jordan wrote the song for me. Her voice vibrates with raw emotion. I need to learn how to play it, and play it, and play it, until my fingers bleed. "I'm gonna sleeps alone for the ressst of my life, tooooo."

Rachel raised the bottle over her head for a toast. "To Sassss— She knows a thing or two about heartache. Yes—yes, she does!" Rachel guzzled back the wine. The sour taste was a relief.

She wiped her hot tears and her mouth in one fluid movement. *I have to accept this, don't I? Like the accepting Elinor in* Sense and Sensibility *who thought she was going to be a penniless spinster, dutifully, pining after her true love, but Elinor had Jane Austen manipulating her story, didn't she! Morgan and I—we can't overcome the obstacles in our way and we can't remain friends. I can't be his friend. I can't! Not after everything that's happened.*

Maureen thought Rachel's feelings were misguided hero worship. Rick thought Morgan manipulated her, controlled her. Jason shook her senseless years ago trying to get her to see reason, but she fought against the tide, not able to accept the possibility that her love for Morgan could be one-sided. Her resolve had had tremendous moments of doubt. Was she delusional? Was he ever going to see her as more than his in-between girl? Would their history destroy their opportunity? Was she enough? Were some people just lucky? Was she destined to be a bitter old crone? *'Cause it sure seems that way.* Or was she destined to settle for less?

The energy she had wasted trying to answer these questions—it was embarrassing to admit, but she'd believed—so many *fucking* times—she'd believed! That everything would widen out into the yellow brick road that led to happiness. She believed her love was true and passionate—real, and that it would survive the hills and vales of life. Was she wrong? Did true love not conquer all?

Love's unfairness burned a path of rage up Rachel's esophagus and with its release came an ear-splitting scream from the deepest part of her. She whipped the wine bottle at the ugly green wall. It smashed, exploding its bitter brew into an unstable replication of her broken heart. The wine oozed out like blood and guts—evidence that her pain was a living art.

"Wonderful, the pukey walls finally have purpose! A canvasssss of heartbreak! How aproposss," she giggled. Her giggles quickly turned into unadulterated laughter. "Perrrfettt!" Really—it's good! Ap! It's so *fucking* hilarious!"

As quick as her rage became laughter, it rolled into painful sobs that sliced her heart into tinier pieces. *"W'at aa stuuupid foollll I am! Whyyy didn't I ever, ever tell him!"*

Everything that's happened? It was for nothing? It was never meant to be anything but a junk yard of suffering? That can't be right! It can't!

Rachel scraped the tears off her face with a coarse tea towel that made her skin tingle.

No! That's all wrong! No! I saw into him. I felt his heartbeat inside mine. She pounded on her chest. *I felt his joy and pain. It ran through my body.*

She sobbed. *It ran through my body!*

Morgan had brought her from sea to shore countless times, but now the beacon's light was no longer a port of call. The world Rachel had relied on was slashed open and the pain of exposure was humbling. There was no going back; her life had been altered. It had morphed into a gloomy set of changes. Everything moved slower now. She couldn't seem to keep up. People walked in slow motion. Their mouths moved but she couldn't quite make out their words. Rachel needed to grieve until the earth adjusted to the vibration of her pain.

A poem from long ago came to mind:

> And when the fury came
> It took out the lighthouse that had brought her
> from sea to shore
> And she would never be the same
> No shimmer of light caressed the water
> Not even the moon could help this poor daughter

When Rachel was with Morgan, it gave what she felt substance. Loving him made her better than she was by herself. If that made her some kind of feeble little shit—*fine!* She was a feeb. She was going to own her feeb-dom and cry until her eyeballs were raw! She was going to open another stupid bloody bottle of shitty sour wine, and she was going to turn the colour of these shitty green walls into red! She was going to walk around like death until she didn't feel like death anymore, and when she was done with her suck fest, she'd decide what the hell to do about her shitty fucking life. But today? Today, she was lost. She thought she saw into him, thought she felt his heart beat inside hers, but she must have been wrong all these years. Just wrong.

I did! I know it did, I saw into his heart and it does beat inside mine. Rachel pounded on her chest. *I did!* She grabbed her pleated skirt, tugging at it. She felt his joy and pain. She felt his love. *It ran through my body! It did!*

No one knows how you love. No one understands the depth of your love. Or where that love will take you, until it takes you there. No one knows the level of insanity, sacrifice, or indulgence you are prepared to commit, until you are there, naked, your dignity tossed into the fire.

Blinking back her tears, she sucked in a trembling breath. After everything that had happened, Rachel was certain of four things:

- Circumstance is geography, but it often feels like fate.

- When you love someone from the deepest part of yourself, and they leave without objection, a certain kind of sadness breaks a piece off your heart. Rachel was certain, everything she needed to know about life and love was hidden in that broken piece.

- Everything you love? Everything you hate? Same thing.

- Love is a war of extremes.

Rachel had first-hand experience on the war love wages between the extremes: happiness and depression, love and hatred, isolation, and intimacy, and there could be no real consoling in the throes of such beautiful chaos. A distinct loneliness collides with passion. With it comes a siege of emotions not easily understood. Emotions burn and consume even the most rational of minds. When you dust yourself off, you forge through the pain to keep ridicule at bay; you erect barricades like fortresses of natural landscape, just so you can handle survival.

Morgan's heart does beat inside Rachel's—and it has made an enduring imprint of a million tiny arrows that make her bleed like a poor slob in love.

THE END

A Certain Kind of Sadness Playlist

These are the songs I listened to while I wrote this book. They provided me with so much inspiration. I listened to them constantly.

I am a huge Sass Jordan fan. She's an amazing rocker. If you haven't listened, googlize (this is not a spelling mistake. I did it on purpose and yes, it's a made up word that means the act of googling) so googlize Sass, you won't be sorry. Check out her tune, *High Road Easy*, from her *Rats* album. She released an anniversary album last year with an amazing cover. Joni Mitchell is in a class all her own. Her trailblazing career has that wow factor because she's the exception many of us want to be. She came on the music scene in the 70's which was dominated by men, sang in bars in Western Canada and became a music icon. But you love Joni Mitchel because she hits the nail on the head in a unique way. I had to have a lie down after I listened to *Both Sides, Now*. Her honest storytelling about raw emotions in a delicate way is what makes her brilliant. Shania Twain has her own brand of special. From the first time I saw her music video, *Any Man of Mine*, I was a fan. Her humour and down to earth manner made her so relatable, but for me, it was her vulnerability coupled with her self confidence and girl power mantra that set her apart. Matchbox Twenty! I have loved this band from the first song I ever heard. I've seen them in concert many times. My kids know their songs. My friends. The crossing guard on the corner. And when Rob Thomas worked with Santana, Wow! Enough said.

Hope you listen and enjoy.

You Don't Have to Remind Me
I Want to Believe
Sass Jordan

Both Sides, Now
All I Want
Help Me
Joni Mitchell

You're Still the One
The Woman in Me
Shania Twain

Nights in White Satin
Moody Blues

Say Something
A Great Big World

The Reason
Hoobastank

One Love
Mariana Trench

3am
Disease
Mad Season
Matchbox Twenty

Smooth
Santana & Rob Thomas

Sláinte, Jillean M

AUTHOR'S NOTE
OF THANKS

Spinning tales, building family trees and designing motivations to people you invent seem like a strange occupation but oddly it's very cathartic. It often reveals nuances you didn't realize needed attention and sets you on a journey of discovery and awareness through the eyes of a character that isn't you, and yet, you know them without actually knowing them.

However, you craft your creative life, one thing for certain, it takes a village. An enormous thank you to Sands Press, Perry Prete for his humour, patience, and guidance. To my editor, Laurie Carter, for getting me to dig deeper and made the story better. To the smorgasbord of writers whose work has inspired me since Miss McCaffery taught me how to read in primary one.

I can't thank my village enough. From my fantastic friends who agreed to be the first readers of my very rough draft, Maureen Di Sebastiano and Michelle Gomes Hamilton, your enthusiasm and encouragement spurred me on. To dearest Elke Marceau, my writing partner who talks me off the ledge with regularity and without complaint, who pushes me creatively, and who knows me with frightening clarity, and loves me anyway. To mother Marie Gray who was the very best person, my first storyteller, who taught me plot and the art of the yarn. She thought I was the best thing since dipped bread – no loves you like your mum. She was the greatest mother a girl could have and it made me wonder what it would feel like if I didn't have a Marie.

Thank you to the detective and tactical sergeant who were generous with their time in answering my questions. Any legal or police procedural mistakes made or creative liberties taken are mine alone.

Michael McClory. My partner in life who insisted, from our first adorable little house near the lake, that I needed a creative space with a window. He was the first to say – writers need to write, so write. To my talented and inspiring daughters Lydia and Bridget who I want to be when I grow up. To my hilarious family of characters – and no you are not in the book – but with certainly provide a wealth of inspiration you crazy asses.

To my wonderful dad, the sweetest man alive, George Gray, my cheerleader from the beginning and always, who bought me a 315 Underwood typewriter when I was ten after I told him I wanted to be a writer. To my surrogate Mums, Aunt Pat, and Aunt Bridie. Aunt Pat who sang Mary Ann McGee to me while skipping down Avenue Road, and taught me the art of rhythm. Aunt Bridie who she saw me struggling to type on my 315 and taught me how to type, with an enormous amount of patience. She stressed the importance of focus and that advice has carried me throughout my life.
To my village, with much love, thank you.

Sláinte Jillean